Anna B. Williams

The Regerenes

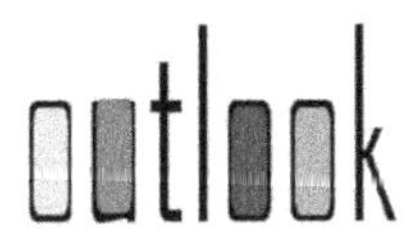

Anna B. Williams

The Regerenes

1st Edition | ISBN: 978-3-75235-233-7

Place of Publication: Frankfurt am Main, Germany

Year of Publication: 2020

Outlook Verlag GmbH, Germany.

THE ROGERENES

BY

ANNA B. WILLIAMS

INTRODUCTION.

While spending the summer at New London, in 1894, we were requested to aid Mr. John R. Bolles, in the capacity of reader and amanuensis, he being compelled, by reason of impaired sight, to depend upon such assistance. The work upon which he was engaged was a vindication of the Rogerenes. Having, from what we had read and heard concerning this colonial sect, regarded them as fanatics whose idiosyncrasies bordered upon lunacy, we could neither understand Mr. Bolle's interest in the subject, nor why he was so willing to call public attention to the fact that certain Rogerene leaders were among his ancestors. Nevertheless we could not refuse to render the small service required of us.

The chief sources upon which Mr. Bolles depended for information were Miss Caulkin's "History of New London" and a number of Rogerene works, nearly two hundred years old, dating from their first publication, which were in possession of family friends. It was necessary for us to read these works to Mr. Bolles. Much to our surprise, we found them to be of an exceedingly intelligent, logical character, far removed from the fantastic and visionary. Although written during periods of severest persecution, they were perfectly calm and dispassionate in tone, even in the few pages where reference was made to Rogerene sufferings "for conscience's sake"; these being passed over, for the most part, with the remark that "it would take a large volume to contain them all." In these volumes was almost nothing of Rogerene history; but here stood out, in bold relief, such features of Rogerene faith and principles as dearly separated this sect from other people of their day and were calculated to excite bitter enmity and opposition on the part of the ruling and popular party. It was now easy to understand why these dissenters were portrayed to their own and succeeding times as brainless enthusiasts. Those in advance of their age are as cranks and fanatics in the esteem of their contemporaries, and rumor is ever busy blackening the character of unpopular people.

The Rogerene leaders appeared, in their writings, as consistent Christians, contending, by word and example, for the religion set forth in the New Testament, a religion depending not upon the observance of forms or of days, but upon love to God and the neighbor. They maintained that the civil government had no right to dictate in matters of religion; that the Christian church had but one lawgiver and judge, the Lord Himself. The divine commands regarding religion as set forth in the New Testament they would strictly obey, but they would, "for conscience's sake," obey no command of men in this regard. The purely civil laws they held themselves bound to observe, according to Christ's command. Had Sunday laws been instituted for avowedly sanitary and moral purposes, and for the convenience and protection of church-going people, none would have conformed to such laws more conscientiously than the Rogerenes, such obedience being in the line of their preaching and practice regarding the civil laws. But because they were commanded to keep this day "sacred," as a religious duty and necessity, and such observance was accounted a vital part of a religious life, they would not join in what seemed to them to be more of the nature of heathen idolatry than of the religion instituted by Jesus Christ.

At a period when extreme regard for the first day "Sabbath" was one of the most readily accepted signs of a religious life, and no laws were more rigidly enforced than those which guarded that "sacred" day from desecration, the Rogerenes conscientiously ignored its sacredness. At a period when the materia medica was founded largely upon erroneous ideas and practices, when surgery was bungling and blundering and he who called a physician was, frequently, more liable to die of the so-called remedy than of the disease, the Rogerenes elected to trust their health and their lives to Nature and to Nature's God, in the manner prescribed in the New Testament, and they appear to have profited by their choice.[1] At a period when no men were more in favor of war than those who preached—in parts—the gospel of Him who bade His followers to forgive their enemies, to love them and pray for them and to return good for evil, the Rogerenes stood for uniform peace and good will on the part of Christians, according to the spirit and the letter of the Master's teachings. At a period when the law called upon all to support a state church, the Rogerenes refused to pay towards the support of a church of whose teachings they largely disapproved, or to either give or take anything for a ministry which Christ established as a free gift from those gifted by Him. Driven by the intolerance of their times to protect their obnoxious sect from extinction at the hands of powerful enemies, as best they could, the Rogerenes employed, at critical periods, a peaceable yet effective mode of defense, in the line of Gospel testimony, which enraged their opponents while it kept them fairly at bay. This was the climax of their offences.

Here was enough, and more than enough, to account for the misrepresentations given of this sect.

The death of Mr. John R. Bolles occurred soon after his attempt to place the Rogerenes in a more correct light was completed. The logic employed by this author was of the best, his style was forcible, his quotations were important; but his lack of new light upon the subject in the shape of additional facts in Rogerene history was much to be regretted. It did not seem best that his work should be published until some attempt had been made to secure further authentic information. Our leisure time for a number of succeeding summers was devoted to research in this obscure direction. Thorough examination was made of the town records and records of the colonial courts of Connecticut, also of contemporary writings having any bearing upon the subject. When the mass of material thus secured was chronologically arranged, it was discovered that portions fragmentary and obscure in themselves were supplemented by other fragments, and this to such a degree that even the records of the inimical courts, where evident pains had been taken to omit particulars liable to tell for the side of the Rogerenes, aided in disclosing the true facts. As a dissected picture is made intelligible by the correct arrangement of its parts, this at first seemingly chaotic collection of fragmentary items, by a mere arrangement according to dates, resolved itself into a presentation of the Rogerene leaders as actors in a series of highly romantic scenes, in which were dearly displayed the true character and principles of these dissenters and the calumnious nature of the descriptions which had been given of them. Here were heroes and situations deserving not only the attention of historians, but that of poets and artists. Here were facts that outromanced fiction. Here was something new for lovers of old-time tales and images, and much bearing upon New England history at large, as well as remarkable examples of Christian heroism. Here were questions for the Christian scholar and statesman.

As they came to us out of the old records and writings, we present the following facts concerning the Rogerenes to readers of this generation as before a court of appeal. The enemies of this sect have said their worst of them, largely by aid of false statements. Now, for the first time, is presented, by many valid evidences, the case for the Rogerenes.

Precedence has been given in this volume, to the work of the senior author. That and the historical portion will be found largely supplementary, each of the other.

The task which Mr. Bolles had undertaken was chiefly in correction of certain erroneous statements which had been made in newspaper articles and printed sermons, issued in his locality, most of which statements had been derived from ecclesiastical authors, who had found it expedient to adopt various current representations and traditions which had appeared on the church side of the controversy rather than to enter upon any research in this matter. As will be seen, some portion of Mr. Bolle's vindication had been published in a local paper. This is comprised in the first chapter.

In compiling the History, careful search was made for every item of reliable information concerning John Rogers and the Rogerenes, and every fact that was discovered is set plainly before the reader, in chronological order.

It would be quite possible for a reader to view the entire material that has been examined for the production of this History. The County Court records are at the county clerk's office in Norwich. The records of the Superior Court are in the secretary's office, in the State House, at Hartford. The records of the General Court have been published and are to be found in many public libraries. The Rogerene books still extant are very rare, so much so that they could only be seen as a whole by going here and there among the owners. The titles of these works will be found at the end of the Appendix, together with statement of where single copies may be found.

Some of the material used for the History is from "Letters of Mr. Samuel Hubbard." The portions of these letters quoted in this work may be seen in Benedict's "History of the Baptists." The "Journal of William Edmundson" and "The Life and Travels of Samuel Bownas" have furnished some important particulars. These two works are rare outside of Quaker libraries. Miss Caulkin's "History of New London," from which quotations will be found, is in many public libraries in New England and elsewhere.

The scandalous work of Peter Pratt, "The Prey Taken from the Strong," is in the Prince collection in the Boston Public Library and in the Massachusetts Historical Society's Library in Boston. A copy of "The Reply of John Rogers 2nd" is in the Connecticut Historical Library at Hartford. The last half of the original manuscript of the Hempstead Diary is in the Historical Rooms at New London, while the first half is at the "Old Hempstead House," at New London. This Diary has recently been published in book form by the New London Historical Society.

"An Account of the Debate between Rev. Mather Byles and The Brethren" of the Congregational Church of New London may be seen in the New London Public Library.

An interesting side-light was furnished by Mr. Julius F. Sachse, in his work entitled "The Ephrata Cloister," Vol. II, Chapter IV.

As for spurious accounts of the Rogerenes to be found here and there, in ecclesiastical and town histories, the falsity of which is established in the course of this volume, mention of their authorship will be found in the places of refutation. Other minor references will be credited as they occur.

Our thanks are due to the Connecticut state librarian and his assistants, to clerks in the secretary's office, and to Mr. Bates of the Connecticut Historical Library at Hartford, for the polite and obliging manner in which they placed before us books and manuscripts having a bearing upon this subject. Like courtesy was shown us in the county clerk's office, in Norwich, the town clerk's office in New London, and by the secretary of the New London Historical Society. In the Yale College Library, we were shown a copy of "An Answer to a Pamphlet," by John Rogers, 2d, which is the only copy we have discovered.

By researches in new lines, we have discovered some mistakes regarding the Rogerenes made by that gifted and honored historian, Miss Fanny M. Caulkins. Miss Caulkins was the first historian to attempt careful and intelligent search in this obscure direction. In her "History of New London" she has given a large amount of accurate information concerning the Rogerenes, much of which is quoted with advantage, in Part First, by Mr. Bolles. It is to be hoped that we, in our turn, may be supplemented by some historian favored with sources of information unknown to ourselves, who will shed a still clearer light upon this subject, by presentation of facts outside of our own field of observation.

A. B. W.

PART I.
A VINDICATION

BY

JOHN R. BOLLES.

THE PATHWAY OF THE YEARS.

An onward path we have to tread,
    We cannot see the way.
Faith, love and hope their radiance shed,
Here and thus far the years have led;
But of the steps that lie ahead
    We know not one to-day.

Then pause, look back and courage take;
    How bright the road appears!
Each foot that trod there helped to break
Rough places down, and for our sake
Were lived the lives that shining make
    The pathway of the years.

Backward it reaches, firm and sure
    The steps that trod the way,
In simple homes, with purpose pure,
Faith to inspire, hope to allure;
Men wrought for ends that still endure
    And make us strong to-day.

The days to come are all unread,
    Unguessed by hopes or fears;
But press with courage high ahead,

For still there grows beneath our tread,
The highway grand, by pilgrims made,
    The pathway of the years.
We come of heroes! Be each soul
    Loyal like theirs, and free,
A shrine of honor, a white scroll;
That, as life's pages fresh unroll,
They who then read, may find the goal
    We sought was heavenly.

MARY L. BOLLES BRANCH.

A VINDICATION.

CHAPTER I.

This chapter contains the substance of several letters, originally published in the *New London Day* (1860), in reply to an article which had previously appeared in that paper, misrepresenting the teachings and conduct of the Rogerenes.

A communication in the *New London Day* of December 9, 1886, speaks of John Rogers and his followers, the Rogerenes, whose distinctive existence spread over a period of more than a century in the history of New London. The writer of the article referred to followed the example of his predecessors who have spoken derisively of this "sect," either in not knowing whereof he affirmed or in purposely misrepresenting these dissenters. We prefer to ascribe the former, rather than the latter, reason.

Trumbull, in his "History of Connecticut," charged John Rogers with crimes from which the grand jury fully exonerated him, as by its printed records may be seen. These false and scandalous charges have been reiterated, again and again, and have found a place in Barber's "Historical Collections of Connecticut" against the clearest testimony. His withdrawal from the standing religious order of the day aroused such hatred that many false accusations were made against him, which, like dragon's teeth sown over the land, have been springing up again and again.

The article which called forth these remarks doubtlessly derived its errors from those sources. I will point out a few of its inaccuracies.

The author says, "The Rogerenes are a sect founded by John Rogers in 1720." John Rogers died in 1721, after a most active dissemination of his principles for a period of about fifty years, gathering many adherents during that time.

Again, he says, "They entered the churches half naked." He must have confounded the Boston Quakers with the Rogerenes, as nothing of the kind was ever known of the latter. It is true that Trumbull makes an assertion of this sort; but even Dr. Trumbull cannot be regarded by close students as an example of accuracy—certainly not as regards Rogerene history.

The inhabitants of New London plantation were not sinners above other men. At the time James Rogers, senior, his wife, sons and daughters were thrust into prison in New London, John Bunyan was held in jail in England and said he would stay there till the moss grew over his eyebrows, before he would deny his convictions or cease to promulgate them. In the light of to-day, neither of these committed any offense whatever. Hundreds of the best of men suffered in like manner in England, and for a long period of time; and some were given over to death. The reverend father of Archbishop Leighton was, for conscience's sake, held imprisoned for more than twelve years, and not released until his faculties, both of body and mind, were seriously impaired. Rev. John Cotton, one of Boston's earliest preachers, came out of prison to this country. Religious thought was drenched, so to speak, with false notions, and many, even of those who had escaped from persecution in the Old World, became persecutors in the New.

Great praise is due to such men as Roger Williams, who fled from Salem to the wilderness to escape banishment for his principles, hibernating among Indians "without bed or board," as he expressed it, and whose ultimate settlement in Rhode Island made that State the field of religious liberty. Equal praise is due to John Rogers and his associates, at a later day, for boldly enunciating the same principles, and bravely suffering in their defense, ploughing the rough soil of Connecticut and sowing the good seed there.

Nor was the treatment of the Rogerenes comparable for cruelty with that of the Quakers at Boston, a few years prior to the Rogers movement. We hear nothing of the cutting off of ears, boring the tongue with a red-hot iron, banishment, selling into slavery or punishment by death, which disgraced the civilization of the Massachusetts colony and which was Puritanism with a vengeance, almost leading us to sympathize with their persecutors in England. New London plantation was disgraced by no such heathenism as this.

St. Paul boasted that he was a citizen of no mean city. We shall find that the Rogerenes are of no mean descent, sneered at and held in derision though they have been, by men of superficial thought.

James Rogers, senior, a prosperous and esteemed business man of Milford, Conn., had dealings in New London as early as 1656, and soon after became a resident. Says Miss Caulkins:—

He soon acquired property and influence and was much employed, both in civil and ecclesiastical affairs. He was six times representative to the General Court. Mr. Winthrop had encouraged his settlement in the plantation and had accommodated him with a portion of his own house lot next the mill, on which Rogers built a dwelling house of stone. He was a baker on a large scale, often furnishing biscuit for seamen and for colonial troops, and between 1660 and 1670 had a greater interest in the trade of the port than any other person in the place. His landed possessions were very extensive, consisting of several hundred acres on the Great Neck, the fine tract of land at Mohegan, called the Pamechaug Farm, several house lots in town and 2,400 acres east of the river, which he held in partnership with Col. Pyncheon of Springfield.[2] Perhaps no one of the early settlers of New London numbers at the present day so great a throng of descendants. His five sons are the progenitors of as many distinct lines. His daughters were women of great energy of character. John Rogers, the third son of James, having become conspicuous as the founder of a sect, which though small in point of number has been of considerable local notoriety, requires a more extended notice. No man in New London County was at one time more noted than he; no one suffered so heavily from the arm of the law, the tongue of rumor and the pens of contemporary writers.

John and James Rogers, Jr., in the course of trade, visited Newport, R.I., and there first embraced Sabbatarian principles and were baptized in 1674; Jonathan in 1675; James Rogers, senior, with his wife and daughter Bathsheba, in 1676, and these were received as members of the Seventh Day Church at Newport.[3]

As James Rogers, senior, against whom even the tongue of slander has been silent, was among the first to feel the ecclesiastical lash, a few words more concerning him from the pen of Miss Caulkins are here given:—

The elder James Rogers was an upright, circumspect man. His death occurred in February, 1688. The will is on file in the probate office in New London in the handwriting of his son John, from the preamble of which we quote.

"What I have of this world I leave among you, desiring you not to fall out about it; but let your love one to another appear more than to the estate I leave with you, which is but of this world; and for your comfort I signify to you that I have a perfect assurance of an interest in Jesus Christ and an eternal happy estate in the world to come, and do know and see that my name is written in the book of life, and therefore mourn not for me as they that are without hope."

Hollister, in his "History of Connecticut," speaks of James Rogers in high terms; although, in an evidently faithful following of historical errors, he gives the common estimate of John Rogers and his followers. Says Miss Caulkins:—

In 1676 the fines and imprisonments of James Rogers and his sons, for profanation of the Sabbath,[4] commenced. For this and for neglect of the established worship, they and some of their followers were usually arraigned at every session of the court, for a long course of years. The fine was at first five shillings, then ten shillings, then fifteen shillings. At the June court, 1677, the following persons were arraigned and each fined £5:—James Rogers, senior, for high-handed, presumptuous profanation of the Sabbath, by attending to his work; Elizabeth Rogers, his wife, and James and Jonathan, for the same. John Rogers, on examination, said he had been hard at work making shoes on the first day of the week, and he would have done the same had the shop stood under the window of Mr. Wetherell's house; yea, under the window of the meeting house. Bathsheba Smith, for fixing a scandalous paper on the meeting house. Mary, wife of James Rogers, junior, for absence from public worship.

Again, in September, 1677, the court ordered that John Rogers should be called to account once a month and fined £5 each time; others of the family were amerced to the same amount, for blasphemy against the Sabbath, calling it an idol, and for stigmatizing the reverend ministers as hirelings. After this, sitting in the stocks and whipping were added.

This correspondent says, "The Rogerenes despised the authority of law." But only that which infringed upon their natural rights and honest convictions of duty. To all other laws they were obedient. Says Miss Caulkins:—

John Rogers maintained obedience to the civil government, except in matters of conscience and religion. A town or county rate the Rogerenes always considered themselves bound to pay; but the minister's rate they abhorred, denouncing as unscriptural all interference of the civil power in the worship of God.

The Rogerenes were the first in this State to denounce the doctrine of taxation without representation, the injustice of which is now universally acknowledged. All their offences may be traced to a determination to withstand and oppose ecclesiastical tyranny. Pioneers in every great enterprise are sufferers, and pioneers in thought are no exception to this rule. Other men have labored, and we have entered into their labors. That principle for which these heroes and heroines so valiantly and faithfully contended, in the grim face of suffering and hate, the total divorcement of Church and State, is now established. Has it not become the boast and glory of the nation, the torch of liberty held aloft in the face of the world? And does it not show the march of civilization that the right of all to equal religious freedom, then so obnoxious, is now fully confessed and sweet to the ear as chime of silverbells?

The venerable James Rogers, senior, with his wife, three sons and two daughters, were, as we have seen, arraigned and fined £5 each at one session of the court, within two years from the time of their alliance with the Seventh Day Baptist Church of Newport. Other arraignments followed, and in the case of John Rogers, the court ordered that he should be called to account every month and fined £5 each time. Draco's laws were said to have been written in blood; Caligula set his on poles so high they could not be read; but it was reserved for a New England court, in the perilous times of which we are speaking, to pass sentence before the offense was committed or trial had!

Nor have we but just entered into the vestibule of that temple of ignorance, tyranny, and crime, which, even in the New London plantation, reared its front and trailed its long shadow down a century. But on the ashes of oppression thrives the tree of liberty. Religious freedom was then emerging from the incrustation of ages, as the bird picks its way through the shell to light and beauty. Whippings and sittings in the stocks afterwards took place, yet we hear of but a single attempt on the part of the Rogerenes to interrupt the public worship of their enemies, until nearly eight years of persecution had elapsed, and it should be remembered that such interruption was not uncommon in those days; Quakers doing the same in Boston, under like treatment.

We quote from the records of the court, 1685:—

John Rogers, James Rogers, Jr., Samuel Beebe, Jr., and Joanna Way are complained of for profaning God's holy day with servile work, and are grown to that height of impiety as to come at several times into the town to rebaptise several persons; and, when God's people were met together on the Lord's Day to worship God, several of them came and made great disturbance, behaving themselves in such a frantic manner as if possessed with a diabolical spirit, so affrighting and amazing that several women swooned and fainted away.[5] John Rogers to be whipped fifteen lashes and for unlawfully re-baptising, to pay £5. The others to be whipped.

The Quakers at Boston had been charged with having a similar spirit, and, almost simultaneously with this complaint, witches, so-called, were hung at Salem. Mr. Burroughs, a preacher, being a small man, was charged with holding out a long-barrelled gun straight with one hand. He defended himself by saying that an Indian did the same thing. "Ah! that's the black man!" said the judge, meaning the devil helped him do the deed. Burroughs was hung! It was said of Jesus of Nazareth, "He hath a devil."

There was no printing-press at that time in New London, and had there been it would have served the will of the dominant power, not that of the persecuted few. Bathsheba Smith had been previously fined £5 for attaching a paper to the side of the meeting-house, setting forth their grievances. If John Rogers had undertaken to harangue an audience in the street, it might have been regarded as a still greater offense. It may be said to be an unlawful act to present their case and assert their rights in this manner; but an unlawful act is sometimes justified by circumstances. It would be an unlawful act to go to your neighbor's house in the night, knock loudly at his door, disturb the inmates and call out to them while quietly sleeping in their beds; but, if the house were on fire, it would be a right and merciful act. Great exigencies justify extraordinary conduct. What would be wrong under certain conditions would be right under others.

It may be said that this course would not be tolerated at the present day.

Neither, we add, would the acts that led to it. The prophet was at one time commanded to speak unto the people, whether they would hear or whether they would forbear. With our imperfect knowledge of the circumstances of the case, it may be impossible, at this date, to judge rightly of its merits. Elizabeth Rogers was charged with stigmatizing the reverend clergy as hirelings, and with calling the Sabbath an idol. She was fined five pounds. There was not much freedom of speech in those days. As to calling the Sabbath an idol, that was no more than saying it was unduly reverenced. It was so among the Jews, at the time our Saviour endeavored to disabuse them of the fallacy and to teach them that "the Sabbath was made for man and not man for the Sabbath." The brazen serpent ordained of God for the healing of the people, when it became an object of idolatrous worship, was ordered to be taken to pieces.

Miss Caulkins says:—

One of the most notorious instances of contempt exhibited by Rogers against the religious worship of his fellow-townsmen was the sending of a wig to a contribution made in aid of the ministry.

This was in derision of the full-bottomed wigs then worn by the Congregational clergy.

We sympathize with him in his contempt of the ornament, if such it may be called, of which the portraits of the Rev. Mr. Saltonstall present a rich specimen. An ancient bishop refused to administer the rite of baptism to one thus garnitured, saying, "Take that thing away; I will not bless the head of a dead man." John Rogers made an apologetic confession of this offense, which may be seen upon the town records to-day, viz.:—

Whereas I, John Rogers of New London, did rashly and unadvisedly send a periwigg to the contribution of New London, which did reflect dishonor upon that which my neighbors, ye inhabitants of New London, account the ways and ordinances of God and ministry of the Word, to the greate offense of them, I doe herebye declare that I am sorry for the sayde action and doe desire all those whom I have offended to accept this my publique acknowledgment as full satisfaction.

JOHN ROGERS.

A young man, sensible that his life had not been what it ought to have been, and resolving upon amendment, sought his father and made frank acknowledgment of his faults. Having done so, he said, "Now, father, don't you think you ought to confess a little to me?" We think some confessions were also due from the other side.

The nest in which is hatched the bird of Jove is built of rough sticks and set in craggy places. Again, it is stirred up that the young eaglet may spread its wings and seek the sun. The victor's laurels are not cheaply gained; conflict and struggle are the price. Sparks flash from collision. Lightnings cleanse the air. The geode is broken to free the gem that lies within. Diamonds are cut and polished ere they shed forth their splendor. Great good is usually ushered in by great labor and sacrifice. It is so with liberty. Let us tread about its altars with reverence, with unshod feet; altars from which have ascended flames so bright as to illumine earth, and offerings so sweet as to propitiate heaven. The unjust and tyrannical laws by which the early battlers for religious freedom in this section were assailed have long since been erased from the statutes of the State. The tide of public sentiment had swollen to such height, in which all denominations except the standing order were a unit, that they were wiped out, and their existence was made impossible in the future. That the Rogerene movement largely contributed to bring about this result will be shown. Of the hardships, loss of liberty, loss of property, etc., which the Rogerenes endured for conscience's sake, Miss Caulkins speaks thus:—

Attempts were made to weary them out and break them up by a series of fines, imposed upon presentments of the grand jury. These fines were many times repeated, and the estates of the offenders melted under the seizures of the constable as snow melts before the sun. The course was a cruel one and by no means popular. At length, the magistrates could scarcely find an officer willing to perform the irksome task of distraining.

The demands of collectors, the brief of the constable, were ever molesting their habitations. It was now a cow, then a few sheep, the oxen at the plow, the standing corn, the stack of hay, the threshed wheat, and, anon, piece after piece of land, all taken from them to uphold a system which they denounced.

Further details of their sufferings will be omitted in this place; but the famous suit of Rev. Gurdon Saltonstall against John Rogers demands and shall receive dose attention.

It was while Rev. Gurdon Saltonstall was minister of the church of New London, and through his influence, that John Rogers was expatriated, so to speak, and mercilessly confined three years and eight months in the jail at Hartford, "as guilty of blasphemy." Shortly after his release, Rev. Mr. Saltonstall brought a suit against John Rogers for defaming his character. The following is the record of the court:—

At a session of the County Court, held at New London, September 20th, 1698, members of the court, Capt. Daniel Wetherell, esq., Justices William Ely and Nathaniel Lynde, Mr. Gurdon Saltonstall, minister of the gospel, plf. pr. contra John Rogers, Sr., def't, in an action of the case for defamation.

Whereas you, the said John Rogers, did some time in the month of June last, raise a lying, false and scandalous report against him, the said Mr. Gurdon Saltonstall, and did publish the same in the hearing of diverse persons, that is to say, did, in their hearing, openly declare that the said Saltonstall, having promised to dispute with you publicly on the holy Scriptures, did, contrary to his said engagement, shift or wave the said dispute which he promised you, which said false report he, the said Saltonstall, complaineth of as to his great scandal and to his damage unto such value as shall to the said court be made to appear. In this action the jury finds for the plaintiff £600 and costs of court £1 10s.

The £600 damages, equal perhaps to $10,000 at the present day, was not more remarkable than the suit itself, which had no legal foundation. Lorenzo Dow tells "how to lie, cheat and kill according to law." But here is a deed—ought we not to call it a robbery?—done under cover, without the authority, of law. For the words alleged to have been spoken, action of slander was not legal. That this may be made clear to the general reader, we quote the language of the law from Selwyn's "Digest":—

An action on the case lies against any person for falsely and maliciously speaking and publishing of another, words which directly charge him with any crime for which the offender is punishable by law. In order to sustain this action it is essentially necessary that the words should contain an express imputation of some crime liable to punishment, some capital offense or other infamous crime or misdemeanor. An imputation of the mere defect or want of moral virtues, moral duties, or obligations is not sufficient.

To call a man a liar is not actionable; but the offensive words charged upon Rogers do not necessarily impute as much as this. There might have been a mistake or a misunderstanding on both sides, or Mr. Saltonstall may, for good reason, have changed his purpose. No crime was charged upon him, which we have seen is necessary to support the action. "Where the words are not actionable in themselves and the only ground of action is the special damage, such damage must be proved as alleged." In this case no special damage, is alleged and of course none proved. The causes of the suit were too trifling for further discussion. Falsehood need not rest upon either. Duplicity was no part of Roger's character, and, since we have spoken a word for him, we will let the Rev. Gurdon Saltonstall speak for himself, as quoted by Mr. McEwen in his "Bi-Centennial Discourse":—

"There never was," said Gov. Saltonstall in a letter to Sir Henry Ashurst, "for this twenty years that I have resided in this government, any one, Quaker or other person, that suffered on account of his different persuasion in religious matters from the body of this people."

We may suppose that Mr. Saltonstall thought he had done a brilliant act, to recover from John Rogers a sum equal to about six year's salary. But there are scales that never grow rusty and dials that do not tire. Time, the great adjuster of all things, will have its avenges.

While the least peccadilloes of the Rogerenes have been searched out as with candles and published from pulpit and from press, no one of their enemies has ever found it convenient to name this high-handed act of oppression, as shown in the suit referred to. Perhaps they have viewed it in the light that the Scotchman did his text, when he said, "Brethren, this is a very difficult text; let us look it square in the face and pass on." They may not even have looked it in the face.

Last, if not least, of the unauthenticated anecdotes narrated by Mr. McEwen of the Rogerenes, in his half-century sermon, which we would not care to unearth, but which has recently been republished in *The Outlook*, is here given:—

One of this sect, who was employed to pave the gutters of the streets, prepared himself with piles of small stones, by the wayside, that when Mr. Adams was passing to church, he might dash them into the slough, to soil the minister's black dress. But, getting no attention from the object of his rudeness, who simply turned to avoid the splash, the nonplussed persecutor cried out, "Woe unto thee, Theophilus, Theophilus, when all men speak well of thee!"

When we remember that Mr. Adam's name was not Theophilus, and that, if it was on Sunday that the preacher was going to church, the gutters would not have been in process of paving, a shadow of doubt falls upon this story.

But Mr. McEwen throws heavier stones at the Rogerenes, which we are compelled to notice, and shall see what virtue there is in them.

Why, in speaking of the Rogerenes, in his half-century sermon, does he say: "To pay taxes of any sort grieved their souls"? when they were so exact to render to Cæsar the things that are Cæsar's, and unto God the things that are God's? Miss Caulkins fully exonerates them from this charge. We repeat her words:—

He (John Rogers) maintained also obedience to the civil government, except in matters of conscience and religion. A town or county rate the Rogerenes always considered themselves bound to pay; but the minister's rate they abhorred.

Why should they not? Would not the Congregational church at that time have abhorred such a tax imposed upon them to support the Baptist ministry?

Until we are willing to concede to others the rights that we claim for ourselves, we are not the followers of Him who speaketh from heaven. But the most glaring wrong done to these dissenters by the standing order, outvying perhaps Gov. Saltonstall's groundless suit for damages, is found in the course taken by the magistrates, unrebuked, who, however small was the fine or however large the value of the property distrained, returned nothing to the victims of their injustice.

Says John Rogers, Jr.:—

For a fine of ten shillings, the officer first took ten sheep, and then complained that they were not sufficient to answer the fine and charges, whereupon, he came a second time and took a milch cow out of the pasture, and so we heard no more about it, by which I suppose the cow and the ten sheep satisfied the fine and charges.

As showing the absurd and unjust treatment that John Rogers endured at the hands of the civil and ecclesiastical power, we quote from Miss Caulkins. Clearly he was right with regard to the jurisdiction of the court:—

In 1711, he was fined and imprisoned for misdemeanor in court, contempt of its authority and vituperation of the judges. He himself states that his offense consisted in charging the court with injustice for trying a case of life and death without a jury. This was in the case of one John Jackson, for whom Rogers took up the battle axe. Instead of retracting his words, he defends them and reiterates the charge. Refusing to give bonds for his good behavior until the next term of court, he was imprisoned in New London jail. This was in the winter season and he thus describes his condition:—

"My son was wont in cold nights to come to the grates of the window to see how I did, and contrived privately to help me to some fire, etc. But he, coming in a very cold night, called to me, and perceiving that I was not in my right senses, was in a fright, and ran along the street, crying, 'The authority hath killed my father'; upon which the town was raised, and forthwith the prison doors were opened and fire brought in, and hot stones wrapt in cloth and laid at my feet and about me, and the minister Adams sent me a bottle of spirits, and his wife a cordial, whose kindness I must acknowledge.

"But when those of you in authority saw that I recovered, you had up my son and fined him for making a riot in the night, and took, for the fine and charge, three of the best cows I had."

John Bolles, born in 1677, a disciple of John Rogers, in his book entitled "True Liberty of Conscience is in Bondage to No Flesh," makes this statement, on page 98:—

To my knowledge, was taken from a man, only for the costs of a justice's court and court charge of whipping him for breach of the Sabbath (so-called) a mare worth a hundred pounds, and nothing returned, and this is known by us yet living, to have been the general practice in Connecticut.

His biographer adds, "Mr. Bolles was doubtless that man."

We quote further from John Bolles:—

And as he (John Rogers) saith hitherto, so may we say now, fathers taken from their wives and children, without any regard to distance of place, or length of time. Sometimes fathers and mothers both taken and kept in prison, leaving their fatherless and motherless children to go mourning about the streets.

When a poor man hath had but one milch cow for his family's comfort, it hath been taken away; or when he hath had only a small beast to kill for his family, it hath been taken from him, to answer a fine for going to a meeting of our own society, or to defray the charges of a cruel whipping for going to such a meeting, or things of this nature. Yea, £12 or £14 worth of estate hath been taken to defray the charges of one such whipping, without making any return as the law directs. And this latter clause in the law is seldom attended.

Yea, fourscore and odd sheep have been taken from a man, being all his flock; a team taken from the plough, with all its furniture, and led away. But I am not now about giving a particular account; for it would contain a book of a large volume to relate all that hath been taken from us, and as unreasonable and boundless as these.

Mr. McEwen says derisively:—

Their goods were distrained; their cattle were sold at the post, and some of their people were imprisoned. But, emulating the example of the apostles, they took joyfully the spoiling of their goods; yea, they gloried in bonds and imprisonment.

It was not the apostles, but the Hebrews, to whom the apostle wrote, who took joyfully the spoiling of their goods. A small matter, it may seem, to correct; but accuracy of Scripture quotation may be a Rogerene trait, and the writer will be proud if it be said, "Surely, thou art also one of them, for thy speech bewrayeth thee."

The subject on which we have entered opens and broadens and deepens before us, blending with all history and all truth. It is not exceptional, it is not isolated. It may not be blotted from memory, as it cannot be blotted from existence, painfully interwoven as it is with the mottled fabric of time. The world's greatest benefactors have often been its greatest sufferers. Socrates was made to drink the fatal hemlock, for not believing in the gods acknowledged by the state. Seneca, the moralist, was put to death by his ungrateful pupil, Nero. The first followers of Christ were persecuted, tortured and slain by the heathen world. Attaining to civil power, Christians treated in like manner their fellow Christians. Ecclesiastical history, wherever there has been an alliance of church and state, is blackened with crimes and cruelties too foul to be named. Recall the nameless horrors of the Inquisition, perpetrated under such rule. Think of Smithfield and the bloody queen.

Is it to be wondered at that the Rogerenes, meeting persecution at every turn, should have been aroused to a sublimity of courage, perhaps of defiance, against the tide of intolerance which had swept over the ages and was now wildly dashing its unspent waves across their path? Not until more than a century later did the potent word of Christian enlightenment go forth, "Hitherto shalt thou come, but no further; and here shall thy proud waves be stayed."

Passing a period of fifty years, darkened with wrongs and cruelties, the following notice of whipping is here given. It is necessary to present facts, that we may form a true judgment of the character and mission of this sect, which had at least the honor, like that of the early Christians, of being "everywhere spoken against."

From the "Life of John Bolles" we take the following:—

I have before me a copy of the record of proceedings, in July, 1725, before Joseph Backus, Esq., a magistrate of Norwich, Conn., against Andrew Davis, John Bolles, and his son Joseph Bolles (a young man of twenty-four years), John Rogers (the younger), Sarah Culver and others, charged with Sabbath breaking, by which it appears that for going on Sunday, from Groton and New London, to attend Baptist worship in Lebanon, they were arrested on Sunday, imprisoned till the next day and then heavily fined, the sentence being that if fine and costs were not paid they should be flogged on the bare back for non-payment of fine, and then lie in jail till payment of costs. As none of them would pay, they were all flogged, the women as well as the men, John Bolles receiving fifteen stripes and each of the others ten.

According to the statement of one of the sufferers, Mary Mann of Lebanon wished to be immersed, and applied to John Rogers (the younger) and his society for baptism. Notice was publicly posted some weeks beforehand that on Monday, July 26th, 1725, she would be baptised and that a religious meeting would be held in Lebanon on Sunday, July 25th, "the day," says Rogers, "on which we usually meet, as well as the rest of our neighbors."[6] When the Sunday came, a company of Baptists, men and women, from Groton and New London, set out for Lebanon, by the county road that led through Norwich. The passage through Norwich was so timed as not to interfere with the hours of public worship. After they had passed through the village, they were pursued and stopped, brought back to Norwich, imprisoned until Monday, and then tried, convicted and sentenced for Sabbath breaking. It must be added that a woman who was thus stripped and flogged was pregnant at the time, and that the magistrate who ordered the whipping stood by and witnessed the execution of the sentence. This outrage was much talked of throughout New England, and led to the publication of divers proclamations and pamphlets.

Deputy Governor Jenks, of Rhode Island, the following January, having obtained a copy of the proceedings against Davis and the others, ordered it to be publicly posted in Providence, to show the people of Rhode Island "what may be expected from a Presbyterian government," and appended to it an indignant official proclamation.

GOVERNOR JENK'S PROCLAMATION.

I order this to be set up in open view, in some public place, in the town of Providence, that the inhabitants may see and be sensible of what may be expected from a Presbyterian government, in case they should once get the rule over us. Their ministers are creeping in amongst us with adulatious pretense, and declare their great abhorrence to their forefather's sanguinary proceedings with the Quakers, Baptists and others. I am unwilling to apply Prov. xxvi, 25, to any of them; but we have a specimen of what has lately been acted in a Presbyterian government, which I think may suppose it sits a queen and shall see no sorrow. I may fairly say of some of the Presbyterian rulers and Papists, as Jacob once said of his two sons, Gen. xlix, 5 and 6 verses, "They are brethren, instruments of cruelty are in their habitations! O, my soul, come not thou into their secret! Unto their assembly, mine honor, be thou not united!" Amos v, 7, "They who turn judgment into wormwood and leave off righteousness in the earth." Chapter vi, 12, "For they have turned judgment into gall, and the fruit of righteousness into hemlock!" And I think in whomsoever the spirit of persecution restest there cannot be much of the spirit of God. And I must observe that, notwithstanding the Presbyterian pretended zeal to a strict observance of a first day Sabbath was such that those poor people might not be suffered to travel from Groton to Lebanon on that day, on a religious occasion, as hath been minded, but must be apprehended as gross malefactors and unmercifully punished; yet, when a Presbyterian minister, which hath a great fame for abilities, hath been to preach in the town of Providence, why truly then the Presbyterians have come flocking in, upon the first day of the week, to hear him, from Rehoboth, and the furthest parts of Attleborough, and from Killingly, which is much further than John Rogers and his friends were travelling; and this may pass for a Godly zeal; but the other must be punished for a sinful action. Oh! the partiality of such nominal Christians!

JOSEPH JENKS, *Dep. Gov.*

CHAPTER II.

In the contemplation of noble deeds, we become more noble, and by the just anathematizing of error our love of truth is made stronger. As the bee derives honey from nauseous substances, so we would extract good even from wrongdoing. It is with no spirit of animosity towards any one that we pursue this subject.

No word of palliation for the acts of the Rogerenes, no admission of wrong done to them by their opponents, is heard from the ecclesiastical side. Perhaps even the severity of the statements made against them may be an evidence in their favor.

The Rev. Mr. Saltonstall began his ministry in New London in 1688, at the age of twenty-two. This was about twelve years after the prosecutions against the Rogers family, for non-conformity, had commenced. In 1691, he was ordained, and continued to preach until 1708, when he was chosen governor of the State and abandoned the ministry altogether. Bred in the narrow school of ecclesiasticism, and of a proud and dominant spirit, the day-star of religious liberty seems not even to have dawned upon his mind.

He was virulent in his enmity to John Rogers from the beginning. The Furies have been said to relent; his rancor showed no abatement.

In 1694, he presented charges of blasphemy against John Rogers, without the knowledge of the latter, and while he was confined in New London jail. We copy the following extract, from a statement made by John Rogers, Jr., writing in defence of his father, which shows how closely he was watched by his adversaries, that they might find grounds of accusation against him.

Peter Pratt, of whom we shall say more hereafter, an author mainly quoted by historians on the subject we are discussing, in a pamphlet traducing the character of John Rogers, and written after his death, had said of his treatment in Hartford: "His whippings there were for most audacious contempt of authority; his sitting on the gallows was for blasphemous words."

To which John Rogers, Jr., thus replies:—

First, he asserts that his whippings there—viz., at Hartford—"were for most audacious contempt of Authority"; but doth not inform the reader what the contempt was; making himself the judge, as well as the witness, whereas it was only his business to have proved what the contempt was, and to have left the judgment to the reader.

And forasmuch as his assertion is altogether unintelligible, so may it reasonably be expected that my answer must be by supposition, and is as follows:—

"I suppose he intends that barbarous cruelty which was acted on John Rogers, while he was a prisoner at Hartford, in the time of his long imprisonment above mentioned, which was so contrary to the laws of God and kingdom of England, that I never could find that they made a record of that matter, according to Christ's words, John iii, 20, 'For every one that doeth evil hateth the light,' etc.

"But John Rogers has given a large relation about it, as may be seen in his book entitled, 'A Midnight Cry.' From pages 12-15, where he asserts that he was taken out of Prison, he knew not for what, and tied to the Carriage of a great gun, where he had seventy-six stripes on his naked body, with a whip much larger than the lines of a drum, with knots at the end as big as a walnut, and in that maimed condition was returned to prison again; and his bed, which he had hired at a dear rate, taken from him, and not so much as straw allowed him to lie on, it being on the eighteenth day of the eighth month, called October, and very cold weather."

And although myself, with a multitude of spectators, who were present at Hartford and saw this cruel act, can testify to the truth of the account which he gives of it, yet I cannot inform the reader on what account it was that he suffered it, or what he was charged with; for, as I said before, I never could find a record of that matter.

But if it was for contempt of Authority, as Peter Pratt asserts, then I think those that inflicted such a punishment were more guilty of contempt against God than John Rogers was of contempt against the Authority; for God in his holy law has strictly commanded Judges not to exceed forty stripes on any account, as may be seen, Deut. xxv, 3, "So that for Judges to exceed forty stripes is high contempt against God."

In the next place, he adds that "his sitting on the gallows was for blasphemous words."

Reply:—

Here again he ought to have informed the reader what the words were, which doubtless would have been more satisfaction to the reader than for Peter Pratt to make himself both witness and judge, and so leave nothing for the reader to do but to remain as ignorant as before they saw his book.

And he might as well have said of the Martyr Stephen that his suffering was for blasphemous words, as what he says of John Rogers, for it was but the judgment of John Roger's persecutors that the words were blasphemous, and so it was the judgment of the Martyr Stephen's persecutors that he was guilty of speaking blasphemous words, as may be seen, Acts vi, 13, "This man ceaseth not to speak blasphemous words," etc. Whereupon they put him to death.

In the next place, I shall give the reader an account of what these words were for which John Rogers was charged with blasphemy; the account of which here follows:—

He being at a house in New London where there were many persons present, was giving a description of the state of an unregenerate person, and also of the state of a sanctified person; wherein he alleged that the body of an unregenerate person was a body of sin, and that Satan had his habitation there. And, on the contrary, that the body of a sanctified person was Christ's body, and that Christ dwelt in such a body.

Whereupon, one of the company asked him whether he intended the humane body, to which he replied that he did intend the humane body. Whereupon, the person replied again, "Will you say that your humane body is Christ's body?" to which he replied, clapping his hand on his breast, "Yes, I do affirm that this humane body is Christ's body; for Christ has purchased it with His precious blood; and I am not my own, for I am bought with a price."

Whereupon, two of the persons present gave their testimony as follows: "We being present, saw John Rogers clap his hand on his breast and say, 'This is Christ's humane body.'" But they omitted the other words which John Rogers joined with it.

And because I was very desirous to have given those testimonies out of the Secretary's Office, I took a journey to Hartford on purpose but the Secretary could not find them; yet, forasmuch as myself was present, both when the words were spoken, and also at the trial at Hartford, I am very confident that I have given them verbatim. And whether or no this was blasphemy, I desire not to be the judge, but am willing to leave the judgment to every unprejudiced reader.

The words of John Rogers were perfectly scriptural, as will be understood by every intelligent reader of the Bible.

The Apostle speaks of the church as the body of Christ. Again, "Know ye not that your bodies are the members of Christ?" And other passages to the same effect.

The cry of blasphemy has been a favorite device with murderers and persecutors in all ages.

When Naboth was set on high by Ahab to be slain, proclamation was made, "This man hath blasphemed God and the King."

"For a good work we stone you not," said the Jews to Christ, "but for *blasphemy*." And the high priest said of Christ himself, "What need we any further witness? Have we not heard his blasphemy from his own mouth?"

Miss Caulkins, in her "History of New London," although inclined to favor the ecclesiastical side, says: "The offences of the Rogerenes were multiplied and exaggerated, both by prejudice and rumor. Doubtless a sober mind would not now give so harsh a name to expressions which our ancestors deemed blasphemous."

It will be remembered that in 1677, "the court ordered that John Rogers should be called to account once a month and fined £5 each time," irrespective of his innocence or guilt, and without trial of either. This unrighteous order would seem to have been in force fifteen years later, viz., in November, 1692. "At that time," says Miss Caulkins, "besides his customary fines for working on the Sabbath and for baptizing, he was amerced £4 for entertaining Banks and Case (itinerant exhorters) for a month or more at his house."—"Customary fines!"

In the spring of 1694, Rogers was transferred from the New London to the Hartford Prison. Why was this transfer made? Perhaps that the charges of blasphemy brought against him might with more certainty be sustained where he was not known. Perhaps that the sympathies of the people would not be as likely to find expression there as they sometimes did at his outrageous treatment in New London; as will be seen. Or, by a more rigorous treatment he might be made to submit.

In Hartford he was placed in charge of a cruel and unprincipled jailer, who was entirely subservient to the will of his enemies, and who told John Rogers *he* would make him comply with their worship, if the authorities could not.

What prompted, we might ask, the unusual and merciless treatment that he received during this imprisonment at Hartford? He had not offended the authorities nor the people there; he was a stranger in their midst. The same remorseless spirit that had delivered him up to them as guilty of blasphemy was doubtless the moving, animating cause of such savage conduct. Scarcely four months had elapsed after his release from the Hartford prison where he had been confined nearly four years, before the Rev. Gurdon Saltonstall brought a suit of defamation against him, for the most trivial reasons, as we have seen (Chapter I), and upon no legal grounds whatever; yet a parasitical jury awarded the august complainant damages in the unconscionable sum of £600. Of this proceeding, Miss Caulkins, in her "History of New London," says: "Rogers had not been long released from prison, before he threw himself into the very jaws of the lion, as it were, by provoking a personal collision with Mr. Saltonstall, the minister of the town."

"Jaws of the lion!" Perhaps Miss Caulkins builded wiser than she knew. We had not ourselves presumed to characterize Mr. Saltonstall as the king of beasts; but, since John Rogers, so far as we know, was never charged with deviation from the truth, except in the above mentioned suit, while the Rev. Mr. Saltonstall was not above suspicion, as will appear by the false charge of blasphemy he brought against Rogers, and by other acts of which we shall speak hereafter, we will leave the reader to judge on which side the truth lay in this case.

It should be remembered that years had elapsed after the fines, imprisonments, etc., of Rogers had commenced—for non-attendance at the meetings of the standing order, for baptizing, breach of the Sabbath, etc.—before he was charged with entering the meeting-house in time of public worship and remonstrating there with the people. It was not in self-defence alone, it was in defence of justice that he spoke. Who were the first aggressors? Who disturbed him in the performance of the baptismal rites? Who interfered with his meetings? Who entered them as spies, to lay the foundation for suits against him? These things have not been referred to; they have not been confessed; they have not been apologized for, on the part of the standing order. If John Rogers was such a terrible sinner for what he did to them, how much greater accountability will they have to meet who, without any just cause, made their attack upon him!

There are fires burning in the heart of every good man that cannot be quenched. As well undertake to smother the rays of the sun or to confine ignited dynamite. We would not justify breach of courtesy, or any other law not contrary to the law of God; but there are times when to be silent would be treason to truth.

John Roger's father was the largest taxpayer in the colony, and had himself alone been subjected to the payment of one-tenth part of the cost of building the meeting-house, while John Rogers and his adherents, who were industrious, frugal, and thrifty people—or they never could have sustained the immense fines imposed upon them without being brought to abject poverty—had probably paid as much more; so we may suppose that at least one-fifth of the meeting-house, strictly speaking, belonged to them, while they were constantly being taxed for the support of this church of their persecutors.

The meeting-house was, in those times, quite often used for public purposes; in fact, the courts were frequently held there. How, upon a week day, could he have found an audience of his persecutors, or permission to address them? If he had published a circular it would have been deemed a scandalous paper, for which he might have been fined and imprisoned. He could scarcely get at the ear of the people in any other way than by the course he took, and he could in no other way put as forcible a check upon the church party persecutions of his own sect.

There are volcanoes in nature; may there not be such in the moral world? Who knows but they are safety valves to the whole system. It cannot be denied that the church gave ample and repeated occasion to call from these reformers something more than the sound of the lute. These moral upheavings must tend to a sublime end, and like adversity have their sweet uses. We are now breathing the fragrance of the flower planted in the dark soil of those turbulent times. Of the Puritanism of New England, we must say it is bespattered with many a blot, which ought not to be passed over with zephyrs of praise. "Fair weather cometh out of the north. Men see not the bright light in the cloud. The wind passeth over and cleanseth them." Let us revere the names of all who, in the face of suffering and loss, have dared to stand up boldly in truth's defence.

To impress men to haul an apostle of liberty from jail to jail, break into the sanctity of family relations, imprison fathers and mothers, purloin their property, for no just cause whatever, leaving their children to cry in the streets for bread, and this under the cloak of religion, is an offence incomparably greater than to make one's voice heard in vindication of truth, even in a meeting-house.

The offences of John Rogers, whatever they may have been, encountering opposition with opposition, in which facts were the only swords, and words the only lash, are as insignificant as the fly on the elephant's back compared with the treatment that he and his followers received from those who had fled from persecution in the Old World to stain their own hands with like atrocities in the New.

Of the almost unprecedented suffering and cruelties which John Rogers endured for conscience's sake, and in the cause of religious freedom, for many years, and particularly of his confinement in the Hartford prison, he here tells the story, written by himself about twelve years after his release from that prison. See "Midnight Cry," pages 4-16:—

Friends and Brethren:—

I have found it no small matter to enter in at the straight gate and to keep the narrow way that leads unto life; for it hath led me to forsake a dear wife and children, yea, my house and land and all my worldly enjoyment, and not only so, but to lose all the friendships of the world, yea, to bury all my honor and glory in the dust, and to be counted the off-scouring and filth of all things; yea, the straight and narrow way hath led me into prisons, into stocks and to cruel scourgings, mockings and derision, and I could not keep in it without perfect patience under all these things; for through much tribulation must we enter into the kingdom of God.

I have been a listed soldier under His banner now about thirty-two years, under Him whose name is called the Word of God, who is my Captain and Leader, that warreth against the devil and his angels, against whom I have fought many a sore battle, within this thirty-two years, for refusing to be subject to the said devil's or dragon's laws, ordinances, institutions and worship; and for disregarding his ministers, for which transgressions I have been sentenced to pay hundreds of pounds, laid in iron chains, cruelly scourged, endured long imprisonments, set in the stocks many hours together, out of the bounds of all human law, and in a cruel manner.

Considering who was my Captain and Leader, and how well He had armed me for the battle, I thought it my wisdom to make open proclamation of war against the dragon, accordingly I did, in writing, and hung it out on a board at the prison window, but kept no copy of it, but strangely met with a copy of it many years after, and here followeth a copy of it. (See Part II, Chapter IV.) This proclamation of War was in the first month, and in the year 1694. It did not hang long at the Prison window before a Captain, who also was a Magistrate, came to the prison window and told me he was a Commission Officer and that proclamations belonged to him to publish; and so he took it away with him, and I never heard anything more about it from the Authority themselves; but I heard from others, who told me they were present and heard it read among the Authority, with great laughter and sport at the fancy of it.

But the Dragon which deceiveth the whole world, pitted all his forces against me in a great fury; for one of his ministers, a preacher of his doctrine, not many days after this proclamation, made complaint to the Authority against me, as I was informed, and after understood it to be so by the Authority, and that he had given evidence of Blasphemy against me; though nothing relating to my proclamation; and this following Warrant and Mittimus was issued against me, while I was in New London prison, which I took no copy of also; but the Mittimus itself came to my hands as strangely as the copy of the Proclamation did; of which here followeth a copy:—

Mittimus.

"Whereas John Rogers of New London hath of late set himself in a furious way, in direct opposition to the true worship and pure ordinances and holy institution of God; as also on the Lord's Day passing out of prison in the time of public worship, running into the meeting-house in a railing and raging manner, as being guilty of Blasphemy.

"To the Constable of New London, or County Marshal, these are therefore in their Majestie's name to require you to impress two sufficient men, to take unto their custody the body of John Rogers and him safely to convey unto Hartford and deliver unto the prison-keeper, who is hereby required him the said John Rogers to receive into custody and safely to secure in close prison until next Court of Assistants held in Hartford. Fail not: this dated in New London, March 28th, 1694."

By this Warrant and Mittimus I was taken out of New London Prison, by two armed men, and carried to the head jail of the Government, where I was kept till the next Court of Assistants, and there fined £5 for reproaching their ministry, and to sit on the gallows a quarter of an hour with a halter about my neck; and from thence to the prison again, and there to continue till I paid the said £5 and gave in a bond of £50 not to disturb their churches; where I continued three years and eight months from my first commitment. This was the sentence. And upon a training day the Marshall came with eight Musqueteers, and a man to put the halter on, and as I passed by the Train Band, I held up the halter and told them my Lord was crowned with thorns for my sake and should I be ashamed to go with a halter about my neck for His sake? Whereupon, the Authority gave order forthwith that no person should go with me to the gallows, save but the guard; the gallows was out of the town. When I came to it, I saw that both gallows and ladder were newly made. I stepped up the ladder and walked on the gallows, it being a great square piece of timber and very high. I stamped on it with my feet, and told them I came there to stamp it under my feet; for my Lord had suffered on the gallows for me, that I might escape it.

From thence, I was guarded with the said eight Musqueteers to the prison again. Being come there, the Officers read to me the Court's sentence and demanded of me whether I would give in a bond of £50 not to disturb their churches for time to come, and pay the £5 fine. I told them I owed them nothing and would not bind myself.

About five or six months after, there was a malefactor taken out of the prison where I was and put to death, by reason of which there was a very great concourse of people to behold it; and, when they had executed him, they stopped in the street near to the prison where I was, and I was taken out (I know not for what) and tied to the carriage of a great gun, where I saw the County whip, which I knew well, for it was kept in the prison where I was, and I had it oftentimes in my hand, and had viewed it, it being one single line opened at the end, and three knots tied at the end, on each strand a knot, being not so big as a cod-line; I suppose they were wont, when not upon the Dragon's service, not to exceed forty stripes, according to the law of Moses, every lash being a stripe.

I also saw another whip lie by it with two lines, the ends of the lines tied with twine that they might not open, the two knots seemed to me about as big as a walnut; some told me they had compared the lines of the whip to the lines on the drum and the lines of the whip were much bigger. The man that did the execution did not only strike with the strength of his arm, but with a swing of his body also; my senses seemed to be quicker, in feeling, hearing, discerning, or comprehending anything at that time than at any other time.

The spectators told me they gave me three score stripes, and then they let me loose and asked me if I did not desire mercy of them. I told them, "No, they were cruel wretches." Forthwith, they sentenced me to be whipped a second time. I was told by the spectators that they gave me sixteen stripes; and from thence I was carried to the prison again; and one leg chained to the cell. A bed which I had hired to this time, at a dear rate, was now taken from me by the jailer, and not so much as straw to lie on, nor any covering. The floor was hollow from the ground, and the planks had wide and open joints. It was upon the 18th day of the 8th month that I was thus chained, and kept thus chained six weeks, the weather cold. When the jailer first chained me, he brought some dry crusts on a dish and put them to my mouth, and told me he that was executed that day had left them, and that he would make me thankful for them before he had done with me, and would make me comply with their worship before he had done with me though the Authority could not do it; and then went out from me and came no more at me for three days and three nights; nor sent me one mouthful of meat, nor one drop of drink to me; and then he brought a pottinger of warm broth and offered it to me. I replied, "Stand away with thy broth, I have no need of it."

"Ay! ay!" said he, "have you so much life yet in you?" and went his way. Thus I lay chained at this cell six weeks. My back felt like a dry stick without sense of feeling, being puffed up like a bladder, so that I was fain to lie upon my face. In which prison I continued three years after this, under cruel sufferings.

But I must desist; for it would contain a book of a large volume to relate particularly what I suffered in the time of this imprisonment. But I trod upon the Lion and Adder, the young lion and the dragon I trampled under my feet, and came forth a conqueror, through faith in Him who is the King of Kings and Lord of Lords, and hath overcome death itself for us, and him that hath the power of it also, who is the devil. But this long war hath kept me waking and watching and looking for the coming of the bridegroom and earnestly desiring that his bride may be prepared and in readiness to meet Him in her beautiful garments, being arrayed in fine linen, clean and white, which is the righteousness of the saints.

We are glad to set before the gaze of the world an example of moral heroism, courage and endurance, strongly in contrast with the spirit of this pleasure-loving, gain-seeking age. A light shining in a dark place, which the storms of persecution could not extinguish nor its waves overwhelm.

Mr. McEwen says, in his Half-Century Sermon:—

During the ministry of Mr. Saltonstall, and reaching down through the long ministry of Mr. Adams, and the shorter one of Mr. Byles, a religious sect prevailed here whose acts were vexatious to this church and congregation. I have no wish to give their history except so far as their fanaticism operated as a persecution of our predecessors in this place of worship.

On the side of the oppressor there was power, said Solomon. These people were powerless from the beginning, so far as the secular or ecclesiastical arm was concerned. The power lay in the church and state, and was freely exercised by both, in a cruel and most tyrannical manner, as undisputed history attests.

Mr. McEwen admits that the Rogerenes held the doctrine of non-resistance to violence from men. Referring to this sect in the time of Mr. Byles,[7] he says:—

"They were careful to make no resistance, showing their faith by their works," and relates an anecdote which reflects no credit upon the officers of the law at that day. He says:—

One constable displayed his genius in putting the strength of this principle of non-resistance to a test. He took a bold assailant of public worship down to the harbor, placed him in a boat that was moored to a stake in deep water, perforated the bottom of the boat with an auger, gave the man a dish and left him to live by faith or die in the faith.

Quoting the words of Satan, Mr. McEwen adds, "Skin for skin, all that a man hath will he give for his life." The faith of the man was strong, yet he was saved not by faith, but by bailing water.

Mr. McEwen is quick to condemn the infringement of the law when charged upon the Rogerenes, but makes no objections to the constable's outrage upon law, and no reference to the hundred years of oppression, in fines, whippings, imprisonments, etc., which the Rogerenes had then endured; fines which, with, interest, would have amounted to millions of dollars at the time Mr. McEwen was speaking.

But, notwithstanding the principles of non-resistance so publicly professed by the Rogerenes, from whom the weakest had nothing to fear, Mr. McEwen dwells strongly upon the terrors which they inspired. He says:—

Mr. Saltonstall and Mr. Adams were brave men. Mr. Byles was a man of less nerve and he suffered not a little from their annoyances. He was actually afraid to go without an escort, lest he should suffer indignities from them.

We have shown (Chapter I) the transparent groundlessness of another statement made of their rudeness by Mr. McEwen, which we need not repeat; but the trials into which Mr. Byles was thrown and the escort deemed necessary present such a comical aspect that the following lines from Mother Goose seem appropriate to the case:—

Four and twenty tailors

Went to kill a snail,

The best man among them

Durst not touch its tail;

It stuck up its horns,

Like a little Kyloe cow;

Run! tailors, run! or it

Will kill you all just now.

Mr. Byles, who was ordained in 1757, seems to have been as much displeased with the church as with the Rogerenes themselves; for in 1768 he left New London, renounced the Congregational church and abandoned its ministry altogether. (See Part II, Chapter XII.)

Herod and Pilate were men of note in their day. What are they thought of now? The records of history show many examples of this sort. Quakers were once persecuted and slain. Men are now proud of such ancestry. Let the calumniated wait their hour. The progress of truth adown the ages is slow, but its chariot is golden and its coming sure.

CHAPTER III.

As round and round it takes its flight,
That lofty dweller of the skies,
And never on the earth doth light,
The fabled bird of Paradise;
So would we soar on pinions bright,
And ever keep the sun in sight,
That sun of truth, whose golden rays
Are as the "light of seven days."

Falsehood is the bane of the world. It links men with him who was a liar from the beginning. We would bruise a lie as we would a serpent under our feet. Not so much to defend persons as to vindicate justice do we write.

It has been said that toleration is the only real test of civilization. But toleration is not the word; all men are entitled to equal religious freedom, and any infringement thereof is an infringement of a God-given right.

Who was the most calumniated person the world has ever seen,—stigmatized as a blasphemer, as a gluttonous man, as beside himself, as one that hath a devil? From his mouth we hear the words: "Blessed are ye when men shall persecute and revile you, and say all manner of evil against you falsely."

John Rogers and his disciples, who, in the face of so much obloquy, nurtured the tree of liberty with tears, with sacrifices and with blood, would seem to be entitled to this blessing.

Is it not strange, as we have before said, that Mr. McEwen should say, "To pay taxes of any kind grieved their souls"?

Ought a public teacher to state that which a little research on his part would have shown him to be false?

Miss Caulkins sets this matter in its true light, as already shown, and it will be further elucidated by the words of John Rogers, 2d, here given:—

Forasmuch as we acknowledge the worldly government to be set up of God, we have always paid all public demands for the upholding of the same, as Town Rates and County Rates and all other demands, excepting such as are for the upholding of hireling ministers and false teachers, which God called us to testify against.

Now when the worldly rulers take upon themselves to make laws relating to God's worship, and thereby do force and command men's consciences, and so turn their swords against God's children, they then act beyond their commission and jurisdiction.

Thus it is by misrepresentations without number that the name and fame of these moral heroes have been tarnished.

We will again refer to the false statements in Dr. Trumbull's History, nearly all of which aspersions are taken from that volume of falsehoods written by Peter Pratt after Roger's death, from which we shall presently make quotations that, we doubt not, will convince the intelligent reader that this author was unscrupulous to a degree utterly incomprehensible, unless by supposition of a natural tendency to falsehood.

Yet it is from this book of Pratt's that historians have drawn nearly all their statements regarding the Rogerenes.

Trumbull (quoting from Pratt) says: "John Rogers was divorced from his wife for certain immoralities."

The General Court divorced him from his wife without assigning any cause whatever, of which act Rogers always greatly complained. It was left for his enemies to circulate the above scandal, with the intent to blacken his character and thus weaken Rogerene influence. John Rogers, 2d, testifies that his mother left her husband solely on account of his religion. He says ("Ans. to Peter Pratt"):—

I shall give the reader a true account concerning the matter of the first difference between John Rogers and his wife, as I received it from their own mouths, they never differing in any material point as to the account they gave about it.

Although I did faithfully, and in the fear of God, labor with her in her lifetime, by persuading her to forsake her adulterous life and unlawful companions; yet, since her death, should have been glad to have heard no more about it, had not Peter Pratt, like a bad bird, befouled his own nest by raking in the graves of the dead and by publishing such notorious lies against them "whom the clods of the valley forbid to answer for themselves;"[8] for which cause I am compelled to give a true account concerning those things, which is as follows:—

John Rogers and his wife were both brought up in the New England way of worship, never being acquainted with any other sect; and although they were zealous of the form which they had been brought up in, yet were wholly ignorant as to the work of regeneration, until, by a sore affliction which John

Rogers met with, it pleased God to lay before his consideration the vanity of all earthly things and the necessity of making his peace with God and getting an interest in Jesus Christ, which he now applies himself to seek for, by earnest prayer to God in secret and according to Christ's words, Matt. vii, 7, 8, "Ask and it shall be given you, seek and ye shall find, knock and it shall be opened unto you. For every one that asketh receiveth, and he that seeketh findeth," etc.

And he coming to witness the truth of these scriptures, by God's giving him a new heart and another spirit, and by remitting the guilt of his sins, did greatly engage him to love God with all his heart, and his neighbor as himself, as did appear by his warning all people he met with to make their peace with God, declaring what God had done for his soul.

Now his wife, observing the great change which was wrought in her husband, as appeared by his fervent prayers, continually searching the scriptures, and daily discoursing about the things of God to all persons he met with, and particularly to her, persuading her to forsake her vain conversation and make her peace with God, did greatly stir her up to seek to God by earnest prayer, that he would work the same work of grace in her soul, as she saw and believed to be wrought in her husband.

After some time, upon their diligent searching the holy scriptures, they began to doubt of some of the principles which they had traditionally been brought up in; and particularly that of sprinkling infants which they had been taught to call Baptism; but now they find it to be only an invention of men; and neither command nor example in Scripture for it. Upon which, they bore a public testimony against it, which soon caused a great uproar in the country.

And their relations, together with their neighbors, and indeed the world in general who had any opportunity, were all united in persuading them that it was a spirit of error by which they were deluded.

But the main instrument which Satan at length made use of to deceive John Roger's wife, was her own natural mother, who, by giving her daughter an account of her own conversion, as she called it, and telling her daughter there was no such great change in the work of conversion as they had met with; but that it was the Devil had transformed himself into an angel of light, at length fully persuaded her daughter to believe that it was even so.

Whereupon, she soon publicly recanted and renounced that Spirit which she had been led by, and declared it to be the spirit of the Devil, and then vehemently persuaded her husband to do the like, telling him, with bitter tears, that unless he would renounce that spirit she dare not live with him. But he constantly telling her that he knew it to be the Spirit of God and that to deny it would be to deny God; which he dare not do.

Whereupon she left her husband, taking her two children with her, and with the help of her relations went to her father's house, about eighteen miles from her husband's habitation.

And I do solemnly declare, in the presence of God, that this is a true relation of their first separation, as I received it from their own mouths, as also by the testimony of two of their next neighbors is fully proved. (See Chapter IV, 1st Part.)

So doubtful was she herself of the lawfulness of her subsequent marriage with the father of Peter Pratt, that she never signed her name Elizabeth Pratt to any legal document; but "Elizabeth, daughter of Matthew Griswold," many instances of which are on record.

This charge made against John Rogers, in Dr. Trumbull's History, is further shown to be false by the record of the Court at Hartford, May 25, 1675; the grand jury returning that they "find not the bill." Yet, in the face of this patent fact, has this false charge been perpetuated by ecclesiastical historians and their followers. We note, however, one shining exception, contained in the Saulisbury "Family Histories," under the Matthew Griswold line, treating of the divorce of his daughter Elizabeth, which is here given:—

In 1674, her first husband departed from the established orthodoxy of the New England churches, by embracing the doctrines of the Seventh Day Baptists; and, having adopted later "certain peculiar notions of his own," though still essentially orthodox as respects the fundamental faith of his time, became the founder of a new sect, named after him Rogerenes, Rogerene Quakers, or Rogerene Baptists. Maintaining "obedience to the civil government," he denounced as unscriptural all interference of the civil power in the worship of God.

It seemed proper to give these particulars with regard to Rogers, because they were made the ground[9] of a petition by his wife for divorce, in May, 1675, which was granted by the "General Court," in October of the next year, and was followed in 1677 by another, also granted, for the custody of her children, her late husband being so "hettridox in his opinions and practice."

The whole reminds us of other instances, more conspicuous in history, of the narrowness manifested by fathers of New England towards any deviations from the established belief, and of their distrust of individual conscience as a sufficient rule of religious life, without the interference of civil authority. There is no reason to believe that the heterodoxy "in practice" referred to in the wife's last petition to the Court, was anything else than a nonconformity akin to that for the sake of which the shores of their "dear old England" had been left behind forever by the very men who forgot to tolerate it themselves, in their new Western homes. Of course, like all persecuted, especially religious, parties, the Rogerenes courted, gloried in, and profited by, distresses.

In Trumbull's History, we also find the scandalous statement, to which we have previously referred: "They would come on the Lord's day into the most public assemblies nearly or quite naked."

Nothing could be further from the truth. There is no evidence on record, or tradition, concerning any such act. Among the hundreds of prosecutions against the Rogerenes, no such thing is alluded to on the records, etc. Miss Caulkins in her History makes no reference to this stigma. Yet Mr. McEwen, in his Half-Century Sermon, says: "Dr. Trumbull and perhaps some others give us some historical items of the Rogerenes."

By thus referring to Dr. Trumbull's History, he virtually, we would hope not intentionally, indorses all the errors concerning this sect, which are contained in that work.

But, like the entablature of a column, crowning all the rest, are the words of Rev. Mr. Saltonstall, credited to same 'History,' and which we have before quoted:—

There never was, for this twenty years that I have resided in this government, any one, Quaker or other person, that suffered on account of his different persuasion in religious matters from the body of this people.

Why were the Rogerenes fined for observing the seventh day instead of the first day of the week, consistently with their profession? Why fined for absenting themselves from the meetings of the Congregational church? Why forbidden to hold meetings of their own? Why was John Rogers fined for every one he baptized by immersion, and for entertaining Quakers, as we have seen? And why did the Hartford jailer say to him: "I will make you comply with their worship if the Authority cannot"?

Miss Caulkins, though writing in partial defence of the Church, speaks truthfully on this subject when she says:—

It was certainly a great error in the early planters of New England to endeavor to produce uniformity in doctrine by the strong arm of physical force. Was ever religious dissent subdued either by petty annoyance or actual cruelty? Is it possible to make a true convert by persecution? The principle of toleration was, however, then less clearly understood.

This self-justification of Mr. Saltonstall would seem to vie for insincerity with the language used by papists, as they handed over heretics to the civil power, asking that they be treated with mercy and that not a drop of blood be shed, meaning that they be burned.

It is not unlike what that most cruel persecutor, Philip II of Spain, husband of Bloody Mary, said of himself: "that he had always from the beginning of his government followed the path of clemency, according to his natural disposition, so well known to the world;" or what Virgilius wrote of the merciless Duke of Alva, while the latter was carrying out some of the most diabolical devices of the Inquisition, under the orders of this same king Philip: "All," said Virgilius, "venerate the prudence and gentleness of the Duke of Alva."

Mr. Saltonstall's words also run in a groove with those of Peter Pratt, the great traducer. "In short," says Pratt, "he never suffered the loss of one hair of his head by the Authority for any article of his religion, nor for the exercise of it."

To which John Rogers, 2d, replies:—

In answer to this last extravagant assertion, which the whole neighborhood knows to be false, I shall only mention the causes of some few of his sufferings, which I am sure that both the records and neighborhood will witness the truth of.

In the first place, he lost his wife and children on the account of his religion, as has been fully proved.

The next long persecution, which both himself and all his Society suffered for many years, was for refusing to come to Presbyterian meetings; upon which account, their estates were extremely destroyed and their bodies often imprisoned.

Also the multitude of fines and imprisonments which he suffered on the account of baptizing such as desired to be baptized after the example of Christ, by burying in the water. All which fines and imprisonments were executed in the most rigorous manner. Sometimes the officers, taking him in the dead of winter, as he came wet out of the water, committed him to prison without a spark of fire, with many other cruel acts, which for brevity I must omit.

Moreover, the many hundreds of pounds which the collectors have taken from him for the maintainance of the Presbyterian ministers, which suffering he endured to the day of his death and which his Society still suffers.

But, forasmuch as his sufferings continued more than forty years, and were so numerous that I doubt not but to give a particular account of them would fill a larger volume than was ever printed in New England, I must desist.

But the same spirit of persecution under which he suffered, is yet living among us; as is evidenced by what here follows:—

The last fifth month called July, in the year 1725, we were going to our meeting, being eight of us in number, it being the first day of the week, the day which we usually meet on as well as the rest of our neighbors; and as we were in our way, we were taken upon the king's highway, by order of Joseph Backus, called a justice of the peace, and the next day by his order cruelly whipped, with an unmerciful instrument, by which our bodies were exceedingly wounded and maimed; and the next first day following, as we were returning home from our meeting, we were again, three of us, taken upon the king's highway, by order of John Woodward and Ebenezer West of Lebanon, called justices of the peace, and the next day by them sentenced to be whipped, and were accordingly carried to the place of execution and stripped in order to receive the sentence; but there happened to be present some tender-spirited people, who, seeing the wounds in our bodies we had received the week before, paid the fines and so prevented the punishment.

And also the same John Woodward, soon after this, committed two of our brethren to prison, viz., Richard Man and Elisha Man, for not attending the Presbyterian meeting, although they declared it to be contrary to their consciences to do so. Neither have their persecutors allowed them one meal of victuals, nor so much as straw to lie on, all the time of their imprisonment; although they are well known to be very poor men.

But, to return to the matter I was upon, which was to prove Peter Pratt's assertion false, in saying John Rogers never suffered the loss of one hair of his head by the Authority for any article of his religion, nor for the exercise of it. And had not Peter Pratt been bereft as well of reason as conscience, he would not have presumed to have asserted such a thing, which the generality of the neighborhood knows to be false.

In further proof of the falsity of Mr. Saltonstall's assertions, and as showing also the spirit of those times, we quote the following from Dr. Trumbull's History:—

But though the churches were multiplying and generally enjoying peace, yet sectaries were creeping in and began to make their appearance in the Colony. Episcopacy made some advances, and in several instances there was a separation from the Standing Churches. The Rogerenes and a few Baptists made their appearance among the inhabitants; meetings were held in private houses, and laymen undertook to administer the sacraments. This occasioned the following act of the General Assembly, at their sessions in May, 1723.[10]

"Be it enacted, &c., That whatsoever persons shall presume on the Lord's

Day to neglect the public worship of God in some lawful congregation, and form themselves into separate companies in private houses, being convicted thereof before any assistant or Justice of the Peace, shall each of them on every such offense, forfeit the sum of twenty shillings, and that whatsoever person (not being lawfully allowed minister of the Standing Order) shall presume to profane the holy sacraments by administering them to any person or persons whatsoever, and being thereof convicted before the County Court, in such County where such offense shall be committed, shall incur the penalty of £10 for every such offense and suffer corporal punishment, by whipping not exceeding thirty stripes for each offense."

Previous to this act, the penalty for baptizing by immersion was £5, which penalty was often inflicted upon John Rogers, as we have seen.

In the Boston plantation, for merely speaking against sprinkling of infants the like penalty was incurred. Thus thick was the cloud of bigotry and ignorance which had settled down on the people at that day and which John Rogers, and his followers by the light of truth labored to disperse, deserving honor instead of the reproaches which they have suffered from prejudiced and careless historians and narrow-minded ecclesiastics.

Still, in the face of facts like these, "all of which he saw and a large part of which he was," the Rev. Gurdon Saltonstall asserts "that no man hath suffered on account of his religious opinions," etc.

Dr. Trumbull says, "Mr. Saltonstall was a great man."

"They helped every one his neighbor; so the carpenter encouraged the goldsmith."—*Isaiah.* "And the great man he uttereth his mischievous desire: so they wrap it up."—*Micah.*

CHAPTER IV.

One has said that an angel would feel as much honored in receiving a commission to sweep the streets as though called to a service higher in the world's estimation. We confess to something like a street-cleaning duty in removing the scandals which have settled about the name of John Rogers.

Since the enemies of Rogers have mainly taken their artillery from Pratt's work, the falsity of which has in part been shown, we now proceed to give it further notice and refutation. Base coin is sometimes passed around and received as genuine; put to the test, its worth vanishes. Written in a malignant spirit, with no regard to truth whatever, the untrustworthiness of Pratt's book can scarcely be overstated.

We will continue to quote from this book, and John Rogers, 2d's "Reply" to the same.

It remains (says Pratt) that I speak of the third step in Quakerism taken by John Rogers, who received his first notions of spirituality from Banks and Case, a couple of lewd men[11] of that sort called Singing Quakers. These men, as they danced through this Colony, lit on John Rogers and made a Quaker of him; but neither they nor the Spirit could teach him to sing. However, he remained their disciple for a while, and then, being wiser than his teachers, made a transition to the church of the Seventh Day Baptists. But, the same spirit not deserting him, but setting in with the disposition of his own spirit to a vehement affectation of precedency, he resolved to reach it, though it should happen to lead to singularity; whereupon, after a few revelations, he resolved upon Quakerism again, though under a modification somewhat new. I call it Quakerism, not but that he differed from them in many things, yet holding with them in the main, being guided by the same spirit, acknowledging their spirit and they his, he must needs be called a Quaker.

Reply of John Rogers, Jr.:—

Every article of this whole paragraph (so far as it relates to John Rogers) is notoriously false; for the proof of which I have taken these following testimonies from two of his ancient neighbors, which though they have always been enemies to his principles, yet have been very free in giving their testimonies to the truth, signifying their abhorrence of such an abuse done to a dead man.

"The testimony of Daniel Stubbins, aged about eighty years, testifieth, that from a lad I have been near neighbor and well acquainted with John Rogers, late of New London, deceased, to his dying day, and do testify that the time he first pretended to spiritual conversation and declared himself to be a converted man, upon which he broke off from the Presbyterian church in New London and joined with the Seventh Day Baptists, and his wife therefore left him and went to her father, Matthew Griswold of Lyme, was about the year 1674, and the time that Case and Banks, with a great company of other ranters, first came into this Colony was about twelve years after; and I never heard or understood that J. Rogers ever inclined to their way, or left any of his former principles on their account.

DANIEL STUBBINS."

Dated in New London, June 27, 1725.

"The testimony of Mary Tubbs, aged about seventy-seven years, testifieth, that I was a near neighbor to John Rogers, late of New London, deceased, at the time when his wife left him and went to her father, Matthew Griswold of Lyme, and I had discourse with her the same day she went, and she informed me that it was because her husband had renounced his religion and was joined with the Seventh Day Baptists, and this was about the year 1674, and it was many years after that one Case and Banks, with a great company of ranters, first came into this Colony and came to New London and were some days at the house of James Rogers, where John Rogers then dwelt; but I never understood that John Rogers inclined to their way or principles, or countenanced their practices, but continued in the religion which he was in before.

MARY TUBBS."

Dated in New London, June 29, 1725.

Now the first falsehood which I shall observe in this place is his asserting that "the first notions of spirituality taken by John Rogers were from Case and Banks," etc. Whereas the above witnesses testify that he had broke off from the church of New London and joined with the Seventh Day Baptists; upon which his wife had left him, and that all this was many years before Case and Banks came into this Colony.

The second falsehood is his saying, "These men lit on John Rogers and made a Quaker of him." Whereas these witnesses testify that he never inclined to their way, nor countenanced their practices, but continued in the religion which he was in before.

The third falsehood is his saying, "He remained their disciple for awhile;" since it is fully proved that he never was their disciple at all.

The fourth falsehood is his saying that "after he had remained their disciple awhile he made a transition to the church of the Seventh Day Baptists." Whereas it is fully proved that his joining with the Seventh Day Baptists was many years before those people first came into this Colony.

And among his other scoffs and falsehoods, he asserts that John Rogers "often changed his principles." To which I answer that upon condition that Peter Pratt will make it appear that John Rogers ever altered or varied in any one article of his religion, since his separating from the Presbyterian church and joining with the Seventh Day Baptists, which is more than fifty years past (excepting only as to the observation of the seventh day), I will reward him with the sum of £20 for his labor. No, verily, he mistakes the man; it was not John Rogers that used to change his religion, but it was Peter Pratt himself.

Here follow more of the false statements made by Peter Pratt, which have been repeated by Trumbull, Barber, and others:—

Great part of his imprisonment at Hartford was upon strong suspicion of his being accessory to the burning of New London meeting-house.

To which John Rogers, 2d, replies:—

As to this charge against John Rogers concerning New London meeting-house, were it not for the sake of those who live remote, I should make no reply to it; because there are so many hundreds of people inhabiting about New London who know it to be notoriously false, and that John Rogers was a close prisoner at Hartford (which is fifty miles distant from New London) several months before and three years after said meeting-house was burnt. And that this long imprisonment was for refusing to give a bond of £50, which he declared he could not in conscience do, and to pay a fine of £5, which he refused to do, for which reason he was kept a prisoner, from the time of his first commitment, three years and eight months, and then set at liberty by open proclamation, is so fully proved by the records of Hartford that I presume none will dare contradict.

And now, in order to prove Peter Pratt's affirmation to be false, in that he affirms that "great part of his imprisonment at Hartford was upon strong suspicion of his being accessory to the burning of New London meeting-house," take these following testimonies:—

"The testimony of Thomas Hancox, aged about eighty years, testifieth, That when I was goal keeper at Hartford, John Rogers, late of New London, deceased, was a prisoner under my charge for more than three years; in which time of his confinement at Hartford, New London meeting-house was burnt, and I never heard or understood that the Authority, or any other person, had any mistrust that he was any way concerned in that fact, nor did he ever suffer one hour's imprisonment on that account.

THOMAS HANCOX, Kinsington, Sept. 17, 1725."

"Samuel Gilbert, aged sixty-two years, testifieth and saith: That at the time when John Rogers, late of New London, deceased, was a prisoner several years at Hartford, I did at the same time keep a public house of entertainment near the prison, and was well knowing to the concerns of the said Rogers all the time of his imprisonment, and I do farther testify that New London meeting-house was burnt at the time while he was a prisoner in said prison, but no part of his imprisonment was upon that account.

SAMUEL GILBERT, October, 1725."

Thus it plainly appears that this affirmation concerning New London meeting-house is a positive falsehood.

He (Pratt) further says that "Rogers held downright that man had no soul at all, and that though he used the term, yet intended by it either the natural life, or else the natural faculties, which he attributed to the body, and held that they died with it, even as it is with a dog."

In answer to this notorious falsehood charged upon John Rogers, I shall boldly appeal to all mankind who had conversation with him in his lifetime; for that they well knew it to be utterly false: and for the satisfaction of such as had not acquaintance with him, I shall refer them to his books, and particularly in this point to his "Exposition on the Revelations," beginning at page 232, where he largely sets forth the Resurrection of the Body, both of the just and unjust, and of the eternal judgment which God shall then pass upon all, both small and great. All which sufficiently proves Peter Pratt guilty of slandering and belying a dead man, a crime generally abhorred by all sober people; and so shall pass to his 3d chapter, judging that by these few remarks which have been taken, the reader may plainly see that the account he pretends to give of John Roger's principles is so false and self-contradictory that it deserves no answer at all, and that it was great folly in Peter Pratt so to expose himself as to pretend to give an account of John Roger's principles in such a false manner; since John Rogers himself has largely published his own principles in print, which books are plenty, and will fully satisfy every one that desires satisfaction in that matter of what I have here asserted.

In page 48 he (Pratt) tells the reader as follows: "But John Rogers held three ordinances of religious use; viz., Baptism, the Lord's Supper, and imposition of hands." Again, "that all worship is in the heart only, and there are no external forms."

Here the reader may observe that, first, he owns that Rogers held three external ordinances, viz., Baptism, the Lord's Supper, and imposition of hands; and in the very next words forgets himself and tells the reader that Rogers held all worship to be in the heart only, and that there were no external forms. See how plainly he contradicts himself.

Here we ought to say, without soiling our pen with his obscene language, that what Peter Pratt said and others have quoted about John Roger's "maid" has reference to his second wife, an account of his marriage to whom, with other facts of the case, we now give to the reader, in the words of John Rogers, 2d, in his "Reply" to Peter Pratt:—

After John Roger's first wife had left him, on account of his religion, he remained single for more than twenty-five years, in hopes that she would come to repentance and forsake her unlawful companions. But, seeing no change in her, he began to think of marrying another woman, and, accordingly, did agree upon marriage with a maid belonging to New London, whose name was Mary Ransford. They thereupon agreed to go into the County Court and there declare their marriage; and accordingly they did so, he leading his bride by the hand into court, where the judges were sitting and a multitude of spectators present, and then desired the whole assembly to take notice that he took that woman to be his wife; his bride also assenting to what he said. Whereupon, the judge offered to marry them in their form, which John Rogers refused, telling him that he had once been married by their Authority, and by their Authority they had taken away his wife again and rendered him no reason why they did it. Upon which account, he looked at their form of marriage to be of no value, and therefore would be married by their form no more, etc. And from the court he went to the Governor's house with his bride, and declared their marriage to the Governor,[12] who seemed to like it well enough, and wished them much joy, which is a usual compliment.

And thus having given a true and impartial relation of the manner of his marriage to his second wife, which I doubt not but every unprejudiced person will judge to be as authentic as any marriage that was ever made in Connecticut Colony, in the next place, I shall proceed to inform the reader in what manner he came to be deprived of this his second wife; for, after they had lived together about three years and had had two children, the court had up John Roger's wife and charged her with fornication, for having her last child, pretending no other reason than that the marriage was not lawful; and thereupon called her Mary Ransford, after her maiden name. And then vehemently urged her to give her oath who was the father of her child, which they charged to be by fornication, her husband standing by her in court, with the child in his arms, strictly commanding her not to take the oath, for these three following reasons:—

First, because it was contrary to Christ's command, Matt. v, 34, "But I say unto you, swear not at all," etc.

A second reason was because it was a vain oath, inasmuch as they had been married so publickly, and then lived together three years after, and that he himself did not deny his child, nor did any person doubt who was the father of the child, etc.

A third reason was, he told her, they laid a snare for her, and wanted her oath to prove their charge, which was that the child was by fornication; so that her swearing would be that he was the father of that child by fornication, and so it would not only be a reproach to him and the child, but also a false oath, forasmuch as the child was not by fornication.

For these reasons, he forbid her taking the oath, but bid her tell the court that her husband was the father of that child in his arms. He also told her in the court that if she would be ruled by him, he would defend her from any damage. But if she would join with the court against him, by being a witness that the child was by fornication, he should scruple to own her any more as a wife.

But the court continuing to urge her to take the oath, promising her favor if she took it, and threatening her with severity if she refused to take it, at length she declared she would not be ruled by John Rogers, but would accept of the court's favor, and so took the oath; and the favor which the court granted her was to pass the following sentence:—

New London, at a County Court, the 15th of September, 1702.

Mary Ransford of New London, being presented by the grandjurymen to this court, for having a child by fornication, which was born in March last, and she being now brought before this court to answer for the same, being examined who was the father of her child, she said John Rogers senior of New London, to which she made oath, the said Rogers being present.

The court having considered her offense, sentence her, for the same, to pay unto the County Treasurer forty shillings money, or to be whipt ten stripes on the naked body. She is allowed till the last of November to pay the fine.

A true copy of the Record, as far as it respects the said Mary Ransford, her examination and fine.

Test. JOHN PICKET, *Clerk.*

And now the poor woman found that by her oath she had proved her child illegitimate, and thereby denied her marriage, and that her husband dare not own her as a wife; for I think that no woman can be said to be a wife (though ever so lawfully married) if she turn so much against her husband as not only to disobey his most strict commands, but also to prove by her oath that his children are by fornication, as it was in this case. She was also greatly terrified on account of her whipping, to avoid which she some time after made her escape out of the Government, to a remote Island in Rhode Island Government, called Block Island; and in about eight years after she had thus been driven from her husband she was married to one Robert Jones, upon said Island, with whom she still lives in that Government.

Whereupon, John Rogers again lived single twelve years, which was four years after she was married to Robert Jones, and then he made suit to one Sarah Coles of Oyster Bay, on Long Island, a widow, and by reason of the many false reports which had spread about the Country, as if he had turned away his second wife, etc., he offered the woman to carry her to Block Island, where she might know the truth of the matter, by discoursing with the woman herself, as well as the Authority and neighbors, which accordingly he did; by which means she was so well satisfied that she proposed to be married before they came off; and accordingly was married, by Justice Ray.

There are other scandalous stories quoted nearly verbatim from Pratt's book by Trumbull, which neither space, nor the patience of the reader, nor delicacy permits us to repeat, all of which have been completely refuted by John Rogers, 2d, in his "Reply" to the same.

We will presently entertain the reader with Pratt's poetical effort deriding baptism by immersion, concerning which John Rogers, 2d, replies. It should be remembered that Peter Pratt was the son of John Roger's first wife, by her second husband, and was much at the house of John Rogers, Sr., on visits to his half brother, John, 2d. He was baptized (viz., rebaptized by immersion) by Rogers, and even suffered imprisonment, at one time, with other Rogerenes, but apostatized under persecution and returned to the Congregational church, from which, after the death of Rogers, he threw at him those poisonous shafts of which the reader has seen some specimens.

Here follow Pratt's verses, quoted in "Reply" of John Rogers, 2d:—

And now as to his songs and other verses, I shall be very brief, only mentioning some of the gross blasphemies which they contain, not doubting that all sober Christians, together with myself, will abhor such profaneness as may be seen in page 36, and is as follows:—

That sacramental bond,
By which my soul was tied
To Christ in baptism, I cast off
And basely vilified.
I suffered to be washed
As Satan instituted,
My body, so my soul thereby,
Became the more polluted.

I suppose he intends by that sacramental bond by which he says his soul was tied to Christ, that non-scriptural practice of sprinkling a little water out of a basin on his face in his unregenerate state. Now the scriptures abundantly show us that the Spirit of God is the bond by which God's children are sealed or united to him; as Eph. i, 13, Eph. iv, 3 and 30, John iii, 24. Thus it plainly appears it is the Spirit of God that is the bond by which God's children are united to Christ, and not by sprinkling a little elementary water on their faces, as Peter Pratt has ignorantly and blasphemously asserted.

Whereas he says he suffered his body to be washed as Satan instituted, I suppose he intends his being baptized according to the rule of Scripture of which he gives us an account, page 18, how that he was stirred up to this ordinance from those words, Acts xxii, 16, "And now why tarriest thou? arise and be baptized and wash away thy sins," and that accordingly he was baptized by burying his body in the water.

As to the first institutor of this ordinance, we know that John the Baptist was the first practiser of it, therefore let us take his testimony as to the institutor of it, which is to be seen John i, 33, "And I knew Him not, but He that sent me to baptize with water, the same said unto me, upon whom thou shalt see the Spirit," etc.

And here I suppose none but Peter Pratt will dare deny that it was God Almighty that instituted this ordinance and sent John the Baptist to administer it.

Having given a specimen of Peter Pratt's poetical effusions, we will further entertain the reader with some verses by John Rogers, 2d, which precede his "Reply" to Pratt's book:—

A POETICAL INQUIRY INTO WHAT ADVANTAGE P. PRATT COULD PROMISE HIMSELF BY HIS LATE ENGAGEMENT WITH A DEAD MAN.

I marvel that when Peter Pratt, in armor did appear,
He should engage, in such a rage, a man that's dead three year.
Could he suppose for to disclose his valour in the field?
Or by his word, or wooden sword, to make his en'my yield?
Did he advance, thinking by chance, and taking so much pain,
To fright away a lump of clay, some honour for to gain?
Was his intent by argument, some honour for to have?
Or gain repute by making mute a man that's in his grave?
Why did he strain his foolish brain, and muse upon his bed,
To study lies, for to despise a man when he is dead?
Why did he flout his venom out against the harmless dirt,

Which when alive did never strive to do the creature hurt?

No manly face, or Godly grace such actions will uphold,

Yet 'tis not new; apostates crew did do the like of old.

When Cain let in that dreadful sin which never can be pardoned,

He then did hate his loving mate, because he was so hardened.

Though Saul before did much adore his well-belovèd David,

Yet in the state that I relate his life he greatly cravèd.

In Judas we may also see another strange disaster,

Who for small gain did take such pain to sell his blessèd Master.

Apostates then, the vilest men, they're always most forlorn;

Because such deeds from them proceeds which other men do scorn.

Such raging waves Satan depraves of all humanity;

They can embrace no saving grace, nor yet civility.

Had but this strife been in the life of his supposèd foe,

Then Peter Pratt would like a rat into a corner go;

Or flee apace, or hide his face, although that now he glories

To trample on one dead and gone, with his debauchèd stories.

A certain tribe of Indians would not allow the burial of any one until some person could speak a word in his praise. On one such occasion, silence long reigned, when a squaw arose and said, "He was a good smoker." What can we say of Peter Pratt, that the right of sepulture may be granted him? This may be said: He at one time thought he had discovered the "wonderful art of longitude," by which he expected to be made famous the world over, and presented his scheme to the faculty of Yale College, who regarded it as the product of an hallucinated mind. Upon this, Pratt gave up the fallacy, which should be spoken to his praise. The following testimony which he gave in his book regarding John Rogers, 2d, and incidentally in favor of John Rogers senior, should also be put to his credit:—

My near alliance to John Rogers (then junior) who is my brother, viz., the son of my mother, proved an unhappy snare to me. He being, naturally, a man as manly, wise, facetious and generous perhaps as one among a thousand, I was exceedingly delighted in and with his conversation. He also endeared himself to me very much by his repeated expressions of complacency in me, by which I was induced to be frequently in his company and often at his house, where his father would be entertaining me with exhortations to a religious life, warning me of the danger of sin, and certainty of that wrath which shall come on all that know not God. I would sometimes, for curiosity, be inquiring into his principles, and othertimes, for diversion, be disputing a point with him; but I knew not that the dead were there, Prov. ix, 18. I was not religious enough to be much concerned about his principles, but pitiful enough to be extremely moved with the story of his sufferings. I had also a reserve in his favor, that it was possible he might be a good man (the strangeness of his doctrine notwithstanding), especially seeing all his sufferings were not able to shake his constancy, or oblige him to recede from the least part of his religion.

And here a just tribute may be paid to John Rogers, 2d, from whom we have so largely quoted. The appreciative reader will agree with us in saying he was a son worthy of the father, in defence of whose honor he wrote. Clear in his statement of facts, conclusive in his reasoning, and abundantly supplied with authority in proof of his assertions, his words bear the sacred impress of truth. Malice has raised no aspersions against his character. "Notwithstanding," says Miss Caulkins, "his long testimony and his many weary trials and imprisonments, he reared to maturity a family of eighteen children, most of them, like their parents, sturdy Rogerenes." As soon as he was able to make choice for himself, about the age of sixteen, he left the home of his grandfather, Matthew Griswold of Lyme, the ancestor of many noted men, and chose to live with his father. His sister did the same thing at the age of fourteen, and was married at her father's house. A purer, sweeter, and higher tribute could scarcely be paid to that heroic defender of religious liberty and great sufferer for conscience' sake.

John Rogers, 2d, was the author of several other books besides his "Reply to Peter Pratt," each of them being of the same able character.

CHAPTER V.

"Nine and twenty knives."—Ezra i, 9. It would take more than that number of knives to sever the many threads of falsehood and malice wound about the name of John Rogers, a name that may yet emerge as the royal butterfly from its chrysalis, to dwell in the light and atmosphere of heaven.

We must now charge the Rev. Gurdon Saltonstall, governor of the State of Connecticut, and judge of its Superior Court, with concocting a plan whereby he and his ecclesiastical accomplices might incarcerate John Rogers in the Hartford jail, exclude him from the light, and hide him from the public thought. Had this nefarious scheme succeeded, Rogers would doubtless have been held a close prisoner for life; but he was apprised of it and enabled to make his escape, like as St. Paul was let down in a basket from the wall of Damascus to elude the fury of his enemies. The governor's suit against him for slanderous words—not slanderous in law—for which a subservient jury awarded him damages in the sum of £600, proves with what malign purpose Roger's conduct was watched by him.

Here follows an account of the above mentioned plot and other matters, in Roger's own words, copied from his address to the civil authorities and particularly to Gov. Saltonstall, in which he recounts some of the atrocious wrongs he had received from them,—wrongs which could hardly gain credence had they not been openly published at the time, during the life of Gov. Saltonstall, and not denied by him.

The last fine you fined me was ten shillings. All that I did was expounding upon a chapter in the Bible between your meetings, after the people were gone to dinner, which you call a riot. I went into no other seat but that which I was seated in by them whom the town appointed to seat every one. The building of the meeting-house cost me three of the best fat cattle I had that year and as many sheep as sold for thirty shillings in silver money. For which said fine of ten shillings, the officer took ten sheep, as some told me that helped to drive them away. The sheep were half my son's. They were marked with a mark that we marked creatures with that were between us, which said mark had been recorded in the town book, I suppose for above twenty years. And after they were sold, the officer went into my son's pasture, unbeknown to him, and took a milch cow which was between us (my part he hired), all upon the same fine of ten shillings. Such things as these have been frequently done upon us; but my purpose is brevity, and such things as these would contain a great volume; therefore I think to mention but one more. I was fined £20 by a Superior Court for charging an Inferior Court with injustice for trying upon life and death without a jury. The judge of the Superior Court that fined me was this present Governor, who also denied me a jury, though I chose the jury then panelled. For which £20 and the charges, an execution was laid upon land which I bought for my son, with his own money, and after it was taken away by said execution, he went and bought it of you this present Government, and gave you the money down for it, and you gave him a patent for it I think as substantial as your patent from the crown of England for your Government, upon all accounts, being sealed with your seal and with your present Governor's hand and your Secretary's to it. The patent cost 19s. to the Governor for signing it. And when you had got his money for it, and given him said patent, then you took this very individual land from him, and kept his money also, and left him nothing but said patent in his hand; for said Governor kept the deed which the man of whom I bought it gave, and keeps it to this day, I think for that end that my son may not help himself of said deed; for the man of whom I bought it lives in another Government.

I prosecuted the judges of your said Inferior Court before your General Court for judging upon life and death without a jury, it being by your own law out of their jurisdiction to judge in so high a fact without a jury; the fact also charged to be done in New York government; to wit, the stealing of three servants out of a man's house on Long Island in the night. But you non-suited me in your Court of Chancery and laid all the charge upon me and fined me £20. So that if the poor man had not obtained justice in Boston Government, he had lost his wife and children by you, as I had mine; for he had tried in Rhode Island Government before, and had got bondsmen to answer all damages, if he did not make good his right and title to his wife and children. But said Governor of Rhode Island sent them back to this present Governor; but, by the good hand of God, they were after transported into Boston Government, by which means the poor man came at justice.

I thought to have concluded with what is above written; but, upon consideration that it is but two things among many, I shall set before you this last to the end of it. The said Inferior Court did proceed and pass judgment in a case that was upon life and death by the law of God, the law of England and your own law, upon a fact charged in another government, as above said, and without witness. And when I saw they would proceed, I then drew up the following protest and gave it unto your court.

The Protest of John Rogers, senior, of New London, against the proceedings of the present Court, against myself and John Jackson, being a pretended fact done upon Long Island, within the bounds and limits of the Government established there for to do justice and judgment within their limits and territories, and do appeal to their Court of Justice for a trial where I have evidence to clear myself of any such fact.

June 1 , 171 .	JOHN ROGERS, Sr.

A true copy, testified George Denison, County Clerk.

June 28, 171 .

And I do declare unto you, in the presence of God, that I was not at that time upon Long Island, when the fact was charged to be done, though I was at that time within the government of New York. But when I heard the said Court's sentence, I did declare it to be injustice and rebellion against the laws of the crown of England; upon which charge, the said court demanded of me a bond of £200 to answer it at the next Superior Court. And when the Superior Court came, I desired to be tried by a jury, and chose that jury then sitting. But this present Governor, being judge of this Superior Court, denied me a jury and fined me £20 and required of me a great bond for my good behavior till the next Superior Court, which I refused to give, upon this reason that I would not reflect upon myself, as if I had misbehaved myself, as I had not. Whereupon, I was committed to prison, and kept a close prisoner in the inner prison, where no fire was allowed me, and that winter was a violent cold winter and there was no jailer, but the sheriff kept the keys, who lived half a mile distant from the prison, and my own habitation full two miles distant; so that it was a difficult thing for my friends to come at me; the prison new and not under-pinned, and stood upon blocks some distance from the ground; the floor, being planked with green plank, shrunk much and let in the cold. My son was wont in cold nights to come to the grates of the window to see how I did, and contrived privately in cold nights to help me with some fire (for the sheriff said he had order that no fire be allowed me), but could not find any way to make it do by giving it in at the grates, they being so close, and no place to make it within. But he, coming in a very cold night, called to me, and perceiving that I was not in my right senses, was in a fright, and ran along the street, crying, "The Authority hath killed my father!" and cried at the sheriff's, "You have killed my father!" Upon which, the town was raised and my life was narrowly preserved, for forthwith the prison doors were opened and fire brought in, and hot stones wrapt in cloth and laid at my feet and about me, and the minister Adams sent me a bottle of spirits and his wife a cordial, whose kindness I must acknowledge. And the neighbors came about me with what relief they could, all which kindness I acknowledge. But when those of you in authority saw that I recovered, you had up my son and fined him for making a riot in the night, and he desired to be tried by a jury, but you dismissed the jury that was in being and panelled a jury purposely for him, as I was informed,—and since have seen it to be so by your own court record,—and took for the fine and charge three of the best cows I had.

In which prison I lay till the next Superior Court and in the sheriff's house. The time of the bond demanded by them being out, I was dismissed. I think the next day, I was going to baptize a person,[13] and, as I was going to the water, the sheriff came to me and desired to speak with me. His house being close by, I went in with him. He went through two rooms and came to the door of the third, and then told me the Superior Court had ordered him to shut me up. Upon that, I made a stop and desired him to show me his order. He said it was by word of mouth. He keeping a tavern, there were many present who told him he ought not to shut me up without a written order. He then laid violent hands upon me to pull me in, but the people rescued me; and then he told me he would go to the court and get it in writing. And so he left me and brought this following Mittimus, this present Governor being judge of this Superior Court also.

"To the Sheriff of the County of New London, or to his Deputy:

"By special order of her Majesty's Superior Court, now holden in New London, you are hereby required, in her Majesty's name, to take John Rogers, Sr., of New London, who, to the view of said Court, appears to be under a high degree of distraction, and him secure in her majesty's jail for the County abovesaid, in some dark room or apartment thereof, that proper means may be used for his cure, and till he be recovered from his madness and you receive order for his release.

"Signed by order of the said Court, March 26, 1712. In the 11th year of Her Majesty's reign.

"Vera Copia, Testified

JONATHAN LAW, *Clerk.*
JOHN PRENTIS, *Sheriff.*"

And upon this Mittimus, he carried me to prison and put me into the inner prison and had the light of the window stopt. Upon this, the common people was in an uproar, and broke the plank of the window and let light in. And one of the lieutenants that came out of England told me he had been with the said Superior Court and desired that I might be brought forth to their view, and they would see that I was under no distraction, and that they had ordered that I should be brought out to the Governor in the evening. When it was dark night, I was taken out by the sheriff and carried to the Governor's House, into a private room, and the sheriff sent out by the Governor to see that the yard was clear; but it is too much to write what was done to some that were found standing there; but the body of them ran away. The Governor ordered the sheriff to take me home with him, and keep me at his house. Accordingly he did so, and gave me charge not to go out of his yard, but set nobody to look after me; he himself tended on the said court. About two days after, I was told that the sheriff told a friend of his that he was ordered, after the court was broke up and the people dispersed, to carry me up to Hartford prison and to see me shut up in some dark room, and that one Laborell, a French doctor, was to shave my head and give me purges to recover me of my madness. I hearing of this, desired the sheriff to give me a copy of the Mittimus, and after I told him what I heard privately, he owned the truth of it. The night following, I got up and got a neighbor to acquaint my son how matters were circumstanced, who brought £10 of money for me, and hired hands to row me over to Long Island, and pulled off his own shirt and gave me.

I got to Southold, on Long Island, in the night, and, early in the morning (it being the first day of the week), I went to a justice, to give him an account of the matter, having told him that I got away from under the sheriff's hand at New London. He replied, "It is the Sabbath; it is not a day to discourse about such things." So I returned to the tavern, and I suppose it was not above an hour before the constable came and set a guard over me, till about nine or ten of the clock the next day, and then took me where three justices were sitting at a table, with a written paper lying before them, who read a law to me that it was to be counted felony to break out of a constable's hand. I then presented a copy of the Mittimus. They read it and desired to be in private. Being brought before them again, they told me they did not look at me to be such a person as I was there rendered, and so discharged me, without any charge.

I told them my design was to their Governor for protection; and that I expected *Hue and Cries* to pursue me, and requested of them to stop them if they could. They promised me they would, and afterwards I heard they did stop them. I got a man and horse to go with me to York, with all the speed I could, and the first house I went into was Governor Hunter's, in the fort. I showed him the Mittimus and gave him an account of the matters. He told me he would not advise me to venture thither again, and that I should have safe protection. I told him I expected *Hue and Cries* to come after me. He told me I need not fear that at all, "For," said he, "I have heard you differ in opinion from them, and they will be glad to be rid of you. It is evident you are no such man as they pretend."

But, the next day, about ten of the clock, there came two printed *Hue and Cries* in at the tavern where I was, and I got them both, and went directly to the Governor, who was walking alone on the wall of the fort, and delivered one of them to him, who read it and then called to a little man walking on the pavement of the fort, saying, "Mr. Bickly, Mr. Bickly, come hither." And when he was come he read it, and said he, "I grant protection to this man, he shall not be sent back upon this *Hue and Cry*," and saith he, "I will write to the Governor of Connecticut," and to me he said, "You are safe enough here; I will grant you protection." I told him I did believe no answer would be returned him. He found my words true, and advised me to go for England and make my complaint, and told me there was a ship then going from Pennsylvania. A merchant being then present told me if I wanted money he would lend it to me, and if I should never be able to pay him he would never trouble me for it. All this kindness have I met with from strangers; but have thought it my wisdom to commit my cause to the all-seeing God.

And after I had continued in York about three months, I returned home, and, after I was recruited, with great difficulty I prosecuted the judges of said Inferior Court, for you had made it so difficult to summon them that none could give forth a summons but your General Court in such a case; but when I with great difficulty brought it to your Court of Chancery, you non-suited me and ordered me to pay all the charges and fined me £20. All which causes me to suspect your pretended care expressed in your printed *Hue and Cries* to cure me of my distraction. And here follows a copy for you to view:—

ADVERTISEMENT.

Whereas John Rogers, Sr., of New London, being committed to the custody of her Majesty's Goal, in the County of New London, which is under my care, with special orders to keep him in some dark apartment thereof, until proper means be used for the cure of that distraction which he appears (to her Majesty's Court of said County) to be under in a very high degree, hath, by the assistance of evil persons, made his escape out of the said custody, these are therefore to desire all persons to seize and secure the said Rogers and return him forthwith unto me, the subscriber, sheriff of the said County, and they shall be well satisfied for the trouble and charge they may be at therein.

Dated in New London, March 31, 1712.	JOHN PRENTIS.

After I returned home, I went to the printer to know who it was that drew this advertisement up, and he showed me the copy, and I took it to be Governor Saltonstall's own hand.

New London, 15th of the 7th month, 1721.	J. ROGERS.

Matt. x, 26. "Fear them not therefore, for there is nothing covered that shall not be revealed, and hid that shall not be known."

We will say a few words in this place concerning the crime of falsely charging persons with insanity, whether from personal dislike or from motives of a pecuniary or other nature. Depravity can scarcely find a lower depth, or infamy wear a deeper brand. Even now such atrocities are not uncommon, and should be guarded against with the utmost vigilance. Nearly every one of long and large experience has been made cognizant of some such diabolism, where the laws have been too lax in reference to this matter. In the State of Connecticut, until recently, nothing was required but the certificate of a physician to secure the incarceration of any one in a lunatic asylum, with the superintendent's consent. But by the law passed, May, 1889, the defect has been thoroughly remedied. It is also enacted, Section 23, that "Any person who wilfully conspires with any other person unlawfully to commit to any asylum any person who is not insane, and any person who shall wilfully and falsely certify to the insanity of such person, shall be punished by a fine not exceeding one thousand dollars, or by imprisonment in the State Prison not exceeding five years, or both."

To charge a sane person with insanity, and then devise methods for his cure which would tend to deprive a sane person of reason! Could the blade of enmity be drawn to a keener point?

CHAPTER VI.

It is with regret that we are compelled to make the following strictures upon "The Discourse Delivered on the Two Hundredth Anniversary of the First Church of Christ, in New London, by Thos. P. Field, 1870." Amiable as was its author, and highly esteemed, yet in this discourse, so far as it relates to the Rogerenes, he has followed in the footsteps of his predecessors, showing how much easier it is to float on the surface, with the tide, than to dive deep and bring up gems from the bottom of the sea. We shall briefly quote from this discourse and make reply.

Mr. Field says: "During the ministry of Mr. Saltonstall, peculiar disturbances arose in the church," referring to the sect called Rogerenes.

Since we have shown the falsity of many of the statements concerning the Rogerenes which are repeated by Mr. Field in this discourse, it is needless to take further notice of them here. But is it not a matter of surprise that Mr. Field should have spoken with seeming favor concerning the malicious suit brought by Mr. Saltonstall against John Rogers for slander? His words are: "On one occasion, when John Rogers circulated some false report about him, he brought an action in the county court for defamation and obtained a verdict of the jury in his behalf."

He does not tell us the verdict was the enormous sum of £600, and that there was no legal basis for the action, even had the charge been true; neither does he state that this suit was brought against Rogers but a few months after release from his long confinement, of three years and eight months, in Hartford jail, where he had been placed at the instance of Mr. Saltonstall, on charge of blasphemy for words truly scriptural. Mr. Field's reference to this suit shows how superficially he had looked into the subject.

We must also express surprise that the statement, so falsely and unblushingly made by Mr. Saltonstall, should be quoted and indorsed in Mr. Field's discourse:—

There never was, for the twenty years that I have resided in this government, any one, Quaker or other person, that suffered on account of his different persuasion in religious matters from the body of this people.

A note appended to Mr. Field's discourse, may be presumed to contain his maturest thought, or rather absence of thought. "Lucus a non lucendo." The note reads:—

Some who heard the discourse thought the Rogerenes were not sufficiently commended for what was good in them, and especially for their protest against the improper mingling of civil and religious affairs. It is the belief of the writer that there were a great many who entertained similar views with the Rogerenes on that subject, but who would not unite with them in their absurd mode of testifying against what they deemed erroneous.

"Belief of the writer!" Belief is of little consequence, unless based upon authority or knowledge; and the person who thrusts forward his simple belief, to command the assent of others, seems to proffer a valueless coin. But what if there were such among the people? They were not heard from; and Seneca says, "He who puts a good thought into my heart, puts a good word into my mouth, unless a fool has the keeping of it."

There were a few, however, who did protest against the tyrannical treatment of the dissenters and in favor of religious freedom; but they were heavily fined and laid under the ban of the church, as the blind man who had received his sight was cast out of the temple by the Jews. From Miss Caulkin's history, we quote the protest:—

While Rogers was in prison, an attack upon the government and colony appeared, signed by Richard Steer, Samuel Beebe, Jr., Jonathan and James Rogers, accusing them of persecution of dissenters, narrow principles, self-interest, spirit of domineering, and saying that to compel people to pay for a Presbyterian minister is against the laws of England, is rapine, robbery and oppression.

"A special court was held at New London, Jan. 25th, 1694-5, to consider this libellous paper. The subscribers were fined £5 each."

Mr. Field goes on to say, "There can be no justification of their conduct in disturbing public assemblies as they did, which would not justify similar conduct at the present day." So much has been said about their disturbing public assemblies, and to such varied notes has the tune been played, that the paucity of other arguments against the Rogerenes is thereby evinced. Fame, with its hundred tongues, has no doubt greatly exaggerated these offences, if such they were. There are some Bible commands that might seem to justify conduct like that above referred to; as, "Go cry in the ears of this people." Fines, whippings, imprisonments, setting in stocks, etc., for no crime, but simply for non-conformity to the Congregational church, were grounds for their conduct which do not now exist. Did Mr. Field suppose that an intelligent audience would give credence to his above assertion? or had he taken lessons of the teacher of oratory who told his pupils to regard his hearers as "so many cabbage stumps"?

"No justification of their conduct" at that time "which would not justify similar conduct at the present day!"

There was an evil to be assailed then that has now passed away. The man who should enter a meeting-house now with a plea for religious liberty might properly be regarded as a lunatic. But, if the old abuses were revived, some Samson would again arise, to shake the pillars of tyranny.

Mr. Field closes his remarks by saying:—

There is no evidence that their testimony or their protestations had the slightest influence in correcting any of the errors of the times in respect to the relation of civil and ecclesiastical authority.

Had Mr. Field said that there was no evidence within his knowledge, we should have taken no notice of this statement. Confession of ignorance, like other confessions, may sometimes be good for the soul. But when he presumes to assert that a fact does not exist of which other people may be cognizant, he transcends the bounds of prudence.

Proof is abundant, that the Rogerenes and their descendants were foremost in advocating the severance of church from state and the equal rights of all to religious liberty. Their uniform testimony in Connecticut, for more than a century, in defence of true liberty of conscience, which awakened so much discussion throughout the State, could not have been without its enlightening influence.

But we will be more minute by mentioning some of the things which were said and done by Rogerenes,[14] and by those into whose minds their doctrines had been early and effectually instilled.

John Bolles, whom Miss Caulkins calls "a noted disciple of John Rogers," wrote largely on the subject of religious liberty. In his work, entitled "True Liberty of Conscience is in Bondage to No Flesh," this point is amply discussed. In his address to the Elders and Messengers of the Boston and Connecticut Colonies, concerning their Confessions of Faith, which were one and the same, he says:—

First, the Elders and Messengers of each Colony have recommended them to the Civil Government, and the Civil Government have taken them under their protection to defend them. And now God hath put it into my heart to reprove both Governments.

After showing by Scripture that the civil government is ordained of God to rule in temporal affairs, and not for the government of men's consciences in matters of religion, he goes on to say:—

Thus it is sufficiently proved that God hath set up the Civil Government to rule in the Commonwealth, in temporal things; and as well proved that he hath not committed unto them the government of his church. I have proved that the Civil Government as they exercise their authority to rule only in temporal things are the ministers of God, and that God hath not committed to them the government of his Church, or to meddle in cases of conscience.—And now I speak to you, Elders and Messengers; as you have recommended your Confessions of Faith; and to you, Rulers of the Commonwealth, as you have acknowledged them, and established them by law, and defend them by the carnal sword; I speak, I say, to both parties, as you are in fellowship with each other in these things, and so proceed to prove that exercising yourselves in the affairs of conscience and matters of faith towards God, you do it under the authority of the dragon, or spirit of antichrist.

And you, Elders and Messengers (as you are called), as you stand to maintain and defend the said confessions, are not Elders and Messengers of the churches of Christ, but of antichrist. And you, Rulers of the Commonwealth of each Government, as you exercise yourselves as such in the affairs of conscience, and things relating to the worship of God, you do it not under Christ; but against Christ, under the power of antichrist, as by the Scripture hath been fully proved. In the form of church government in Boston, Confession, Chapter 17, par. 6, they say: "It is the duty of the Magistrate to take care of matters of religion, and improve his civil authority for observing the duties commanded in the first, as well as for observing the duties commanded in the second table." And further say, "The end of the Magistrate's office is not only the quiet and peaceable life of the subject in matters of righteousness and honesty, but also in matters of Godliness, yea, of all godliness." The gospel was preached and received in opposition to the civil magistrates, as is abundantly recorded: And the encouragement Christ has given to his followers is by way of blessing under persecution: "Blessed are they which are persecuted for righteousnes's sake, for theirs is the kingdom of heaven." And for any people professing the Christian faith to set up a form of Godliness, and establish it by their human laws, and defend it by the authority of the Magistrate, is to exclude Christ from having authority over his Church, and themselves to be the supreme head thereof.

The book from which we quote was published about 1754. The following, from the same book, has reference to the persecutions in New England, of the Rogerenes and others:—

Now, Boston and Connecticut, let us briefly inquire into the doings of our forefathers[15] towards those that separated themselves from them for conscience' sake, and testified against their form of godliness. To begin with Connecticut: they punished by setting in stocks, by fining, whipping, imprisoning and chaining in prison, and causing to set on the gallows with a halter about the neck, and prohibiting the keeping Quaker books, and that such books should be suppressed, as also putting fathers and mothers both in prison from their children, and then enclosing the prison with a boarded fence about ten foot high, with spikes above, points upwards, and a gate kept under lock and key to prevent any communication of friends or relations with the prisoners, or communicating anything necessary for their support; but must go near half a mile to the prison keeper to have the gate opened.

At New Haven, a stranger, named Humphrey Norton, being put ashore, not of his own seeking, was put in prison and chained to a post, and kept night and day for the space of twenty days, with great weights of iron, without fire or candle, in the winter season, and not any suffered to come to visit him; and after this brought before their court, and there was their priest, John Davenport, to whom said Norton endeavored to make reply, but was prevented by having a key tied athwart his mouth, till the priest had done; then, said Norton was had again to prison, and there chained ten days, and then sentenced to be severely whipped, and to be burned in the hand with the letter H. for heresy, who, my author says, was convicted of none; and to be sent out of the Colony, and not to return upon pain of the utmost penalty they could inflict by law. And the drum was beat, and the people gathered, and he was fetched and stripped to the waist, and whipped thirty-six cruel stripes and burned in the hand very deep with a red-hot iron, as aforesaid, and then had to prison again and tendered his liberty upon paying his fine and fees.—See George Bishop: "New England Judged," page 203, 4.

These and other like things were done in Connecticut.

Now let us hear what was done in Boston Government, as it is to be seen in the title-page of said Bishop's history, touching the sufferings of the people called Quakers: "A brief relation," saith he, "of the suffering of the people called Quakers in those parts of America, from the beginning of the fifth month, 1656, the time of their first arrival at Boston from England, to the latter end of the tenth month, 1660, wherein the cruel whippings and scourgings, bonds and imprisonments, beatings and chainings, starvings and huntings, fines and confiscation of estates, burning in the hand and cutting off ears, orders of sale for bond-men and bond-women, banishment upon pain of death, and putting to death of those people are shortly touched, with a relation of the manner, and some of the most material proceedings, and a judgment thereupon." They also burned their books by the common executioners (see Daniel Neal's "History of New England," Vol. I., page 292). They also impoverished them by compelling them to take the oath of fidelity, which they scrupled for conscience' sake, and for their refusing of which they were fined £5 each or depart the Colony; but they, not departing, and under the same scruple, came under the penalty of another £5; and so from time to time, and many other fines were imposed on them, as for meeting by themselves. (See said History, page 320.)

And in said book is contained a brief relation of the barbarous cruelties, persecutions and massacres upon the Protestants in foreign parts by the Papists, etc. And now I return to Boston and Connecticut, with reference to what was said touching the doings of our forefathers; they notbeing repented, nor called in question, but a persisting in acts of force upon conscience in some measure to this day. But it is the same dragon, and same persecuting spirit that required the worshipping of idols, and persecuted the primitive church, that now professes himself to be a Christian, and furnishes himself with college-learned ministers, nourished up in pride through idleness and voluptuous living; and these are his ministers; and they are the same set of men that Christ thanked God that he had hid the mysteries of the kingdom of God from, Matt. xi, 25. And he, the dragon, assures the rulers of the commonwealth that God hath set them to do justice among men, and to take under their care the government of the church also.

In 1754, I went to the General Court at Hartford, and also to the General Court at Boston, considering their Confessions were both one, and that both Governments lie under the same reproof,—and I have published three treatises already, touching these things; but there has been no answer made to any, and this is the fourth; after so much proof, I think it may truly be said of them, as in Rev. ii, 2, "And thou hast tried them which say they are apostles, and are not, and hast found them liars."

In a word, to rule the church by the power of the magistrate is to destroy the peace of both church, families and commonwealths. But, on the contrary, Christ is said to be the Prince of Peace. Isaiah ix, 6. And all that walk in His spirit follow His example, to live peaceably towards all men, as also towards the Commonwealth, as he did, for peace' sake, rather than to offend.

Perhaps we cannot give a better idea of the extent and versatility of Mr. Bolle's efforts in this direction, which extended over a long period, than by transcribing some portion of what is said of him by his biographer (in "Bolles Genealogy"):—

John Bolles, third and only surviving son of Thomas and Zipporah Bolles, was born in New London, Conn., August 7, 1767. At the age of thirty, he became dissatisfied with the tenets of the Presbyterian church, in which he had been educated. That church was the only one recognized by law. Its members composed the standing order, and, from the foundation of the colony until the adoption of a state constitution and the principle of religious toleration, in 1818, every person in Connecticut, whatever his creed, was compelled by law to belong to or pay taxes for the support of the standing order. It was as complete an "Establishment" as is the "Established Church of England." Mr. Bolles became a Seventh Day Baptist,[16] and was immersed by John Rogers, the elder. Well educated, familiar with the Bible, independent in fortune, earnest in his convictions and of a proselyting spirit, bold and fond of discussion, Mr. Bolles engaged very actively in polemical controversy, and wrote and published many books and pamphlets; some of which still extant prove him to have been, as Miss Caulkins, the historian of New London, describes him, "fluent with the pen and adroit in argument." From one of his books in my possession, it appears that his escape when his mother and her other children were murdered by Stoddard, and his deliverance from other imminent perils, "when," to use his own words, "there was but a hair's breadth between me and death," made a deep impression on his mind and caused him to feel that God had spared him for some special work. This belief is expressed in some homely verses, Bunyan-like in sound, closing with the following couplet:

> "Yet was my life preserved, by God Almighty's hand
> Who since has called me forth for His great truth to stand!"

Under the spur of this conviction, he devoted himself to the great cause of religious freedom, encountering opposition and persecution, and suffering fines, imprisonments and beating with many stripes.

After referring to several of his books his biographer says:—

I have another of his books, called "Good News from a Far Country," whose argument is to prove that the Civil Government "have no authority from God to judge in cases of conscience," to which is added "An Answer to an Election Sermon Preached by Nathaniel Eells." Another, dated from New London 11th of 7th month, 1728 (March being then the first month of the year), is a pamphlet containing John Bolle's application to the General Court, holden at New Haven, the 10th of the 8th month, 1728, informing that honorable body, "in all the honor and submissive obedience that God requires me to show unto you," etc., that he had examined the Confessions of Faith established by them and found therein principles that seem not to be proved by the Scriptures there quoted, and had drawn up some objections thereto, etc. He published many other works, and from 1708 to 1754 hardly a year elapsed without his thus assailing the abuses of the established church and vindicating the great principle of "soul-liberty." Once a year, as a general rule, he mounted his horse, with saddle-bags stuffed full of books, and rode from county to county challenging discussion, inviting the Presbyterian Elders to meet him, man-fashion, in argument,[17] or confess and abandon their errors. "But," says he, in one of his books, "they disregarded my request." He even made a pilgrimage to Boston, Mass., in 1754, to move the General Court of Massachusetts in this behalf, as he had often endeavored to move the Connecticut Legislature. This last exploit, a horseback ride of two hundred miles, in his 77th year, may be regarded as a fit climax to a long life of zealous effort in the cause of truth. It is no extravagant eulogy to say that John Bolles was a great and good man.

His works are his best epitaph. No man knoweth of his grave unto this day; but the stars shine over it.

With all the humble, all the holy,

All the meek and all the lowly,

He held communion sweet;

But when he heard the lion roar,

Or saw the tushes of the boar,

Was quick upon his feet:

And what God spake within his heart

He did to man repeat.

So much from one of the early Rogerenes against the union of church and state and in favor of equal religious liberty; thoughts, sentiments, principles which lie at the basis of our new constitution; published and scattered throughout the land at an early period, instilled into the hearts of children, blossoming out in speech and inspiring efforts which aided the complete establishment of religious liberty in Connecticut. Descendants of John Bolles were among the very foremost, ablest, and most efficient workers in this cause, baptized, as it were, into these sacred truths. A few examples will be given; but we can hardly hope that the despisers of the Rogerenes will find in them "evidence that their testimony or their protestations had the slightest influence in correcting any of the errors of the times, in regard to the relations of civil and ecclesiastical authority."

To show that early descendants of the Rogerenes were trained in goodness, as well as in argument, we will speak of John Bolles of later times, brother of Rev. David Bolles and grandson of the John Bolles of whom we have said so much. He was the founder, and for forty years a deacon, of the First Baptist

Church of Hartford, of which Rev. David Bolles was one of the first preachers. We quote some interesting passages concerning him from Dr. Turnbull's "Memorials of the First Baptist Church, Hartford, Conn.," which were read by Dr. Turnbull as sermons, after the dedication of the new church edifice, May, 1856:—

There was no man, perhaps, to whom our church, in the early period of its history, was more indebted than John Bolles.... He was a Nathaniel indeed, in whom there was no guile. And yet, shrewd beyond most men, he never failed to command the respect of his acquaintances. Everybody loved him. Decided in his principles, his soul overflowed with love and charity. Easy, nimble, cheerful, he was ready for every good word and work. He lived for others. The young especially loved him. The aged, and above all the poor, hailed him as their friend. He was perpetually devising something for the benefit of the church or the good of souls. How or when he was converted he could not tell. His parents were pious, and had brought him up in the fear of God, and in early life he had given his heart to Christ, but all he could say about it was that God had been gracious to him and he hoped brought him into his fold. On the relation of his experience before the church in Suffield, the brethren, on this very account, hesitated to receive him; but the pastor, Rev. John Hastings, shrewdly remarked that it was evident Mr. Bolles was in the way, and that this was more important than the question when, or by what means, he got in it; upon which they unanimously received him. He was very happy in his connection with the church in Suffield. The members were all his friends. He would often start from Hartford at midnight, arrive in Suffield at early dawn, on Sabbath morning, when they were making their fires, and surprise them by his pleasant salutation. After breakfast and family prayers, all hands would go to church together.

Of course, he was equally at home with the church in Hartford, and spent much of his time in visiting, especially the poor of the flock. He had a kind word and a ready hand for every one. One severe winter, a fearful snow-storm had raised the roads to a level with the tops of the fences. A certain widow Burnham lived all alone, just on the outer edge of East Hartford. The deacon was anxious about her; he was afraid that she might be covered with the snow and suffering from want. He proposed to visit her; but his friends thought it perilous to cross the meadows. But, being light of foot, he resolved to attempt it. The weather was cold, and the snow slightly crusted on the top. By means of this he succeeded, with some effort, in reaching the widow's house. As he supposed, he found it covered with snow to the chimneys. He made his way into the house and found the good sister without fire or water. He cut paths to the woodpile and to the well, and assisted her to make a fire and put on the tea-kettle. He then cut a path to the pig-pen and supplied the wants of the hungry beast, by which time breakfast was ready. After breakfast, he read the word of God and prayed, and was ready to start for home. In the meanwhile, the sun had melted the crust of snow, and, as he was passing through the meadows, he broke through. He tried to scramble out, but failed; he shouted, but there was no one to hear him. The wind began to blow keenly; he did not know but he must remain there all night and perish with cold. But he committed himself to God, and sat down for shelter on the lee-side of his temporary prison. He finally made a desperate effort, succeeded in reaching the edge, and found, to his joy, that the freezing wind had hardened the surface of the snow, which enabled him to make his way home.

On a pleasant Sabbath morning, some seventy years ago, might be seen a little group wending their way from Hartford, through the green woods and meadows of the Connecticut valley, towards the little church on Zion's Hill. Among them was a man of small stature, something like Zaccheus of old, of erect gait, bright eye and agile movement. Though living eighteen miles from Suffield, he was wont, on pleasant days, to walk the whole distance, beguiling the way with devout meditation; or, if some younger brother chose to accompany him, with pleasant talk about the things of the Kingdom. This was Deacon John Bolles, brother of Rev. David Bolles, and uncle of the late excellent Rev. Matthew Bolles, and of Dr. Lucius Bolles so well known in connection with the cause of foreign missions.

In the year of our Lord 1790, just about the commencement of the French Revolution, this good brother and a few others came to the conclusion that the time had arrived to organize a Baptist Church in the city of Hartford. Previous to that, they had held meetings in the court-house and in private houses. On the 5th of August, 1789, the first baptism, according to our usage, was administered in this city. On September 7, it was resolved to hold public services on the Sabbath in a more formal way. Accordingly, the first meeting of this kind was held, October 18, in the dwelling-house of John Bolles. These services were continued, and in the ensuing season a number of persons were baptized on a profession of their faith in the Lord Jesus Christ. On the 23d of March, 1790, sixteen brothers and sisters were recognized as a church of Christ, by a regularly called council, over which Elder Hastings presided as Moderator.

When the Baptists began to hold public services, an over-zealous member of Dr. Strong's society (the Centre Congregational Society) called upon him and asked him if he knew that John Bolles had "started an opposition meeting." "No," said he. "When? Where?" "Why, at the old court-house." "Oh, yes, I know it," the doctor carelessly replied; "but it is not an opposition meeting. They are Baptists, to be sure, but they preach the same doctrine that

I do; you had better go and hear them." "Go!" said the man, "I am a Presbyterian!" "So am I," rejoined Dr. Strong; "but that need not prevent us wishing them well. You had better go." "No!" said the man, with energy, "I shan't go near them! Dr. Strong, a'n't you going to do something about it?" "What?" "Stop it, can't you?" "My friend," said the doctor, "John Bolles is a good man, and will surely go to heaven. If you and I get there, we shall meet him, and we had better, therefore, cultivate pleasant acquaintance with him here."

Dr. Bushnell, many years after, paid him a sweet tribute, in his sermon "Living to God in Small Things." "I often hear mentioned by the Christians of our city (Hartford) the name of a certain godly man, who has been dead many years; and he is always spoken of with so much respectfulness and affection that I, a stranger of another generation, feel his power, and the sound of his name refreshes me. That man was one who lived to God in small things. I know this, not by any description which has thus set forth his character, but from the very respect and homage with which he is named. Virtually, he still lives among us, and the face of his goodness shines upon all our Christian labors."

Dr. Samuel Bowles, founder of the *Springfield Republican*, says in his "Notes of the Bowles Family:" "Deacon John Bolles of Hartford, one of the most godly men that ever lived, a descendant of Thomas Bolles, was a contemporary and neighbor of my father, and used to call him 'cousin Bowles.'"

Judge David Bolles, son of the Rev. David Bolles before named, was prominent for many years as an active advocate of religious freedom. We quote the following historical statement concerning him:—

David Bolles, Jr., first child of Rev. David and Susannah Bolles, was born in Ashford, Ct., September 26, 1765, and died there May 22, 1830. He first studied and practised medicine, and afterwards law. At the time of his death he was judge of the Windham County Court. He received the honorary degree of A.M. from Brown University in 1819. He was a Methodist in religion, and to his long continued and zealous services, as advocate of "the Baptist Petition," before successive legislatures, was Connecticut largely indebted for the full establishment of religious liberty in 1818.

He was the author of the famous "Baptist Petition" above referred to, the original copy of which, written by his own hand, was shown to the author by his nephew, Gen. John A. Bolles.

Judge David Bolles was extensively known throughout the State as the earnest advocate of the liberal movement. The following anecdote was told the writer by one who sat at a dinner with him. Calvin Goddard, the late distinguished lawyer of Norwich, then a young man, said to Judge Bolles on the occasion, "You will blow your Baptist ram's horn until the walls of Jericho fall."

Rev. Augustus Bolles, another brother of Judge Bolles, a Baptist preacher, many years a resident of Hartford and for some time associated with the *Christian Secretary* published there, referring to the great controversy for equal religious rights in the State of Connecticut, said to the writer, more than fifty years ago, "The Bolleses were perfect Bonapartes in that contest." Where was Mr. Field then? Perhaps he wasn't born.

That ably conducted paper, the *Hartford Times*, was established in 1817, by Frederick D. Bolles, a descendant of John Bolles, for the express purpose of meeting this question. From the first number of said paper, we copy the following:—

Anxious to make the *Times* as useful and worthy of public patronage as possible, the subscriber has associated himself with John M. Niles, Esq., a young gentleman of talent. The business will be conducted under the firm of F. D. Bolles & Co., and they hope, through their joint exertions, to render the paper acceptable to its readers.

F. D. BOLLES.

The subject of religious rights was the main topic of discussion in this paper. A subsequent number, August 12, 1817, has a long article signed, "Roger Williams." It is headed, "An Inquiry Whether the Several Denominations of Christians in the States Enjoy Equal Civil and Religious Privileges."

From the "History of Hartford County," we quote the following:—

The *Hartford Times* was started at the beginning of the year 1817. Its publisher was Frederick D. Bolles, a practical printer, and at that time a young man full of confidence and enthusiasm in his journal and his cause. That cause was, in the party terms of the day, "TOLERATION." First, and paramount, of the objects of the Tolerationists was to secure the adoption of a new Constitution for Connecticut. Under the ancient and loose organic law then in force, people of all forms and shades of religious belief were obliged to pay tribute to the established church. Such a state of things permitted no personal liberty, no individual election in the vital matter of a man's religion; and it naturally created a revolt. The cry of "Toleration" arose. The Federalists met the argument with ridicule. The "Democratic Republicans," of the Jefferson fold, were the chief users of the Toleration cry, and the *Hartford Times* was established on that issue, and in support of the movement for a new and more tolerant Constitution. It proved to be a lively year in party politics. The toleration issue became the engrossing theme. The *Times* had as associate editor, John M. Niles, then a young and but little known lawyer from Poquonock, who subsequently rose to a national reputation in the Senate at Washington. It dealt the Federalists some powerful blows, and enlisted in the cause a number of men of ability, who, but for the peculiar issue presented—one of religious freedom—never would have entered into party politics. Among them were prominent men of other denominations than the orthodox Congregationalists; no wonder; they were struggling for life. There was a good deal of public speaking; circulars and pamphlets were handed from neighbor to neighbor; the "campaign" was, in short, a sharp and bitter one, and the main issue was hotly contested. The excitement was intense. When it began to appear that the Toleration cause was stronger than the Federalists had supposed, there arose a fresh feeling of horrified apprehension, much akin to that which, seventeen years before, had led hundreds of good people in Connecticut, when they heard of the election of the "Infidel Jefferson" to the Presidency, to hide their Bibles—many of them in hay-mows—under the conviction that that evident instrument of the Evil One would seek out and destroy every obtainable copy of the Bible in the land.

The election came on in the spring of 1818, and the Federal party in Connecticut found itself actually overthrown. It was a thing unheard of, not to be believed by good Christians. Lyman Beecher, in his Litchfield pulpit and family prayers, as one out of numerous cases, poured out the bitterness of his heart in declarations that everything was lost and the days of darkness had come.

Was not the soul of John Rogers marching on?

In fact, it proved to be the day of the new Constitution—the existing law of 1818—and under its more tolerant influence other churches rapidly arose; the Episcopalians, the Baptists, and the Methodists all feeling their indebtedness to the party of Toleration.

The *Times*, successful in the main object of its beginning, after witnessing this peaceful political revolution, continued, with several changes of proprietors. It was about sixty years ago that the paper became the property of Bowles and Francis, as its publishing firm; the Bowles being Samuel Bowles, the founder, many years later, of the *Springfield Republican*, whose son, the late Samuel Bowles, built up that well-known journal to a high degree of prosperity.

Mrs. Watson, of East Windsor Hill, daughter of Frederick D. Bolles, the founder of the *Hartford Times*, who courteously furnished us with the above quotations, also sent us a paper containing the following tribute to John M.

Niles, early associated with her father in the publication of the *Times*.

Mr. Niles, then a young man, who perhaps had not dreamed at that time of becoming a Senator of the United States and of making speeches in the Senate Chamber, which, however dry in manner, were to be complimented by Mr. Calhoun as being the most interesting and instructive speeches he was accustomed to hear in the Senate—this then unknown young man was one of the editors. The *Times* was established on the motto of "Toleration"—the severance of church from state—the exemption of men from paying taxes to a particular church if they did not agree with that church in their consciences. The reform aimed at the establishment of a more liberal rule in Connecticut; a rule which would let Baptists, Methodists, and other denominations rise and grow, as well as the one old dominant and domineering church that had so long reigned, and with which party federalism had become so incorporated as to be looked upon practically as part of its creed and substance. The cause advocated by the *Times* triumphed; the constitution framed in 1818 established a new order of things. Both Mr. Bolles and Mr. Niles have passed out of the life of earth; but the work which was accomplished by the agitation of the "Toleration" question, sixty years ago, has remained in Connecticut and grown. The old intolerant influence also is not dead; its spirit remains, but its old power for intolerant rule has passed away.

A terrible weight of prejudice rested upon the Rogerenes who first planted that seed in Connecticut, whose outshoot, ingrafted into the constitution of every State in the Union, has become a great tree of religious liberty spreading its branches over all the land, under the shadow of which not only we but immigrants from every clime sit with delight.

This weight of superstition and intolerance was not wholly removed when Mr. Field wrote of the Rogerenes, which is the only excuse we can offer for the statements made by him in his "Discourse Delivered on the Two Hundredth Anniversary of the First Church of Christ, in New London, October 19, 1870." Compared, however, with what John Rogers and his early followers endured at the hands of a tyrannical, bigoted, blinded church, and the falsehoods and scoffs which ecclesiastical historians have promulgated, Mr. Field's utterances are lighter than a feather.

CHAPTER VII.

We had not intended to make further reply (see Chapter II) to Mr. McEwen's Half-Century Sermon; but lest our silence should be construed by some as implying an inability to do so, we turn to it again.

"The elder Gov. Griswold," he says, "acted at one time as prosecuting attorney against the Rogerenes." If this was so, he was prosecuting his somewhat near relatives, so far as the descendants of John Rogers, 2d, were concerned, Henry Wolcott and Matthew Griswold, Sr., being their common ancestors.

Is it not strange that ministers of religion should delight in showing the powers of this world to be their support, as if to add honor and respectability to the church? "Who is she that"—without secular pomp—"looketh forth as the morning; fair as the moon, clear as the sun, and terrible as an army with banners?"

Mr. McEwen proceeds, "I have not yet spoken of scourging, nor of the effect of it; which, in the consummation of judgments, actually befell these crusaders against idolatry," referring to the "outbreak" of 1764-6.

Neither does Mr. McEwen speak of fines, imprisonments, setting in stocks, and other barbarous cruelties practised upon John Rogers and his followers; but he adds: "What the law could not do, in that it was weak, lynching did." We wonder that Mr. McEwen should have made this admission; but we honor him for it, although he gives away his cause. "Lynching did." Here is an acknowledgment that the church and government of that day, regardless even of their own laws, resolved themselves into a mob.

Says Mr. McEwen:—

Historical fidelity constrains me, though with reluctance and sadness, to say that our forefathers of this congregation, in the extremity of their embarrassment, took the disturbers of public worship out, tied them to trees, and permitted the boys to give them a severe whipping with switches taken from the prim bush.

This treatment was made more disgraceful from the fact, admitted by Mr. McEwen, that the Rogerenes, "in common with Quakers, held the doctrine of non-resistance to violence from men," as an example of which, he says:—

A constable often took out a lusty man and with a twine tied him to a tree. He was studious not to break the ligature; but stood, conscientiously, until the close of divine service, when he was officially released.

He continues:—

The affirmation of the Rogerenes is that the shrub has never vegetated in this town since that irreligious and cruel use of it.[18] It is to be feared that the moral effect upon the boys was worse than the blasting effect upon the prim bush.

Mr. McEwen goes on to say, as palliating their conduct: "But our fathers had not the Sabbath School."

Was the preaching of the gospel a less potent influence than the Sabbath School? They had Moses and the prophets and the teachings of Christ. The persecutors of the Christians in all former ages had not the Sabbath School; but who ever before offered this excuse in their behalf? And even this apology he does not extend to the Rogerenes; but holds them to the strictest account, notwithstanding that they also had not the Sabbath School.

"The Rogerenes," he adds, "have dwindled to insignificance."

Should he not know that the work of these reformers is accomplished? The principles for which they contended have become universal; their distinctive existence is no longer needed. The citadel of religious bigotry which they assailed has been demolished. While the dark night of superstition and intolerance overspread the land, the Rogerenes, like stars and constellations, pierced the gloom. Leo and the Great Bear shone in the heavens; but when the sun arose they made obeisance and retired. The trumpet of Luther is not now blown in Protestant churches. The Anti-Slavery Society, once potent, has ceased to exist; slavery is abolished. Would Mr. McEwen doom the Rogerenes to endless labor, like Sisyphus? He rolled up the stone to have it roll back again; they helped to roll the stone to the top of the mountain, the headstone, brought forth with shoutings, to rest there forever.

Mr. McEwen says: "A small remnant of their posterity, almost unknown, exists in an adjacent town, with hardly a relic of their earth-born religion. 'A small remnant' will be noted hereafter."

"Earth-born religion!" In regard to doctrinal points in religion they differed not from the Congregational church. Mr. Field himself said, in the discourse from which we have before quoted, "In their opinions concerning the doctrines of religion generally they coincided with other Christians, and they did not abandon, as do the Quakers, the ordinances of Baptism and the Lord's Supper." And Miss Caulkins, in her history, says that John Rogers was strenuously orthodox in his religious views, as all his writings clearly show. The Rogerenes baptized by immersion, it is true, and much of their suffering was on that account. Benedict, in his Church History, speaks of them as "Rogerene Baptists." This feature of their belief, ancient though it may be, against which the Congregational church a century or two ago set itself in such violent opposition, has now become current and popular. With the progress of religious freedom and of gospel truth, the Rogerenes have long since affiliated with other denominations and are as one with them. We shall, presently, show to the reader that prominent ministers, in different denominations, have been of Rogerene descent.

"But why," says Mr. McEwen, "you may be ready to ask, rake from oblivion a sect devised for nothing but to destroy the religion of the gospel and destined to vanish away?"[19]

In view of what we have already said and shown, we are now somewhat at a loss which of Solomon's rules to adopt (see Proverbs xxvi, 4 and 5), and therefore deem it the part of wisdom to make no answer at all. Had Mr. McEwen attempted to rear a monument to his own ignorance, he could not have succeeded better than by uttering the words above quoted.

"Our answer is," he continues, "to confirm our faith in the Almighty Saviour, who said, 'Every plant which my Heavenly Father hath not planted shall be rooted up.'"

We are glad that our faith needs no such confirmation. Said the apostle, "We know whom we have believed." But what have the ages preceding the Rogerene movement not lost, who lived and passed away before this new means of confirming the truth of the gospel was discovered!

"Shall be rooted up." If he refers to the principles advocated by the Rogerenes, to the seed of equal religious rights sown by them, these are deeper rooted in the hearts, consciences and understandings of men to-day than ever before at any period in the world's history.

To quote further from Mr. McEwen's discourse:

"Men and women of low minds, in regions of darkness, now invent religions."

An insinuation, perhaps, that the Rogerenes were "men and women of low minds." They did not invent a new religion, as we have fully shown, and, for intelligence, for wealth, for moral rectitude, were not behind others, as will further appear.

Mr. McEwen spoke of "a small remnant of their posterity, almost unknown, in a neighboring town," seeming to intimate, perhaps unintentionally, that all, or nearly all, "their posterity" were in that "town" and "almost unknown."

We will mention some of their numerous posterity outside of this "neighboring town," where in fact are and have been comparatively few of their descendants, showing first and chiefly how numerous and well known are descendants of James Rogers, Sr., and his son John Rogers, founders of this sect, in the town in which Mr. McEwen resided and where he delivered this sermon.

First, we will mention Miss Frances Manwaring Caulkins, of pleasant memory, author of "The History of New London," and also Pamela, her amiable sister, for many years an acceptable teacher in this city. They were descendants of James Rogers, Sr., as was also their brother, Henry P. Haven, so well known in religious and commercial circles, to whose munificent gift, and that of his daughter, Mrs. Anna Perkins, we are indebted for our Public Library, a noble monument to their memory. The mother of Henry P. Haven and the Misses Caulkins was a sister of Christopher Manwaring, formerly a well-known citizen of this town, whose father, Robert Manwaring, married Elizabeth Rogers, daughter of James[4]. Miss Caulkins was also of Rogerene descent on her father's side, in the line of Joseph, son of James, Sr.

The late Dr. Robert A. Manwaring, son of the above Christopher Manwaring, was, by both his parents, honored by Rogers descent, his mother being daughter of Dr. Simon Wolcott, of Windsor, who married Lucy Rogers a descendant of James[2] and settled in this place.

Capt. Richard Law also married a daughter of Dr. Simon Wolcott and Lucy Rogers; his descendants include the later branches of the Chew family, also the children of William C. Crump and of Horace Coit.

J. N. Harris, one of New London's most enterprising citizens, is a descendant of James Rogers, Sr.

Ex-Lieut.-Gov. F. B. Loomis was a descendant in the same line, as was the eminent Professor of Astronomy, the late Elias Loomis, of Yale College, and also his brother, Dr. Loomis, of New York.

Rev. Nehemiah Dodge, formerly so well known in New London as the talented minister of the First Baptist Church, who afterwards adopted the doctrines of Universalism, was a descendant of James Rogers; as, of course, was his brother, Israel Dodge, father of Senator Henry Dodge of Wisconsin and grandfather of Senator Augustus C. Dodge, first governor of the Territory of Iowa, and afterwards minister to Spain. Rev. Nehemiah was remarkable for his wit and quickness of repartee, and of him many anecdotes might be told. One may suffice, as showing his abundant humor.

As Mr. Dodge was driving his horse and sleigh through a narrow passage, high banks of snow on both sides, he was approached by a person, also in a sleigh, coming in the opposite direction. Mr. Dodge, who was a large, stalwart man, arose, and, lifting his whip loftily, said, "Turn out, you rascal, or I'll serve you as I did the last man I met." The poor fellow, his horses floundering in the snow, replied, "How did you serve the last man you met?" "I turned out for him," was Mr. Dodge's jovial reply, as he drove past.

The wife of Dr. Nathaniel Perkins and her sister, Miss Jane Richards, may be mentioned as of Rogers ancestry.

The children of the late Thomas Fitch, one of New London's most enterprising citizens, are descendants of James Rogers, in the line of his daughter, Bathsheba Smith, their mother being sister of the famous whaling captains of this place, Robert Smith and Parker Smith, also James Smith, the popular captain of the Manhansett.

The descendants of Henry Deshon, one of the early residents of New London, are doubly of Rogers ancestry, being descendants of John Rogers and also of his sister Bathsheba, by marriage of daughter of latter to John Rogers, 2d. The late Capt. John Deshon, the children of B. B. Thurston, and also Augustus Brandagee, on his mother's side, are in this line ofdescent.

John Bishop, government contractor, builder and first proprietor of the Pequot House, Charles, Henry and Gilbert Bishop, of the enterprising firm of Bishop Bros., and the late Joseph B. Congdon may be named as descendants of John Rogers.

The children of Ex-Gov. T. M. Waller and the children of Frank Chappell are descendants of John Rogers, in the Bishop line.

The children of Alfred Chappell are descendants of John Bolles, in the Turner line.[20]

Peter C. Turner, for some time cashier of the whaling bank in New London, and afterwards of the First National Bank, was a descendant of John Bolles; as are also, in the same line, the Weavers and Newcombs of the later generations.

Elisha and Frank Palmer, of New London, large manufacturers at Montville, Fitchville, etc., are descendants of James Rogers and of John Bolles, as are also Reuben and Tyler Palmer, of New London, manufacturers. Mr. George S. Palmer of Norwich is of the same line.

The late enterprising brothers, President and George Rogers, of New London, were descendants of James Rogers, 2d, and of John Rogers.

The late Mrs. Marvin, of New London, daughter of Job Taber, was a descendant of John Rogers and John Bolles, by marriage of a son of the latter (Ebenezer) with a daughter of John Rogers, 2d.

William Bolles (brother of the writer) was for many years engaged in the printing, publishing and book-selling business in New London. He was author and compiler of several books, among which was Bolle's "Phonographic and Pronouncing Dictionary," royal octavo, admitted to be the best dictionary in this country previous to Webster's Unabridged. From the "History of New London County" we quote the following:—

It is a fact worthy of notice, as displaying the originality and versatility of New England thought and enterprise, that the paper mill at Bolle's Cove, a few miles out of New London, was erected by William Bolles, who there made the paper for his dictionary, which was printed and bound by the concern of which he was senior partner.

William Bolles was a foremost abolitionist, when to speak against slavery was to call down ridicule and opposition of a very serious nature. William Bolles was a descendant of John Rogers and John Bolles, who, one hundred and fifty years before, tenaciously maintained the equal right of all to religious liberty.

Joshua Bolles, brother of above, was a prominent business man of New London, being not only a partner in the book publishing firm and bookstore, but also concerned in banking and brokerage. Of his transactions as a broker, he was able to say that he never sold stock which he considered unsafe to any man without fully stating to the applicant his own opinion of the same, and that even after such warning, he had never sold such stock unless fully confident that the would-be purchaser was able to lose the amount thus risked.

Peter Strickland, Consul to Goree-dakir, Senegal, conspicuous for fidelity in discharging the duties of that office, which he has held for twenty years, and equally honored as a captain sailing between Boston and foreign ports, is a descendant of John Rogers and James Rogers, 2d. His skill in seamanship and fertility of resource when his vessel was dismantled in a gale, and which he brought safely into Boston, though it might lawfully have been abandoned, won him great praise and a gold medal from the underwriters whose interests he had so faithfully served.

Among lawyers of John Bolles descent: David Bolles, whose labors were so efficient in the defence of religious liberty more than half a century ago, to which we have before referred; John A. Bolles (son of Rev. Matthew Bolles), first editor of the *Boston Daily Journal*, and for many years a prominent lawyer in that city. He received the degree of LL.D. from Brown University, and was Secretary of State of Massachusetts. He was author of the prize essay on a Congress of Nations, published by the American Peace Society, also of many magazine articles. He was a member of Gen. John A. Dix's staff during the Civil War, and afterwards Judge Advocate General and solicitor of the Navy Department.[21] His son, Frank Bolles, was a lawyer, although better known as Secretary of Harvard College. To his superior qualities of mind and heart no words of ours can do justice. He was the author of works illustrative of nature, among which are "The Land of the Lingering Snow" and "Back of Beaucamp Water." Of his recent death, the *Boston Journal* said: "The birds and flowers have lost their best historian." The following lines to his memory were written by George B. Bancroft:—

All the world loves a lover,
Proclaims our poet seer.
So, Nature's sweet interpreter—
We hold thy memory dear.
And all the world, with myriad tongues,
Rejoices to proclaim,
With insight true, and clear as thine,
Thy fair and spotless fame,
Which lifted high on mighty pens
On every side is heard,
Wherever sounds an insect note
Or carol of a bird.
On opening leaf of tree and plant
He who has eyes may see
The imprint of the secrets rare
It whispered unto thee.
Thy life, so short, compared with ours,
Seems very full and long,
Crowned with the mystic harmony
Of wild melodious song.
The gentle river, drifting slow,
Its verdant banks between,
Reflects the pines that bear thy name
And keeps them ever green.

H. Eugene Bolles (son of William Bolles mentioned above), now an active lawyer in Boston, of large practice, is a descendant of John Rogers and John Bolles.

There are seven lawyers of the present date in New London who are descendants of John Rogers, viz., Hon. Augustus Brandagee, Frank Brandagee, Tracy Waller and brothers, Abel Tanner and the writer. There are three others who are descended from James Rogers, Sr., in other lines, viz., Clayton B. Smith, W. F. M. Rogers and Richard Crump.

Benjamin Thurston, a distinguished lawyer in Providence, and his brother, also a lawyer, are descendants of John Rogers.

We will now speak of ministers, and first of Rev. Peter Rogers, descendant of James Rogers, 2d, and John Rogers, 2d, his father being a grandson of the former and his mother a granddaughter of the latter. We give the following extract from an obituary notice[22] of this early New England Baptist minister.

Elder Peter Rogers was born in New London, Conn., June 23, 1754, and died at Waterloo, Munroe Co., Illinois, Nov. 4, 1849, at the age of 95 years. His father was a seafaring man and commanded a vessel; his mother was a devout, praying woman and made a lasting impression upon his character. Yet he grew up worldly and thoughtless, and at an early period in the Revolutionary War, enlisted in the army as a musician and became attached to the corps denominated "Washington's Life Guards." After three year's service in the army, he was honorably discharged and then commanded a government vessel, in which he performed valiant deeds and took three prizes from the enemy.

His conviction of sin was instrumentally produced by the life of faith and happy death of his first wife (we think she lived to rejoice in his conversion, but died soon after) and remembrance of the prayers and instruction of his mother. He was baptized by Eld. Amos Crandall and soon began to "improve his gift," as the Baptist phrase was in early times. In 1790, he was ordained by Elder Zadoc Darrow, Sr., Jason Lee and Christopher Palmer. His ministry was distinguished by revivals.

For a number of years, Eld. Rogers was a retailing merchant, while his gratuitous labors were abundant as an evangelist and pastor.

He lived and preached in New London, Killingly and Hampton, in Connecticut, in Leicester, Mass., and Swanzey, N. Ham., from 1789 to 1828, when he removed to Munroe County, Illinois.

For a few years, he was partially sustained as a pastor; but for a large part of sixty years he performed the warfare at his own charges, as did nearly all the Baptist ministers of New England in that day. Several hundred were converted and baptized under his ministry, a much larger number, in that day and in that part of the country, than by other Baptist ministers.

He was past threescore and ten when he came to Illinois, yet for a number of years he labored much in the gospel and was highly esteemed and beloved by all his brethren.

He delighted in Christian society, and, like a memorable patriarch of a former age, his presence, counsel and kindness were welcome in all our circles. "He fell like a shock of corn fully ripe in its season," strong in faith, full of hope, and abundant in joy and consolation.

Dr. Lucius Bolles (Rev., D.D., and S.T.D.) was a descendant of John Bolles. He was for more than twenty-two years pastor of the First Baptist Church in Salem, Mass., and for many years Secretary of the American Baptist Board of Foreign Missions and Fellow of Brown University. Of him it is said, "No man of his denomination occupied a more prominent position, or exercised an influence more strong and universal."

James A. Bolles, D.D., Episcopalian, for many years pastor of the Church of the Advent, Boston, was a descendant of John Bolles. He was author of several pamphlets and books on church matters.

Edwin C. Bolles, D.D., a talented preacher of New York City (Church of the Eternal Hope), whose sermons are embellished more with the precepts of the Bible than with sectarian tenets, is a descendant of John Bolles.

Four ministers born in New London during the present century were descendants of John Rogers, among them Rev. John Brandagee and Father Deshon of good fame.

Rev. John Middleton was a descendant of James Rogers, 2d.

Rev. Charles H. Peck, of Bennington, Vt., is a descendant of James Rogers, 2d. He is the son of Mrs. E. P. Peck, of New London, daughter of our late esteemed fellow-townsman, Daniel Rogers, to whose interest in genealogical researches many besides ourselves are indebted for information concerning early inhabitants of New London.

As to physicians of Rogerene descent, we recall very few at time of this writing. Their ancestors largely discarded medicines, and this sentiment may have been handed down. But we will mention William P. Bolles, M.D., of Boston, brother of Lawyer H. E. Bolles above mentioned, who by his skill in surgery and medical practice, and also by literary work in the same lines, has brought honor to himself and his profession.

The writer will here relate a conversation which was held with a prominent physician of the present day.

"If you had lived," said we, "two hundred years ago, would you have chosen the attendance of a physician or the good care of friends in sickness?"

"I would have preferred the good care of friends," was the reply. "The science of medicine was not so well understood then as at the present day."

A tacit acknowledgment that the Rogerenes were right, although the doctor knew not the purpose for which the question was asked. Certain it is that much less medicine is administered now than formerly, and statistics show that longevity has increased.

Mr. McEwen has not failed to ridicule the belief of the Rogerenes concerning the non-use of medicine, and perhaps the best reply is given by Mrs. Caulkins, when she says of John Rogers, 2d, as before quoted, "Notwithstanding his long testimony and his many weary trials and imprisonments, he reared to maturity a family of eighteen children, most of them, like their parents, sturdy Rogerenes."

And of John Bolles in this connection we have only to say, he had fifteen children, the average age reached by whom was more than seventy-six years. He himself lived to be ninety.

We are not disposed to deny the fact that the Rogerenes held the sentiments ascribed to them on this subject, and, not to spoil a joke for relation's sake, we will relate an anecdote which was told us by the late Edward Prentice, with much glee on his part.

Joshua Bolles, youngest son of John Bolles (and grandfather of the writer), then living on Bolles Hill, was badly injured by a ferocious animal on his place, and brought to the house insensible. Mr. Frink, his nearest neighbor, immediately sent for Dr. Wolcott, who came to his assistance. When Mr. Bolles recovered consciousness, he saw Dr. Wolcott in the room and said to Mr. Frink, who was standing near him, "What's Wolcott here for?" Mr. Frink replied, "I sent for him; if I had not, you would have been dead by this time." "Then you should have let me die!" was Mr. Bolle's answer. Joshua Bolles lived to be eighty-three years of age; only one of his fifteen children died in childhood. Several lived to be eighty and upwards, and all but one of the others to past middle age.

Since we have introduced Joshua Bolles, we will make the reader acquainted with a few more of his descendants.

Andrew W. Phillips, the distinguished Professor of Mathematics in Yale College, is a descendant of Joshua Bolles; as are also Rev. Joshua Bolles Garritt, Professor of Greek and Latin in Hanover College, Indiana, his son, Joshua Garritt, missionary in China, and his daughter, Mrs. Coulter, well known in missionary and philanthropic circles, wife of John M. Coulter, formerly Professor of Natural Sciences in Wabash College, and now President of the Indiana State University.[23]

Of professors in the Rogers line, we will mention Hamilton Smith, son of Anson Smith, formerly of New London. He early gave his attention to telescopic observations, and is a well-known professor of astronomy in Hobart College, N.Y. He is a descendant of John Rogers.

William Augustus Rogers, a descendant of James Rogers, 2d, also deserves honorable notice. He is a graduate of Brown University. He was Professor of Mathematics and Industrial Mechanics at Alfred University, N.Y., where he secured the building of an observatory which he equipped at his own expense. Afterwards, he was for fifteen years Assistant Professor of Astronomy at Harvard College. In 1880, he received from Yale College the honorary degree of A.M., in recognition of his services to astronomy; was elected member of the American Academy of Arts and Sciences and Fellow of the Royal Microscopical Society, London; and is now (1895) a professor in Colby University, Maine.

Prof. Nathaniel Britton, of Columbia College, New York, Professor of Botany, is a grandson of David S. Turner, of New London, a descendant of John Bolles. David Turner, son of the latter, is a prominent journalist in Florence, Italy.

Of wealthy merchants and brokers of Rogerene descent in the Rogers and Bolles line there have been and still are several millionaires.

William Bolles, of Hartford, recently deceased, whose estate was valued at more than a million, was a grandson of Joshua Bolles.

As an example of sterling business integrity we will mention Matthew Bolles, of Boston, well known in commercial circles at home and abroad, a descendant of John Bolles.

Of artists, we will name John W. Bolles, of Newark, N.J., Miss Amelia M. Watson and Miss Edith S. Watson, of Windsor, granddaughters of Frederick D. Bolles, also Miss Thurston, of Providence, formerly of New London, and daughter of Hon. B. B. Thurston, a descendant of John Rogers.

A young architect, of high promise and achievement, should not be overlooked, Charles Urbane Thrall, of the Perth Amboy Terra Cotta Works. He is grandson of Mrs. Urbane Haven, of New London, who is doubly of John Rogers descent.[24]

Of editors and authors: Frederick D. Bolles, founder and first editor of the *Hartford Times*, a descendant of John Bolles.

Joshua A. Bolles, son of the late Joshua Bolles of New London (before mentioned), editor and proprietor of the *New Milford Gazette*, a descendant of John Rogers and John Bolles.

John McGinley, editor of the *New London Day*, is a descendant of John

Bolles.

Anna Bolles Williams, author of a number of popular works, is a descendant of John Rogers and John Bolles.

Mrs. Mary L. Bolles Branch (daughter of the writer), author of many acceptable articles for periodicals, both in prose and verse, is a descendant of John Rogers and John Bolles.[25]

Among teachers, we must not fail to mention Mrs. Marion Hempstead Lillie, so long the efficient and popular Principal of the Coit Street School, also a prominent member of the L. S. Chapter of the D. A. R. and other social and literary circles, in which her genial manners and brilliant conversational powers have won her many friends and admirers. She is a descendant of John Rogers, also of Bathsheba Rogers.

Miss Jennie Turner, so favorably known, and for many years Assistant Principal of the Young Ladie's Institute of New London, is a descendant of John Bolles.

The last four were fellow-students at the Young Ladie's Academy of New London, under the instruction of Mr. Amos Perry, afterwards consul to Tunis, and now (1894) Secretary of the Rhode Island Historical Society. They were members of an advanced class formed by him, of which, as the names are now recalled, we discover that nearly all were of Rogerene descent, viz.: John Bolles, John Rogers, or both.

Goodness should not less receive its meed of praise. We present in this place the name of one who from childhood was called to display sweet ministries in all the walks of life, and by gentlest influence to lead the hearts of others to that which is purest and best. We speak of our own sister, Delight Rogers Bolles, admired and loved by all, and whose influence ceases not to be felt at the present day.

When about twenty years of age, she listened to a discourse delivered by a preacher of some eminence, which was praised by all who heard it. After returning home, for her own benefit and that of others, she wrote down the sermon as nearly as possible as it was delivered, which was read by many. Fifty years afterwards, Mr. Charles Johnson, President of the Norwich Bank, formerly a resident of the town of Griswold, in which she resided at the time, spoke of it to us with fresh admiration, saying, "Every word of the sermon was written to a dot." Afterwards she married and lived in Hampton for several years, where her excellence of character won for her hosts of friends. Although a Baptist by profession, she uniformly partook of the sacrament of the Lord's Supper with the Congregational Church on Hampton Hill, no Baptist meeting being within several miles of that place, for which she received no censure from the church to which she belonged, to their praise be it spoken. Goodness and love overshadowed all distinction. We should remember that the robe of Christ was seamless. Having so beautifully served her day and generation, she still lives, though her obsequies were celebrated at the Congregational church at Hampton seventy years ago. We never heard an unpleasant word spoken to or by the subject of this memoir. She kept a diary. When eleven years of age, we cast a glance upon one of its pages and read these words: "What shall I do to glorify Thee this day?" This awakened in me a little surprise at the time, wondering what a person in so small a sphere could do to glorify the great God of the universe. But we have long since found that the smallest offerings are acceptable to Him who makes his abode with the humble and the contrite.

The list of persons of Rogerene descent might be much enlarged, even within the limits of New London. Outside of this city, it might be almost indefinitely extended. But we have here given enough, we think, to show that Mr. McEwen's words, "a small remnant," were not well chosen.

It is surprising to note how many of the dwellers on State Street, in New London, have been, and are, of Rogerene descent. Even the agent from Washington employed by the government to select a lot on that street for the new postoffice, and other public uses, was a descendant of John Rogers.

Instead of a "small remnant," the words of Scripture would be much more appropriate:—

"There shall be a handful of corn in the earth, on the top of the mountain, and the fruit thereof shall shake like Lebanon."

Here the writer may be indulged in a little pleasantry, and hopes the reader will not regard it as ungermane to the subject.

As we throw our searchlights upon the past, we are pleased to note that the lot on which the First Congregational Church now stands was formerly owned by Stephen Bolles (grandson of John Bolles) and then called Bolles Hill.[26] It was purchased from him in the year 1786, by "The First Church of Christ," and a meeting-house built thereon; Stephen Bolles contributing one-third of the price of the lot towards its erection. At and after this period, it would seem that the church was more lenient toward the Rogerenes; although they were not permitted to enter into full enjoyment of equal religious liberty until 1818, when the New Constitution spread its broad ægis over all alike, to the consummation of which glorious end, the descendants of the pioneers in the Rogers movement acted such an efficient part.

Thus, the First Congregational Church, leaving the spot where had been enacted so much injustice towards the dissenters, planted itself on Bolles Hill, where the fresh breezes of liberty seemed to give it a higher and a purer life, reminding us of the old saying, "If the mountain will not come to Mahomet, Mahomet will go to the mountain."

A fine granite structure now stands upon the old hill. May all its future utterances be worthy of its foundation. Long may it live to make the *amende honorable*, till the brightness of its future glory shall hide the shadows of the past. None will be more ready to publish its praises than the numerous posterity of the persecuted Rogerenes, remembering the motto, "To err is human, to forgive divine."

We will close this chapter with a poem by Mary L. Bolles Branch, one of her earlier productions which has been widely circulated in this and other countries. Is not the same oftentimes true of character; hidden long in obscurity under masses of prejudice and scorn, yet destined, some day, to be presented, in all its lines of beauty, to the gaze of men?

THE PETRIFIED FERN.

In a valley, centuries ago,
Grew a little fern-leaf, green and slender,
Veining delicate and fibres tender,
Waving when the wind crept down so low.
Rushes tall and moss and grass grew round it,
Playful sunbeams darted in and found it,
Drops of dew stole down by night and crowned it;
But no foot of man e'er trod that way;
Earth was young and keeping holiday.

Monster fishes swam the silent main,
Stately forests waved their giant branches,
Mountains hurled their snowy avalanches,
Mammoth creatures stalked across the plain;
Nature revelled in grand mysteries,
But the little fern was not of these,
Did not number with the hills and trees,
Only grew and waved its wild, sweet way.
No one came to note it, day by day.

Earth one time put on a frolic mood,
Heaved the rocks and changed the mighty motion
Of the deep, strong currents of the ocean;
Moved the plain and shook the haughty wood;
Crushed the little fern in soft, moist clay—
Covered it, and hid it safe away.
O the long, long centuries since that day!
O the changes! O life's bitter cost,
Since the useless little fern was lost!
Useless? Lost? There came a thoughtful man
Searching for Nature's secrets, far and deep;
From a fissure in a rocky steep,
He withdrew a stone, o'er which there ran
Fairy pencillings, a quaint design,
Leafage, veining fibres, clear and fine,
And the fern's life lay in every line!
So, I think, God hides some souls away,
Sweetly to surprise us, the last day.

Shortly after mention, in this chapter, of some of the descendants of the Rogerene leaders, Mr. John R. Bolles was called to join those heroes whose vindication he had so conscientiously undertaken, in the cause of justice and of truth. It remains to add to the above list of descendants some notice of this deceased writer, who not only bore the names of both of the principal Rogerene leaders, but was a direct descendant of both, his mother being a daughter of John Rogers, 3d, and his father a grandson of John Bolles. For this purpose is here presented the briefest of the several obituary notices that appeared in New London papers, being an editorial in the *Daily Telegraph*, of February 26, 1895.

The death of John Rogers Bolles removes from the people one who might be regarded almost as a relic of the old times when men were inspired to bear messages to the world. He was a bold and persistent fighter of what he deemed wrong and an active and indefatigable warrior for the right; any cause in which he was engaged was certain to have the whole benefit of his energies. The achievements of Mr. Bolles for his city and state have been fully set forth in the number of brilliant and graphic papers he contributed to *The Telegraph* and which were read with the widest interest, not only by those here but in other states. But it was not left for himself to chronicle his work. Some of the greatest men of the nation have been his friends and have repeatedly testified their admiration and respect for his remarkable qualities of mind. Mr. Bolles had a memory that was something prodigious. He was able to correct with the utmost ease the most trivial misplacements of a word in a MS. of many thousands, and his familiarity with the Book and all authors, ancient and modern, was also little less than a marvel, considering his lack of sight in later years. His reasoning powers were keen and wonderfully swift, he could anticipate and provide means against an emergency in an inconceivably short time, and as a tactician in the fight for New London's rights he was one of the most skilful and adroit of managers. Had he devoted his life to other than the work which was his sole aim, he would undoubtedly have won national pre-eminence. But after leaving the business of publishing, in which he was very successful and which he brought to a high degree of excellence here, he went with all his energies for the development of the Navy Yard, and in the pursuit of this object he spared nothing, himself least of all. He was very fluent in speech. His figures were always grand and forcible, and the magnetic power of his utterance carried away his audience. His pen is well known. There was a wonderful power of imagery in him, and he often expressed himself in verse of no mean order. His capacity for doing literary labor was something enormous; he could turn out a volume that would stagger an industrious man, and yet be fresh to tackle another subject after five or six consecutive hours of steady application. New London owes a great deal to John R. Bolles, how much it will understand more fully as time goes on.

But apart from his mental endowments, the grand simplicity and purity of the man deserves the highest commendation. He hated vice. He lived in virtue. His faith might not have been that of the creed follower, but he had a sublime and unshaken confidence in God and belief in His love for him and all true followers of His rules. Simple, sincere, innocent as a babe of wrong thought or act, John R. Bolles ended his long life a firm believer in the goodness and mercy of the Creator whom all that life he had worshipped with the worship of faith and act and example. In Christ he lived and in Christ he fell asleep.

PART II.
HISTORY OF THE ROGERENES.

BY

ANNA B. WILLIAMS.

THE GREAT LEADERSHIP.

CHAPTER I.

1637-1652.

Among noticeable young men in the Colony of Connecticut, previous to 1640, is James Rogers.[27] His name first appears on record at New Haven, but shortly after, in 1637, he is a soldier from Saybrook in the Pequot war.[28] He is next at Stratford, where he acquires considerable real estate and marries Elizabeth, daughter of Samuel Rowland, a landed proprietor of that place, who eventually leaves a valuable estate to his grandson, Samuel Rogers, and presumably other property to his daughter, who seems to have been an only child. A few years later, James Rogers appears at Milford. His wife joins the Congregational church there in 1645, and he himself joins this church in 1652.

He has evidently been a baker on a large scale for some time previous to 1655, at which date complaint is made to the General Court in regard to a quantity of biscuit furnished by him, which was exported to Virginia and the Barbadoes, upon which occasion he states that the flour furnished by the miller for this bread was not properly ground. The miller substantially admits that he did not at that time understand the correct manner of grinding.

In the course of ten years, Milford proves too small a port for the operations of this enterprising and energetic man, whose business includes supplies to seamen and troops. Governor Winthrop is holding out inducements for him to settle at New London. In 1656 he is empowered by the General Court to sell his warehouse at Milford, with his other property, provided said building be used only as a warehouse. He now begins to purchase valuable lands and houses at New London, and so continues for many years, frequently adding some choice house-lot, Indian clearing, meadowland, pasture or woodland to his possessions. In 1659 he sells to Francis Hall, an attorney of Fairfield, "all" his "lands, commons and houses in Stratford, Milford and New Haven."—(*History of Stratford.*)

At New London, in addition to his large baking business, he has charge of the town mill, by lease from Governor Winthrop, at the head of an inlet called Winthrop's Cove and forming Winthrop's Neck, which neck comprises the home lot of the governor. That James Rogers may build his house near the mill,[29] the Governor conveys to him a piece of his own land adjoining, upon which Mr. Rogers builds a stone dwelling. He also builds a stone bakery by the cove and has a wharf at this point.[30]

The long Main street of the town takes a sharp turn around the head of the cove, past the mill and to the house of the Governor, the latter standing on the east side of the cove, within a stone's throw of the mill.

The native forest is all around, broken here and there by a patch of pasture or planting ground. One of the main roads leading into the neighboring country runs southerly five miles to the Great Neck, a large, level tract of land bordering Long Island Sound. Another principal country road runs northerly from the mill, rises a long hill, and, after the first two or three miles, is scarcely more than an Indian trail, extending five miles to Mohegan, the headquarters of Uncas and his tribe. Upon this road are occasional glimpses, through the trees, of the "Great River" (later the Thames).

James Rogers is soon not only the principal business man of this port, but, next to the Governor, the richest man in the colony. His property in the colony much exceeds that of the Governor. He is prominent in town and church affairs, he and his wife having joined the New London church; also frequently an assistant at the Superior Court and deputy at the General Court. His children are receiving a superior education for the time, as becomes their father's means and station. Life and activity are all about these growing youth, at the bakery, at the mill, at the wharf. Many are the social comings and goings, not only to and from the Governor's house,[31] just beside them, but to and from their own house. His extensive business dealings and his attendance at court have brought James Rogers in contact with intelligent and prosperous men all over the colony, among whom he is a peer. His education is good, if not superior, for the time. He numbers among his personal friends some of the principal planters in this colony and neighboring colonies.

1666.

In 1666 James Rogers retires from active business. His sons Samuel and Joseph are capable young men past their majority. Samuel is well fitted to take charge of the bakery. Joseph inclines to the life of a country gentleman. John, an active youth of eighteen, is the scholar of the family. He writes his father's deeds and other business documents, which indicates some knowledge of the law. Besides being sons of a rich man, these are exceptionally capable young men. That there is no stain upon their reputations is indicated by the favor with which they are regarded by certain parents of marriageable daughters. In this year occurs the marriage of Samuel to the daughter of Thomas Stanton, who is a prominent man in the colony and interpreter between the General Court and the Indians. The parents of each make a handsome settlement upon the young people, James Rogers giving his son the stone dwelling-house and the bakery. This young man has recently sold the farm received from his grandfather, Samuel Rowland. Having also grants from the town and lands from his father (to say nothing of gifts from Owaneco), together with a flourishing business, Samuel Rogers is a rich man at an early age.

Somewhat before the marriage of Samuel, his father, in anticipation of this event, established himself upon the Great Neck, on a farm bought in 1660, of a prominent settler named Obadiah Bruen. This is one of the old Indian planting grounds so valuable in these forest days. Yet James Rogers does not reside long on the beautiful bank of Robin Hood's Bay (now Jordan Cove), for in this same year his son Joseph, not yet twenty-one years of age, receives this place, "the farm where I now dwell" and also "all my other lands on the Great Neck," as a gift from his father. All the "other lands" being valuable, this is a large settlement. (It appears to mark the year of Joseph's marriage, although the exact date and also the name of the bride are unknown. The residence of James Rogers for the next few years is uncertain; it is not unlikely that he takes up his abode in one of his houses in town, or possibly at the Mamacock farm, on the Mohegan road and the "Great River," which place was formerly granted by the town to the Rev. Mr. Blinman, and, upon the latter's removal from New London, was purchased by Mr. Rogers.)

The next marriage in this family is that of Bathsheba, a beloved daughter. She marries a young man named Richard Smith. A prominent feature in the character of this daughter is her fidelity to her parents and brothers, and especially to her brother John.

1670.

Matthew Griswold is a leading member in the church of Saybrook. He resides close by the Sound, at Lyme, on a broad sweep of low-lying meadows called Blackhall, which is but a small portion of his landed estate. His wife is a daughter of Henry Wolcott, one of the founders and principal men of Windsor, and a prominent man in the colony. Matthew Griswold is, like James Rogers, a frequent assistant and deputy. There are many proofs that he and his wife are persons of much family pride, and not without good reasons for the same. When, in 1670, they enter into an agreement with James Rogers for the marriage of their daughter Elizabeth to his son John, it is doubtless with the knowledge that this is a very promising young man, as well as the son of a wealthy and generous father.

How far from the mind of the young lover, when, on the night before the happy day when he is to call Elizabeth his bride, he pens the writing[32] which is to give her the Mamacock farm, recently presented to him by his father, is a thought of anything that can part them until death itself. To this writing he adds: "I do here farther engage not to carry her out of the colony of

Connecticut." This sentence goes to prove the great fondness of the parents for this daughter, her own loving desire to live always near them, and the ready compliance of the young lover with their wishes. He marries her at Blackhall, October 17, and takes her to the beautiful river farm which upon that day becomes her own. He does not take her to the farmhouse built by Mr. Blinman, but to a new and commodious dwelling, close by the Mohegan road, whose front room is 20 by 20, and whose big fireplaces, in every room, below and above, will rob the wintry blasts of their terror. The marriage settlement upon the young couple, by James Rogers and Matthew Griswold, includes provisions, furniture, horses, sheep, and kine.[33]

1673.

In 1673, James Rogers, Jr., is of age. No large gift of land to this young man is recorded; for which reason it seems probable that his principal portion in the lifetime of his father is the good ship of which he is master. His ability to navigate and command a foreign bound vessel at such an age is sufficient guarantee of the skill and enterprise of this youth. In 1674, the young shipmaster has (according to tradition in that branch of the family—*Caulkins*) among his passengers to Connecticut a family emigrating from Ireland, one member of which is an attractive young woman twenty years of age. Before the vessel touches port, the young captain and his fair passenger are betrothed, and the marriage takes place soon after.[34]

1674.

Although John Rogers resides at Mamacock farm, he is by no means wholly occupied in the care of that place; a young man of his means has capable servants. As for years past, he is actively interested in business, both for his father and himself. At Newport, in the year 1674, he meets with members of the little Sabbatarian church of that place, recently started by a few devout and earnest students of the Bible, who having, some years before, perceived that certain customs of the Congregational churches have no precedent or authority in Scripture, resolved to follow these customs no longer, but to be guided solely by the example and precepts of Christ and his apostles. In attempting to carry out this resolve, they renounced and denounced sprinkling and infant baptism and attached themselves to the First Baptist Church of Newport. About 1665, they were led, by the teachings of Stephen Mumford, a Sabbatarian from England, to discern in the first day Sabbath the authority of man and not of God. Under this persuasion, the little company came out of the First Baptist Church, of Newport, and formed the Sabbatarian Church of that place. Mr. Thomas Hiscox is pastor of this little church, and Mr. Samuel Hubbard and his wife (formerly among the founders of the First Congregational Church of Springfield, Mass.) are among its chief members. During this year, under the preaching and teachings of this church, John Rogers is converted.

Hitherto this young man and his wife Elizabeth have been members of the regular church, as ordinary membership is accounted, and their two children have been baptized in that church, at New London. If children of professed Christians, baptized in childhood, lead an outwardly moral life, attend the stated worship and otherwise conform to the various church usages, this is sufficient to constitute them, as young men and young women, members in good and regular standing. The daughter of Elder Matthew Griswold has been as ignorant of the work of regeneration as has been the son of James Rogers.

The conversion of John Rogers was directly preceded by one of those sudden and powerful convictions of sin so frequently exemplified in all ages of the Christian church, and so well agreeing with Scriptural statements regarding the new birth. Although leading a prominently active business life, in a seaport town, from early youth, and thus thrown among all classes of men and subjected to many temptations, this young man has given no outward sign of any lack of entire probity. Whatever his lapses from exact virtue, they have occasioned him no serious thought, until, by the power of this conversion, he perceives himself a sinner. Under this deep conviction the memory of a certain youthful error weighs heavily upon his conscience.

He has at this time one confidant, his loving, sympathetic and deeply interested young wife, who cordially welcomes the new light from Newport. In the candid fervor of his soul, he tells her all, even the worst he knows of himself, and that he feels in his heart that, by God's free grace, through the purifying blood of Jesus Christ, even his greatest sin is washed away and forgiven.

Does this young woman turn, with horror and aversion, from the portrayal of this young man's secret sin? By no means.[35] She is not only filled with sympathy for his deep sorrow and contrition, but rejoices with him in his change of heart and quickened conscience. More than this, understanding that even one as pure as herself may be thus convicted of sin and thus forgiven and reborn, she joins with him in prayer that such may be her experience also. They study the New Testament together, and she finds, as he has said, that there is here no mention of a change from a seventh to a first day Sabbath, and no apparent warrant for infant baptism, but the contrary; the command being first to believe and then to be baptized. Other things they find quite contrary to the Congregational way. In her ardor, she joins with him to openly declare these errors in the prevailing belief and customs.

Little is the wonder that to Elder Matthew Griswold and his wife the news that their daughter and her husband are openly condemning the usages of the powerful church of which they, and all their relatives, are such prominent members, comes like a thunderbolt. Their own daughter is condemning even the grand Puritan Sabbath and proposes to work hereafter upon that sacred day and to worship upon Saturday. They find that her husband has led Elizabeth into this madness. They accuse and upbraid him, they reason and plead with him. But all in vain. He declares to them his full conviction that this is the call and enlightenment of the Lord himself. Moreover, was it not the leading resolve of the first Puritans to be guided and ruled only by the Word of God and of His Son, Jesus Christ? Did they not warn their followers to maintain a jealous watchfulness against any belief, decree or form of worship not founded upon the Scriptures? Did they not urge each to search these Scriptures for himself? He has searched these Scriptures, and Elizabeth with him, and they have found a most astonishing difference between the precepts and example of Christ and the practice and teachings of the Congregational church.

Elder Matthew Griswold is ready with counter arguments on the Presbyterian side. But "the main instrument" by which Elizabeth is restored to her former church allegiance is her mother, the daughter of Henry Wolcott. This lady is sister of Simon Wolcott, who is considered one of the handsomest, most accomplished and most attractive gentlemen of his day. Although she may have similar charms and be a mother whose judgment a daughter would highly respect, yet she is evidently one of the last from whom could be expected any deviation, in belief or practice, from the teachings and customs of her father's house. That her daughter has been led to adopt the notions of these erratic Baptists is, to her mind, a disgrace unspeakable. She soon succeeds in convincing Elizabeth that this is no influence of the Holy Spirit, as declared by John Rogers, but a device of the Evil One himself. Under such powerful counter representations, on the part of her relatives and acquaintances, as well as by later consideration of the social disgrace attendant upon her singular course, Elizabeth is finally led to publicly recant her recently avowed belief, despite the pleadings of her husband. At the same time, she passionately beseeches him to recant also, declaring that unless he will renounce the evil spirit by which he has been led, she cannot continue to live with him. He, fully persuaded that he has been influenced by the very Spirit of God, declares that he cannot disobey the divine voice within his soul.

One sad day, after such a scene as imagination can well picture, this young wife prepares herself, her little girl of two years and her baby boy, for the journey to Blackhall, with the friends who have come to accompany her. Even as she rides away, hope must be hers that, after the happy home is left desolate, her husband will yield to her entreaties. Not so with him as he sees depart the light and joy of Mamacock, aye, Mamacock itself which he has given her. He drinks the very dregs of this cup without recoil. He parts with wife and children and lands, for His name's sake. Well he knows in his heart, that for him can be no turning. And what can he now expect of the Griswolds?

Although his own home is deserted and he will no more go cheerily to Blackhall, there is still a place where dear faces light at his coming. It is his father's house. Here are appreciative listeners to the story of his recent experiences and convictions; father and mother, brothers and sisters, are for his sake reading the Bible anew. They find exact Scripture warrant for his sudden, deep conviction of sin and for his certainty that God has heard his fervent prayers, forgiven his sins and bestowed upon him a new heart. They find no Scripture warrant for a Sabbath upon the first day of the week, nor for baptism of other than believers, nor for a specially learned and aristocratic ministry. They, moreover, see no authority for the use of civil power to compel persons to religious observances, and such as were unknown to the early church, and no good excuse for the inculcating of doctrines and practices contrary to the teachings of Christ and his apostles. Shortly, James, the young shipmaster, has an experience similar to that of his brother, as has also an Indian by the name of Japhet. This Indian is an intelligent and esteemed servant in the family of James Rogers, Sr.

At this time, the home of James Rogers is upon the Great Neck. By some business agreement, his son Joseph resigned to his father, in 1670, the lands upon this Neck which had been given him in 1666. In this year (1674), his father reconfirms to him the property bought of Obadiah Bruen, by Robin Hood's Bay. The younger children, Jonathan and Elizabeth, are still at home with their parents. Bathsheba and her family are living near, on the Great Neck, as are also Captain James and his family.

Although John may still lay some claim to Mamacock farm, while awaiting legal action on the part of the Griswolds, it can be no home to him in these days of bitter bereavement. Warm hearts welcome him to his father's house, by the wide blue Sound, and here he takes up his abode. Never a man of his temperament but loved the sea and the wind, the sun and the storm, the field and the wood. All of these are here. Here, too, is his "boat," evidently as much a part of the man as his horse. No man but has a horse for these primitive distances, and in this family will be none but the best of steeds and boats in plenty.

Near the close of this eventful year, Mr. James Rogers sends for Mr. John Crandall to visit at his house. Mr. Crandall has, for some time, been elder of the Baptist church at Westerly, an offshoot of the Baptist church of Newport. He has recently gone over with his flock to the Sabbatarian church of Newport. If the subject of possible persecution in Connecticut is brought up, who can better inspire the new converts with courage for such an ordeal than he who has been imprisoned and whipped in Boston for daring to avow his disbelief in infant baptism and his adherence to the primitive mode by immersion? The conference is so satisfactory, that Mr. Crandall baptizes John Rogers, his brother James, and the servant Japhet.—(*Letter of Mr. Hubbard.*)

News of the baptism of these young men into the Anabaptist faith by Mr. Crandall, at their father's house, increases the comment and excitement already started in the town. The minister, Mr. Simon Bradstreet, expresses a hope that the church will "take a course" with the Rogers family. The Congregational churches at large are greatly alarmed at this startling innovation in Connecticut. The tidings travel fast to Blackhall, dispelling any lingering hope that John Rogers may repent of his erratic course. Immediately after this occurrence, his wife, by the aid of her friends, takes steps towards securing a divorce and the guardianship of her children. From her present standpoint, her feelings and action are simply human, even, in a sense, womanly. He who is to suffer will be the last to upbraid her, his blame will be for those who won her from his view to theirs, from the simple word of Scripture to the iron dictates of popular ecclesiasticism.

If John Rogers and his friends know anything as yet of the plot on the part of the Griswolds to make the very depth of his repentance for an error of his unregenerate youth an instrument for his utter disgrace and bereavement, their minds are not absorbed at this time with matters of such worldly moment.

1675.

In March, 1675, James Rogers, Sr., and his family send for Elder Hiscox, Mr. Samuel Hubbard and his son Clarke, of the Sabbatarian church of Newport, to visit them. Before the completion of this visit, Jonathan Rogers (twenty years of age) is baptized. Following this baptism, John, James, Japhet and Jonathan are received as members of the Sabbatarian church of Newport, by prayer and laying on of hands.—(*Letter of Mr. Hubbard.*)

This consummation of John's resolves brings matters to a hasty issue on the part of the Griswolds, in lines already planned. There is no law by which a divorce can be granted on account of difference in religious views. In some way this young man's character must be impugned, and so seriously as to afford plausible grounds for divorcement. How fortunate that, at the time of his conversion, he made so entire a confidant of his wife. Fortunate, also, that his confession was a blot that may easily be darkened, with no hindrance to swearing to the blot. At this time, the young woman's excited imagination can easily magnify that which did not appear so serious in the calm and loving days at Mamacock, even as with tear-wet eyes he told the sorrowful story of his contrition. Thus are laid before the judges of the General Court, representations to the effect that this is no fit man to be the husband of Elizabeth, daughter of Matthew Griswold. The judges, lawmakers and magistrates of Connecticut belong to the Congregational order—the only elite and powerful circle of the time; this, taken in connection with the unfavorable light in which the Rogerses are now regarded in such quarters, is greatly to the Griswold advantage.

Yet, despite aversion and alarm on the part of the ruling dignitaries regarding the new departure and the highly colored petition that has been presented to the court by the daughter of Matthew Griswold, there is such evident proof that the petitioner is indulging an intensity of bitterness bordering upon hatred towards the man who has refused, even for her sake, to conform to popular belief and usages, that the judges hesitate to take her testimony, even under oath. Moreover, the only serious charge in this document rests solely upon the alleged declaration of John Rogers against himself, in a private conference with his wife. This charge, however, being represented in the character of a crime[36] (under the early laws), is sufficient for his arrest. Very soon after his reception into the Sabbatarian church, the young man is seized and sent to Hartford for imprisonment, pending the decision of the grand jury.

Although John Rogers has been a member of the Sabbatarian church but a few weeks, he is already pastor of a little church on the Great Neck (under the Newport church) of which his father, mother, brothers and sisters are devout attendants, together with servants of the family and neighbors who have become interested in the new departure. Who will preach to this little congregation, while its young pastor is in Hartford awaiting the issue of the Griswold vengeance? Of those who have received baptism, James is upon the "high seas," in pursuance of his calling, and Jonathan is but a youth of twenty. Yet Mr. James Rogers does not permit the Seventh Day Sabbath of Christ and His disciples to pass unobserved. The little congregation gather at his house, as usual, and sit in reverent silence, as in the presence of the Lord.[37] Perchance the Holy Spirit will inspire some among them to speak or to pray. They are not thus gathered because this is the Quaker custom, for they are not Quakers; they are simply following a distinct command of the Master and awaiting the fulfilment of one of His promises.

William Edmundson, the Quaker preacher, driven by a storm into New London harbor on a Saturday in May, 1675, goes ashore there and endeavors to gather a meeting, but is prevented by the authorities. Hearing there are some Baptists five miles from town, who hold their meetings upon that day, he feels impressed with a desire to visit them. Meeting with two men of friendly inclinations, who are willing to accompany him, he goes to the Great Neck and finds there this little congregation, assembled as described, "with their servants and negroes,"[38] sitting in silence. At first (according to his account) they appear disturbed at the arrival of such unexpected guests; but, upon finding this stranger only a friendly Quaker, they welcome them cordially.

After sitting with them a short time in silence, the Quaker begins to question them in regard to their belief and to expound to them some of the Quaker doctrines. He sees they are desirous of a knowledge of God and finds them very "ready" in the Scriptures. He endeavors to convince them that after the coming of Christ a Sabbath was no longer enjoined, Christ having ended the law and being the rest of His people; also that the ordinance of water baptism should long ago have ended, being superseded by the baptism of the Holy Ghost. Although in no way convinced (as is afterwards fully demonstrated), they listen courteously to his arguments and to the prayer that follows. Not only so, but, by his declaration, they are "very tender and loving." The next day, this zealous Quaker, having obtained leave of a man in New London, who is well inclined towards the Quakers, to hold a meeting at his house, finds among his audience several of the little congregation on the Great Neck. In the midst of this meeting, the constable and other officers appear, and break it up forcibly, with rough handling and abuse, much to the indignation of those who have been anxious to give Mr. Edmundson a fair hearing.

The week after his visit to New London, Mr. Edmundson is at an inn in Hartford, where he improves an opportunity to present certain Quaker doctrines to some of those stopping there, and judges that he has offered unanswerable arguments in proof that every man has a measure of the Spirit of Christ. Suddenly, a young man in the audience rises and argues so ably upon the other side as to destroy the effect of Mr. Edmundson's discourse. This leads the latter to a private interview with his opponent, whose name he finds to be John Rogers, and who proves to be "pastor" of the people whose meeting he had attended at New London, on the Great Neck. He also learns from this pastor that he was summoned to Hartford, to appear before the Assembly, for the reason that, since he became a Baptist, the father of his wife, who is of the ruling church, had been violently set against him and was endeavoring to secure a divorce for his daughter on plea of a confession made to her by himself regarding "an ill fact" in his past life, "before he was her husband and while he was one of their church," with which, "under sorrow and trouble of mind," he "had acquainted her" and "which she had divulged to her father."

Mr. Edmundson informs the young man that he has been with his people at New London and "found them loving and tender."—(*Journal of Mr. Edmundson.*)

Since John Rogers remains at the inn for the night, he is evidently just released from custody. So interwoven were truth and misrepresentation in this case, that either admission or denial of the main charge must have been difficult, if not impossible, on the part of the accused. Moreover, there is for this young man, now and henceforth, no law, precedent or example, save such as he finds in the New Testament, through his Lord and Master. That Master, being asked to declare whether he was or was not the King of the Jews, a question of many possible phases and requiring such answer as his judges neither could nor would comprehend, answered only by silence. Ought this young man to repeat before these judges the exact statement made to his wife, in the sacred precincts of his own home, even if they would take the word of a despised Anabaptist like himself? It is not difficult to see the young man's position and respect his entire silence, despite all efforts to make him speak out in regard to the accusation made by his wife in her petition.[39]

The case before the grand jury having depended solely upon the word of a woman resolved upon divorce and seeking ground for it, they returned that they "find not the bill," and John Rogers was discharged from custody. Yet, in view of the representations of Elizabeth in her petition regarding her unwillingness, for the alleged reasons, to remain this young man's wife, backed by powerful influence in her favor, the court gave her permission to remain with her children at her father's for the present, "for comfort and preservation" until a decision be rendered regarding the divorce, by the General Court in October. No pains will be spared by the friends of Elizabeth to secure a favorable decision from this court.

The Rev. Mr. Bradstreet, bitter in his prejudice against the young man by whose influence has occurred such a departure from the Congregational church as that of James Rogers and his family and such precedent for the spread of anti-presbyterian views outside of Rhode Island, writes in his journal at this date: "He is now at liberty, but I believe he will not escape God's judgment, though he has man's."

Mr. Bradstreet reveals in his journal knowledge that the charge advanced against this young man related to a period previous to his marriage and conversion, and rested upon a confession that he had made to his wife under conviction of sin and belief in the saving power of Christ, which cleanses the vilest sinner.[40] Yet knowing this, he says: “I believe he will not escape God’s judgment.” Truly New England Puritan theology and the theology of the New Testament are strangely at variance in these days.

CHAPTER II.

1675.

Week by week, the little band of Bible students on the Great Neck are becoming more and more familiar with the contents of the New Testament. Heretofore they have, like the majority, accepted religion as it has been prepared for them, as naturally as they have accepted other customs, fashions and beliefs. Now that they have begun to search and examine for themselves, it is in no half-way fashion. Doubtless to a bold, direct, enterprising mode of thought and action James Rogers owed his worldly success. It is evident that his children, by inheritance and example, possess like characteristics. Through the mystic power of conversion they have come "to see and to know"[41] the truth of the Gospel of Jesus Christ. They believe that the Scriptures were inspired by God himself, in the consciousness of holy men, and by His providence written and preserved for the instruction of succeeding generations; that, accordingly, what is herein written, by way of precept or example, is binding upon the regenerate man, and no command or example of men contrary to this Word should be obeyed, whatever the worldly menace or action may be.

John Rogers has already begun to work on the first day of the week. Moreover, in order to conform with exactness to the New Testament command and example relating to preachers of the Gospel, he has taken up a handicraft, that of shoemaking. At this date, all handicrafts are held in esteem, some of the most prominent men in a community having one or more; yet the large dealings of Mr. James Rogers have called for an active business life on the part of this son, who appears to have been his "right-hand man." In taking up this handicraft, John Rogers appears not to neglect other business (in 1678 we shall find him fulfilling a contract to build a ship costing £4,640[42]), but to be busily employed at the bench in what might otherwise be his leisure hours, and especially upon that day which has been declared "holy" by man and not by God.

How closely this movement is watched by the Connecticut authorities appears by a law enacted in May of this year, in which it is ordered that no servile work shall be done on the Sabbath, save that of piety, charity or necessity, upon penalty of 10*s*. fine for each offense, and "in case the offence be circumstanced with high-handed presumption as well as profaneness the penalty to be augmented at the discretion of the judges." What "high-handed presumption" and "profaneness" consist of, in this case, will soon be evident.

The hesitation of the New London church in dealing with the Rogerses can readily be understood. Mr. James Rogers is the principal taxpayer, his rates for church and ministry are largest of all, to say nothing of those of his sons. Not only this, but the family has been one of the most respected in the town. Perchance they may yet see the error of their ways, especially when they have decisive proof of what is likely to proceed from the civil arm, if this foolhardiness is continued.

1676.

Despite the ominous law aimed at themselves and their followers, James Rogers, his wife and their daughter Bathsheba Smith, are preparing for a final consecration to the unpopular cause. In September, 1676, John, Capt. James, Japhet and Jonathan, the four New London members of the Newport church, visit that church, and on their return, September 19, bring with them Elder Hiscox and Mr. Hubbard.—(*Letter of Mr. Hubbard.*)

The Great Neck is still in midsummer beauty, with delicate touches of autumnal brightness, when the hospitable mansion of James Rogers is reopened to the friends who were here on a like mission in the chilly days of winter. Grave and earnest must be the discourse of those gathered on this occasion. That Connecticut is resolved to withstand any inroad of new sects from Rhode Island, appears certain. But James Rogers and his sons are men not to be cowed or driven, especially when they judge their leadership to be from on High. This little family group is resolving to brave the power and opprobrium of Connecticut backed by Massachusetts.

If there is a hesitating voice in this assembly, it is probably that of Samuel Rogers, whose wife's sister is the wife of Rev. James Noyes of Stonington, and who is similarly allied to other prominent members of the Congregational order. Yet his sympathies are with the cause he hesitates to fully espouse. (We shall find the next meeting of this kind at his house.) As for Bathsheba, surely nothing but the waiting for father and mother could so long have kept her from following the example of her brother John.

In front of the house lies the wide, blue Sound. It is easy to picture the scene, as the earnest, gray-haired man and his wife and daughter accompany Elder Hiscox down the white slope of the beach to the emblem of cleansing that comes to meet them. No event in the past busy career of James Rogers can have seemed half so momentous as the present undertaking. There are doubtless here present not a few spectators, some of them from the church he has renounced, to whom this baptism is as novel as it is questionable; but they must confess to its solemnity and a consciousness that the rite in Christ's day was of a similar character. Those who came to smile have surely forgotten that purpose, as the waters close over the man who has been so honorable and honored a citizen, and who, despite the ridicule and the censure, has only been seeking to obey the commands of the Master, and, through much study, pious consideration and fervent prayer, has decided upon so serious a departure from the New England practice.

A summons for James Rogers and his wife and daughter to appear before the magistrate is not long in coming. But they are soon released. It cannot be an easy, pleasant or popular undertaking to use violent measures against citizens of such good repute as James Rogers and his family, whose earnest words in defense of their course must have more genuine force than any the reverend minister can bring to bear against it.

There is another Bible precedent wholly at variance with the Congregational custom that this little church zealously advocates. The apostles and teachers in the early church exacted no payment for preaching the gospel, receiving—with the exception of the travelling ministry—only such assistance as might any needy brother or sister in the church. This practice was eminently suitable for the promulgation of a religion that was to be "without money and without price," and well calculated to keep out false teachers actuated by mercenary motives. So great a religion having been instituted, among antagonistic peoples, by men who gave to that purpose only such time as they could snatch from constant struggles for a livelihood, and all its doctrines and code having been fully written out by these very men, could not the teachers and pastors of successive ages so, and with such dignity, maintain themselves and their families, giving undeniable proof that their calling was of God and not of mammon?

We have seen the young man, John Rogers, preparing himself for such a life as this. He has laid aside the worldly dignity and ease that might be his as the son of a rich man, to work at the humble trade of shoemaking; that he may place himself fully with the common people and give of the earnings of his own hands to the poor, as did the brethren of old.

The General Court has heretofore discovered no sufficient reason for granting the petition of Elizabeth Griswold for a divorce. It is probable that, up to this date, it has looked for some relenting on the part of the young nonconformist, rather than movements so distinctly straightforward in the line of dissent. But now that James Rogers and family have openly followed his lead to the extent of engaging in manual labor upon the first day of the week, and certain others on the Great Neck, who are members of the Congregational church, are regarding the movement with favor, the sympathy of this practically ecclesiastical body is fully enlisted for the Griswolds.

This Court, which, for nearly a year beyond the time appointed for its decision, has hesitated to grant the divorce to Elizabeth, now, with no further ground than that first advanced, except this evidently fixed determination of John Rogers and his relatives to persist in their nonconformity, "doe find just cause to grant her desire and doe" (Oct. 12, 1676) "free her from her conjugal bond to John Rogers."

Among the documents kept on file relating to trials and decisions, the petition of Elizabeth does not appear in evidence, that the public may examine it and discover the nature of the charge put forward for the divorce. This petition and other evidence are kept state and family secrets. There is a law by which particulars of any trial which it is desired to keep secret must not be divulged by speech or otherwise, under penalty of a heavy fine for each such offense. Well may John Rogers and his son by Elizabeth Griswold ever declare that this divorce was desired and obtained for no other cause than "because John Rogers had renounced his religion."

At the meeting of the County Court in January of this year, John Rogers, Capt. James Rogers, Joseph Rogers, Richard Smith (husband of Bathsheba), and one Joseph Horton are fined 15*s*. each for non-attendance at church. All except John and Capt. James Rogers offer excuse for this offense.

1677.

In the following February, James Rogers, Sr., and his wife Elizabeth, Capt. James and his wife, Joseph and his wife, John, Bathsheba and Jonathan, are each fined 15*s*. at the County Court for non-attendance at church.

At the next County Court, in June, besides non-attendance at church, John Rogers is charged with attending to his work on the first day of the week, in May last, and with having upon that day brought "a burthen of shoes into the town." Upon this occasion, he owns to these facts in court, and further declares before that assembly that if his shop had stood under the window of Mr. Wetherell (magistrate) or next to the meeting-house, he would thus have worked upon the first day of the week. Capt. James and his brother Jonathan being arraigned at the same court for non-attendance at church and for work upon the first day of the week, assert that they have worked upon that day and will so work for the future. James Rogers, Sr., being examined upon a like charge, owns that he has not refrained from servile work upon the first day of the week "and in particular his plowing." "He had," says the record, "been taken of plowing the 6th day of May," by which it appears that he has been imprisoned from that time until this June court, as has John also, since his apprehension with the load of shoes. To have secured bail they must have promised "good behavior"—viz. cessation of work on the first day—until this session of the court, which they could not do, being resolved upon this same regular course.

Mary, wife of Capt. James Rogers, herself a member of the Newport church, is presented at the same court for absenting herself for the last six months from public worship. Bathsheba Smith is presented for the same, and also for a "lying, scandalous paper against the church and one of its elders" set up "upon the meeting house." This paper was evidently occasioned by the abovementioned imprisonment of her father and brother on account of their having substituted the Scriptural Sabbath for that instituted centuries later by ecclesiastical law.

The court "sees cause to bear witness against such pride, presumption and horrible profaneness in all the said persons, appearing to be practiced and resolved in the future," and order that "a fine of £5 apiece be taken from each of them and that they remain in prison at their own charge until they put in sufficient bond or security to no more violate any of the laws respecting the due observance of the first day of the week," or "shall forthwith upon their releasement depart and remain out of the colony." Bathsheba is fined £5 for non-attendance at church and the "scandalous paper," and Mary and Elizabeth 10*s*. each for non-attendance at church.

It is evident that a crisis has now arrived; the sacred Puritan Sabbath has been ignored in an amazingly bold manner by this little band of dissenters, who openly declare, in court, their intention of keeping a seventh day Sabbath, and that alone, whatever be the menace or the punishment.

In these early days, £5 is so large a sum as to be of the nature of an extreme penalty. Truly, the "discretion of the judges" is beginning to work. How James Rogers and his two sons escaped from prison at all, after this sentence, does not appear; certainly they did not give any bonds not to repeat their offenses nor any promise to remove from the colony. Proof of their release is in the fact that they are all again before the court at its very next meeting, in September, together with Elizabeth, Mary, Joseph and his wife, all for non-attendance at church; and upon this occasion, John declares that he neither does nor will attend the Congregational church, nor will he refrain from servile work on the first day of the week, upon which the court repeats the fine of £5 "for what is past" and recommends to the commissioners that the delinquent be called to account by a £5 fine "if not once a week yet once a month." This, if strictly carried out, means almost constant imprisonment for John at his own charge, since it is against his principles to pay any such fines, or to give any of the required promises. Even could he be at large, £60 a year would seem to be more than he could earn by shoemaking. (At this period, £60 would buy a good farm "with mansion house thereon.")

Besides the arraignment of the Rogers family at the June court, as previously described, a suit is brought by Matthew Griswold for damages to the amount of £300. A part of this sum is for the Mamacock farm, which John Rogers very naturally declined to deliver up to the marshal on demand of the divorced wife, which refusal is denominated by Mr. Griswold in this suit a "breach of covenant." Another part is for the Griswold share of articles comprised in the marriage settlement of the fathers upon the couple. In this sum of £300 is also included a considerable charge for the maintenance of Elizabeth and her children at her father's, during the time between her leaving her husband's house and the date of the divorcement by the General Court; also board for her and her first child three months at her father's house, during an illness following birth of said child (see ChapterXIV, "Dragon's Teeth").

Thus the divorced husband is asked to deliver up the farm he gave Elizabeth in full expectation of her remaining his wife, to repay all that her father gave them during the four years of their happy married life, to pay her board during a visit to her father's house by solicitation of her parents,[43] and also to recompense her father for the maintenance of herself and children at the same place after she had deserted her husband and forcibly taken away his children.

It is to the credit of this County Court that, although incensed at the audacity of John Rogers in bringing a load of shoes into town on the first day of the week, together with his other "offenses," it decides this case wholly in favor of the defendant.

An appeal is taken by Mr. Griswold. In the following October his suit comes before the Superior Court at Hartford. This court reverses the decision of the County Court as regards the farm, which is to "stand firm" to Elizabeth "during her natural life."

At the October session of the General Court, Elizabeth Griswold petitions that her children may be continued with her and brought up by her, their father "being so hettridox in his opinions and practice."

The court, "having considered the petition, and John Rogers having in open court declared that he did utterly renounce all the visible worship of New England and professedly declare against the Christian Sabbath as a mere invention," grants her petition "for the present and during the pleasure of the court." John Rogers is to pay a certain amount towards the support of his children at Matthew Griswold's, for which the Mamacock farm is to stand as security.[44]

The various forms of stringency lately in operation are so little deterrent to the new movement that on Saturday, Nov. 23, Elder Hiscox and Mr. Hubbard are again at New London, holding worship with the Rogerses.[45] The next day, Joseph's wife, having given a satisfactory account of her experience, is to be baptized. In this instance, John Rogers proposes that they perform the baptism openly in the town. This earnest and zealous young man overcomes the objections of the saintly but more cautious Mr. Hubbard. Moreover, his father, mother, Joseph and Bathsheba are on his side, and there is evident readiness on the part of the person to be baptized. If they have, at much peril and loss, begun a good work in this region, by setting aside inventions of men and substituting the teaching and practice of Christ and his apostles, it is no true following of the Master to hide their light under a bushel.

No mention is made of objection on the part of Elder Hiscox to going into town on this occasion, and he is found preaching there before the baptism, out of doors by the mill cove, with an alarming number of hearers. He is soon arrested and brought before a magistrate and the minister, Mr. Bradstreet. The latter has "much to say about the good way their fathers set up in the colony," upon which Mr. Hubbard replies that, whereas Mr. Bradstreet is a young man, he himself is an old planter of Connecticut and well knows that the beginners of this colony were not for persecution, but that they had liberty at first to worship according to their consciences, while in later times he himself has been persecuted, to the extent of being driven out of this Colony, because he differed from the Congregational church.

Some impression appears to be made upon the magistrate; since he asks them if they cannot perform this obnoxious baptism by immersion elsewhere, to which Mr. Hubbard assents. They are then released and proceed to the house of Samuel Rogers, by the mill cove.

The time consumed in going from the presence of the magistrate to the house of his brother is sufficient to fix the resolve of John Rogers that no man, or men, shall stand between him and a command of his Master. For more than two years he has been an acknowledged pastor of the New London Seventh Day Baptist Church, under the church at Newport. If the older pastor from Newport cannot perform a scriptural baptism in the name of the Master, for fear of what men can do, in the way of persecution, then that duty devolves upon himself. Upon reaching his brother's house, he offers an earnest prayer; then, taking his sister by the hand, he leads her down the green slope before his brother's door, to the water, and himself immerses her, in the name of Father, Son and Holy Ghost, in the glistening water of thecove.

Doubtless the crowd that gathered during Mr. Hiscox's discourse and the after-disturbance has not yet dispersed, for the magistrate is directly informed of what has taken place. Supposing Mr. Hiscox to be the daring offender, he is straightway apprehended. But John Rogers appears before the magistrate, to state that he himself is the author of this terrible act, upon which Mr. Hiscox is released and the younger pastor is held in custody.

This new action on the part of the fearless and uncompromising youth, increases the excitement and comment. If the majority of the townspeople condemn him, there are yet some, even of Mr. Bradstreet's congregation, to wonder and admire. James Rogers, Sr., and his family undoubtedly rejoice that John is not to be turned aside by the hesitation of others, or for fear of what men can do to him. As for Jonathan, who is engaged to Naomi Burdick, granddaughter of Mr. Hubbard, it is not strange if he has hesitated to approve of a move made contrary to Mr. Hubbard's judgment.

It soon further appears that the New London church is not studying to conform to that at Newport, but to know the very doctrines and will of Christ himself, as revealed by His own words and acts and by those of His disciples.

In the course of their study of the New Testament, the Rogerses find distinct command against long and formal prayers like those of the prescribed church, so evidently constructed to be heard and considered of men, and of a length that would probably have appalled even the Pharisee in the temple.[46]

They also carefully consider the command given by Christ to the disciples, and to believers in general, in regard to healing the sick, and the explicit directions given by James, the brother of Christ in the flesh, to the church at large: "Is any sick among you," etc. They see that other directions in this same chapter are held by the churches as thoroughly binding upon Christians of to-day; yet here is one, which, although perfectly agreeing with the teachings and practice of Christ and of the other apostles, is now commonly ignored. Indeed, should anyone attempt to exactly follow this direction of James, he would be considered a lunatic or a fool. Carefully does James Rogers, Sr., consider this matter, with his two sons, the one his logical young pastor and the other his practical, level-headed young shipmaster. Turn it as they may, they cannot escape the conclusion that if any of the New Testament injunctions are binding upon the church, all of them must be, so far as human knowledge can determine.

Whether Mr. Hiscox or Mr. Hubbard agrees with them in the above conclusions does not concern these conscientious students of Scripture. Not so with Jonathan, the young lover. He is ready to believe that a religion good enough for so conscientious and godly a man as Mr. Samuel Hubbard is good enough for him. He judges that his father and brothers are going too far, not only in this, but in braving constant fines and imprisonments by so openly working upon the first day of the week.

Evidently, Jonathan cannot remain with the little church of which John is the pastor. Yet in dropping him, by his own desire, from their devoted band, they merely leave him in the church of Newport, of which they themselves are yet members (and will be for years to come), although they have made their own church a somewhat distinct and peculiar branch.[47] There is no sign of any break with the beloved son and brother, in friendliness or affection (now or afterwards), on account of this difference of opinion.

1678.

In March, 1678, Jonathan is married to Naomi; he brings her to the Great Neck, to a handsome farm by the shore, provided for them by his father, close bordering the home farms of his father and brothers.[48] This is an affectionate family group, despite some few differences in religious belief. It is evident enough to these logicians that He who commanded men to love even their enemies, allowed no lack of affection on the part of relatives, for any cause.

When the church at Newport learns that the name of Jonathan Rogers has been erased from the roll of the Connecticut church, because of his more conservative views, representatives are sent to New London to inquire into the matter. Here they learn of still another departure of this church from their own, in that this church have omitted the custom of oral family worship, because they find no command for any prayers except those directly inspired by the occasion and the Spirit, but direct condemnation of all formal prayer, as tending to lip service rather than heart service, and to be heard of men rather than of God.

What can the Newport church offer in protest, from scriptural sources? To excommunicate persons for not following the teaching of Christ is one thing; to excommunicate them for obeying such teaching is another. The Newport church takes no action in these matters, although evidently much perplexed by this conscientiously independent branch of their denomination.

Accounts of the intolerance towards the Seventh Day sect in Connecticut having led Peter Chamberlain[49] to write a letter regarding this matter to Governor Leete of Connecticut, the latter replies, in a studiously plausible manner, that the "authority" has shown "all condescension imaginable to us" towards the New London church ("Rogers and his of New London"), having given them permission to worship on the seventh day, "provided they would forbear to offend our conscience."

The letter of Governor Leete contains also the following ingenious sophistry:—

"We may doubt (if they were governors in our stead) they would tell us that their consciences would not suffer them to give us so much liberty; but they would bear witness to the truth and beat down idolatry as the old kings did in Scripture."[50]

This speciously worded sentence is deserving of some reply. Suppose the little band of Rogerenes to have attained the size and power necessary for religious legislation, and to be able to do by their opponents exactly as the latter have done by them. They must exact of these the keeping of a seventh day Sabbath, demand aid for the support of seventh day churches, and enact that none shall go to or from their homes on the seventh day, except between said homes and seventh day churches. In case any of these laws be broken, or any dare speak out in first day churches against the tyranny and bigotry of this seventh day legislation, such shall be fined, imprisoned, scourged and set in the stocks. Could any person really suppose such a course possible for these conscientious students of New Testament teachings, who are not only opposed to any religious legislation, but long before this date have given marked attention to the gentle, peaceable doctrines of the Gospel, and listened with respect and interest to the expositions of the Quakers, one of whom at the start had found them "tender and loving". Close upon this date, the Rogerenes are found openly and zealously advocating the non-resistant principles of the New Testament.

A fact not revealed by court records (but which must frequently be taken into account in this history) is detected in this letter of Governor Leete: "*if they would forbear to offend our conscience*," etc., "we would give them no offence in the seventh day worshipping," viz.: until such time as the Rogerenes will forbear to labor upon the first day of the week, they must expect, not only fines, imprisonment and stocks, but to have their Saturday meetings broken up, according to the pleasure or caprice of the authorities.[51] Constant liability to punishment by the town authorities, for failure to pay fines for holding their Saturday meetings, is one of the aggravating features of this warfare. (All the power used by the magistrates "at their own discretion" was exercised wholly in the dark, so far as any records are concerned, and the periods of greatest severity in its exercise can only be discerned by effects which can be attributed to no other cause.)

Continual breaking up of their meetings, together with fines and imprisonments for breach of the first day Sabbath—to say nothing of the license allowed the ever mischievous and merciless mob to aid in indignities —is at length beginning to tell on this people in a manner quite opposite to that looked for by their opponents.

In June, 1678, James Rogers, Sr., and his sons, John and James, enter the

New London meeting-house and take their seats in the pews set off to them, that of James, Sr., being, presumably, the highest of all, since he is the largest taxpayer in the town. It may be supposed by some that their spirits are at length subdued by the three years of incessant persecutions and annoyances. But presently they rise, one by one, in the midst of the service, and declare their condemnation of a worship in the name of Christ, which upholds persecution of those worshipping in the same name, and by the same book, who, in this name and this book, find no command for a first day Sabbath. To bring such arguments into the midst of a Congregational meeting is more effectual than any violence of constable or mob; yet, so far from being contrary to any command of the Gospel, it is a direct maintenance of the command there set forth to testify to the truth, regardless of consequences. At last, these distressed people have devised a method by which even this powerful ecclesiastical domination may be held in check.

From the church they are taken to prison, from prison to trial. They are fined £5 each. Payment of the fine being refused, imprisonment ensues, at their own expense,[52] for such a period as will as effectually deplete their purses. Fines and imprisonments are to them common experiences; but the church party understand that here, at last, is an effective weapon in the hands of these people, with blade of no lesser metal than the words of the Master himself.

(For nearly five years after this countermove, no disturbance of meeting and no serious molestation of the Rogerenes appears on record. Evidently during that period the commissioners are not displaying such zeal in breaking up seventh day meetings as was the case previous to this appearance in the meeting-house.)

1679.

In October, 1679, there appears in the records of the General Court, an effort on the part of Samuel Rogers to clear a stigma from the reputation of his wife. She has been charged, by a man who has lost some money, with having appropriated it, and the County Court, by weight of circumstantial evidence, decided the case in favor of the plaintiff. In the case before the General Court, at this date, a man who has been imprisoned, on charge of being the true culprit, not being appeared against by Samuel Rogers, is released. (During the four years following this release, Samuel Rogers is at much expense in endeavoring to establish his wife's innocence. In 1683, he presents such clear proof of the falsity of the charge that the General Court grants him 300 acres of land, towards compensation for time and money expended in clearing his wife's name. In this instance, Samuel Rogers makes an address to the court, the substance of which does not appear on record.)

By this time there are a considerable number of Sabbatarians on the Great Neck, some of whom have come from Rhode Island. Any who object to the ultra movement of which John Rogers is the exponent, can attend the meetings of the less radical Mr. Gibson. Both of these pastors appear, however, to be working largely in unison, and they are both arraigned before the County Court, in September of this year, for servile labor on the first day of the week, together with James Rogers, Sr., and Capt. James. John Rogers is fined 20*s*., and the others 10*s*. each, and "the authority of the place" is desired "to call these or any others to account" for future profanation of the Sabbath, and to punish them according to law. On this occasion, Mr. Gibson states that he usually works upon the first day of the week. It is presumable that Jonathan Rogers also works, although not conspicuously.

This is one of the spasmodic efforts to check this growing community of nonconformists, by punishment of the bolder offenders, despite the fact that the child is growing too sturdy and strategic to be handled with perfect impunity.

In the latter part of this year, Mr. Hubbard, having come to the Great Neck on a visit (probably to the home of his granddaughter, Naomi Rogers), finds that Mr. James Rogers has recently been severely injured, by a loaded cart having passed over his leg, below the knee, for which injury he has allowed of no physician, "their judgment being not to use any means." A cart in these days being of no delicate mechanism, it is not improbable that a physician would have advised amputation. Mr. Rogers appears to be well on the way to recovery at the date of Mr. Hubbard's visit.

1682.

Save the moderate fine in September, 1679, for a single non-observance of the first day of the week, which non-observance has been occurring with every recurring Sunday, no recorded effort to suppress the sect occurs from the date of the appearance of James Rogers and his sons in the Congregational meeting-house, 1678, until late in 1682, when William Gibson, John Rogers, James, Sr., Capt. James, Joseph, Bathsheba and her husband, Richard Smith, are presented before the County Court for "prophanation of the Sabbath," upon which occasion John Rogers declares that he worked the last first day, the first day before, and the first day before that, and so had done for several years. James, Sr., and Capt. James express themselves to the same effect. Bathsheba and her husband "own" that this is their practice also, and aver that, "by the help of God," they shall so continue.

The court, not only "for the offense" but for the "pride, obstinacy and resolution" displayed in regard to continuance of the offense, fines each of the offenders 30*s*. apiece,—except Joseph, whom they fine 20*s*.,—and to continue in prison until they shall give good security for the payment of those fines. A bond of £20 each is also required, for their good behavior for the future and abstinence from all servile work on the first day of the week.

Here is the bringing up of a fast horse with dangerous suddenness. But for the imprisonment, it is almost certain that the next Sabbath would see another interruption of the Congregational services. As it is, Joseph and Captain James break out of the prison, for which the latter is fined £3 and the former £5. Undoubtedly they are speedily apprehended and returned to prison. (It is entirely unlikely that any of the fines are paid or bonds given; so that how these people finally escape from durance, unless after very long imprisonment, cannot be conceived.)

1683.

In this year occurs the death of Richard Smith, husband of Bathsheba. Also the will of James Rogers is written, at his dictation, by his son John. In this year James Rogers confirms to his son Joseph all his lands at "Poquoig or Robin Hood's Bay," within certain boundaries of fence, ledge and "dry pond." This land appears to be a part of the gift of land returned by Joseph to his father, in 1670.

CHAPTER III.

1684.

A youth is growing up at Lyme, in regard to whom Matthew Griswold and his daughter Elizabeth may well feel some concern, although it afterwards appears that he is one of the brightest and manliest boys in the colony. This is none other than John Rogers, Jr. For five years past, his mother has been the wife of Peter Pratt, of Lyme, who has a son by this marriage. That gentleman is doomed to suffer no little trouble of conscience in regard to his marriage to the wife of John Rogers, having himself come to doubt that any valid reasons for the divorce ever existed.[53]

In May, 1684, Matthew Griswold and his daughter petition the General Court "for power to order and dispose of John Rogers, Jr., John Rogers still continuing in his evil practises," which "evil practices" were set forth, in the previous permission of the court regarding the continuance of the children of John Rogers with their mother, in these words: "he being so hettridox in his opinion and practice." Their request is granted, the youth "to be apprenticed by them to some honest man."

John Rogers, Jr., is now barely ten years of age, and must be a forward youth to be apprenticed so young, unless we suppose this a mere device to put him under stricter control of his mother's family. He has surely heard nothing in favor of his father from those among whom he has been reared, unless perhaps from his stepfather. Yet neither mother nor grandparents can keep his young heart from turning warmly towards the dauntless nonconformist at New London.

If it has been hoped that, by another attempt at more heroic treatment than the spasmodic onslaughts of the town magistrates, a death-blow may yet be dealt to the Rogerenes, it must soon become evident that such is unlikely to be the case. Not only so, but there is danger that some of the principal members of the New London Congregational church, and those among the most moneyed, may be won over to the new persuasion. Samuel Beebe, Jr., eldest son of one of the most substantial citizens, has recently married Elizabeth, daughter of James Rogers, and is conforming to the faith and usages of that family. Several from the Congregational church have recently been rebaptized by the new sect.

1685.

The prospect of further injury to the New London church, as well as to general church conformity in the colony, becomes such that, in the spring of 1685, another resolute attempt is made by the New London authorities, "by advice of the Governor and Council," to put a stop to the performance of servile labor on the first day of the week, as also baptism—and rebaptism by immersion.

On Sunday, April 12, 1685, several of the leading spirits are imprisoned for working on the first day of the week. The court records show that some of these escape, and enter the meeting-house in time of public service, to denounce such persecution of followers of the Lord, by those who pretend to worship in His name.

Two days after (April 14), John Rogers, Capt. James Rogers, Samuel Beebe, Jr., and Joanna Way are complained of before the County Court for servile work in general upon the first day of the week "and particularly upon the last first day (12th), although they have and may enjoy their persuasion undisturbed" (here is a revelation of the fact that their Saturday meetings have not been interrupted of late, and possibly not since the institution of the countermove in 1678); also "for coming into town at several times to rebaptize persons" and "for recently disturbing public worship," and because "they go on still to disturb and give disturbance."[54]

Upon examination, John Rogers is found guilty of servile work upon that first day and on many others, "by his own confession," and "will yet go on to do it," regardless of the law forbidding. The court also finds him guilty of "disturbing God's people in time of public worship." For all this, they order that he receive fifteen lashes upon the naked body. He is then complained of for baptizing a person contrary to law, "having no authority so to doe," for which he is fined £5.

Captain James is complained of for servile work, "by his own confession," that he worked on the last Sunday, "and would doe it again." Also he came into the meeting-house, in time of worship, "where he behaved himself in a frantick manner to the amazing of some and causing some women to swounde away," for which he is to have fifteen lashes on the naked body. He is also fined £5 for baptizing a negro woman.

Samuel Beebe is complained of for work on the first day and for declaring that he will continue in that practice as long as he lives. He also is to receive fifteen lashes on the naked body and to pay a fine of £5, although he is charged neither with disturbance of meeting nor with baptizing. Why this double punishment, unless because this young man has recently left the Congregational church to join the nonconformists? Such punishment may intimidate others who are thus inclined. That "discretion" granted the judges appears very prominent in this case.

Joanna Way, for servile work, for declaring that she will still continue in that practice, and for giving disturbance in the meeting-house, is sentenced to receive fifteen lashes on the naked body.

Here we find four persons, one of them a woman, receiving fifteen lashes each on the naked body for working on the first day, while keeping the seventh day, and for venturing the one sure mode of holding their persecutors in check.

In this disturbance of the meeting, Capt. James Rogers is the only one accounted guilty of "amazing" the congregation and causing women to "swounde." He is not charged with having attempted any violence in the church, and has before this become a convert to the peaceable doctrines of the Quakers. The courtrecord gives no hint of the words used on this occasion by Captain James, or why the women were induced to "swounde."[55]

Despite the £5 fine, in less than two months thereafter (June) John Rogers is complained of for baptizing, found guilty, "on his own confession," and again fined £5.

(Although the Rogerenes continue steadfastly and openly to perform servile labor on the first day of the week, as well as to baptize, there appears no further arraignment before the court for these causes for a good while to come; the entrance into the meeting-house, April 12, 1685, proving, like the entrance of 1678, an effectual check upon their enemies.)

About the first of June of this same year, messengers are sent to New London from the Sabbatarian church at Newport, "to declare against two or more of them that were of us who are declined to Quakerism, of whom be thou aware, for by their principles they will travel by land and by sea to make disciples, yea sorry ones too. Their names are John and James Rogers and one Donham."[56] What have these two young men been doing now? They have ventured to adopt and to preach the principle of non-resistance, and so, by this long-forward step, have "declined to Quakerism." This adoption of peace principles appears, in the estimation of the gentle and saintly Mr. Hubbard,—recorder of the above bulletin,—to have completed their downfall. He sufficiently expresses the attitude of the Newport church towards Quakers and their non-resistant principles. John and James Rogers have not been to the Quakers to learn these principles, but have taken them directly from the New Testament, where the Quakers themselves found them.

That John and James have been baptizing persons in the town, and probably at the very mill cove where John, over seven years before, baptized his sister-in-law, is apparent. Captain James is not only baptizing, but also, as shown by Mr. Hubbard's letter, preaching and proselyting. Mr. Hubbard does not complain of his baptizing or preaching, by which it appears that he did these in Sabbatarian order, but only of his preaching a Quaker doctrine. The names of John and Captain James still remain on the roll of membership of the Newport church. To drop them for preaching the pacific principles of the Gospel is no easier than to drop them for having accepted the principle of healing by prayer and faith as set forth in that Gospel.

In this year, Elizabeth, daughter of John Rogers, now fourteen years of age, is, at her own request, allowed by her mother and the Griswolds to return to her father; she who left him a child of three years. She is still the only daughter of her mother, and, by affirmation of both her brothers, John Rogers, 2d, and Peter Pratt,[57] a most lovable character.

Her free committal of this girl child to the care and training of John Rogers, gives proof conclusive that "Elizabeth, daughter of Matthew Griswold," however she may disapprove of her former husband's religious course, knows well of the uprightness of his character and the kindness of his heart.

1687.

In December, 1687, "Elizabeth, former wife of John Rogers," resigns her claim to Mamacock, on condition of certain payments, in instalments, signing herself, "Elizabeth, daughter of Matthew Griswold." (*New London Records.*)

1688.

James Rogers, Sr., is in declining health and fast nearing the end. November 17, 1687, he was unable to sign a deed of exchange of land. It was witnessed as his act by his sons John and James. Administration on his estate commences September, 1688. He leaves a large estate to his children, all of whom have received bountiful gifts from him in his lifetime, and all of whom are intelligent, conscientious, temperate and industrious.

While James Rogers was leading the busy life of a man of varied interests, worldly honor for his children must have been as much a stimulus as the accumulation for their sakes of money and of lands. That honor was relinquished in the cause which he and his espoused.

The esteem in which this man and his wife have been held is shown, among other things, by the failure of the Congregational church to expel them. In fact, where could that church lay a finger upon any violation, on the part of these members, of the teachings of Him in whose name that church was founded? Their names remain on the roll of Congregational church members. Yet by brethren in that church they have been scorned and injured, and their children have been lashed for venturing to follow with exactness New Testament precepts and examples.

In trouble and sorrow, under the despotism that had assumed the very authority of that Lord whom he himself had learned to trust so unreservedly, the mortal life of James Rogers approached its close. Yet, wondrously upheld by faith in God the Father, Christ the Saviour, and the presence of that Comforter which had been promised to all true believers, he was enabled to look far beyond all earthly gain or losses, all worldly disappointment and the injustice and uncharitableness of men, to the eternal blessings and rewards of heaven. Although religious preambles to wills are not unusual at this period, they are generally of a set form, with slight variations; but that which James Rogers dictated, to his son John, was an evident expression of his religious faith couched in his own words: "I do know and see that my name is written in the book of life."[58]

A noticeable feature of this will is the evidently anxious intention of the testator that the court shall have as little as possible to do with the settlement of his estate, and that his children shall carefully avoid any litigation concerning it. (Part I, Chap. I.)

Five years elapsed between the writing of the will and the decease of the testator; and in the meantime a codicil was attached to it.

[It is certainly very lamentable that even one of the children of James Rogers considered it necessary to set aside the last request of so loving and generous a father, by entering upon any suit at law in regard to the settlement of his estate, and this after the first so amicable agreement on the part of each to fully abide by the terms of the will. But it is still more lamentable that, through lack of careful examination into the facts of the case, those children who positively refrained from the slightest action contrary to this request of their father, should be included in the sweeping statement of the New London historian (*Miss Caulkins*): "his children, notwithstanding, engaged in long and acrimonious contention regarding boundaries, in the course of which earthly judges were often obliged to interfere and enforce settlement."[59]

The including of all the children in this statement is not its only error; "earthly judges" being in no way "obliged to interfere" or "enforce," otherwise than by carrying on in the usual manner the business presented to the court.

Because of this erroneous statement, often quoted by other historians, it will be necessary to burden this work with exact note of every case in which any child of James Rogers has any connection with court dealings regarding the settlement of this estate, which settlement, on account of the longevity of the widow, extends over a long period, evidently much longer than was anticipated by the testator, she having been in an impaired condition for some time prior to his decease. This impairment appears to have been more of a mental than physical character, however, and of an intermittent description, indicating whole or partial recovery at intervals. When the intense strain upon mind and heart which this wife and mother must have endured ever since 1674 is considered, one cannot but suspect this to be the cause of an impairment of her mental powers while she still retained so much recuperative vigor even to unusual longevity.]

For some years previous to the date of his death, the home farm of James Rogers was upon that beautiful portion of the shore lands of the Great Neck called Goshen, and here his widow continues to reside. His son Jonathan's place is adjoining on the south. Captain James lives in the same vicinity, and is now to have the Goshen farm lands, under the will. Although Bathsheba has a farm in this locality, received from her father, she appears to be living—with her children—at her mother's, and her brother John is there also, with a life right in the house, under the will. Samuel Beebe resides in the same neighborhood, and Joseph at his Bruen place, near by, on Robin Hood's Bay.

September 15, 1688, the widow executes a deed of trust (New London Probate Records) giving to her son John and daughter Bathsheba the oversight and management of the entire estate of her husband (it having been left subject to her needs for her lifetime), "even my whole interest," fully agreeing to the complete execution of her husband's will, as relating to herself, by these two children, according to the terms of the codicil, which gives the entire estate into their hands during the lifetime of the widow. Her son-in-law, Samuel Beebe, appears to be the justice on this occasion. Two persons, not of the family, testify to her "being apparently in her right mind," and "speaking very reasonably." All the children have previously entered into an agreement to carry out the plan of their father, as relates to settlement out of court, by executorship of John and his guardianship, with Bathsheba, of their mother.

In this year Peter Pratt, second husband of Elizabeth Griswold, dies at Lyme, leaving her with a son who bears his name.

In this year also, Elizabeth, daughter of John Rogers, now seventeen years of age, is married, at her father's home, to a young man named Stephen Prentis, the son of a principal planter of New London.[60]

John Rogers, Jr., is permitted by his mother to attend the wedding of his sister. He is now, for the first time, with his father and his father's family friends. It is an excellent opportunity for the boy of fourteen to make the acquaintance and judge of the characters of these relatives for himself. The result is that he elects to remain with his father, and soon obtains his mother's permission to do so.[61] Thus ends the effort to keep the grandchildren of Mr. Matthew Griswold from the contaminating influence of John Rogers.

Account of the year 1688 should not close without mention of the appearance on this scene of a young dignitary well calculated to rekindle any flickering embers on either side of this controversy. Rev. Mr. Bradstreet having died, a new minister has been hired in the person of Gurdon Saltonstall, a young man inheriting the aristocratic and autocratic spirit of a family of rank and wealth without the gentler and more liberal qualities that adorned the character of his ancestor, Sir Richard Saltonstall. Although only twenty-two years of age, he is already a rigid, uncompromising ecclesiastic, holding the authority and prestige of the Congregational church paramount, even beyond the ordinary acceptation of the time.

There is such general opposition to church taxation in the community at this very time, that an attempt has recently been made to raise funds for the Congregational church by subscription, but the amount subscribed having proved very inadequate, the old method is continued.—(*Caulkins.*) This shows that Congregationalism in this town is, at the best, a yoke imposed upon a majority by a powerful minority. The effort, as well as the failure, to raise church money by subscription is ominous. Should such popular indifference continue, what may not befall the true church, with "hettridoxy" let loose in the land and Rhode Islandisms further overrunning the Colony?

It cannot be long before John Rogers and the zealous young advocate of Congregational rule are carefully observing and measuring each other. Fifty years ago, Congregationalist ("Independent") leaders cropped their hair close to their heads and eschewed fine clothing; now, forsooth, nothing is too good for them, and their curling locks (wigs) are more conspicuous than those of the Cavaliers with whom Cromwell's Roundheads fought to the death. This young man in fine ministerial garb, and with flowing wig, whom they have called to New London to preach the unworldly Gospel of Jesus Christ, is seemingly so immature that John Rogers, the man of forty, can afford to hold his peace for a space, while he goes his way, working upon the first day of the week and resting and preaching upon the seventh. The young minister, being on trial himself, awaiting ordination, cannot for some time to come venture very conspicuously on the war-path.

1690.

In 1690, extensive improvements are made in the Congregational church meeting-house. The interior is furnished with the approved style of pews, which are, as usual, assigned to the inhabitants of the town, those paying the highest rates having the highest seats. Accordingly, John Rogers and his brothers, and all the other Seventh Day people, have seats assigned them. In addition to the minister's rates, they are assessed for these church improvements, which include a new bell, that all may be in good style for the ordination of Mr. Saltonstall. Of course, John Rogers and his followers do not pay these "rates"; but their cattle and other goods are seized and sold at auction, none of the extra proceeds being returned to them. As yet, however, there is no disturbance, although, in addition to the new rates, the town magistrates are imposing fines and inflicting punishments, from time to time, on the seventh day observers, "at their discretion." (The terms of imprisonment of John Rogers aggregated over fifteen years, a very much longer time than the total recorded on court records. This indicates an extraordinary exercise of the delegated power accorded to local officials in his case.[62])

While the period of calm (upon the court records) since the last (and second) entry into the meeting-house, in 1685, is still continuing, and before the young ecclesiastic is in a position to begin his attack, let us take a general glance at the Rogers family, and first at the enterprising and wealthy Samuel Rogers, allied by marriage to some of the most prominent Congregational church members in the colony, yet himself appearing to cultivate no intimate association with the New London church, the reason for which may well be divined. He is now making active preparations for leaving New London altogether, as soon as his son Samuel is old enough to assume control of the bakery, having chosen for his future home a large tract of land in the romantic wilds of Mohegan (New London "North Parish,"—now Montville). He is a great favorite with the Mohegan chief, Owaneco, son of Uncas. The popularity of Samuel Rogers with the Indians is but one of many indications of the amiable and conciliatory character of this man. His simply standing aloof from the church against whose autocratic dictum his father and brothers judged it their duty to so strenuously rebel is characteristic of the man.

On the Great Neck, Jonathan Rogers and his wife, and those of their particular persuasion, are quietly holding their meetings on Saturday, paying their Congregational church rates with regularity, however unwillingly, and working on the first day in no very noticeable manner. There is frequent interchange of visits between them and the many relatives and friends of Naomi in Newport and Westerly.

Although Captain James and wife and Joseph and his wife seem to be adhering faithfully to the radical party, there are growing up in their family several young dissenters from the Seventh Day cause.

Samuel Beebe and his wife Elizabeth remain firm in the Sabbatarian faith.

John Rogers, Jr., although brought up in the house of Mr. Matthew Griswold and kept carefully from all Rogers contamination, works on the days upon which his father works, rests on the day when his father rests, and in all other ways follows his father's lead.

Bathsheba Smith ardently adheres to the religious departure instituted by her father and her brothers. Her son, James Smith, is fifteen years of age at this date. He and his cousin John, Jr., are well agreed to follow on in the faith. Among the children of his aunt Bathsheba there is one dearest of all to John, Jr.; this is Bathsheba Smith the younger.

Others of the third generation of Rogerses are now old enough to begin to observe, reason and choose for themselves. It is not surprising if, by this time, quite a number of Rogers lads, of the James and Joseph families, frequently enter the Congregational church, with other young people, and sit in the pews assigned to their fathers. The principles of John Rogers, Captain James and others of their persuasion would prevent the issue of any command tending to interfere with individual judgment and action in such matters, whatever the anxious attempt to instill strictly scriptural opinions and conduct, by precept and example.

1691.

Preparations for the ordination of the Rev. Gurdon Saltonstall being completed, that event transpires, November, 1691. About a month after this ceremony, occurs the first tilt on record between John Rogers and the ecclesiastic. In this instance, the gauntlet is thrown by the dissenter, in the shape of a wig, on the occasion of a "Contribution to the Ministry."[63]

John Rogers has, apparently, beheld the magisterial headgear of the young minister as long as he feels called upon to do so without some expression of dissent regarding such an unwarrantable sign of Christian ostentation. The unwelcome gift is a peaceable yet significant remonstrance from the leader of a sect determined from the outset to fearlessly express disapproval of any assumption of practices or doctrines in the name of the Christian religion that are foreign to the teachings and example of Christ. One would think that both minister and congregation might be thankful that the additional "rates" (such as cattle and other goods beyond all reason) forcibly taken from the dissenters to fit the Congregational church edifice for its elegant, wigged minister had not brought a delegation of Rogerenes to the meeting-house, to orally complain of being forced to assist in this ordination.

That John Rogers so graciously makes the apology, which is speedily demanded of him for this token of dissent, and assents to its immortalization upon the town records, is explainable in no other way than because it gives him an opportunity of publicly emphasizing the gift and his reasons therefor. The covertly facetious wording of this Apology, amounting in short to a full re-expression of the donor's sentiments in durable form, is a refreshing relief amid all the tragedy of this man's life.[64]

After the ordination of Mr. Saltonstall, his influence in this community, as a clergyman of unusual learning and ability, is fully established. He makes many friends both in and out of the colony, as a staunch and talented advocate of Congregational church rule, especially among the clergy, which is an element of great influence in the General Court, and other courts as well. He will soon be in a position to wreak upon John Rogers dire vengeance, not only for the wig, but for that general nonconformity so likely to disturb the ecclesiastical polity which it is his purpose to vigorously and uncompromisingly maintain.

In this year "Elizabeth, daughter of Matthew Griswold," marries Matthew Beckwith of Lyme, a man much older than herself, and eleven years the senior of her former husband, John Rogers.

CHAPTER IV.

1691.

The children of James Rogers having petitioned the General Court to divide their father's estate according to his will,—which was entered on record with their agreement thereto,—certain persons are now appointed to make this division. At the same time, the court "desire John Rogers and Bathsheba Smith doe take the part doth belong to widow Rogers under their care and dispose that a suitable maintainance for her, etc."

1692.

In July, 1692, there is copied upon the land records a disposition by the widow of James Rogers of certain alleged rights in her husband's estate, viz.: such rights as would have been hers by the will had there been no codicil thereto. In this document she claims a certain thirteen acres of land on the Great Neck[65] to dispose of as she "sees fit," also all "moveables" left by her husband, with the exception of £10 willed therefrom to her daughter Elizabeth Beebe. She states that she has already sold one-half of this thirteen acres to her son-in-law, Samuel Beebe. By this singular document, she not only completely ignores the codicil to her husband's will (already acknowledged by herself, by the other heirs and by the probate court), but her recorded deed of trust, by which, in 1688, she placed her entire life interest in the estate in charge of John and Bathsheba, whose guardianship under the will had also, by agreement of all the children, been confirmed by the General Court.

In the month previous to this singular act of the widow, the committee appointed by the court, to divide the estate according to the will, announced their division, adding "when John and Bathsheba shall pay out of the moveable estate[66] to Eliz. Beebe the sum of £10," "if the widow so order," the remainder of the estate, real and personal, shall "remain under the care and management of John and Bathsheba during their mother's life for her honorable maintainance," also that, after decease of the widow, the real estate and what shall remain of the personal estate be disposed of according to the will of the testator.

There was a distinct blunder in the words "if the widow so order" regarding the payment of the £10; since the will distinctly says that the £10 are to be paid by the widow to Elizabeth ("out of the moveables") "if she sees good, with the advice of my son John," and the codicil makes no change in regard to this clause. The report of the committee omits the advice of John in this matter, which omission probably seemed not very important to any one at the time. (It will later appear that serious results ensue from this apparently slight and inadvertent court error. See Chapter VII.)

About this time, the widow gives to Elizabeth Beebe (as afterwards appears) the estimate of the £10, in the shape of a little colored girl named Joan, who is classed in the movable estate, and she does this without "the consent of my son John." In so doing, she not only ignores the will of her husband regarding the advice of John, but also the erroneous wording of the committee's report that this £10 is to be paid by John and Bathsheba, at her direction. Had she but permitted these guardians and executors to pay the £10, Joan would not have figured in the transaction, it being no part of the intention of John and Bathsheba (as will later appear) that any of their father's slaves should be sold or given away to remain in lifelong bondage. The two executors and guardians make no complaint to the court of these irregular actions on the part of their mother, or of the wrong wording of the recent report of the committee (nor shall we in any instance find them deviating by a hair's breadth from the request of their father to make no appeal regarding his estate to earthly judges, although such appeal at this early stage would have saved incalculable trouble hereafter). However, Joan is not given over by them to Elizabeth Beebe.[67]

Another part of the erratic document of the widow is that after her death all the "moveables" shall be divided between her son Jonathan and her daughter Elizabeth, again totally ignoring the codicil of the will, which speaks only of John, Bathsheba and Captain James as being concerned in the division of "the moveables" after her death, except that Elizabeth is to have "three cows."[68]

Although the widow has evidently the encouragement and assistance of Samuel Beebe in this proceeding, there is no appearance of any complicity on the part of Jonathan, who exactly conforms to the terms of the will and the executorship of John. Captain James makes no complaint to the court of the fact that Samuel Beebe is already claiming, under this procedure of the widow, a piece of land which is a part of the farm given to himself by the will, for which he is paying rent to his mother by order of the executor. He quietly makes a temporary sale of the thirteen acres to an attorney, of which sale Samuel Beebe complains (New London Records), but evidently in vain.

This is but the beginning of annoyances which certain children of James Rogers are to endure, on account of their determination not to disobey their father's request in regard to any appeal to "earthly judges." Little could the testator foresee that his attempt to keep his estate out of the court would be the very means of litigation, through the vagaries of his mentally diseased widow, unchecked by appeal to the court on the one hand, and encouraged by interested parties on the other.

1693.

Before the close of the year 1693, John Rogers is fined £4 for entertaining two Quakers at his house "for a month or more." He has (by the testimony of his son, see Part I) no fellowship with these men, except as regards his concurrence in the doctrine of non-resistance and some few other particulars. For non-payment of this fine; he is in prison (and remains there well into the next year). This is but the beginning of more stringent measures than have prevailed since the disturbance of the Congregational meeting in 1685, which seems to have won a seven year's respite from severe persecution.

As yet, the ambitious young minister, Gurdon Saltonstall, appears to have found no good opportunity for attempting to suppress this intractable man. But if John Rogers is to be prevented from continuing to scatter, broadcast, doctrines so subversive to a state church, he should be checked without further delay. In this lapse of severer and more public discipline on the part of the authorities, he has been gathering more converts from the Congregational fold, and has even grown so bold as to come into the very heart of the town to preach his obnoxious doctrines. Prominent citizens, who ought to be above countenancing him, are not only among his hearers, but among his converts.

Samuel Fox, a member of the Congregational church and one of the most prosperous business men of the place, has recently married the widow Bathsheba Smith and adopted her faith. He may be very influential in gaining more such followers, unless deterrent measures are soon taken. How long could the Congregational church be maintained, on its present footing, if such a new birth as this man describes should be required before admission; aye, if any conversion other than turning from, or avoidance of, immoral practices be generally insisted upon? Moreover, this ranting against "hireling ministers" is of itself calculated to weaken and destroy a capable and orderly ministry, to say nothing of baptism by immersion, administering the communion in the evening (after the example of Christ), the nonsensical doctrine of non-resistance, and the rest of this man's fanatical notions, all of which, strange to say, are attracting favorable attention in intelligent quarters. There is Mr. Thomas Young, for instance, a man of the highest respectability, and allied to some of the best families in the church and the place; it is even understood that John Rogers is to be invited to preach at his house.

But what shall be done with the man? Despite the regular fine of £5, he goes right on with his baptisms and rebaptisms, sometimes on the very day he is released from imprisonment on this account. Fines and imprisonments for other offenses, also, hold him in check only so long as he is in prison. Moreover, the grand jurymen and other officials have become very indulgent regarding his offenses; certain of them appear to connive in leaving him undisturbed in his defiance of ecclesiastical laws. By what means can he be kept in durance long enough to lose his singular and growing popularity; or how can he be put out of sight and hearing altogether?

At least one aspect is encouraging; some of the Rogers young people are inclining towards the Congregational church, in spite of their elders. James, Jr., (son of Captain James), is evidently not in sympathy with the family departure. Let us make much of this young man; he seems a right sensible fellow. Joseph's sons, with the exception of James (the eldest), appear to be well inclined also. In fact, John Rogers himself is the only one of the original dissenters who is causing any very serious disturbance nowadays. Something of this kind is likely enough to be passing in the mind of Mr. Saltonstall.

In this year, 1693, another difficulty occurs regarding the settlement of the James Rogers estate. The persons appointed to divide the land among the children according to the terms of the will have given Jonathan a farm, "with house thereon," which was included in the lands given to Joseph by his father in 1666. Joseph (as has been shown) resigned all of this gift of land to his father in 1670, but the latter redeeded the most (or supposedly all) of it back to him in 1683. Joseph appears to have understood that this farm was included in the second deed of gift, and it is probable that his father supposed it to have been thus included, by the terms of the deed. Upon examination, however, the committee have decided that this farm remains a part of the estate of the testator, and, by the terms of the will regarding the division of the residue of land between James and Jonathan, it falls to Jonathan. Naturally, Jonathan has nothing to do but to take what is accorded to him by the decision of those to whom the division has been intrusted, who have divided it to the best of their knowledge and ability. Although Joseph is in much the same position, acquiescence in his case is far less easy. He does not find any fault with the will, but simply claims this farm as his own by the deed of gift of his father, and arbiters are appointed to decide the matter. These men appear to labor under no small difficulty in concluding to which of the two the farm should really belong, but finally decide in favor of Jonathan. Joseph is unwilling to abide by this decision, asserting that some of the evidence on the other side has not been of a fair character.[69] Consequently the case is reopened, with considerable favor shown, on the part of the court, to the representations of Joseph. Jonathan's part in the case is to present evidence in favor of his right to the property awarded to him; so that he cannot be said to have gone to law in the matter.

(This attempt of Joseph to regain a farm he had supposed to be his own, is the sole "contention regarding boundaries," which was ascribed by Miss Caulkins to the "children." It in no way concerns the executor, who had no part whatever in designating the boundaries or dividing the land. Joseph appears to have hesitated at first to make any move in the matter; the opening protest was made in 1692 by his wife, in regard to the deed by which her husband returned to his father (in 1670) the first gift of land.[70])

1694.

The time is now come for the Rev. Gurdon Saltonstall to prove what he can do, to stay the progress of this nonconformist movement under the masterly leadership of John Rogers. It is not his intention to confine his efforts to the ineffectual methods heretofore employed, the most public of which have been presentation of leading Rogerenes before the County Court, a procedure that, for some reason (at this date quite obscure), is sure to provoke the dreaded countermove, which has each time accomplished so much for the nonconformists.

The brilliant plan finally matured by Mr. Saltonstall is to capture John Rogers and imprison him at a distance from New London. As in many another contest, the fall of the leader is the death of the cause, or the longer he can be separated from his followers the more will their cause be weakened and the greater the check to his proselyting career, which is just now so alarmingly in the ascendant. There are many dignitaries who share such sentiments with Mr. Saltonstall. A satisfactory plan being matured, it can readily be carried out. Such a plan (which is gradually disclosed in the sequence of events) may be outlined as follows:

For the first part of the program, resort will be had to the old apprehension for servile labor, with arraignment before the County Court. It is presumable, according to precedent, that this will be sufficient to bring out the countermove, which will result in a large fine—with larger bond for good behavior—payment of which being refused, as it undoubtedly will be, the bird will be fully secured in its first cage.

The second part of the plan is, having caught John Rogers in some expression of doctrine or sentiment that will furnish ground for his arrest as a preacher of an unwarrantable sort, to secure his trial before the Superior Court, with adverse verdict and imprisonment in Hartford jail.

According to such a plan, John Rogers will receive a double dose that may prove effectual. The two parts of this plan take place as nearly together as possible, the first standing in abeyance until evidence is secured for the second procedure. This evidence is obtained late in the month of February, 1694, Saturday the 24th.

Upon this date, John Rogers is holding a meeting in town, in the house of

Mr. Thomas Young,[71] a gentleman nearly allied, as has been said, to some of the principal members of the Congregational church, and among them to the Christophers family, several of which family (notably Christopher and John) are very intimate friends of Mr. Saltonstall, as well as prominent officials of New London. The large number gathered to listen to this discourse indicates the drawing power of the speaker. Some of his own Society are present, including his son John. It need scarcely be said that the having interested Mr. Thomas Young so seriously is one of the offenses of which John Rogers is now conspicuously guilty.[71] John Christophers, Daniel Wetherell (another New London official and friend of Mr. Saltonstall) and Rev. Gurdon Saltonstall enter this meeting for a sinister purpose.[72]

The subject selected by John Rogers for his discourse on this occasion is one particularly relating to Rogerene dissent; it is the necessity of a new birth and the wonderful changes wrought in body and soul by that divine miracle.[73] That only by such an operation of the Holy Spirit can a man become in truth one with Christ, is the burden of the theme. Not only has the speaker wealth of scriptural foundation for this discourse, but by his own conversion, so sudden and so powerful, he has internal evidence of the mysterious change set forth in the New Testament. No subject could better bring out the fervor and eloquence of the man. He declares that the body of an unregenerate person is a body of Satan, Satan having his abode therein, and that the body of a regenerate person is a body of Christ, Christ dwelling in such a body. (See account of his son, Part I, Chapter II.)

It is (and is to be) a conspicuous feature of Mr. Saltonstall's ministry that no experience of this kind is to be considered necessary to church membership; such a test as this would never allow of that great ingathering to the state church which he desires to see firmly established and maintained.

The Rev. Gurdon Saltonstall and his accomplices do not listen to this discourse in concealment from the speaker, however they may stand apart from the hearers that gather cordially about the remarkable man in their midst. That these three men are his enemies, none know better than the keen-eyed man who beholds them there; but it may well be judged that their presence gives no tremor to his heart or his voice, but, the rather, adds nerve and emphasis.

Mr. Saltonstall, watching his opportunity, and holding the attention of his accomplices, inquires of the speaker:

"Will you say that your body is the body of Christ?"

The reply of John Rogers shows the quick wit of the man. He evidently perceives the intention to entrap him, and is, moreover, unwilling to allow the expression, which he has been using in a general way, to bear this bald, personal application, with its intended insinuation of irreverence.

"Yes, I do affirm that this human body (bringing his hand against his breast) is Christ's body; for Christ has purchased it with His precious blood, and I am not my own, for I am bought with a price." (See account of his son, Part I, Chapter II.)

Even thus ingeniously and reverently the speaker adheres to his affirmation that the body of a man as well as his soul belongs after regeneration to Christ and is animated by Him.

It was a reply that turned the edge of the enemy's sarcasm and left the speaker free to continue his discourse in no way disconcerted by the trick. He now goes on to picture, with glowing face and words, the brotherhood into which the regenerate man enters; that of Christ, the firstborn of many brethren, and of the disciples and apostles. The light upon his face as he speaks may well border upon a smile, and his voice take on an exultant tone (to be called on the court record "a laughing and a flouting way"). (See Chapter V.)

From this perfectly Scriptural discourse, the spies now manage to construct a charge of blasphemy, which, under good management and by powerful influence, will aid in sending this man to Hartford prison. Red tape, however, is necessary, before this action can be brought. In the meantime, trial will be made of the other portion of the plot, which will imprison him at once in New London jail.

The very next day (Sunday, February 25, 1694), John Rogers is arrested for "carting boards," and Samuel Fox "for catching eels on that holy day." Both are arraigned before the County Court now in session. It is the first arraignment of this kind since 1685. During till these nine years, John Rogers and all of his Society have been working upon the first day of the week, as for the ten years previous to 1685. If the countermove now takes place, according to the plan indicated, John Rogers steps directly into the trap that has been set for him. That he does step into it is certain; that he does it without a clear understanding of the situation is by no means to be inferred. While he may not have counted upon so deeply laid a scheme as that which is shortly to develop, yet he is evidently conscious of a situation which renders it necessary that he, on his part, should act as promptly and boldly in this crisis as it appears to be the intention of his enemies to act.

(We shall soon come upon proof that the town authorities, instigated undoubtedly by the same leader and his friends, have been, for some time past, attacking—"oppressing"—not only the Rogerenes, but the regular

Seventh Day Baptists, despite the quiet, compromising attitude of the latter sect; a fact so uncommon heretofore as to amount, in connection with the other appearances, to proof positive that an unusual emergency is confronting all these nonconformists at this time, and that John Rogers not only steps forward to check the advances upon his own Society, but as the champion of the Seventh Day cause at large. See "Remonstrance," Chapter V.)

Not having paid his fine, there is now nearly a week in which John Rogers may meditate in prison before the next Sunday (March 4) arrives, which he appears to do to good purpose. In some way he manages to communicate with his ever devoted and ready sister Bathsheba, and also with his faithful Indian servant, William Wright. Evidently the 20*s.* fine is sufficient to keep him in prison over this Sunday, and the wait of a week longer would detract from the full force of the countermove. This difficulty must be overcome.

The next Sunday and meeting time arrives. Mr. Saltonstall's service proceeds, to which of its many heads is uncertain. Despite the fact that his opponent is in prison, does every blast of the March wind seem to rattle the meeting-house door ominously?

Some one ought surely, and at the earliest possible moment, to make the olden move. The lot has fallen upon Bathsheba. She enters the church with (apparently) womanly modesty, simply to announce that she has been doing servile work upon this day and has come purposely to declare it. (County Court Record.) She is placed in the stocks. But the end is not yet.

John Rogers himself enters the meeting-house upon this veritable Sunday, March 4. It is in the "afternoon" (County Court Record), and, as shown by his copy of "Mittemus" (Part I, Chapter II), he has by some means escaped from prison for this purpose.

When he appears, it is in a manner calculated to excite in the preacher whose discourse is interrupted, something besides delight at the success of the latter's masterly scheme to entrap him. He enters with a wheelbarrow load of merchandise,[74] which he wheels directly to the front of the pulpit, before any in the assembly can sufficiently recover from their astonishment to lay hands upon him. From this commanding position he turns and offers his goods for sale.[75] The scene that ensues before he is returned to prison must be imagined.

Upon this same Sunday, William Wright, "an Indian servant of John Rogers," makes a "disturbance," "outside of the meeting house," "in time of worship." Refusing to pay a fine for his misdemeanor, he is whipped ten stripes on the naked body. (County Court Record.)

Mr. Saltonstall has one consolation for this certainly unexpected style of entrance. He can hardly, have reckoned upon such a stupendous move to aid in securing the long incarceration of his opponent. The "Proclamation"[76] which John Rogers soon hangs out at his prison window, to keep before the public his steadfast determination to oppose the doctrines and measures of the ruling church, is still further ground for the intended removal to Hartford and trial before that court, which is soon effected through the "Mittemus." (Part I, Chapter II.)

On the part of John Rogers, his procedure, from beginning to end, indicates his knowledge of an important crisis, as regards the Seventh Day cause, and his judgment that the boldest move possible on his part is the wisest at this time.

[For many a year to come, there will be found no presentment at court of any of the Rogerenes for servile work upon the first day of the week. Nevertheless they do not escape. When it becomes doubtful if juries will punish them; the town authorities may be instigated to the task.

The wheelbarrow episode was an extreme measure adopted at a critical time, when, after so long a cessation of violent measures, the battle was begun anew under the leadership of Mr. Saltonstall.]

CHAPTER V.

1695.

In May, at a special session of the Superior Court, at Hartford, John Rogers is tried upon the following charges:—

1. For that in New London, in Feb. last, thou didst lay thy hand upon thy breast and say: This is the humane body of Christ, which words are presumptuous, absurd and of a blasphemous nature.

2. For saying, concerning a wheelbarrow thou broughtest into the meeting house about a week or fortnight before, that Christ drove the wheelbarrow—an impious belying of Christ, accusing him to be the author of sin and was on the Sabbath day.

3. Thou art presented for disturbing the congregation of N. London on the Lord's day, when they were in the public worship of God.

4. Also for saying in court that thou did'st nothing and had said nothing but what thy Lord and Master sent thee to doe etc.[77] which expressions were spoken in answer to the governor, who reproved thee for disturbing God's people in his day and worship.

The evidence against the prisoner in regard to these matters is given by Rev. Gurdon Saltonstall, Daniel Wetherell and John Christophers, and by "an old man in New London prison," who testifies that he heard John Rogers say "that he was in Christ and just and holy, and ministers would carry people to the devil." Stated in record that John Rogers owned to saying he was in Christ, but denied the rest of the statement by the old man. He also denied that he said Christ drove the wheelbarrow into the church.

Messrs. Saltonstall, Christophers and Wetherell testify that ("at Mr. Thomas Young's") they saw John Rogers lay his hand on his breast, and heard him say: "This is the humane body of Christ;" they also heard him say in a "laughing," or "as they thought in a flouting way," "brother Jesus and brother Paul." Owned in court by John Rogers "that he said his body was Christ's" (note this exact agreement with his son's statement, Part I, Chapter II), also that he used the term brother in regard to Christ and Paul.

The opinions of four ministers are taken as to the blasphemous nature of said expressions. The names of these ministers are "Samuel Stow, Moses Noyes, Timothy Woodbridge and Caleb Watson." They judge that the expression, "This is the humane body of Christ," has a high blasphemous reflection. The saying "brother Jesus is also a presumptuous expression, in the manner of his saying it" (viz., as rendered by Gurdon Saltonstall). "The saying that Christ drove the wheelbarrow is an impious belying of Christ" (regardless of the prisoner's denial of having made any such statement). "The reflections on our worship are a slanderous charge against the generation of the righteous, and heretical and impious."[78] They also "apprehend that in every one of the expressions evidenced against him there is a high and abominable profanation of the name of Christ."

Verdict, guilty. Sentence:—

To be led forth to the place of execution with a rope about his neck, and there to stand upon a ladder leaning against the gallows, with the rope about his neck, for a quarter of an hour. And for his evil speaking against the ordinances of God to pay a fine of £5; for disturbing the congregation to be kept in prison until he gives security to the value of £50 for his peaceable behavior and non-disturbance of the people of God for the future and until he pay to the keeper of the prison his just fees and dues.

Here is set forth a term of imprisonment which can be ended only by some change of policy on the part of the authorities; since it is well known by those who have this matter in charge that John Rogers never gives such security or bonds.

By this time, excitement and sympathy on the part of friends, followers and relatives of the prisoner are undoubtedly at their height, and it is probable that these people give somewhat free expression to their indignation, especially regarding the charge of blasphemy and the consequent ignominious punishment. Neither they nor the prisoner expected other than severe measures regarding the wheelbarrow affair, which was a very bold stroke of countermove in an extraordinary emergency.

In June, close following the trial and punishment inflicted upon John Rogers at Hartford, the New London meeting-house burns to the ground.

But for the excitement among the dissenters, this disaster might be attributed to some other cause; but under the circumstances it is a convenient and plausible charge to lay at their door. About the same time, also, Stonington meeting-house is desecrated by "daubing it with filth."

Bathsheba Fox, John Rogers, Jr., and William Wright (the Indian servant before referred to) are arraigned before the Superior Court at Hartford, on suspicion of being "concerned in" both of the above occurrences. The only evidence against John, Jr., and his aunt Bathsheba is of a circumstantial character, to the effect that some conversation transpired previous to these occurrences which it is considered may have instigated the burning and desecration on the part of others, notably of William Wright. The latter is convicted of defiling the Stonington meeting-house.[79]

It is probable that, in the height of their excitement over the treatment John Rogers received at Hartford, Bathsheba, John, Jr., and others expressed great indignation against Mr. Saltonstall and the New London church generally. Yet the burning of the meeting-house was probably as much a surprise to them as to anyone, and certainly as great a financial disaster; since upon them more than upon others, by exorbitant seizure of property, must fall the expense of a new edifice. This latter fact, as well as certainty that suspicion and apprehension must surely fall in their quarter, would naturally deter them from any such undertaking. Also, retaliatory measures of this description are contrary to the principles of this sect.[80]

At this same Superior Court session, John Rogers, Jr., and William Wright are charged with having recently assisted in the escape from the Hartford prison of a man, "Matthews," who was condemned to death.[81] William Wright is charged with assisting Matthews to escape from prison, and John Rogers, Jr., is accused of conveying him out of the colony. He appears to have been soon recaptured, and is again in prison at the time these charges are preferred. This is not the only instance in which John Rogers, Jr., is found running great risk and displaying great courage in a cause which he deems right before God, however criminal in the judgment of men.

For assisting in this escape, William Wright is to pay half the charges incurred in recapturing Matthews. For "abusing" Stonington meeting-house, for not acknowledging to have heard alleged conversations among the Rogerses and their confederates in regard to the burning of New London meeting-house, and for having made his escape from justice (by which he appears to have recently escaped from jail[82]), he is to be "sorely whipped" and returned to Hartford prison.

John Rogers, Jr., for being "conspicuously guilty of consuming New London meeting house" (although no slightest evidence of such guilt is recorded), "for having been in company with some who held a discourse of burning said meeting house" (although no such discourse has been proven), and "that he did encourage the Indian to fly far enough" (this appears to refer to William Wright's "escape from justice"), and "for being active in conveying Matthews out of the colony," is placed under bond for trial. It is shown that his uncle, Samuel Rogers, has appeared and given bail for him. (There is no after record to show that such trial ever took place, and no slightest mention of any further proceeding in the matter.) This act of Samuel Rogers is one of the frequent evidences of cordial friendship between John, Jr., and his uncle.

Bathsheba, for "devising and promoting" the firing of the meeting-house, and the "defiling" of that at Stonington, is to pay a fine of £10 or be severely whipped. This fine is probably paid by Samuel Rogers. It certainly would not be paid by her. The sole evidence against John, Jr., and Bathsheba is in the character of vague rumors of indignant discourse relating to the recent moves against John Rogers, Sr. No proof of any complicity is recorded.

John, Jr., and Bathsheba are freed, but William Wright remains in Hartford jail with his master (and will continue there for three years to come), not for burning the meeting-house, which is not proven against him, nor for defiling that at Stonington (on suspicion of which he has already been punished with the stripes); not (save in part) for the charges incurred by the rescue of Matthews, but (as will be evident three years later) for his averred determination not to submit to the law regarding servile labor on the first day of the week.

In the meantime, Mr. Saltonstall and his friends, who have recently been congratulating themselves on the success of their scheme for keeping John Rogers in Hartford jail, are gravely contemplating the ashes of their meeting-house and the remnants of its new bell, with still further uneasiness in regard to results like enough to ensue from added distrainments of the nonconformists towards the building of another edifice.

Nor is this all. There are prominent members of this very church who have so long been witnesses of wrongs and provocations on the part of the authorities towards the conscientious non-conformists, and have seen these wrongs and provocations so increased of late, that they are willing to join with representatives of those people in an open remonstrance.

In October of this year, occurs the terrible and mysterious public scourging of John Rogers at Hartford, which is best given in his own words and those of his son (see Part I, Chapters II and III), of which act, or cause for it, no slightest mention is to be found on court records. All this is but the beginning of vengeance for his continued refusal to bind himself to what the court terms "good behavior." Close following any such bonds, would be the institution of such procedures against the Rogerenes as would tend to annihilate their denomination. But so long as the dreaded countermove is to be looked for, in times of extremity, some degree of caution must be exercised, even by the rulers of Connecticut.

The "Remonstrance," to which reference has been made, appears in January of this year, and is issued by Capt. James Rogers, Richard Steer, Samuel Beebe and Jonathan Rogers. Appended to it are many names. Briefly stated, it is charged that the Congregational church have been so accustomed to persecute those that dissent from them "that they cannot forbear their old trade;" that the design of the Act of Parliament for liberty to Presbyterians,

Independents, Quakers and Baptists, to worship according to the dictates of conscience

"is violently opposed by some whose narrow principles, fierce inclinations and self interest have wedded to a spirit of persecution and an itch for domineering over their neighbors. That the present actions of the authority show that the king has nothing to do with this colony. That the compelling them to pay towards the maintainance of a Congregational Minister is contrary to law and therefore rapine and robbery. That the rights of peaceable dissenters have been of late, by permission of the authorities, violated, and that the authority has illegally oppressed them."

(Here is proof of recent unusual procedures by the town magistrates, not only against the Rogerenes, but in regard to the quiet dissenters on the Great Neck and elsewhere. This persecution has been going on out of sight of the general public, by action of the town authorities, since no County Court record appears. Undoubtedly it was this revival of indignities that stirred John Rogers to his bold move.)

The "emitters" of this paper are placed under bonds for appearance at the County Court, where they are fined £5 each "for defamation of their Majesties," viz.: "the Gov. of Conn. and others in authority," as well as "breach of His Majesty's peace and disquietude of his liege people."

The "emitters" appeal to the Superior Court, not because they expect any favor from that quarter, but it keeps the cause before that public in whose sense of justice is all their hope.

1697.

Before May of this year, and while another trial of the case regarding the claim of Joseph to land awarded Jonathan is still in progress, occurs the death of Joseph Rogers. It is not unlikely that had both brothers lived they would have come to an amicable adjustment of the difficulty; since the evident perplexity of those charged with examination into the case, indicates reasonable arguments upon either side, and thus a matter well fitted for compromise.

Our glimpses of Joseph Rogers are meagre. He and his wife appear not to have joined the Newport church, but were evidently members of the church of which John Rogers was pastor. (We have seen the wife's baptism, Chapter II.) Yet, of late years, Joseph has been scarcely more noticeable than Jonathan, as regards arraignment for labor on the first day of the week, which, as in case of the latter, appears to prove that his labor was not of an ostentatious character.

That he was steady, thrifty, industrious and enterprising is very evident. He added largely, by purchase, to the lands given him by his father, and had become proprietor of a saw-mill and corn-mill at Lyme. He died intestate, and his widow, Sarah, administered on his estate. Sarah Rogers now carries forward the suit in which her husband was engaged. The court appears not unfavorable to her presentation of the case; but, on account of a neglect on her part in regard to certain technicalities, the trial comes to a pause, and, through lack of further action on her part, the case is again decided in favor of Jonathan.

In March, 1697, complaint is made to the Governor and Council that John Rogers and William Wright, who were "to be kept close prisoners," are frequently permitted to walk at liberty, and the complainants (names not stated) declare their extreme dissatisfaction with the jailer and any that connive with him in this matter. It is ordered that said persons be hereafter kept close prisoners, and that the jailer or others who disobey this order be dealt with according to law. Has John Rogers made such friends with the prejudiced and cruel jailer of 1694? Even so (see Part I., Chapter IV., for testimony of Thomas Hancox, and Part I, Chapter II., for scourging of John Rogers at Hartford and part of same jailer in this abuse).

In 1697, the General Court appoint a committee to revise the laws of the colony and certain "reverent elders" to advise the persons chosen in this affair,[83] and also "to advise this court in what manner they ought to bear testimony against the irregular actions of John Rogers in printing and publishing a book reputed scandalous and heretical."

John Rogers, Jr., is now twenty-three years of age, a young man of brilliant parts and daring courage. Since he is the printer and circulator of this book, he is probably also its author. In this same month of May, "John Rogers, Jr.," is "bound in a bond of £40" "to appear at court" (Superior) "to answer what may be objected against him for bringing a printed book or pamphlet into this colony which was not licensed by authority, and for selling the same up and down the colony, as also for other misdemeanors"—the nature of the latter not indicated. No complaint being presented against him, he is dismissed.

[Could a copy of this pamphlet be found, great light might be thrown upon this stormy period, by revelation of the full circumstances leading up to the desperate entry of John Rogers into the meeting-house in 1694, the plot of Mr. Saltonstall and the "Remonstrance in Behalf of Peaceable Dissenters."

That this book, sold "up and down the colony" by John Rogers, Jr., was for the enlightenment of the people at large regarding the cause, and lack of cause, for the long imprisonment and cruel treatment of his father, with representation of the case for the nonconformists, can scarcely be doubted.

We can picture this talented and manly youth going from place to place, eagerly seeking and finding those who will listen to his eloquent appeal to buy and read this tale of wrong and woe, in the almost single-handed struggle for religious liberty in Connecticut.]

Does the little book create so much sympathy "up and down the colony," that it is no longer wise to keep John Rogers incarcerated, or are his ecclesiastical enemies at last sated by his nearly four years of close imprisonment in Hartford jail? However this may be, at the October session of the Superior Court, 1697, John Rogers is brought from prison and "set at liberty in open court," "in expectation that he will behave himself civilly and peaceably in the future." The promise of good behavior is not required of him, as formerly, but in its place the "in expectation," etc., which is not their expectation at all, unless with the proviso that they themselves observe due caution in the handling of him and his followers. They are apparently mindful of public opinion and of the little book.

William Wright is also brought from prison to this court. He stands here, in the presence of this master, who has just been set at liberty, awaiting his own turn to be freed. For more than three years, these men have been comrades in Hartford prison. They dwelt together at the home of James Rogers, Sr., the Indian a servant of the latter, and, since his death, servant of the executor, John Rogers. The master has been kind and trustful, the servant faithful to a remarkable extent. But for signal proof of heroic allegiance to this nonconformist, he had not been in prison at all.

The master is waiting that his servant may go with him from the court-room as a free man. But no! As the ceremony proceeds, the Indian is offered his freedom only on condition that he will promise to "behave himself civilly and peaceably in future," which would include refraining from servile work upon the first day of the week. They are demanding promises of the despised red man that they dare not exact of the white man, who has no lack of money or of friends.

Well may the warm blood of this master spring crimson to cheek and brow. But not alone the master, the servant himself. They would compel him to desert his master! The blood of the Indian is a match for that of the Saxon.

William Wright, standing in swarthy dignity before this worshipful court, declines his freedom on terms not only unjust to himself, but demanding infidelity to that master and that cause for which he has been so ready to venture and to suffer. He declares before this assembly that he will not submit to the law against servile labor on the first day of the week, that said law "is a human invention," and that he will work upon the first day of the week so long as he lives.

For this admirable fidelity to his religion and his friends, he is sentenced to be returned to prison "until there shall be opportunity to send him out of the colony on some vessel, as a dangerous disturber of the peace," and in case of his return he shall be whipped and again transported.

The wonder is that John Rogers held his peace until the full completion of this sentence. Had an outburst of indignation and condemnation of this unjust sentence not been forthcoming, as this faithful servant was being returned to the close imprisonment of Hartford jail, then might it be said that John Rogers could, for fear or favor, stand silent in the presence of injustice. For such an outburst as this[84] John Rogers is immediately fined £5. This "contempt of court" is briefly rendered on the records as follows:—

"John Rogers upon the above sentence being passed upon William Wright behaved himself disorderly, in speaking without leave and declaring that he did protest against the said sentence."

Since he never pays such fines (except through execution upon his property) he is probably returned to prison with his faithful servant, there to continue until this fine shall be cancelled.

Before the close of this year, Jonathan Rogers is accidentally drowned in Long Island Sound. Our glimpses of this youngest son of James Rogers have been slight and infrequent. That he possessed firmness and independence, is shown by his resolution to continue fully within the Newport church. The fact that this made no break—other than upon religious points—with his Rogerene relatives reveals both tact and an amiable and winning personality. In his inventory are "cooper's tools," "carpenter's tools" and "smith's tools," indicating an enterprising man concerned in several occupations, according to the fashion of his time.

1698.

When John Rogers is finally released from prison, the rancor with which he is still pursued by Mr. Saltonstall, with intent to weaken his financial power to continue his bold stand, is proven by the preposterous suit instituted against him almost immediately (Superior Court) for alleged defamation, in saying that he (Saltonstall) agreed to hold a public argument with him (Rogers) on certain points of scripture, which agreement said Saltonstall failed to fulfil.[85] (This case has been fully presented in Part I., Chapter VI.)

(Motive for any such alleged statement, unless true, being lacking, and a pamphlet being published not long after by John Rogers, giving a detailed account of the whole cause and proceeding, by which the exorbitant sum of

£600 recovery for libel, with costs of court, was levied upon him, it is presumable that enmity and court influence were at the bottom of this suit, if not clearly on the surface. Ecclesiastical power was dominant at this time in all the courts. Ever back of Mr. Saltonstall stood this power, as intent as himself upon the overthrow of this daring nonconformist. Could a copy of the pamphlet by John Rogers,[86] giving details of that remarkable suit, be found, much light would doubtless be cast upon this period in the history of the Rogerenes.)

The death of Elizabeth, widow of James, has recently occurred.[87]

John Rogers has changed his home from the Great Neck to Mamacock farm, North Parish. His sister Bathsheba has also removed to the North Parish, to a place called Fox's Mills, from the mills owned and carried on by her husband, Samuel Fox.

CHAPTER VI.

1698.

The long and close imprisonment of John Rogers in Hartford, attended as it was with a bitter sense of wrong, would seem sufficient to undermine the strongest constitution. To this was added anxiety regarding home affairs, including charge of his father's estate and the care of his mother, which were devolving wholly upon his sister Bathsheba. His mother's death close following his release, and business neglected during the past four years, must have borne hard on his enfeebled system, to say nothing of annoyance and difficulty on account of Mr. Saltonstall's recovery of the £600. Although he has gathered his family (son and servants) about him, at Mamacock farm, and resumed the leadership of his Society, he can scarcely as yet be the man he was four years ago.

It must be sweet to breathe again the open air of freedom, and such air as blows over Mamacock; purest breezes from river and from sea, fragrant with the breath of piney woods, of pastures filled with flowers and herbs, and of fields of new-mown hay, mingled with the wholesome odor of seaweed cast by the tide upon Mamacock shore.

Not far from the house, towards the river, in a broad hollow in the greensward, bordered on the north by a wooded cliff and commanding a view of the river and craggy Mamacock peninsula, is a clear, running stream and pool of spring water. Here yet (1698) the Indians come as of old, with free leave of the owner, to eat clams, as also on Mamacock peninsula, at both of which places the powdered white shells in the soil will verify the tradition for more than two hundred years to come. In this river are fish to tempt the palate of an epicure, and trout abound in the neighboring streams. A strong-built, white-sailed boat is a part of this lovely scene, and such a boat will still be found here for many years to come. (See "Hempstead Diary" for mention of boat.)

1699.

If after the perilous trials, hardships and irritations of the past four years, this man has a mind to enjoy life, as it comes to him at Mamacock, it is not strange.

Nor is it strange that, among his house servants, he soon particularly notices a young woman, lately arrived from the old country, whose services he has bought for so long as will reimburse him for payment of her passage.

Perhaps the chief cause of his interest is in the fact that she herself has taken a liking to the half-saddened man who is her master. Surely he who could so attach to himself a native Indian like William Wright, has traits to win even the favor of a young woman. He is evidently genial and indulgent with his servants, rather than haughty and censorious.

For twenty-five years he has been a widower, except that the grave has not covered the wife of his youth. Through all these years, the bitterest of his calumniators have not raised so much as a whisper questioning his perfect fidelity to Elizabeth, who, since the divorce, has been the wife of two other men and yet ever by this man has been considered as rightfully his own. Such being the case, well may his son wonder that he is becoming interested in this young housemaid, Mary Ransford, even to showing some marked attentions, which she receives with favor. She is a comely young woman, no doubt, as well as lively and spirited. Her master will not object to her having a mind of her own, especially when she displays due indignation regarding the wholesale method of gathering the minister's and church rates. But when she goes so far as to "threaten"[88] to pour scalding water on the head of the collector of rates, as he appears at the front door upon that ever fruitless errand, this master must give her a little lesson in the doctrine of non-resistance, although his eyes may twinkle with covert humor at her zeal. As for the rates, they must be taken out of the pasture.

Evidently this attractive girl, Mary, is willing to assent to anything this indulgent master believes to be right, taking as kindly to his doctrines as to himself. A man of soundest constitution, as proven from first to last, and of great recuperative energy, he is not old at fifty-two, despite imprisonments, stripes and ceaseless confiscations.

It soon becomes plain to John the younger that this is no ordinary partiality for an attractive and devoted maid, but that his father will ask this young woman to become his wife. For the first time, there is a marked difference of opinion between father and son. Mary is perfectly willing to pledge herself to this man, even under the conditions desired. As for him, why should he longer remain single, seeing there is no possible hope of reclaiming the wife whom he still tenderly loves. There are arguments enough upon the other side. John, Jr., presents them very forcibly, and especially in regard to the inconsistency of putting any woman in his mother's place, so long as his father continues to declare that Elizabeth is still, in reality, his wife.

To this latter and chief argument, the father replies that he shall not put Mary in his first wife's place, since that marriage has never been annulled, by any law of God or of man. Did not God, in the olden times, allow two kinds of wives, both truly wives, yet one higher than the other? Under the singular circumstances of this case, being still bound to Elizabeth by the law of God, yet separated from her by the will of men, he will marry Mary, yet not as he married Elizabeth Griswold. He will openly and honorably marry her, yet put no woman in the place of his first wife. To this Mary agrees.

It is but another outcome of this man's character. He fears God and God alone. He takes very little thought as to what man may think or do concerning him. Yet not by a hair's breadth will he, if he knows it, transgress any scriptural law. (In his after treatise "On Divorce," how well can be read between the lines the meditations and conclusions of this period, and chiefly the fact that, in deciding upon a second marriage, he in no wise admitted that Elizabeth Griswold was not still his wife, although so held from him that he might lawfully take another, although under the circumstances a lesser, wife. [89])

Oppose this unpropitious plan as he may, the son, whose influence has hitherto been paramount, cannot prevail to weaken his father's resolution. It is the old and frequent glamour that has bound men and women in a spell from the beginning, making them blind to what others see, and causing them to see that to which others are blind, in the object of their choice. The fact that Mary returns John, Jr.'s, pronounced opposition to the marriage with consequent aversion to the spirited youth, does not necessarily injure her standing with the father. There is but one person for whom favoritism on her part is absolutely necessary. As is usual in such cases, the matter goes on, despite all opposition. He who has so often borne to his mother the tale of his father's unfaltering fidelity, must now acquaint her with this sudden engagement. To the young, the new loves of older people are foolishness. But, in this case, there is still another reason for John, Jr.'s, opposition to this mid-life romance; it is sadly interfering with a very natural intention of his own.

With his usual habit of unhesitatingly executing a plan as soon as it is fully determined upon, John Rogers improves the opportunity offered by the session of the County Court in New London, to present himself with Mary before that assembly (June 6), where they take each other, in the sight and hearing of all, as husband and wife; he, furthermore, stating his reason for marrying her outside the form prescribed by the colony, to which form he declares he attaches no value, since it was not sufficient to secure his first wife to him, although no valid cause was presented for the annulment of that approved ceremony. To fully make this a well-authenticated marriage, he gallantly escorts Mary to the house of the Governor (Mr. Winthrop) and informs him that he has taken this young woman for his wife. The governor politely wishes him much joy.[90]

Much as this second marriage might be lamented, from several points of view, and much trouble as it brought upon both Mary and John, Jr., by their irreconcilable disagreement, to say nothing of the perplexities and sorrows which it inflicted upon John Rogers himself, it is scarcely to be regretted by his biographer; since it brings into bold prominence a striking, and wonderfully rare, characteristic of this remarkable man, viz.: the most reverent and careful deference to every known law of God, combined with total indifference to any law of man not perfectly agreeing with the laws of God.[91] Evidently, what the most august assembly of men that could be gathered, or the most lofty earthly potentate, might think, say or do, would to him be lighter than a feather, if such thought, speech or act did not accord with the divine laws.

1700.

By some agreement the house at Mamacock, cattle on the place, and other farm property, are under the joint ownership of John, Sr., and John, Jr.; the one has as much right to the house and the farm stock as the other. It now appears that the junior partner has himself been intending to furnish a mistress for the house at Mamacock. In January, 1700, seven months after the marriage of his father, he brings home his bride and is forced to place her in the awkward position of one of two mistresses. The young woman who now enters upon this highly romantic and gravely dramatic scene is one with whom John Rogers, Sr., can find no fault, being none other than his niece, Bathsheba, daughter of his faithful and beloved sister of the same name.

In spite of the difficulties sure to ensue, John, Sr., cannot but welcome this favorite niece to Mamacock. Not so with Mary. Whatever estimable and attractive qualities the latter may possess, here is a situation calculated to prove whether or not she is capable of the amount of passion and jealousy that has so often transformed a usually sensible and agreeable woman into the semblance of a Jezebel. The birth of a son to Mary, at this trying period, does not better the situation. Even so courageous a man as John Rogers might well stand appalled at the probable consequences of this venturesome marriage. When he brought Mary home and directed his servants to obey her as their mistress,[92] he in no wise calculated upon her being thus, even partially, set aside. He stands manfully by her, as best he may, though with the evident intention that she shall refrain from any abuse of his son's rights in the case.

Although Mary is fined 40*s*. by the County Court in June, for the birth of her child, it is not declared illegitimate by the usual form, the authorities being nonplussed by the fact she and John Rogers so publicly took each other as husband and wife. She is not called upon to declare who is the child's father, nor is the latter charged with its maintenance, as in cases of illegitimacy. Evidently, John Rogers did not expect any court action, in the case of so public a ceremony. He declines to pay a fine so disgraceful to his wife and child, and appeals to the Superior Court. The court decides that, since the fine was not accompanied by other due forms of law, it is invalid, but refers the matter to the future consideration of the County Court, which results in no further action in regard to this child.

Mary is also summoned before this same June court and fined 10*s*., "for her wicked and notorious language to John Rogers, Jr.," evidently on complaint of the latter. In this crisis, her husband presents himself at the court, partly in her defense and partly in that of his son. He calls attention to a mark upon her face, which he says she declares to have been inflicted by the hand of his son John, during his own absence from home, and that upon this account "she has become so enraged as to threaten the life of somebody, as she has done before from time to time," and he is "fearful that if God or man do not prevent it,"[93] serious consequences may follow. John, Jr., is fined 10*s*. on this evidence of his father. Although the injury to Mary, as indicated by the fine, is nothing serious as a wound, yet it proves how far the young man lost self-control in this instance. John Rogers, Sr., objects to the fine imposed upon Mary under these circumstances, but his statement before the court is evidently intended not only as a defense of his son, but as a check upon herself.

[There is the evidence of a no more partial witness than Peter Pratt that John Rogers never complained, outside his own home, of the domestic troubles resulting from this marriage.[94] In the above instance, he was compelled, by the action of his son, to testify, both in Mary's defense and in excuse of his son. Upon this court record and affidavit is founded Miss Caulkin's statement that appeal was made to the court to "quell domestic broils" arising from this marriage. It is to the advantage of this history that the family affairs of John Rogers were in this instance forced before the public, since we may observe the manner in which the father and husband endeavors to secure an impartial administration of justice, and immunity of any one from harm.]

However this marriage and its consequences may figure upon the printed page of a less primitive period, they appear not to lessen respect for this remarkable man in the eyes of his followers, although these followers are persons of the highest moral character. His blameless life as a single man for the last twenty-five years, and his avowed reasons for taking another wife in the manner he has, are known to all. Moreover, they find no word of God in condemnation.

In this year, John Rogers publishes, in pamphlet form, an account of the dispute agreed upon between himself and Mr. Saltonstall, telling the particulars of that great extortion. (Would that a copy of this might yet come to the light!)

1702.

In September, 1702, the County Court have a good opportunity to exercise the "after consideration" recommended by the Superior Court in 1700, which they improve by dealing with Mary, after the birth of her second child, exactly as they are accustomed to deal with an unmarried woman. Her presentment is in exactly the same wording, a part of which calls upon her to declare under oath, before the court, the name of the father of her child. To prevent their carrying out this form, John Rogers is there in court, with his six-months-old girl baby in his arms, to save it from this disgrace. He has given Mary directions how to proceed, in order to supplement his plan of breaking up the intended procedure. If she refuse to take the oath and to declare John Rogers to be the father of her child, the court will be baffled.[95]

Being ordered to take the oath, she is silent, as her husband has enjoined, while he declares to the court that this her child in his arms is his own. The court knows, as well as the man before them, that his first marriage has not been annulled for any legal cause; that he had reason to refuse a repetition of the ceremony. But while those who make and administer laws may be allowed to ignore them with impunity, lesser people must abide by them; least of all must this man escape, who has imperilled the ecclesiasticism of the land. They threaten Mary with stripes, if she continue her refusal to take the oath. She looks from the judge to the man who stands, so earnest and anxious, with the babe in his arms, bidding her not to take the oath, declaring that, if she obey him, he will shield her from harm. She knows he will do all that he can to protect her; but she has seen marks of the stripes upon his own back; she knows how he has sat for hours in the stocks, and been held for weary years in prison. Can he rescue her from the stripes?

He sees her yielding and pleads with her, pleads that she will save their child from this dishonor. The court sternly repeats the threat. Again he promises to defend her, in case she will obey him; but declares that, if she yield, branding his child as base-born, herself as common, and himself a villain, he needs must hesitate, hereafter, to own her as his wife.

She sees the court will not be trifled with. She knows that John Rogers uses no idle words. Yet will it not be safer to brave his displeasure than that of the court? She takes the oath, and declares John Rogers to be the father of her child. The cloud grows dark upon the father's face. He folds his branded child against his heart and goes his way. All this he risked to hold his first love first, in seeming as in truth; has risked and lost.

The court proceeds as usual in cases of illegitimacy, pronouncing John Rogers the father of the child, and ordering that he pay 2*s.* 6*d.* per week towards its maintenance, until it is four years of age. Mary is allowed until the end of the following month to pay the usual fine of 40*s.*, in case of non-payment of which she shall receive ten stripes on the naked body. In the meantime, she is to be detained in prison. Will John Rogers own his child to be illegitimate by paying this fine? By no means.

1703.

To now take Mary back (even if so allowed by the authorities)[96] would be to brand any other children in the same manner. To marry her by the prescribed form would be to acknowledge these two children to be illegitimate. Yet there is one thing that can be done, and must be done speedily. Mary must be rescued from the prison and thus saved from the lash. There are but two in all this region who will risk an attempt like that. They are John Rogers and his son. Mary escapes to Block Island.

After a safe period has elapsed, Mary is returned from Block Island to New London. Her children are placed with her, somewhere in the town, to give the more effect to her Petition to the General Court, which is presented early in May. It is a long and pathetic document (still to be seen in "Book of Crimes and Misdemeanors," in the State Library, at Hartford), narrating the manner of her marriage to John Rogers; his taking her home and "ordering his servants to be conformable and obedient" to her; the trouble they had, "especially myself," on account of the displeasure of John, Jr., at the marriage; a description of her presentment at court for her second child; her compliance with the court's importunity, although her husband stood there "with it in his arms," and how the result had made their children "base-born," by which her "husband" says he is "grossly abused;" since "he took me in his heart and declared me so to be his wife before the world, and so owned by all the neighbors." She beseeches that the sentence of the court be annulled; so that, "we may live together as husband and wife lawful and orderly," "that the blessing of God be upon us, and your Honor, for making peace and reconciliation between us, may have an everlasting reward." Dated in "New London, May 12, 1703."

The court takes no notice of this appeal. Mary is returned to Block Island and the children to Mamacock. Proof will appear, however, that she is not forgotten nor neglected. Even after her marriage to another man, and years after this hopeless separation, she will say nothing but good of him who first called her his wife and acted faithfully towards her a husband's part.

[Miss Caulkins states that, some months before this period, John Rogers "made an almost insane attempt" to regain his former wife Elizabeth, wife of

Matthew Beckwith. This statement is founded upon a writ against John Rogers on complaint of Matthew Beckwith (Jan. 1702-3), accusing John Rogers of laying hands on Elizabeth, declaring her to be his wife and that he would have her in spite of Matthew Beckwith. The historian should ever look below the mere face of things. For more than twenty-five years, John Rogers has known that Elizabeth, married or unmarried, would not return to him, pledged as he was to his chosen cause. He is, at this particular date, not yet fully separated from Mary, but holding himself ready to take her back, in case a petition to the General Court should by any possibility result favorably. This and another complaint of Matthew Beckwith—the latter in June, 1703—to the effect that he was "afraid of his life of John Rogers"[97] indicate some dramatic meeting between John Rogers and "Elizabeth, daughter of Matthew Griswold," in the presence of Matthew Beckwith, the incidents attendant upon which have displeased the latter and led him to resolve that John Rogers shall be publicly punished for assuming to express any ownership in his, Matthew Beckwith's, wife.

Any meeting between John Rogers and Elizabeth Griswold could not fail of being dramatic. What exact circumstances were here involved is unknown; what attitude was taken by the woman, when these two men were at the same time in her presence, it is impossible to determine. But it is in no way derogatory to the character of John Rogers, that in meeting this wife of his youth, he gives striking proof of his undying affection. Ignoring her marriage to the man before him, forgetful, for the time being, even of Mary, blind to all save the woman he loves above all, he lays his hand upon Elizabeth, and says she is, and shall be, his. Under such circumstances, Matthew Beckwith takes his revenge in legal proceedings. When summoned before the court, John Rogers defends his right to say that Matthew Beckwith's wife—so-called—is still his own, knowing full well the court will fine him for contempt, which process follows (County Court Record).]

John Rogers is fifty-five years of age at this date, and Matthew Beckwith sixty-six. Elizabeth is about fifty.

In this year, a fine of 10*s*. is imposed upon Samuel Beebe (Seventh Day Baptist) for ploughing on the first day of the week (County Court Record). Without doubt the Rogerenes (Seventh Day Baptists also) have done the same thing. At this period John Rogers may do whatever he pleases of this sort on the first day of the week.[98] Nearly four years of imprisonment in Hartford jail, the little book "sold up and down" the colony, and many a tale narrated of his bravery and sufferings in the cause of religious liberty, have won for him such popular sympathy that those who aid and abet ecclesiastical rule in the state councils, are not as yet venturing to resume stringent proceedings against the Rogerenes. The signal failure to secure a promise of "good behavior" from the Rogerene leader is also a prominent factor in the situation.

Although there is no sign that Capt. James Rogers and his wife have receded from their nonconformity, their son, James, Jr., has married a member of the Congregational church and taken the half-way covenant. He is prominent in the community and has political ambitions, the attainment of which would be impossible for one of a nonconformist persuasion. To have won this talented young man, must be counted a signal victory by Mr. Saltonstall. Samuel, son of Samuel, has also married a member of the Congregational church. He is continuing the bakery on its old scale, has landed interests in the neighboring country, and is surveyor for the town of New London.

Samuel, son of Joseph, now of Westerly, has become a member of the Congregational church, while his older brother James, an enterprising young man, is of the Baptist persuasion.

James Smith, son of Bathsheba, is a close follower of his uncle John, although his sister Elizabeth (married to William Camp) is a member of the Congregational church, in which her children are baptized.

During the respite from graver cares, John Rogers has enough to busy him at Mamacock, outside of his duties as preacher and pastor, in caring for the place (in unison with John, Jr.) and other business interests, making shoes, writing books, and attending to the welfare and training of his two little children, to whom he must be both father and mother. John and Bathsheba have a third child now. So here are five little ones in the home at Mamacock. And there is Mary at Block Island. She came from across the sea, and is likely to have only the one friend in America.

In this eventful year, John Rogers visits Samuel Bownas, a Quaker who is detained in jail at Hempstead, L. I., on a false accusation.

Through the whole of a long conversation with the Quaker (narrated by the latter in his Journal), he makes no reference to Mary, the prominent figure in this period of his history. It is not his purpose to reveal to outsiders that, although he and Mary are separated, he has not resigned her to her fate.

Mr. Bownas states that John Rogers is

"chief elder of that Society called by other people Quaker Baptists, as imagining (though falsely) that both in their principles and doctrines they are one with us; whereas they differed from us in these material particulars, viz.: about the seventh day Sabbath, in use of water in baptism to grown persons, using the ceremony of bread and wine in communion, and also of anointing the sick with oil; nor did they admit of the light of truth or manifestation of the Spirit but only to believers, alleging Scripture for the whole."

Upon this latter point, Mr. Bownas and his visitor have a long discussion. On any subject but the Quaker doctrines, Mr. Bownas appears not particularly interested, for which reason he does not furnish much information in regard to the part of the conversation relating to John Roger's sufferings for conscience' sake, which he avers to have been a portion of the converse, and which would have been more edifying to many than the doctrinal views of the Quakers so fully expounded to John Rogers, which are presented to the reader through this account of their conversation.

John Rogers is quoted as describing the manner in which the young people in his Society are trained in knowledge and study of the Scriptures,[99] and stating that women "gifted by the Spirit" are encouraged to take part in their meetings.

Of the Rogerenes, Mr. Bownas says: "They bore a noble testimony against fighting, swearing, vain compliments and the superstitious observation of days."

Although John Rogers, in this narration, is represented as fluent in speech, he is also shown capable of preserving complete silence, allowing a person who is presenting views exactly the opposite of his own to go on uninterrupted, rather than present counter views to no purpose. He is also shown ready to concede much to the Quaker, expresses no annoyance at the other's very positive stand, and even admits possible mistakes on his own part.

In short, the picture given of John Rogers by the Quaker, although less particular than could be desired, is that of a genial, friendly man, discussing questions with great fairness, and without excitement. When he requests Mr. Bownas, if he ever sees Edmund Edmundson, to convey to him his sincere sorrow for having argued against his views that night at Hartford (see Chapter I), the natural gentleman shows plainly in the man. Possibly, his own opinions on the subject of that discussion may have changed.

1705.

There is still a refreshing respite from persecution, beyond the minister's rates and minor prosecutions carried on by the town magistrates (of which latter there is so seldom any clear view), and no attempt to disturb any of the meetings of the Congregational church.

In this year, John Rogers publishes his book entitled "An Epistle to the Church called Quakers." This work, while heartily assenting to many of the Quaker doctrines, is an earnest and logical appeal to these people against the setting aside of such express commands of Christ as the ceremony of Baptism and the Lord's Supper. In this same year he issues "The Midnight Cry" from the same press (William Bradford, New York).

At this time, as for some five years previous, a youth by the name of Peter Pratt is a frequent inmate of the family at Mamacock. This is none other than the son of Elizabeth Griswold by her second husband. Elizabeth could not keep her son John from fellowship with his father, and it appears that she cannot keep from the same fellowship her son by Peter Pratt. This is not wholly explainable by the fact that Peter admires and is fond of his half-brother, John (see Part I., Chapter IV.). Were not the senior master at Mamacock genial and hospitable, Peter Pratt's freedom at this house could not be of the character described (by himself), neither would he be likely (as is, by his own account, afterwards the case) to espouse the cause of John Rogers, Sr., so heartily as to receive baptism at his hands, and go so far in that following as to be imprisoned with other Rogerenes.

According to his own statement, this young man was present at the County Court in 1699, when John Rogers appeared there with Mary Ransford and took her for his wife. He seems at that time to have been studying law in New London, and making Mamacock his headquarters. He had every opportunity to know and judge regarding John Rogers at that exact period. To this young man must also have been known the particulars which led to the complaint of Matthew Beckwith, his step-father, concerning John Rogers.[100] Had Peter Pratt disapproved of either of these occurrences it would have prevented his affiliation with this man. Evidently, nothing known or heard by him concerning John Rogers, Sr., has availed to diminish his respect for him or prevent a readiness to listen to his teachings. (He admits that at this period he "knew no reason why John Rogers was not a good man.")[101]

We have seen proof, by statement of Mr. Bownas, that in 1703 John Rogers was still a faithful observer of the Seventh Day Sabbath. But in the Introduction to his Epistle to the Seventh Day Baptists, written, according to date of publication, about 1705, he states that by continual study of the New Testament, he has become convinced that Christ Himself is the Sabbath of His church, having nailed to His cross all the former ordinances (Col. xi, 14), that, therefore, adherence to the Jewish Sabbath, or any so-called sacred day, is out of keeping with the new dispensation. "Let no man, therefore, judge you in meat or drink, or in respect of an holy-day, or of the new moon, or of the Sabbath."—(Col. xi, 16.) He also states that as soon as he came to this conclusion he gave up the Seventh Day Sabbath and wrote this Epistle to his former brethren of that church.

After the above conclusion on the part of John Rogers and his Society, the Rogerenes begin to hold their meetings on the first day of the week, in conformity with the common custom. Yet, much as they might enjoy making this a day of entire rest, were there not an "idolatrous" law declaring that sacred which was not so declared in the Scriptures, they still consider it their duty to bear sufficient witness against the assumption of its sanctity.

While the Rogerenes were preaching New Testament doctrines antagonistic to the state church, on Saturday, when the rest of the world were busy with secular affairs, not many outsiders would be likely to attend their meetings; but now that these doctrines are preached and taught on Sunday, in public meetings of the Rogerenes,[102] many more are likely to attend these services, and so become interested in this departure, despite the fine that might be risked by such attendance.

Yet there are no indications that any new measures have been adopted, on account of this change on the part of the Rogerenes. They are at least ceasing labor for that portion of the day devoted to religious services, which may possibly appear a hopeful indication, to the view of the ecclesiastical party. At all events, by the silence of the court records and the testimony of John Bolles, the Rogerenes are not now being persecuted as formerly, and we shall find these peaceful conditions existing for some years to come.

CHAPTER VII.

1707.

June 4, of this year, a complaint is made by Samuel Beebe against John Rogers, as executor of his father's estate, for detaining from Samuel Beebe three cows, which, by the codicil of the will, were to be given to his wife Elizabeth after the death of her mother. The cows are evidently given up to him, since nothing further concerning them appears on the court records.

The peculiarity about this complaint is that, while claiming what is given to his wife under the codicil, he is still (as will be seen) firmly adhering to the irregular proceeding of the widow in 1692, which ignores the codicil to the extent of attempting a distribution of the movables—and also a portion of the residue of land—in a manner entirely different from that directed by the testator in this codicil.

The determination of Samuel Beebe to, if possible, prevent the executor from carrying out the full intent of the testator is sufficient to account not only for the detention of the cows, but for the much longer delay made by the executors, John and Bathsheba, in attempting to make the final division indicated by the codicil, a preliminary to which division would be their taking for themselves all of the household goods.[103]

No complaint against the Rogerenes has appeared on the court records during the nine years previous to this date. While this does not imply entire cessation of hostilities on the part of the town authorities, it shows that none of these have been of such a character as to call forth the countermove, which is punishable by the County Court.

John Rogers has recently attracted to his following one of the most intelligent and upright men in the community, who has been a member of the Congregational church. This is John Bolles, a young, married man, only son of Mr. Thomas Bolles, one of the wealthiest and most exemplary of the early settlers of this place, himself oldest son of Joseph Bolles (of an ancient family of the English gentry—Nottinghamshire), who emigrated to Maine previous to 1640, and by the death of his two elder brothers became heir to the family estates in England.[104]

Mr. Thomas Bolles settled in New London at the earnest solicitation of Governor Winthrop.[105]

The wife of John Bolles is daughter of Mr. John Edgecomb, another prominent planter of New London, also of gentle blood of Old England. (Edgecombs of Mount Edgecomb.)

As his father's sole heir and by right of his wife in her father's estate, as well as through his own prudence and enterprise, this young man is destined to be one of the richest men in New London.

On account of a remarkable escape from death while an infant in arms, John Bolles was led, while still a youth, to pledge himself to the service of God. Now, after careful examination into the doctrines of John Rogers, he devotes himself, in obedience to his youthful pledge, reverently and enthusiastically to that cause. (See Part I., Chapter VI.)

The home farm of John Bolles is half a mile south of that of John Rogers, on the same (Norwich) road, on a height of land known as Foxen's Hill (later Bolles Hill), directly overlooking the town of New London, with a further view of Long Island Sound.[106] He has lived for years in the near neighborhood of John Rogers, and has been one of his personal acquaintances and friends. If this extremely conscientious young man knew of any cause to distrust the character of this reformer, even in the days when most maligned on account of his independent marriage to Mary Ransford, he would not (in this year) have been baptized by him and entered upon the unpopular and perilous career of one of his followers.

John Bolles states in his "True Liberty of Conscience" that although the Rogerenes had not been molested of late, yet directly after his leaving the Congregational church for that of the Rogerenes (1707) serious persecutions were reinstituted, directed against the performance of labor upon the first day of the week.[107] Evidently something must be done, to prevent an influence that can still reach within the precincts of the Congregational church, to draw forth to this heretical following some of its brightest and its best.

1708.

In this year Mr. Saltonstall, so popular among the clergy and other leading men of Connecticut, as a staunch and able advocate of Congregational church supremacy, is elected governor, and is succeeded in the ministry at New London by Rev. Eliphalet Adams.

Dissenters of several kinds are now so numerous that it is impossible to disregard their combined outcry against ecclesiastical tyranny. Accordingly, in this year we find the General Court enacting a law allowing those "who soberly dissent" to worship in their own way, "without any let, hindrance or molestation whatever," provided it be well understood that none are excused from paying their full share towards the maintenance of the Congregational and Presbyterian ministry, and that those who desire the liberty of worshipping in other than the Congregational or Presbyterian way, shall "qualify themselves at the County Court, according to an Act, made in the first year of the late King William and Mary, granting liberty of worshipping God in a way separate from that by law established."

The Rogerenes do not derive any benefit from this law; John Rogers and his followers being resolved never to countenance, by their obedience, any civil law whatever which dictates in regard to the worship of God.[108] Baptists, Episcopalians and Seventh Day Baptists build meeting-houses,[109] qualify themselves under this law and hold their services in peace; but meetings of the Rogerenes are still held without legal sanction and so without legal protection.

In this year, the Saybrook Platform, conceived by Mr. Saltonstall and his ecclesiastic friends, becomes a law. By this device, church and state are firmly welded together. Although certain dissenters may secure leave to worship in their own way in their own churches (provided they will pay for both their own and the Congregational ministry), the indifferent or irreligious masses are still subject to the dominant church, as regards compulsory Congregational church attendance and money tribute. All yield except the Rogerenes, who heroically go their way, regardless of menace or punishment. They see their cattle and other property sold at outcrys to satisfy extortion, yet hold their peace, unless some action threatening the continuance of their following of New Testament teachings necessitates an extraordinary show of nonconformity, by way of unusual Sunday labor, or perhaps even brings out the countermove, that last but most efficient means of defense.

1709.

In this year, James Rogers, Jr., is admitted to the bar, and soon becomes a prominent lawyer of this vicinity.

An attempt is made at this time to stop the preaching and proselyting of John Rogers. Among his followers at this period is Peter Pratt, son of Elizabeth Griswold (see Chapter VI.). This young man now experiences the great necessity for courage and endurance on the part of anyone who would faithfully adhere to Rogerene principles; since he is imprisoned with other Rogerenes.[110]

Judging from past indications, the fact of their having gained a new convert from a prominent family of the Congregational persuasion is at any time a sufficient cause for the institution of severer measures against this sect.

But other annoyances are now at hand for John Rogers. There is the still unsettled residue of the estate, so difficult of adjustment on account of the claims of Samuel Beebe, (under the widow's "deed" of 1692. See Chapter III.), which will be put forward as soon as any move is made by the executor to divide the residue of the estate according to the codicil. These claims include certain young slaves, coming under the head of "moveables" belonging to the estate of James Rogers, of which movables, by the widow's deed, one-half was to be given, after her decease, to her daughter Elizabeth Beebe, and one-half to her son Jonathan.

During his executorship, John Rogers has freed a number of his father's slaves. Two of these slaves (called "servants") are mentioned in the inventory of the estate, in 1688, where it is stated that they are to be free in three years. The bond-children owned by James Rogers, as yet of no value, were not mentioned in the will or inventory, but they appear to have been classed with that residue of the estate ("moveables") which, by the terms of the codicil, was to be divided between John, Bathsheba and James.

[There are indications that not only had John Rogers come to regard the keeping of slaves in life bondage as contrary to the teachings of the New Testament, in the line of the Golden Rule; but that his father had come to the same conclusion, and had made plans for freeing all his slaves. His charge to his children—John, Bathsheba and James—in the codicil to his will, to "remember Adam," one of his two able-bodied negro slaves, appears to have been understood by them as referring equally to the children of this slave; since one of the young slaves freed by the executor is proven—by "Hempstead Diary"—to be Adam, son of this Adam (each being called "Adam Rogers"). It is probable that others of the young slaves were Adam's children, while some of them were children of the negro woman, Hager, who, as stated in inventory, was to be freed in three years.]

By various documents on record, it is evident that the administration of the estate by John has gone on in a very methodical manner and strictly according to the tenor of the will. The order of the committee (1693) was that, after the death of the widow, the remainder of the estate should be "disposed of according to the terms of the will," of which the codicil was the part that referred to this residue. The codicil, however, does not contain explicit directions regarding the movable estate, but simply says that John and Bathsheba are to "take" the things about the house, "before the others be divided," and that—after the cows have been given to Elizabeth—the remainder of the movable estate "whatsoever" be divided by John, Bathsheba and James among themselves. The residue of land legacies is clearly defined. The whole estate having been placed under the executorship of John and

Bathsheba, presumes their continuance in that office until the final settlement. This is evidently the expectation of the court and of those concerned, as they continue to be called executors.

No fault has hitherto been found with the executorship, save in the demand of Samuel Beebe for the cows. Yet the executor is well aware of the irregular claims pending, and by his father's request will be held from making appeal to the court against any unjust action which Samuel Beebe may take in this matter.

At this crisis, Captain James comes to the rescue, evidently by aid and advice of his son James, the young lawyer. A method is devised by which the irregular claims may be thwarted and, at the same time, the testator's request in regard to legal proceedings on the part of any of his children be respected.

The first indication of the above intention is found in June of this year, when Captain James makes over to his son James all interest which he himself has in "all the moveable estate" left by his father.

The next step is for James, Jr., to enter complaint (July 13) at the Probate Court that the settlement of the residue ("moveables") of his grandfather's estate—after the death of the widow—has not been attended to by "the formality of the law." Being himself interested in the estate, he desires that "such methods may be taken *as the law directs*." The court, upon consideration of this enigma, finds that the estate was to be settled not by legal form, but by agreement among the children to John's executorship, as approved by the General Court. The Probate Court, therefore, declines to meddle in the matter.

James, Jr., now enters complaint, at the Superior Court, that John Rogers and Bathsheba Fox, administrators on the estate of James Rogers,

"have not administered thereon according to the order of the law, and have not ever yet made and exhibited in the Court of Probates, and recorded there, any inventory of said estate; but dispose thereof at their own will and pleasure without giving account."

The manner of administration of John and Bathsheba regarding the movables and lack of exhibition of any inventory of same to the court, have been in entire accordance with the direction of the testator. Moreover, had James Rogers, Jr., held to the mode of division directed in the codicil, his share would be much larger than by the method now being sought. An ulterior motive is evident from the start. The court undoubtedly understands the full meaning of this outwardly peculiar procedure on the part of James, Jr.

The Superior Court directs the Probate Court to issue a writ summoning

John and Bathsheba to render an inventory, etc., "according to law," and if they do not appear, then the Court of Probate shall grant letters of administration to James, Jr., "or some other person," "to the end that a just division be made."

John and Bathsheba not complying with a demand so contrary to the directions given them by their father, James, Jr., is appointed executor, to complete the settlement, viz.: the division of the movable estate. He now presents an inventory, which inventory is dated as having been taken in 1788; just after the death of James Rogers. The movables, of which he claims that John Rogers should render an account, figure at £100 value. Although the original inventory presented mentions an Indian and his negro wife and a mulatto man, each having about three years to serve, also a negro woman "deaf and dumb," no mention is made of these or of any other slaves by the new executor, and no complaint is made regarding the fact that they and their children have been freed by the former executor.

While this is going on, John and Bathsheba appear in court in regard to Hager, a former slave of John Rogers (the negro wife mentioned in the inventory), who has lost the written discharge from bondage that was given to her years before by the executors. John and Bathsheba testify that, shortly before his decease, their father agreed with William Wright to sell him his negro slave, Hager, for a certain term of service on the part of William Wright, and at the time of this agreement gave her to him for his wife, providing for the couple "a wedding dinner." They also say that long before this agreement with William Wright, their father and mother had promised Hager her freedom at the age of thirty-six years.

"William Wright having been banished before his term of service had expired, we, being intrusted by our deceased father with his whole estate, seeing the support of the woman and her children was more than her service, gave her a written discharge, upon condition she should support her younger children" (her eldest son to be free at the age of twenty-one), "which said writing she hath lost." She is herewith again discharged, with all her children except the above, "by these presents."

The next move by James, Jr., is to attach property belonging to the late executor to the amount of the value of the aforesaid "moveables." Thus, with no appeal to court on the part of any of the children of James Rogers, and with no breach of trust on the part of John and Bathsheba, the residue of the estate passes fully into the hands of the new executor, and is clearly minus any of the "negroes" which the irregular claimants were prepared to demand.

By this time, Samuel Beebe sees that the young lawyer contemplates nothing short of preventing every irregular claim which he may venture to make. Samuel Beebe is no more in need of servants, lands or goods than are the other heirs, having a good estate from his own father and another by gifts to his wife from her father. He is now living at Plumb Island, and in so showy a way that he is called "King Beebe."—(*Caulkins.*) It is apparently, on his part, a game played mainly for the zest of it; as Samuel Beebe might sail a boat of his own against one of Captain James or that at Mamacock. But alas! a young wife and mother is to become a victim of this game.

For about four years now, a young negro woman named Joan, who was born of a slave of James Rogers, Sr., has been the wife of a free colored man named John Jackson, a servant of John Rogers, living in a house on the Mamacock farm. Joan has, by Jackson, one child, a son, about two years old, and is expecting another. While yet a child, Joan was given by the widow of James Rogers to Elizabeth Beebe, in payment of the legacy of £10, which latter was to be paid to said Elizabeth Beebe (according to the terms of the will), by said widow, "with consent of my son John." Said executor not seeing fit to transfer Joan to a man who kept slaves in life bondage, and not doubting that the arrangements for settlement of the estate according to the will and codicil would fully sustain him in not allowing this claim of Samuel Beebe by the unwarranted and unsanctioned act of his mother, freed Joan in due course of time, as he did the rest of the young slaves.

1710.

About October 1, 1710, Samuel Beebe, in some manner not indicated by the court records, succeeds in securing Joan Jackson and her boy and detaining them at Plumb Island.

Unfortunately, and apparently very carelessly (as shown in Chapter IV.), the committee, in their decision of 1693, instead of using the wording of the will in regard to the payment of the £10 by the widow, viz.: "with consent of my son John," rendered it that the £10 be paid to Elizabeth "by John and Bathsheba, when the widow so order."

September 19, 1710, James, Jr., enters complaint at the County Court that Samuel Beebe is illegally detaining from him, present executor of his grandfather's estate, a negro woman, named Joan, who was the property of James Rogers at the time of his death. The defendant claims that the woman was part of the legacy of £10 given his wife.

The court decides in favor of Samuel Beebe, its decision being grounded on the blunder of the committee of division, in 1693. James, Jr., appeals to the Superior Court. The latter court decides that if the settlement of the committee in 1693, in accordance with the terms of the will,

"were in point of law a sufficient conveyance of the negro woman to Eliz. Beebe, without John Roger's consent to said conveyance by his mother, then the jury find the case for Samuel Beebe; but if the consent of John Rogers was, in point of law, under said settlement by said committee, necessary to such a conveyance, then they find the woman for John Rogers."

This calls for the decision of Judge Gurdon Saltonstall, the archenemy of John Rogers, who, naturally, ignores the blunder of the committee and adjudges Joan and her child to Samuel Beebe, as slaves for life.

Two months later, a second child is born to Joan, at Plumb Island, a babe its father may neither claim nor behold. Nearly six months more drag slowly by, in great and grave suspense.

1711.

As for Joan herself, she is not likely to settle down at once, if ever, in meek submission to her fate. Woman-like, her first thought would be to escape, if possible, to her husband and the kind masters at Mamacock, being sure that if she is once upon that shore, they will not willingly return her to Plumb Island. She cannot be supposed to consider, in so dire a strait, the peril they would incur by harboring a runaway slave, such as she now is, by the decision of the Superior Court.

In the latter part of May, 1711, John Rogers, Sr., is in the vicinity of Long Island, and also on the mainland of New York. Southold, L.I., is a common stopping-place for boats from New London. His friend, Mr. Thomas Young, is now of that place.

If John Rogers landed at Southold, Joan might learn of this fact and act upon it. But by nightfall the man for whose assistance she may have hoped is at his objective point on the mainland. She finds conveyance of some kind, however; for, this same night, she escapes from Plumb Island with her two children. Upon his return to Mamacock, the next day, John Rogers finds them there and is accused of so poor a trick as the bringing them to his own home. He may have had in view some scheme for their escape; but if so, his plans have been thwarted by Joan's imprudence, through her eagerness to reach her friends in New London.

At the New London County Court, June 5, Christopher Christophers, one of the chief enemies of John Rogers, being one of the judges, Samuel Beebe enters complaint against John Rogers and John Jackson, "on suspicion that they stole Joan and her two children out of his house the night of May 29th last." The accused men, being now before the court, plead not guilty to the charge of taking Joan from Plumb Island; but acknowledge that, after her arrival at Mamacock, they conveyed her into Rhode Island. Samuel Beebe owns that the woman and her children have since been returned to him by the governor of Rhode Island, and that he has them now.

Upon no further evidence of theft than the fact of the presence of Joan and her children at Mamacock and their conveyance into Rhode Island by John Rogers and John Jackson, and having given the accused parties but a few days to secure testimony, also without regard to the fact that the alleged theft occurred in another colony, or that it is a capital offense, on the law book, this court, without a jury, adjudges John Rogers and John Jackson guilty of stealing Joan and her children, and sentence them to pay twice the amount of the worth of said slaves (£40) and costs of prosecution. In case John Jackson be not able to pay his part, he shall serve Samuel Beebe or his assignee at the rate of £5 per year until the whole amount is cancelled. So that Samuel Beebe not only has the negroes fast, but £40 reward for his complaint against John Rogers.

The record further states that

"John Rogers, upon hearing the above sentence, did, in open court, declare the said sentence to be rebellion against her Majesty, and that it was injustice, and declared that this court are rebels against her Majesty,"

for which contempt, said court

"order said Rogers to give bond of £200 for his appearance at the Superior Court, in Oct. next, to answer for his offense and for keeping her Majesty's peace and being in good behavior in the meantime, and for want of sureties, to be committed to prison until he shall be released by due form of law."

Two of the justices on this occasion are bitter enemies of John Rogers, while the Superior Court that is to try him for contempt has Governor Saltonstall for its judge.

Thus, of the two men not proven to have committed this offense, one departs from the court-room to a long imprisonment, to say nothing of an execution upon his property, and the other to four years of slavery, under dictation of the man who has stolen his wife and children, unless he be able to pay the large sum of £20 for his freedom.

In this dilemma, John Rogers makes an effort for justice. He presents a Petition to the court, in which he objects to a trial in the County Court of New London for a crime alleged to have been committed within the jurisdiction of

Long Island. He asks for a trial in the latter jurisdiction, where he can produce evidence to clear himself from any such charge. No attention is paid to this Petition. (See John Roger's account of this affair, Part I., Chapter V.)

On no account will John Rogers go back of this charge of man-stealing, to enter suit regarding Samuel Beebe's seizure of this freed woman; that would be bringing before the court something relating to the estate of his father. Evidently, for the same reason, he who fears not at his peril to denounce an unjust decision in any court of the land, has made no complaint in regard to the so plainly prejudiced award of Joan to Samuel Beebe, by the judge of the Superior Court. Even thus can this man hold his peace, when he will.

The next move, as revealed by the records, is the sale (June 13, 1711) of Joan and her children "for their natural life" to John Livingston (a prominent attorney); one of the children "a boy of three years named John," the other "a girl of six months," to all of whom Samuel Beebe says he "has full right by judgment of court, viz., for the woman and one negro she had with her when she came" (that is, when, in some way, he secured her) "and the youngest born since."

Captain James Rogers appears to be as much opposed as his brother John to keeping persons in lifelong bondage.[111] James, Jr., will take any legal action yet possible to rescue Joan and her children.

Among other things, outspoken dissent to certain state church doctrines and usages will be far less prominent with John Rogers behind the bars. Popular opinion appears to have proven unfavorable to continued persecution on religious grounds, ever since John, Jr., went "up and down the colony" selling that little book. The case regarding Joan has been a fortunate happening for Governor Saltonstall and his friends.

Although, by the sentence, the trial for contempt was to be before the Superior Court at New Haven in October, we find it taking place at a session of this court in New London, September 25, in the meeting-house.[112]

John Rogers asks to be tried by a jury, choosing the one then sitting, but Judge Saltonstall denies him trial by jury,—John Rogers has too many friends in these parts. There must be no means of escape for the opponent he has so often bled before, and would fain bleed to the death. He pronounces judgment in a fine of £20 and costs of prosecution, and a bond of £100 "for good behavior" until the March session of the same court, with imprisonment at prisoner's expense,—unless he give surety for the bond, which Gurdon Saltonstall well knows he will not do, thereby to acknowledge that he has been "misbehaving" himself. All this is (by the court record) because John Rogers "falsely and slanderously declared in court that the sentence of said court against himself and John Jackson was 'rebellion against her Majesty.'"

They examine the deeds to find suitable land to take in execution for this fine of £20, and discovering such land, by Upper Alewife Cove, that was sold to "John Rogers," they proceed to claim it for the Colony of Connecticut. John, Jr., in vain assures them that he himself bought this land, with his own money, and it is also in vain that he presents the original deed, in the copying of which, upon the town records, the clerk omitted the word Jr. Nor will his father's after affirmation in court that he himself made out this deed, and wrote the Jr. therein, secure its release. Moreover, as John Rogers himself declares (Part I., Chapter VI.), they kept the original deed presented in proof, and, after John, Jr., had paid them their price for the redemption of this land, viz., £20—as proven by court record—they took this very land again for another fine of £20.[113] Here are indications of the bitterest venom on the part of those in power, at this period, yet no complaint on the records regarding "servile labor, etc.," or baptisms, or "blasphemy," or any other nonconformity.

By these signs it may be judged that never was the influence of John Rogers more feared than at this very period, yet never also were the authorities more cautious regarding complaints and actions against him on avowedly ecclesiastical grounds.

CHAPTER VIII.

1711.

We left John Rogers on his way back to prison, there to remain until the March term of the Superior Court, because he would not promise "good behavior" ("as if I had misbehaved myself." Part I., Chapter V.).

Against tyranny in high places, there is ever at hand the one highest appeal, that to the public at large, where is always in reserve a good measure of sympathy and sense of justice. Not only is our hero stirred through and through by this personal and ecclesiastical thrust, under guise of righteous administration of law, on the part of an official who has for so many years occupied the position of a reverend preacher of the gospel of Jesus Christ; but he knows well of this last appeal, which has heretofore stood him in good stead against the bitter edicts of these half—if not wholly—ecclesiastical courts. Though as yet there are no newspapers, there are eyes to see, ears to hear, and tongues to carry fast and far.

What recks this Samson of their paltry "goal"? Somehow, without show of physical force (the least sign of which would surely have been entered on the court record), he makes the sheriff quail. The lightning in his eyes, perchance, the deep tones of a voice that never breathes an oath, even to swear by in a court; uttering ominous words to some such effect as that he "will seal his quarrel with his blood." Should he attempt escape from the sheriff his death could be accomplished, then and there.

The sheriff returns to the court-room (meeting-house) and reports to the court that John Rogers is conducting himself in a "furious" manner, "threatening that the jail shall not hold him and that he will seal his quarrel with his blood"; the sheriff "fears he will break out of jail and do mischief to some of her Majesty's subjects." What subject but himself, through punishment which can be inflicted upon him for breaking away from an officer, which is a capital crime on the law book.

The quickly forthcoming order of the court (Judge Saltonstall) that John Rogers shall be placed in irons at need, "for preventing mischief," is but the beginning of the plot now in contemplation.

By further order of the judge and governor (one and the same) John Rogers is to be conducted from the ordinary prison to the "inner" prison.[114] The latter is not yet finished, and is half a mile from the house of the jailer. It has as yet no underpinning, but stands above the ground on blocks. The green planks of which the floor was made are much shrunken, leaving large cracks for the entrance of the wind, and there is "an open window towards the northwest." There is no fireplace, nor any means for making a fire; moreover, by the orders, no fire is to be allowed this prisoner.[114] It is October and unusually cold and stormy for this time of year.

How does John Rogers, Jr., manage to communicate with his father in this place? He must scale the high fence surrounding the prison yard, to make his way to the "open window" of the prison, whose grates will not admit the passage of any fuel, even if a place could be found within in which to make a fire. This son comes, under cover of the darkness, to give such aid and comfort as he may, and especially in the cold nights, which indicates that he contrives to furnish some slight means of warmth.

Until November 16 of this unusually inclement season, John Rogers, at the age of sixty-three, is a solitary prisoner in this inner prison, with such apology for a fire as his son can provide, by coming two miles after dark to the prison window.

Governor Saltonstall, sitting beside his beaming hearth, already furnished with its huge back-log, gives no pitiful thought to the man whom he has denied an honest trial, and now forbids so much as a fire to keep him from death's door.

On the bitter cold night of November 16, John, Jr., coming the long two miles over the rough Mohegan road, and making his way, by scaling the prison fence, to the grated, open window, finds his father incapable of the usual intelligent response. Over the fence again he hurries, and out into the streets of the sleeping town, calling loudly at the sheriff's house: "You have murdered my father in prison to-night!!!" "The Authority has murdered my father!!!" (County Court Record.) Not only are the sheriff, his instigators and their sympathizers aroused by this loud and ringing cry of alarm in the dead of night, but also some of the many who are friendly to the prisoner. These latter spring with alacrity from their beds, at the news that John Rogers is dead, or dying, on this wild night, in the distant and fireless inner prison, through which the bitter winds are whistling.

Mr. Adams, the minister, a man of a kind heart, despite ecclesiastical fidelity, cannot turn a deaf ear to this report concerning the imprisoned dissenter. He and his wife show their humanity by sending a bottle of wine and a bottle of cordial to the sufferer. At the popular demand, the captive, almost senseless with cold and the malady resulting therefrom, is conveyed to the warm house of the sheriff,[115] where he at length revives.

John Rogers, Jr., is brought before the County Court in New London a fortnight later, on charge of making a disturbance in the night, and fined £3. He is granted a review at the court to be held in June, and required to give bonds for "good behavior," until his trial before the said court shall occur. Refusing to acknowledge, by giving the required bond, that he has done anything wrong, he is consigned to jail until session of the June court.

At this same November court, we find several other cases relating to this history. Samuel Beebe again demands of Capt. James Rogers the land made over to himself by the irregular "deed" of the widow. He and John Keeney and wife (formerly wife of Jonathan Rogers) make claim to all the "moveables" by the same document. These cases go against the plaintiffs. Samuel Beebe appeals to the Superior Court.

At this court, also, James, Jr., makes another effort for poor Joan. The case having already been settled on one presentment, he bases his complaint upon different grounds. He says that, in the preceding June, Samuel Beebe brought a suit against John and Bathsheba, previous administrators, for possession of Joan, on plea that she was given to Elizabeth Beebe by the widow as part payment of the legacy of £10; but that for Samuel Beebe to make claim of John and Bathsheba at that date—he himself being at said date executor of the estate in place of John Rogers—or for John and Bathsheba to appear on a court summons to answer such complaint of Samuel Beebe was irregular procedure. He states that, at the time Samuel Beebe declares this disposal of Joan by the widow to have been made, the latter was incapable of managing any business, or even of taking care of herself, and was under the guardianship of John and Bathsheba, according to the intent of the testator; also, by order of the court, they were her guardians and the managers of the estate; so that she had no right to dispose of Joan, neither had any possession of her at the time. He avers that by John and Bathsheba illegally joining a false issue with Samuel Beebe, in not reminding the court that they were no longer executors,[116] Joan had been adjudged to Samuel Beebe and taken by execution. He demands Joan with damages. It is a good case, but of course it fails. The court is not willing to reverse its former decision. James, Jr., appeals to the Superior Court. But it will be useless to ask the judge of that court to alter a decision by means of which he has been able to incarcerate his opponent. (The case is not brought before the Superior Court, but apparently dropped as a useless endeavor.)

Late in this month of November, occurs the death of Bathsheba (Rogers) Fox.[117] She has been heroically faithful to the departure instituted in 1674, only, at the last, to see this beloved brother again in the iron clutches of ecclesiastical hatred, he who would have been among the first to hasten to her bedside. How bitter to him, in those last days of his devoted sister, must have been the cruel bonds that held him at a distance, while she went down to death.

1712.

Under date of March 7th of this year, we find a deed of gift[118] of some land (adjoining Mamacock farm) from John, Sr., to John, Jr., with the statement therein that this gift is to make up to his son for the land that had been taken from the latter for a fine of £20 imposed upon himself (Part I., Chapter V.), also for a choice cow and a considerable number of sheep that had been taken from his son to satisfy like claims against himself. He states that this gift is also to stand as a testimony of his appreciation of the fact that this son who "was taken from me in his infancy, upon the account of my differing in judgment, and ordered by the Authority to be brought up in their principles, incensing him against me his own father, and thus kept from me till he came to a young man's estate; yet, notwithstanding, last winter now past, hath been an instrument in the hands of God, to preserve my life in an unfinished prison, with an open window facing towards the northwest, I being fined and imprisoned by two several courts without any trial of law by a jury."

It will be remembered that John Rogers is still in prison, awaiting the sitting of the March session of the Superior Court in New London. This now opens, March 25, at the meeting-house.

At the opening of the court, the sheriff announces that he has kept John Rogers safely until now and has him still in custody. The court orders the sheriff to set said prisoner at large.

Samuel Beebe fails to follow up his claim on land of Capt. James at this court, but renews the suit regarding alleged gifts of the widow to his wife, viz., "moveables," including certain young slaves belonging to the estate of James Rogers. He enters suit, by his attorney, Colonel Livingston, against Samuel Fox (husband of Bathsheba) for two negroes with £5 damages, and against John Rogers, Jr., for three negroes; all five being free negroes in employ of said persons. The verdict goes against him. John Keeney and wife also lose a similar suit for similar alleged gifts on the part of the widow

On this same day, James Rogers, Jr., having presented his accounts, etc., to the Probate Court, as executor, said court orders distribution to be made of the residue of the estate (movables), according to regular form of law when a person dies intestate; a double portion to Samuel, as oldest son, the remainder to be equally divided between the other children. This gives James Rogers one-eighth of the movables, instead of the much larger share accorded by the codicil. Evidently self-interest had no part in the move made by James, Jr. Now comes the part of Samuel Rogers in this final issue. He states to the court, "in writing," that he has already, and before his mother's decease, received, by the terms of agreement among the heirs, according to his father's will, all that was due[119] to him from his father's estate, to his full satisfaction, and absolutely quits claim to anything further. Joshua Hempstead is ordered to make distribution.

(N.B. There has now been placed before the reader the sum and substance of all the litigation in regard to the estate of James Rogers, upon which Miss Caulkins founded her statement regarding "contention" among his children.)

The very next day,[120] March 26 (by Superior Court record), while the court is still in session, John Rogers is taking a convert to the Mill Cove for baptism. In doing so, he passes near the house of the sheriff, where he has so recently been a prisoner. Accompanying him are a number of his Society, among them John Bolles, John Rogers, Jr., and James Smith, son of Bathsheba. Time and again, since that notable day in 1677, has John Rogers baptized persons in this Mill Cove, directly under the windows of Governor Saltonstall, so to speak, whose house stands near by on a hillside rising from the cove. Certain lands bordering this cove remain in Rogerene ownership.

If the sheriff and his chief have judged that the heroic treatment of the past eleven months has cooled the ardor of the dissenters, here is unmistakable proof to the contrary. If the sheriff can nip this bold little act in the bud, formally or informally, he may be sure of the governor's co-operation and hearty commendation. On plea of wishing to speak with John Rogers, he persuades him to enter his house (which, as before said, contains the prison). He then endeavors to force him to enter a door leading into the prison. The friends of John Rogers, who have followed him into the house, Upon seeing the latter purpose on the part of the sheriff, surround their leader, to prevent hands being laid upon him, and others in the tavern join them in declaring that no arrest can legally be made without a warrant. The sheriff leaves, with the avowed purpose of going to the court-room (meeting-house) for a "mittimus." Here, within this brief period of time, are two outrages upon the law; first, an attempt to take a prisoner without a warrant; second, to seek warrant for an arrest not authorized by law; the only penalty concerning such baptism being a fine after the occurrence of said baptism; imprisonment following only in event of non-payment of the fine. Well may the victim turn and follow the sheriff to the court-room.

The sheriff, being somewhat ahead, has already made out a case, so far as the judge is concerned; nothing more having been necessary than to state the attempted baptism. Taking into account all that he has suffered of late from unjust and despotic procedures on the part of the courts, John Rogers enters the court-room (meeting-house) fully prepared to denounce this latest outrage. [121]

Vain against the power and determination of Governor Saltonstall are the ringing tones in which this departure from the written law of the land is condemned. But well has John Rogers calculated that, in the presence of all these witnesses, the judge will not venture to issue the illegal warrant for his arrest. The judge goes on, however, to sign a warrant ("mittimus"). Although he dare not arrest John Rogers because of the attempted baptism, he has now a better excuse and more personal determination also; since John Rogers has dared to enter the court-room to again publicly denounce official procedures. He signs a warrant for the arrest of John Rogers, on the charge of MADNESS!

Well might all the proceedings of the past year, capped by this, make mad the sanest man, in both senses of the word. The sheriff claims his prisoner and leads him from the court-room.

A crowd follows sheriff and prisoner to the jail. An uproar ensues when the window of the prison is darkened by a plank, and that same plank is broken down by the mob. The appeal of John Rogers, in the court-room, for the rights of the citizen, has not been made in vain. All praise to that English lieutenant, who goes to the Superior Court, still in session, to ask for an adequate examination of this prisoner, that it may be seen he is under no distraction. The assurance is returned that the prisoner shall be brought before the governor in the evening (when danger from the mob may be avoided) *for a private examination regarding his sanity, by the very man who has invented this charge of lunacy*! Of the absurdity of the promised examination, the lieutenant probably knows little or nothing; but others understand. This evening interview will make the friends of the governor laugh in their sleeves, while friends of John Rogers discern a new insult and injury, under this so transparent cloak of fairness.

Even after dark, the prisoner's convoy to the house of the governor is beset with indignant sympathizers, who follow into the very yard of the governor, where, after the prisoner's entrance to the house, they have to be dispersed.

These two men, under these circumstances, stand face to face, behind closed doors, the one knowing as well as the other that the only fault or distraction of which John Rogers is guilty is the old crime of nonconformity. (Would that this remarkable scene and conversation had been revealed for the benefit of future history.)

After this "examination," the prisoner is returned to the sheriff, to be taken to his "house." With such friendly demonstrations among the people, John Rogers cannot be confined as a common malefactor or madman, in the prison at said "house"; he is even allowed the freedom of the yard during the sheriff's continued attendance upon the court, which is sufficiently significant of the known falsity of the charge of insanity.

Two days after, the sheriff is instructed that, after adjournment of the court, he is to convey John Rogers to the Hartford prison and see that he is shut up in a dark room, where a certain French doctor will "shave his head and give him purges," to cure him of his madness. Such treatment, added to all the memories of past wrongs, would seem enough to give the sanest man the temporary appearance of a maniac. The more he can be made to appear like a maniac, the more plausible will be the excuse for consigning him to a worse than prison cell.

Had it remained for Gurdon Saltonstall to carry out this inhuman purpose, the statement that John Rogers died in Hartford prison, or in a madhouse, would probably have ended this man's history.

Some person, to whom the sheriff confided the inhuman plot, being friendly to the prisoner, John Rogers is informed of the doom prepared for him. He goes directly to the sheriff, to inquire into the truth of the statement, and asks to see the warrant for this new procedure, which the sheriff shows him. He there recognizes the handwriting of Gurdon Saltonstall.

Few men could be readier in resources than the man in custody. A person is quickly found to carry word, this very (Saturday) evening, to John Rogers, Jr., at Mamacock, of the impending peril. The hurried message quite suffices. With all possible speed, before the night is far advanced, John, Jr., is at hand, with a staunch boat, near by, well manned, to convey his father to Long Island. He has also money for his use, and, finding him in need of a suitable shirt, takes off his own and gives him. The boat was easily moored not far from the prison, which is by the Mill Cove, and also not far from the Thames River, into which the cove leads.

This boat, propelled by hands well skilled, pulls out from shore, in cover of the night, and goes to brave the winds and waves of March across Long Island Sound. John, Jr., returns to Mamacock, with thrilling tale of this, so far, successful rescue. Many a follower besides John Bolles anxiously awaits the tidings. Eagerly, no doubt, they gather in the big front room at the Mamacock "mansion house," to talk the matter over and speculate regarding the result, noting the weather betimes and praying for a bon voyage.

Before dawn, John Rogers is landed at Southold, and makes his way to the tavern. It will be seen how much he conducts himself either like a malefactor or a madman. While it is still early morning, he presents himself before a justice, to inform him of his escape from the New London sheriff, and the circumstances of the case. A guard is placed over him until the next day (Monday), when he is taken before the justices and the law is read to him stating it to be felony to break out of a constable's hands. In return, he places before them a copy of the warrant issued by Governor Saltonstall for his arrest on the ground of insanity. The intelligent, self-possessed appearance of the man, as opposed to this singular declaration of lunacy, occasions these officials no little perplexity. They withdraw for a private conference. All agreeing that he is a sane man, they discharge him from custody. He now informs them of his intention of appealing to the Governor of New York for protection, and asks them to stop, if possible, the "Hue and Cry" that will be sent after him, which they kindly promise to do. The remainder of this story is best told in his own words (Part I., Chapter V.).

In June of this year, while the refugee is still in New York, a session of the County Court is being held in New London. The case of John Rogers, Jr., for the disturbance at night (November 16, 1711), by which he saved the life of his father, now comes up for review. He desires to be tried by jury; but the present jury is dismissed and a special jury impaneled for this case. The fine of £3 and costs of the previous court is made to stand good against him, and three of the best cows on Mamacock farm are taken for this fine (see Chapter IV., last part). Although he was sentenced to imprisonment until this court for not giving the required bonds, we have seen him free at the time of his father's escape to Long Island. The bonds were doubtless given by a friend, as frequently happens with the Rogerenes.

At this June court, John Rogers, Jr., John Bolles, and James Smith (son of Bathsheba) are complained of for preventing the sheriff from arresting and imprisoning John Rogers on March 26. The charge is that these persons "opposed, resisted and abused" the sheriff "by threatening words, pushing, hunching, and laying hands on John Rogers," as said sheriff and the constable were apprehending him. A jury having been demanded and by good fortune accorded, a verdict of "not guilty" is rendered, and they are discharged. This shows the method of defence used by the Rogerenes on this occasion. They surrounded their leader, forming a human wall about him, and kept this position in spite of the efforts of sheriff and constable to lay hands upon him.

Although no reply is returned to the message which the authorities of New York have sent to the authorities at New London, in behalf of John Rogers, this proof of friendliness on the part of New York dignitaries towards the refugee from Connecticut, and their evident knowledge that this refugee had been imprisoned on false pretences, has so salutary an effect, that when, after a stay of three months in New York, the nonconformist boldly returns to New London, no attempt is made at reimprisonment.

This indomitable man immediately makes a move to prosecute the judge and justices of the County Court who, in June of the preceding year, not only tried in New London a case of "man-stealing," pretended to have been committed within the jurisdiction of Long Island, but tried a case of this serious nature—even capital upon the law book—without a jury. He must be well aware that such protest on his part is not only likely to be very expensive but wholly ineffectual. Back of this judge and these justices, stands Governor Saltonstall; moreover, any blame attaching to them would attach equally to the governor from having so signally punished the man who had declared against the illegal proceedings of the court at the time. Yet he makes the appeal manfully. Those who have heard the previous circumstances will hear also of the vain effort for justice, and this itself may help to weaken the despotic rule of an ecclesiastical clique.

1713.

In May of this year, at the session of the General Court, the judge and justices of the County Court appear, to answer to the above charges; John Rogers having, by repeated efforts, secured this much of attention. (See his account, Part I., Chapter V.) The defendants stand mainly upon objections regarding time and form of the Petition, on the part of the plaintiff. They say there was nothing in John Roger's petition that showed any appearance of maladministration, and that, had there been any ground for his complaint, it did not come within the time limited by law. This shifting from the main ground to technical points, with denial of any importance to be attached to the significant charges (lack of jury and wrong jurisdiction), call for legal knowledge and adroit argument regarding minor points of the law, by way of evading the question of vital importance. In short, the case is, by legal device, taken away from the plaintiff at the start. As a show of justice, the court offers the plaintiff legal counsel; not to decide whether this case should have been tried where, and as, it was tried, but mainly whether the plaintiff's petition was within the time specified by law. Every difficulty possible had been placed in his way to retard the case, doubtless with this very end in view. The plaintiff refuses to make any reply, since he can reply to nothing but legal evasions. It being proven to the satisfaction of this court that John Rogers has nothing to complain of, he is ordered to pay the expenses of the judge and justices for their attendance on the court.

This man has ever in such cases a last resort, to be used at whatever peril. Then and there, before this assembly, he again charges the County Court held in New London, with "felony, rapine and injustice," and moreover declares the daring truth that the Governor of this Colony, here present, is an abettor of the same. The court, having considered his offense and high misdemeanor, resolve that he shall pay a fine of £20 to the public treasury, and execution upon his property is to be granted by the Secretary.

In November of this year, Capt. James Rogers passes away. To the last, he has been a busy man on land and sea. July 1st he returned from one of his voyages to the Barbadoes ("Hempstead Diary"). He owned and operated a tannery and cooper's establishment at Goshen. He left a large estate, and followed his father's example in desiring his children to settle the same out of court. This settlement proceeded in a perfectly orderly and harmonious manner. Despite the fact that his sons, James and Richard, had become connected with the Congregational church, he and his wife evidently continued in their nonconformist faith, as particularly proven by the remonstrance of 1695.[122]

In December of this year, occurs the death of Samuel Rogers in his 73d year. Although this evidently superior man, by his distaste for controversy and public proceedings, as well as by his busy life in developing the new lands of Mohegan (whereby his name is written all over the early books of New London land records), has succeeded in hiding himself largely from the view of future generations; yet when compelled to present himself to such view, he has always been found acting the manly part. Throughout the early period of persecution, he was plainly in sympathy with his father and brothers, and proofs of continued sympathy with the Rogerene cause are evident to the last. He kept quietly but firmly aloof from the church that persecuted his relatives, despite counter-influences in his own family. For some twenty years of his early manhood, he conducted the bakery business on the former large scale and handed it to his son unimpaired. Besides the enterprises of his pioneer life, he was a shipowner and business man at large. Although possessed of great wealth for his time, he so managed to distribute his property in his lifetime that little more than cattle and movables remained to be disposed of after his death, which personal estate was left to his wife Joanna, the executrix. In his will is the following clause: "one cow and six sheep to be delivered unto John Rogers, son of brother John Rogers, to be disposed of as I have ordered him." Also the executrix is to act with the advice of above said John Rogers and Samuel Fox, "oldest son of my brother Samuel Fox" (husband of Bathsheba). At the writing of this will, February 13, 1713, the testator states that he is in "perfect health."

1714.

Mary, the second wife of John Rogers, was, a number of years since, married to Robert Jones of Block Island.[123] It is now fifteen years since John Rogers took her for his wife and twelve years since their enforced separation. He has recently become attached to an estimable widow, by the name of Sarah Cole, of Oyster Bay, L.I., a member of the Quaker Society of that locality. Although favorable to his suit, she is yet inclined to hesitate, on account of rumors that have been circulated in regard to his separation from Mary. In his prompt, straightforward way, he desires her to accompany him to Block Island, to learn from Mary herself if she has anything to say against him. This request is so reassuring, that the publication of their marriage intentions takes place at New London, July 4, 1714 ("Hempstead Diary"), after which they visit Mary at her home on Block Island. Mary gives Mrs. Cole so favorable an account of John Rogers and the treatment she herself received from him, that the ceremony is performed by Justice Wright before they leave the island.

[There is evidence, from the court records and testimony of Peter Pratt,[124] that this wife, Sarah, was of attractive personality, also that she was a zealous religious co-worker with her husband, and that they lived happily together at Mamacock, with John, Jr., and his family and the two children of Mary.]

CHAPTER IX.

1716.

One of the spasmodic attempts to secure more strict enforcement of ecclesiastical laws is instituted about this period. Edicts have been issued by the General Court charging the various officials to observe greater stringency in the execution of all these laws. That this sudden and severe pull on the rein does not occasion a general and continued uprising on the part of the Rogerenes, is only explainable on the supposition that the first attempt to lay hands on them anew having brought forth the countermove, the authorities have thought best to desist from further serious molestation. The particulars of this countermove are as follows:—

April 22, 1716, there is an entry into the Congregational meetinghouse by John Rogers and his wife Sarah, John Bolles and his wife Sarah, John Culver and his wife Sarah, and several others, names not given. The cause of the disturbance is, as usual in affairs of this kind, studiously ignored on the court records; but evidently—as afterwards indicated—this entry, with scriptural testimony not revealed, was occasioned by the breaking up of Rogerene meetings by the town authorities, with the accompanying feature, a church-party mob. As has been seen, the Rogerene meetings, not being among those allowed by law, can at any time be broken up at the pleasure or caprice of the authorities, and their continued existence has depended, not upon the willing forbearance of the ecclesiastical rulers, nor, to any really saving extent, upon the public sympathy enlisted in their favor; but chiefly upon that formidable reserve power—the entrance into the meeting-house, with scriptural testimony.

Proof of the exact date of this countermove and that the before-mentioned persons were concerned in it, is contained in the "Hempstead Diary" and a record of the General Court in the following month (May). By the latter record, Governor Saltonstall, referring in this assembly to the offense committed by the said persons, states that they are now in New London jail. [125] The governor also states that he learns, from "relatives" of the prisoners, that they were ignorant of the provisions, under the law of 1708 (see Chapter VII.), relating to those who soberly dissent. Probably said relatives have been far more ignorant of this law than have any of the Rogerenes, who are naturally watching all ecclesiastical regulations with lynx-like vigilance and are particularly aware that there is no relief for their Society in this law, as allowed in the Colony of Connecticut. The governor knows just what the Rogerenes know in this regard. But he goes on to order that the said prisoners be released—ostensibly on the ground of this ignorance declared by their friends—and says, in case they behave themselves orderly and rest contented with the liberty of worship given them under said law, they shall not be prosecuted.

All this on the part of the governor doubtless sounds very plausible and very indulgent, to the uninitiated. He is evidently very glad of some excuse to release the prisoners. So much of a hornet's nest has been aroused, about this time, that not even the disturbance of the Congregational meeting, less than two weeks before, is considered sufficient ground for detaining them longer in prison or imposing any more serious fine than payment of their prison fees.

By the joint testimony of Peter Pratt and John Rogers, 2d, it is shown that the governor distinctly stated before the Assembly at this time that the Rogerenes should be allowed to worship God according to their consciences, if they would refrain from disturbing Congregational worship, and that he would punish any who should disturb their worship.[126] Here is something tangible, as opposed to the ambiguity of the court record; it not only indicates that the April countermove was a direct result of interference with Rogerene meetings, but that said countermove had been productive of a decisive advantage. In short, interference with their meetings had caused the countermove, the countermove had forced the governor to himself promise them immunity from further interference of this sort, on condition that they would not exercise their reserve power.

1719.

Three years have now passed, with no record of any disturbance of the Congregational meetings, and of nothing, in fact, to show how matters are progressing that concern Rogerene history, unless it be the total lack of court notice. It is at least a season of patient endurance and forbearance on the part of the Rogerenes, so far as the ordinary distrainments are concerned. About this time, there is talk of a proposed rebuilding, or enlargement, of the Congregational meeting-house, which will occasion a new levy on the Rogerenes, with the usual wholesale seizure of property. But something more serious than this now occurs, the exact nature of which is hidden from our view. The disturbing move is made by the town authorities, under some one of the Sunday laws, and the victim is Sarah, wife of John Bolles, her infringement of this Sunday law being "a matter of conscience" on her part.

It must be borne in mind that under the ecclesiastical laws, to whose unscriptural character it is the mission of this sect to bear testimony at all hazards, punishments far beyond the letter of said laws are frequently being inflicted upon the Rogerenes. The following from John Bolles throws light upon this subject:—

When a poor man hath had but one milch cow for his family's support, it hath been taken away; or when he hath had only a small beast to kill for his family, it hath been taken from him, to answer a fine for going to a meeting of his own Society, or to defray the charges of a cruel whipping for going to such a meeting, or things of this nature. Yea, twelve or fourteen pounds worth of estate hath been taken to defray the charges of one such cruel whipping, without making any return as the law directs. Yea, fourscore and odd sheep have been taken from a man, being all his flock; a team taken from the plow, with all its furniture and led away. But I am not now giving a particular account, for it would contain a book of a large volume to relate all that hath been taken from us, and as unreasonable and boundless as these; besides the cruelties inflicted on our bodies and many long imprisonments….

Here we see something of those things which never appear upon the court records and of whose "boundless"ness we only now and then catch a glimpse, by some side-light like this or by a Rogerene entrance into the meeting-house, the latter effect always pointing to some unbearable wrong as its cause. To continue with this statement of John Bolles:—

"and many long imprisonments, of which I shall mention one woman, when she was condemned by a judge in a case of conscience; because she stopped her ears and would not hearken to his sentence, as not belonging to him to judge in such cases, but with a cheerful spirit sang praises to God, and then turned to the judge and said that if he went on persecuting God's people God's judgments would come upon him and his."

There are among the Rogerenes many sweet singers, who sing hymns and psalms in certain meetings of their Society. It appears (by aid of above statement) that Sarah, wife of John Bolles, is one of these; for, by a Superior Court record of September 22, 1719, it is shown that Sarah Bolles is summoned from prison before that court

"to answer for reflecting upon the proceedings of a court held in New London,[127] in saying to one of the judges thereof, viz.: Rich. Christophers, Esq.: Now look to yourself for God's judgments will surely come upon you, for your unjust judgments for persecuting God's people—Said Sarah, being asked whether she was guilty or not guilty of the crime for which she was committed, refused to make any plea. Whereupon said Sarah Bolles shall suffer two month's imprisonment" (in addition to the four already endured) "and pay the charges of her prosecution and stand committed till the said charge be paid, viz.: £1 19*s*."

So this heroic woman, who has ten children at home, five of whom are under ten years of age, is returned to prison, not only for the two months, but until she pay the charges of her prosecution, which the court, as well as her own people, have good reason to believe she will never pay, thus to encourage the authorities in their unchristian persecution of the Rogerenes. John Bolles goes on to say, regarding this woman, whose name he does notreveal:—

Whereupon said judge condemned her to prison, where after further determination, [viz.: above Superior Court sentence] she was required to remain till she should pay the charge of her prosecution, so called, and there continued six months, till God made way by moving the hearts of the people with compassion for her deliverence, by seeing her affliction; she being not only locked up in prison but also a high boarded fence round the prison, locked also,[128] and the prison keeper living near half a mile from the prison, it being an extreme cold winter, and in the height of it she miscarried, being without any help nor could call for any, her husband living about a mile and a half from the prison and was not suffered to come to her; as if God suffered such things to be done to lay conviction before all faces. But after her release she was carried home on her bed in a cart and after some time she was, thro' God's goodness, restored to health again.

About two weeks previous to this appearance of Sarah Bolles before the Superior Court, there occurred a Rogerene countermove which is directly traceable to her imprisonment. This countermove took place September 6, after Sarah had been nearly four months in prison. It must have been known to the Rogerenes, and to the authorities as well, that she was with child, which, together with the fact that the youngest of the ten children needing her at home is but two years of age,[129] made this long imprisonment in "a matter of conscience," with the impending appearance before the Superior Court on charge of contempt, especially aggravating. The circumstances called for some imperative action on the part of her friends, the more so, because no mercy could be expected from the judge of the Superior Court.

The persons accused of entering the meeting-house on this 6th of September, are John Rogers and his wife, Sarah, wife of John Culver, John Bolles, John Rogers, Jr., Andrew Davis and Esther Culver. The records relative to this countermove are in the minutes of the November session of the County Court in New London. First, that on September 6, while Mr. Adams was at public prayer, John Rogers, Sr., entered the meeting-house and interrupted the service in a loud voice.[130] (No slightest clew is given to the words spoken.) He pleads "not guilty" and is fined £20 and charges, £3. The record states that, upon this (November) trial, he "behaved himself contemptuously, coming into court in a violent manner and raving voice, saying, 'What have you to say to me, etc.' (would we might have the words in place of the 'etc.') and when the indictment (not revealed) was read, he cried out That's a ly, and upon that part of the indictment (part not revealed) when read he again cried out, 'That's a devilish ly,' and by abusing one of the members of the court in saying to him, upon said Justice's affirmation, several times that's a ly, and for several other abusive demeanors" in the court-room (unfortunately not described), he is sentenced to pay 20*s.*—he who so often for no more contempt than this has been fined £20. (Moreover, as late as May 25, of the following year, it is on record that "execution" for this 20*s.* was "returned with nothing acted upon it." In this insignificant fine is visible the sympathy of a jury, and in the lack of "execution" the fact that no collector is willing to collect this fine, although he may be himself fined for the omission.) The record continues:—"John Rogers demands a present appeal to the King's bench." "Court consider that no such appeal lies."

Sarah, wife of John Rogers, is also presented at this November court for having come into the meeting-house, on the same occasion (September 6), and "interrupted Mr. Adams by speaking several words in a loud voice." The court having considered the evidence in this case and that said Sarah has "behaved herself competently well before the court and also pleading ignorance of the laws and methods of this government, and considering her also under covert and that she has been committed to prison until this court," sentence her to pay a fine of 10*s.* and prison fees, £3. Sarah, wife of John Culver, for same offense on same occasion, same fine and fee. John Bolles "for breach of Sabbath" on same day (form of breach not stated), same fine and charge as the women. Andrew Davis, Esther Culver and John Rogers, Jr., same charge and fines as John Bolles.

For the two months previous to this November court, John Rogers and his wife, Sarah Culver, John Bolles and the others have been confined in prison. All these people know, at the date of this November court, that Sarah Bolles has not only lost her child, but is lying at the point of death in the "inner prison." Well might the leader of the Society in whose cause she has so suffered and endured, when he at length escaped from prison and had an opportunity to speak in public, employ such scathing words as befitted the occasion.

(From this court scene as described by Peter Pratt,—see Chapter XIV.,—are derived the statements that John Rogers and his followers were accustomed to accuse dignitaries of lying.)

After all the verdicts in this case have been rendered, Sarah, wife of John Culver, knowing so much more of this season of persecution and the legal (and illegal) proceedings than is possible to outsiders, indignantly exclaims in court: "You are an adulterous generation and I hope God will find you out" (by Court Record), for which the court sentences her to receive fifteen stripes on the naked body and to pay charges for the same.

Nor is this the end of the matter. Sarah Bolles, despite all protest, still lies at the point of death in the cold and dismal "inner prison." What can yet be done by this non-resistant people? They may not, by their principles, even waylay the jailer, seize his keys, hold him for a time in durance, and so rescue Sarah Bolles. But, upheld by the public sympathy now enlisted, they can head a resolved company of men and women, break down the gate of the prison fence, and, aided by the Rogerenes within the jail, force open the prison doors and bring out the helpless captive. This is exactly what takes place.

Before this same November court is at an end, complaint is made to said court by the keeper of the prison, that "John Culver, John Culver, Jr., Bathsheba, wife of John Rogers, Jr., and Mary Rogers, daughter of John Rogers, Sr., did, on the 26th and 27th of this Nov." (viz., at midnight) "stave down part of the prison yard." A significant ending of this record is that for this misdemeanor John Culver and his son are to pay only 10*s.* and charges, and Bathsheba and Mary to pay only the charges of their prosecution, also that John Rogers and the others still in prison are not brought before this court at all. All this shows the extent of public sympathy at the time, especially in regard to those concerned in the September countermove.

The court record does not inform us that Sarah Bolles was rescued from the prison by this raid and carried home in a cart; neither does it inform us that the company headed by the persons tried for this daring deed contained others besides Rogerenes, whose approbation was enlisted by the danger of a second murder being committed in that prison, through cruel neglect. Only by the public sympathy exhibited on this occasion can the facts be accounted for that no action is taken by the court regarding the escaped prisoner and no record of her escape made.

John Rogers had been returned to prison on account of non-payment of the £23, for disturbance of meeting. John, Jr., John Bolles and the others were in prison also for non-payment of smaller fines, for the same offense. Thus the attack from outside the prison lacked the usual leadership; yet that these prisoners were concerned in the rescue, from a position within the prison, is shown by a record of the General Court of November 30, to the effect that, at a special meeting of the Governor and Council, of that date, "it is ordered that the fines and penalties incurred by John Rogers etc." ("etc." doubtless including the others tried with John Rogers for the September countermove) "on account of recent tumultuous and riotous proceedings of which said prisoners have been guilty, be applied—upon collection of same—to the extraordinary charge which they have occasioned the county by said proceedings." This "charge" evidently refers to repairs of the prison which was broken into three days before in behalf of Sarah Bolles. Why the Culvers and Mary and Bathsheba were brought before the County Court (where they were so lightly fined) and "John Rogers, Sr. etc." dealt with by a special court can only be conjectured. It is not unlikely that this raid upon the jail resulted also in the rescue of Sarah Culver from the stripes. The fact that her husband and son acted with the women indicates such a possibility.

As has been seen, the arrest of Sarah Bolles was for some so-called "breach of Sabbath."[131] Certainly she could not have been ploughing or carting. Had she been spinning at the door of her home, or had she ventured to walk some distance over the Norwich road to visit one of her friends? In either case, this would be no more than she had been doing ever since 1707; yet either of these acts would have furnished legal ground for her arrest. The only way to account for the proceedings against her is by supposition of another of the spasmodic attempts to intimidate and repress Rogerene leadership. That Sarah Bolles deserves the name of a leader in this Society is evident.

One of the most serious grievances of the Rogerenes, since they began to hold their services on Sunday, is that, although the Congregationalists are allowed to go long distances to Congregational meetings, the Rogerenes are arrested for travelling any considerable distance to meetings of their own persuasion. From the fact that they hold their meetings in private houses, such services are sometimes at one house and sometimes at another, and, as they are widely scattered (outside the nucleus at Quaker Hill), some of the members are always liable to travel some distance.

On Sunday, December 13, two weeks after the November trial just described, a young Rogerene, by the name of John Waterhouse, has the audacity to appear at the door of the Congregational meeting-house, and, "standing within the ground sill, in sermon time," to exclaim: "I am come to enter complaint that I am stopped on the King's highway."[132] He has availed himself of the one efficient mode of defense, the Rogerene countermove.

1720.

The proof of this courageous stand of John Waterhouse, while the leading Rogerenes are in prison, is from records of the County Court, June, 1720. By these records it is also shown that some three months after the above offense (and apparently while out on bail, pending trial in June) this same young man "blew a horn or shell near the meeting-house, while the congregation were singing," and, refusing to give bond for appearance at the County Court in

June, "with good behavior in meantime," is arrested and imprisoned.

At this same June court, the offender is brought from prison, and being charged with the first offense, of December 13, refuses to reply to the question "guilty or not guilty."[133] The court now proceeds to give judgment, "on a nihil dicit," of £20 fine, with charges of prosecution, and if he do not immediately pay or give surety he "shall be let out," until the same is paid. The same judgment, upon a nihil dicit, is pronounced in regard to the blowing of the horn, viz.: fine of £20, which if not paid he is to be let out, etc.

Yet this very act of blowing a horn on Sunday near a meeting-house, in time of service, is among the offenses enumerated upon the law book as finable by only 40*s*., which is all the young man had reason to expect. Here are more than £40 for this young man to pay, or go to common servitude for a long period.

Nor is this all that is charged against John Waterhouse at this June court. He is examined on suspicion of being concerned in a most astonishing performance, in the month previous (May 4), viz.: the "opening and carrying away of the doors of the prison" to which the clarion blast had consigned him, and in which he had been confined something over a month. At date of this June court, said doors have "not yet been found." It is also stated that, during this imprisonment, he had made his escape from the prison several times—and, of course, he had escaped again at the time of the opening of the doors. He pleads "not guilty" regarding the doors, probably, as do other Rogerenes in such cases, admitting no guilt in doing that which they consider right, however contrary it may be to the law. Fortunately for the romance, he does not satisfy the court that he had no hand in said damage and disappearance. The jailer is to recover from him the value of the prison doors "as they were, with the locks on them," which is £5. With charge of prosecution and another fine of £20 for this offense, added to his previous fines, more than £70 are required of this young man at this June court. £70 represents a snug little fortune (at this date), enough to buy a good farm "with mansion house thereon." This is the more preparing him for life-long opposition to ecclesiastical government, an opposition which is to be transmitted undiminished to his descendants. (For this young man is to be the founder of the Quakertown community, that "remnant" which, in the words of Rev. Abel McEwen, "exists in a neighboring town.")

Since John Waterhouse is to be so potent a factor in Rogerene history, let us scrutinize him as closely as the scanty glimpses permit. Is he not some young scapegrace, allied to the Rogerenes for love of their so venturesome and exciting life? So he might be judged, but for the preamble of one old deed of gift on the New London records, despite the fact that he is a son of Jacob

Waterhouse and grandson of Mr. Robert Douglass,[134] two of the most substantial citizens of New London and members of the Congregational church. Jacob Waterhouse, in 1717, singled out this son John to receive, by deed of gift, the family homestead, "my father's habitation,[135] near the mill bridge," as well as a valuable tract of land at "Foxen's Hill" on the river; not because he was his oldest son, but "for love and appreciation of his dutiful behavior." It is, then, the dutiful son of a wealthy and honorable citizen of New London who was arraigned as above at the June court in 1720. Surely it would not be wise to omit visiting upon this renegade youth dire punishment for his bold espousal of Rogerene faith and Rogerene methods, lest other promising young men of the Congregational fold should dare to venture upon a like career.

But we are not yet through with this interesting June court. John Bolles is here arraigned, on a like suspicion of being concerned in opening and carrying away those prison doors "that have not yet been found." For declining, at the time of their disappearance, "to give any reply to inquiries made of him concerning that matter" he has been imprisoned until now. He now pleads "not guilty," which of itself might mean that he acknowledges no guilt in the matter; but his wife is present to testify that he was at home upon the night of this romantic occurrence, also Esther Waterhouse,[136] "who lodged at John Bolle's that night," testifies to the same effect; upon which John Bolles is to be discharged, on payment of costs of prosecution and prison fees. One can but marvel that John Bolles did not in the first place avail himself of this so convenient testimony, and thus escape imprisonment and expense. Also, why were not those noted prison breakers, John Rogers, Sr. and Jr., arraigned, on suspicion of complicity in this matter? Had they no hand in this achievement, or were their tracks so well covered that no slightest clew could be discovered by the authorities? Did John Bolles, knowing he had evidence to clear himself at sitting of the June court, allow himself to be imprisoned on this suspicion, in order to draw attention from the true culprits?

Sometime in this year is printed, in Boston, "The Book of the Revelation of Jesus Christ," by John Rogers, Sr.[137]

CHAPTER X.

1721.

1721. *Feb. 26, Sunday.*—The Quakers at Meeting made a great disturbance; especially Sarah Bolles.—*Hempstead Diary.*

Mr. Hempstead, in his usual brief style of chronicle, gives no further light upon this matter. By the records of the County Court, in the following June, it is shown that the Quakers referred to in the Diary were John Bolles, his wife Sarah and John Waterhouse, and that the impelling reason for this countermove was because John Waterhouse had been seized and maltreated for baptizing Joseph Bolles, eldest son of John and Sarah, now twenty years of age, who, on entering upon a religious life, had, with the approval of his father and mother and the rest of the Society to which his whole family belonged, selected this young leader to baptize him.

Had any Rogerene been selected to perform this baptism other than the "dutiful" son who had recently left the Congregational church to join the nonconformists, it is probable there would have been no such unusual interference; since such baptisms have been constantly taking place for years, and there is no record of any other disturbance of this character.

Extensive improvements have now been completed in the Congregational meeting-house, almost equivalent to a rebuilding of that edifice. From the Rogerenes has been taken the usual unreasonable amount of property on this account; in the case of John Rogers, three of his best fat cattle together with shoes that, sold cheap at an "outcry," brought 30*s*. It seems high time, after so many years of exorbitant tribute to a ministry of which these people have no approbation, that some more effectual effort should be made than the simple refusal to pay such taxes, which has practically greatly increased their loss, by leaving them utterly at the mercy of the collectors.

A plan is now devised to fit this emergency, yet one much less aggressive than the ordinary countermove and indicative of a spirit of compromise on the part of the Rogerenes, despite the fact that one of their recent baptisms has been so seriously interfered with and their friends concerned therein are to be tried at the next sitting of the County Court. A representative number of them will appear at noontime in the meeting-house, which they have been forced to assist in rebuilding, and endeavor to hold a meeting of their own between the regular services. Undoubtedly, they expect to be prevented from entering the church at all; but the appeal for their rights in the premises will be made none the less evident and eloquent by such prevention. If they do succeed in entering, the familiar riot will ensue, occasioned by putting them out in a violent manner, carrying them to prison, etc. In that case, they will be fined "for making a riot," and tried and sentenced for the same; but their cause will be all the better advertised, at home and abroad.

April 23, 1721, Sacrament Day.—John Rogers came into the meeting-house and preached between meetings, his crew with him.—*Hempstead Diary.*

By this, it is shown that the first attempt at this new style of countermove was on the above day, and, by the absence of any court record regarding this occurrence, it further appears that, either because it was "sacrament day," or because the governor was out of town, or from both causes, no resistance was made to this noon entry or to the preaching by John Rogers that followed, each of the Rogerenes occupying his or her own seat as set off in the meeting-house.

Upon the next Sunday, they appear in like manner,[138] just as the Congregational service is breaking up. As Mr. Adams and the others come out, they politely state their purpose of holding another meeting of their own between the Congregational services. No objection being made, they enter and take their places in the seats assigned them. The governor is surely at hand on this occasion, and none can be more expectant of dire consequences to the offenders than are the heroic band themselves. But even Governor Saltonstall cannot well proceed without the issue of a warrant, which he must hasten to procure. In these critical circumstances, the dauntless leader proceeds to expound certain Scriptures to his little audience of twelve Rogerenes, with, doubtless, some curious spectators also.

A constable soon appears upon the scene, and the excitable and riotous portion of the church party are now at liberty to make an uproar and assist in the seizure and abuse. John Bolles is carried out and to jail by the arms and legs, face downward. His wife Sarah and one of the Rogerene men, Josiah Gates, hasten to the house of the governor, near by, where they remind him of his public promise (Chapter IX.) not to break up their meetings provided they do not disturb the Congregational church services, and Mrs. Bolles begs that her husband may not be thus abused.

Considering the towering rage of the governor over this strategic move on the part of the nonconformists, and the plea of the petitioners regarding non-disturbance of Congregational services, the box on the ear which Josiah Gates receives from the hand of the governor and the summary turning of the two petitioners out of doors is a natural sequence.

The next day, the governor binds John Rogers and John Bolles over to the

June court.

By the records of the County Court in June, we find John Rogers and John Bolles called to answer "for unlawful and riotous entrance into the meeting-house on April 30, with other persons to the number of twelve." They plead "not guilty" (viz.: to any riotous entering or to any guilt in entering). The court finds both guilty; John Bolles is to pay a fine of £5, and cost of prosecution £3. John Rogers, having taken the precaution to demand trial by jury, is to pay a fine of only 10*s.*, and cost of prosecution £1 18*s.*, which gives us the popular verdict in the case. Yet for this fine the sheriff took ten sheep and a milch cow. In this way, the executives got the better of a sympathetic jury.

At this June court, John Bolles and his wife are arraigned for having disturbed the congregation "in February last" (upon occasion of the Congregational interference with the baptism of their son Joseph by John Waterhouse). The court, "having heard what each has to offer and the evidence against them, adjudge each to pay a fine of £20 and costs of prosecution £1."

As for John Waterhouse, he is first tried for having disturbed the Congregational meeting (after the church interference with said baptism, February 26) and is to pay same fine and charges as John Bolles and wife for this offense. Accordingly the cost of Joseph's baptism reaches £65. No wonder that Joseph Bolles is to become a leader among the Rogerenes and eventually prominent in a great countermove that is to shake the Congregational church of New London.

John Waterhouse is also tried for "assuming a pretended administration of the ordinance of baptism to one Joseph Bolles of New London" and "that in time thereof he made use of these words: 'I baptize thee into the name of the Lord Jesus Christ.'" "The matter of fact against him being fully proven" and "he having been imprisoned" (apparently until the sitting of this court), he is now sentenced to be whipped ten stripes on the naked body for having performed this baptism.

It is well for the Rogerene Society that so courageous and talented a man as John Waterhouse has given himself to the Christian service in this contest for religious liberty. The days of their great leader are now numbered, although he is still, at seventy-three years of age, in full health and vigor, despite his fifteen years of imprisonment during the last forty-six years, and many other trials and sufferings induced by merciless punishments.

Prominent among the noticeable facts in this man's history is his faithful Christian ministry, a ministry copied closely from New Testament precept and example. Here is a pastor who in obedience to the command to visit the sick has been ever ready to hasten fearlessly to the bedsides of victims of the most dreaded contagion, to render aid temporal or spiritual; although not himself an immune, unless God so decree. He could be called upon in any circumstance of misfortune, wherever a friend was needed, to serve, to comfort, or advise He has assisted the poor from the earnings of his own hands. He has visited the widows and the fatherless and those in prison. He has been at all the charges of his own ministry, by the fruits of his own industry. Since it has been claimed by him and his followers, on Scriptural authority, that faith and prayer are more efficacious in the healing of the sick than are the advice and prescriptions of earthly physicians, how often for this purpose must his prayers have been required.

A few months later than the events narrated in previous portions of this chapter, occurs the great smallpox pestilence in Boston. At this time, John Rogers is having published in that city his book entitled "A Midnight Cry," and also his "Answer to R. Wadsworth." If he has need to go to Boston, on business connected with these publications, it is certain, by the character of the man, that he will not hesitate, but rather hasten, that he may, in the general panic there, render some assistance. Even if he has no business occasion for such a visit, it will not matter, provided he judges the Master's command to visit the sick calls him to Boston. Since his conversion in 1674, he has made a practice of visiting those afflicted with this contagion so shunned by others, yet has never been attacked by the disease. He believes the promise that God will preserve His faithful children to the full age of threescore years and ten unless called to offer up their lives in martyrdom, and that when, at last, in His good pleasure, He shall call them, it matters not by what disease or what accident He takes them hence. Surely death could come in no better way than in some especial obedience to His command.[139]

If after an immunity of more than forty years, not only to himself but to his household, he takes cheery leave of family and friends, ere mounting his horse for the long journey, it is no wonder, nor if they take a like cheerful view of his departure. The Lord may bring him safely back, as so often before, even though his seventieth year is past. Yet—it may be that this call of the Master is to prove his faithfulness unto death.

His horse stands saddled by the roadside, with portmanteau packed for a brave and kindly stay, God willing, with the suffering and the forsaken. He is ready even to his jackboots, and his faithful watch tells him it is time for the start.[140] We look for no tremor here, even when he speaks the last farewell, but for the cheery word, the tender glance, the fervent grasp of the hand, the committal to God of those he holds dearest on earth, the agile spring to the saddle, and a still erect and manly figure vanishing at the turn of the road. It is not unlikely that a cavalcade of brethren accompany him some miles on his way.

On and on, from the health-giving breezes of Mamacock, towards the plague-stricken city. Once there,—would we might follow him in his ministrations, even to that day when he remounts his horse for the homeward journey. Has the contagion so abated by the middle of October that he is no longer needed, or can he indeed be aware that he himself is attacked by the disease? Would it be possible for a man, after he had become sensible that the malady was upon him, to take the journey on horseback from Boston to New London? All that is known for a certainty is that after he reaches home the disease has developed. It seems probable that he was permitted to complete his mission in Boston and to leave there unconscious of the insidious attack awaiting him. Why was he stricken down at the close of this faithful effort to obey the command of the Master in the face of scorn and peril? One important result is to ensue. The unfaltering trust of the Rogerenes in an all-powerful and all-loving God is to be shown remaining as firm as though John Rogers had returned to them unscathed, and this unswerving trust in God's promises, under circumstances calculated to shake such a trust to the uttermost, is to be attested over and over by the records of Connecticut.

Fast and far is spread the alarm that John Rogers, just returned from his foolhardy visit to Boston, is prostrated at Mamacock with the dread contagion. There are in the house, including himself, thirteen persons. Adding the servants who live in separate houses on the place, it is easy to swell the number to "upwards of twenty." The large farm, spreading upon both sides of the road, is itself a place of isolation. On the east is a broad river, separating it from the uninhabited Groton bank. On the north is wooded, uninhabited, Scotch Cap.[141] There is possibly a dwelling within half a mile at the northwest. A half-mile to the south is the house of John Bolles. What few other neighbors there may be, are well removed, and there are dwellings enough on the farm to shelter all not required for nursing the sick. To what degree the family might take the usual precautions, if left to themselves, or how efficacious might be their scriptural methods, can never be known; since the authorities take the matter in hand at the start.

Had this illness occurred in the very heart of a crowded city, greater alarm or more stringent measures could not have ensued. There is a special meeting of Governor and Council at New Haven, October 14, on receipt of the news that John Rogers is ill at Mamacock with the smallpox, and that "on account of the size of the family, upwards of twenty persons, and the great danger of many persons going thither and other managements" (doubtless referring to scriptural methods of restoration and precaution) "there is great liability of the spread of the infection in that neighborhood." It is enacted that "effectual care be taken to prevent any intercourse between members of the family and other persons, also that three or four persons be impressed to care for the sick."

There are a number of meetings of the Governor and Council over this matter (for full accounts of which see the published records of the General Court of Connecticut). Were it not for the court records, coming generations would be at loss to know whether the members of the family themselves, also John Bolles, John Waterhouse, John Culver and their wives, and others of the Rogerenes held firmly to their principles in this crisis, or whether they stood willingly and fearfully aloof, not daring to put their faith and theory to so dangerous and unpopular a test. Fortunately for Rogerene history, the testimony furnished by records of the special sittings of the Governor and Council on this occasion, fully establishes not only the fidelity of the Rogerenes to New Testament teachings, but also their attachment and loyalty to their leader.

Three days after the official order that every relative and friend be banished from his bedside, and so with no one near him but the immunes pressed into the service, John Rogers yields up his life unto Him whom he has faithfully striven to obey, fearing not what man or any earthly chance might do to him. Thus dies John, the beloved and trusted son of James Rogers, and the last of that family.

John Rogers departed this life October 17th, the anniversary day of his marriage to Elizabeth Griswold. She cannot fail to note that fact, when the news reaches her. She is less than woman if, in the hour of that discovery, she does not go aside to weep.

The day after this death, at another special meeting of Governor and Council, it is enacted that "constant watch be kept about the house, to seize and imprison all persons who may attempt to hold any intercourse with the quarantined family." Little do those who have been forced to take charge at Mamacock and to punish all friendly "intruders about the premises" appreciate the deep sorrow and sympathy of these long-time neighbors and friends, who desire to hear the particulars, to show respect for the departed and to render aid to the family. Rudely rebuked, no doubt, are the most reasonable efforts on the part of these friends, to prove their love and fellowship in grief, although as yet no one else has the contagion and all thoughts are centred on this one great bereavement.

When shortly Bathsheba, wife of John Rogers (now 2d) and their eldest son, John, are stricken, the dark shadows deepen over Mamacock, and friends of the family would fain show some sign of fearless fidelity, not only to those afflicted, but to the teachings of the New Testament and the Old, in regard to the power and good will of God to hold even the direst pestilence in His hand. Much of the endeavor on the part of these friends appears to be to provide the family with such necessaries for their comfort as have not yet been supplied by the authorities.

John Waterhouse and John Culver come over from Groton to secure news regarding the sick and bring something likely to be needed in the quarantine. The slightest attempt at such friendly aid excites indignation and terror on the part of the authorities.

At one of the special meetings of Governor and Council (October 31)

"action is taken regarding the fact that several of the followers of John Rogers have, contrary to express orders to the contrary, presumed to go into the company of some that live in the Rogers house, and further express orders are issued to these obdurate persons, particularly John Culver and wife, John Waterhouse and wife of Groton, Josiah Gates and wife of Colchester and John Bolles and wife."

That friends of the family have endeavored to supply them with necessaries, on account of very tardy red tape regarding such provision by the authorities, is strongly suggested by an order accompanying the above, commencing: "Whereas it appears that a meeting of the selectmen is necessary in order to their taking care of the sick family," it is hereby ordered "that notice shall be given the selectmen to meet and consider what is fit to be done for such as are confined in said families." Yet it is not until the next special meeting, over three weeks later (November 24), that it is ordered that two suitable persons shall be constantly in attendance "to lodge at the house of Jonas Hamilton or John Bolles" and "by relieving each other, watch and ward night and day to understand the state of the sick there and give information of what is needed." After this order, although other meetings are held by the Governor and Council on the same account, there is no mention of any further endeavors on the part of friends of the family to hold communication with them.

Two more of the family die of the disease, Bathsheba, wife of John Rogers, 2d, and John, their son. When all is over, John Rogers, 2d, is called upon to pay the expenses of official nurses, guards, provisions and medicines, a large bill, on which he is allowed no reduction.

John Rogers having died intestate, his son John is appointed administrator. The only heirs allowed by the court are the widow, John Rogers, 2d, and Elizabeth Prentice, "only son" and "only daughter," among whom the estate is divided by due course of law. When this form is ended, John Rogers, 2d, ignoring the fact that he, as only son under the law, has "a double portion," and Gershom and Mary, the two children by Mary, are awarded nothing of this estate, pays to each of these a liberal sum out of his own portion for "share in" their "father's estate" (as is still to be seen on the town records). Well may Mary, if living, forgive this honorable man for some things that displeased her in the past. He claims her children as his father's before the world; he claims them as brother and sister of his own. He afterwards buys of them land at Mamacock, which was given them by their father, Gershom's land "having a house thereon."

To the ecclesiastic view, John Rogers has fallen, as to that view he has lived, a fanatic, striving for such an impracticable end as to resurrect the first Christian era into the seventeenth and eighteenth centuries. But the friends and followers of this leader are sure that a Christian hero has passed from their midst, in no ignoble way.

Here was a man who, had he chosen to fight worldly battles, in forum or in field, might well have made a mark that all men had acknowledged; but who, for the truth that is in the Gospel of Jesus Christ, elected to lead through life a forlorn hope, humanly speaking, as of one against a thousand or a score against a host. It matters not that he but voiced the sentiments of a large number of his own day (and a multitude of ours); it is a silent minority, that dare not even to applaud a man who speaks their views, while the popular leadership and power are on the other side.

Mamacock farm has been much enlarged since, by that name; it was the old Blinman farm, and as such given to Elizabeth Griswold; it has taken in lands to the north, south and west (across the Norwich road). In a southeast corner of its present (1721) boundaries, close by the river bank, are three graves that mark the earthly loss to family and friends of that fearless visit to Boston. The sentiments of the Rogerenes who view those mounds are: "The Lord hath given and the Lord hath taken away, blessed be the name of the Lord." They gather closer to fill this great vacancy in their ranks and press on under the same banner. If John Rogers, 2d, be not the next leader-in-chief (as perchance he is) that banner will never falter in his hands. John Waterhouse, as a preacher of rare eloquence and power, wears the mantle well. John Bolles is in the prime of life, being but forty-four years of age at the time of the death of his chief. He will labor in this cause for many a year to come, with ready voice and pen. Under his training and that of his wife Sarah, a bevy of bright and energetic boys are growing up strong in the faith, to join hands with the sons of John Rogers, 2d. Young Joseph Bolles is soon to come to the front. Shortly another elder and preacher rises, in the person of Andrew Davis. Here are enough to hold the present band together and labor for its enlargement.

The authorities cannot take much encouragement, after the fall of the great leader. He has builded for time to come.

In 1722 is passed an act directing dissenters to qualify under the law of 1708, and such persons as neglect the public worship of God in some lawful congregation, and form themselves into separate companies in private houses, are to forfeit the sum of 40*s*. A fine of £10 and a whipping to any person not a minister who shall dare to administer the sacraments.

However this may be aimed at the Rogerenes, it evidently does not reach them. If the authorities should endeavor to strictly enforce this law in New London, there would undoubtedly be court records in plenty regarding countermoves, and an overflowing prison, as will be seen during a later attempt (1764-6) to enforce arbitrary laws of this kind. For more than forty years previous to 1722 the Rogerenes have ignored similar laws, and will continue the same course to the end.

CHAPTER XI.
YEARS OF TRUCE.

For some years after the death of John Rogers, no serious interference with the customs of the Rogerenes is recorded. The countermoves directly preceding that death should, by all precedents, be sufficient to secure them from molestation for a considerable time to come.

September, 1724, occurs the sudden death of Governor Saltonstall, by apoplexy. His family continue to reside in New London and to form an important part of the leading membership of the Congregational church.

Under the ministry of Mr. Saltonstall the half-way covenant was in full force,[142] and under his administration as governor this policy was applied to the colony at large.

For forty years after the death of Governor Saltonstall, nothing regarding the Rogerenes appears on the records of either of the three courts. Yet there is abundant evidence that these people are steadfastly continuing in the faith and practices of their sect, holding their own meetings, in New London, Groton and elsewhere, preaching their purely scriptural doctrines, and publishing books in defense of their principles. Although not presented before the County Court in this period, they are (as shown by the writings of John Rogers, 2d, and John Bolles) frequently disturbed by the town magistrates, who deal with them "at their own discretion." That entrance into the meeting-house was a last resort is shown by its extreme infrequency as compared with the more or less constant and severe aggravations to which they are subjected. The only evidence of virulent measures in this period is the pitiless scourging inflicted by Norwich authorities (1725) upon the Sunday party on their way to Lebanon. (See Part I., Chapter I.) The officers and others concerned in this proceeding appear to have been members of the Norwich church, from which, as has been seen, were wont to issue pursuers of the Rogerenes.[143]

The following from the "Hempstead Diary" shows an imprisonment of one or more Rogerenes at this period, and, in consequence, a Rogerene attendance in Congregational church. The speaking appears to have been so timid as not to disturb the services.

1725. *Sunday, Oct. 31.*—Walter and John Waterus spake aloud att ye Same Instant and said you Blaspheme the name of Christ or to that effect. Jno. Rogers and Bolles and his wife sd Nothing till meeting was over and yn complained much of the french barber striking over one of their crew at the prison and brot the stick wch he sd he Struck him with.

The offenses for which the Rogerenes are most liable to magisterial punishment at this time appear to be travelling upon Sunday, when they have occasion to attend a distant meeting, and performing sufficient observable labor upon that day to assure their opponents that they continue to deny its sanctity; although they take a suitable portion of it for religious services. From them are regularly collected fines for not training. These fines being demanded by Cæsar (the purely civil government) are probably paid without protest.[144] The church rates they never pay, no matter how many fold more than the amount due is collected by execution on their property, and still, as heretofore, they never appeal to the court on account of the surplus retained.

A considerable number of Rogerenes are located in the northeastern part of Groton, among whom John Waterhouse and John Culver are leaders. This is a sparsely populated district, where the nonconformists are less exposed to such molestation and extortions as assail those of New London. These Groton Rogerenes have Baptists for their nearest neighbors, a sect agreeing with them in certain particulars, but equally with the ruling order holding to the observance of a "holy Sabbath." It is certain that the Groton Rogerenes have, sooner or later, some grievance against these Baptists, evidently in connection with the question of Sunday sanctity.

In 1728, John Bolles issues his "Application to the General Court of Connecticut," "in all the honor and submissive obedience that God requires me to show to you,"—in which he states that he discovers in the "Confession of Faith" which this court has established, "principles that seem not to be proven by the Scriptures there quoted," and that he has drawn up some objections thereto which he desires to be considered and "reply to be returned," also that he has "taken a journey for no other end but to deliver these objections to one of the elders in each county in the colony." As he afterwards expresses it, "they disregarded my request." In this pamphlet he mentions various instances of cruel persecution to which he and his friends have been subjected, and ends with these words:—

But we, on our parts, have had the witness of a good conscience towards God in all our sufferings and loss of all these things, and do make it our care to live inoffensively towards all men, except in the case of Daniel, Chap. 6, Verse 5.[145] And whether this be not oppressing and afflicting them that have no power to help themselves for conscience's sake,[146] let God be judge. Pray peruse what is above written, and let it have a due sense upon your minds; and so act and do in all the particulars above mentioned, as you may have confidence and boldness to hold up your heads before the great and terrible and righteous judge of all the earth, when He shall come with his mighty angels in flaming fire, taking vengeance on them that know not God and obey not the Gospel of our Lord Jesus Christ.

That the religious standard of some of the principal members of the Congregational church has not advanced since the time of Governor Saltonstall is indicated by the following, from the "Hempstead Diary":—

1734. *Sunday, Sept. 29.* The late Gov. Saltonstall's Pew stove down the Door and 2 Pannels, it seems to be the effects of a Contention between the two Brothers wives which of ye females shall have the upper hand.[147]

It is not surprising that an aristocracy so autocratic as to contend with near relatives for supremacy of this kind should be bitterly antagonistic to the Rogerenes, who not only shun worldly position for themselves but refuse to be subject to its rule in all matters pertaining to the Christian religion. Youth of the Congregational church, who are to grow up under influences of the above description, are destined, thirty years from this date, to be church members themselves and to take part with their elders, as advocates of a "holy Sabbath," in a movement against the Rogerenes which is to result in the great countermove of 1764-66, and the retaliatory measures adopted in that contest.

We find in the "Hempstead Diary":—"July 17, 1743, Hannah Plumb,[148] a young woman, was baptized in ye river at ye town beach by Samuel son of John Rogers." This not only shows Samuel Rogers (son of John, 2d) to be a leading Rogerene, but is one of the proofs that some of the Plumb family, the elder members of which are prominent in the town and Congregational church, are of Rogerene persuasion; also that the Rogerenes have got beyond the Mill Cove for baptisms

About 1735, John Culver and wife, with their sons and families, together with other Rogerenes of Groton, emigrated to New Jersey, where they founded a Rogerene settlement. (The cause of this removal is unknown. The theory that it was to escape persecution is weakened, not only by proof that the Culvers had proven themselves of heroic mould in this struggle, but by the fact that there was a cessation of virulent persecution at this time.) In the course of a few years, they are found, with quite a following, at Waretown[149] (in the southern part of what is now Ocean County), holding their meetings in a schoolhouse. A man by the name of Weair, the founder of Waretown, is one of their Society; an enterprising business man, who is described as a most worthy Christian.[150]

The location of this little Rogerene community is about one hundred and forty miles from Ephrata, Pa., where is a Society of Dunkers, among whom are certain brethren who dwell apart from the secular portion of the community, in a cloister. This Society observe the seventh day as a Sabbath, and hold closely to New Testament teaching and example, not discarding healing by faith and prayer and the anointing with oil. The brethren of the cloister appear to believe in direct enlightenment being accorded to such as lead devout lives. They have acquired the name and fame of "holy men." John Culver has visited these brethren of the cloister, and a mutual friendship and interest have resulted.

In 1744, a number of these Ephrata brethren, being on a pilgrimage in the vicinity of the New Jersey Rogerenes, pay them a visit. The reputation of these "holy men," in regard to healing by prayer, and also the fidelity of the Rogerenes to this scriptural mode, is shown by the fact, recorded by the Pilgrims, that the New Jersey Rogerenes brought their sick to them, in the hope that they might be restored to health.[151]

The Culvers urge the Pilgrims to visit the Rogerenes of New London, and with such effect that the brethren embark for Connecticut. They land at Blackpoint, where they are received by a Rogerene of that vicinity, who later escorts them to Bolles Hill, where they make their headquarters at the house of John Bolles. They speak, in their journal, of the Rogerenes as leading "a quiet life apart," in the country, and state that they had with them a "most peaceful visit." From the country they are escorted into the town, where they are entertained at the house of Ebenezer Bolles (son of John), whom they describe in their journal as "a blessed virtuous man." They advise him not to marry, not knowing that he is engaged to Mary, the seventeen-year-old daughter of John Rogers, 2d, and has made his house ready for the bride who is very shortly to occupy it.

Notwithstanding the fact that the town, by description of the tourists, is in a state of agitation and excitement, on account of rumors of war with Spain and the religious differences and public disputes occasioned by the presence and preaching of the New Light evangelists, the citizens vie with the Rogerenes in kindly and interested attentions to the strangers, who speak highly of the hospitality of the people and describe New London as "a fruitful garden of God." When the day for their departure arrives, the Rogerenes provide passage for them to New York, to which "gifts" of some kind are added, by reason of which the Pilgrims state that they took away with them more than they brought. There is mention of these strangers in the "Hempstead Diary," under date of October 10, 1744, where they are described as men with beards eight or nine inches long, without hats and dressed in white. By their own description, a crowd followed them in New London wherever they went.

No mention is made by the Pilgrims of any unpleasantness between the Rogerenes and their neighbors, unless the "quiet life apart" of the former can be thus construed. That the Rogerenes sympathize with the New Lights to a considerable degree is more than probable; yet they seem to go their own way, undisturbed and unexcited by the surrounding ferment.[152]

New ecclesiastical laws have recently been enacted, largely on account of the advent of the New Lights, and old laws are to be more strictly enforced. The rulers are tightening the reins, and the Rogerenes with other nonconformists are likely to receive a cut of the lash. In 1745, Joshua Hempstead writes in his Diary:—

Sunday, June 16.—John Rogers and Bolles and Waterus and Adrw Daviss and about 20 more of their Gang, came Down into Town with a cart and oxen and were taken up by the officers and Committed to Prison, also 4 Women of their Company Came to ye Meetinghouse and began to preach and were taken away to Prison also.

No clew is given to the cause of this move. A phalanx of Rogerenes passing, on Sunday, slowly along the principal street of the town in a cart drawn by oxen, each one of these non-combatants calmly and cheerfully prepared to pay for their spectacular move by seizure, imprisonment and fines, is fully as comical as it is tragic. Though some of the spectators are in a rage, others must be overcome with laughter, while sympathizers too politic to laugh outright smile in their sleeves. The after-appearance, at or in the neighborhood of the meeting-house, of four Rogerene women, fluent in Gospel "testimony" regarding the unchristian proceedings of the "authority," is a fitting climax to this non-resistant menace.

No wonder that for nine years to come the entries in the "Hempstead Diary" will contain no hint of any collision with the Rogerenes.

The generally tolerant spirit towards the Rogerenes during the last twenty years is largely to be attributed to the conciliatory character of the Rev. Mr. Adams, who, although he may not have felt himself in a position to oppose the autocratic policy of Governor Saltonstall, appears never to have instigated any attack upon the nonconformists or taken an observable part in any such move. Nor, on the other hand, do we find indication of any hard feeling towards this minister on the part of the Rogerenes.

Who, it may be asked, are the Rogerenes of this period? Foremost among the leaders on the New London side are John Rogers, 2d, and John Bolles. There is a considerable following of families and individuals in the town and vicinity, in no way allied to these by relationship. The region about Mamacock and districts farther north have, within the century, become largely occupied by families from Rhode Island, who, being of Quaker and Baptist sympathies, are well fitted for affiliation with the Rogerenes. It is not unlikely that many of them have been attracted hither by that sect. Among these are descendants of some who, having been persecuted by the ruling church of Massachusetts, had retreated to Rhode Island for security. Such would be nothing loath to aid in the bold stand so well instituted in Connecticut. There are Rogerenes in Groton, Montville, Colchester, Lebanon and Saybrook.[153]

How many more converts are at this date "scattered throughout New England" none could tell so well as John Bolles, who has travelled extensively over the country selling Rogerene books and expounding Rogerene doctrines. But the solid nucleus of this Society is in the neighborhood of Mamacock and just north of there, where the John Rogers and John Bolles families and their neighboring followers are as a phalanx. They are, in the main, a people of broad acres and ample means, industrious and energetic; their young women are sought in marriage by promising youth of other denominations, and their young men, evidently with full parental consent, improve opportunities to take wives from some of the best families in New London of wholly different persuasions from their own. James, son of John Rogers, 2d, a young Rogerene of great business ability, marries a daughter of Mr. Joseph Harris, and permits his wife to have her child baptized in the Congregational church,[154] of which she is a member. Evidently, the New London Rogerenes agree with St. Paul in this regard. 1 Cor. vii, 14. About 1740, Capt. Benjamin Greene, of Rhode Island—a younger brother of Gov. William Greene—established a home farm near Mamacock, at the point called "Scotch Cap." He is not only a shipmaster but the owner of several vessels and their cargoes. His brother, the governor, is a frequent visitor at Scotch Cap. The wife of Captain Greene is of the Angell family of Rhode Island. Delight, daughter of Capt. Benjamin Greene, marries John, son of John Rogers, 2d. The Greenes are of both Quaker and Baptist sympathies. Samuel Rogers, son of John, 2d, marries a daughter of Stephen Gardner, from Rhode Island, whose family are of Quaker origin. The other marriageable son of this date weds a daughter of Mr. John Savol (or Saville), a prominent member of the Congregational church, afterwards of Norwich. One daughter of John Rogers, 2d, marries a son of John Bolles; another marries a young man of Groton whose father is an enterprising business man from Rhode Island; the other four daughters marry sons of members of the Congregational church (New London and elsewhere), of high standing and ample means.

The sons of John Bolles have not all taken wives from among the Rogerenes, but are less allied to those of Congregational persuasion; outside of their own sect they have most favored Baptist women. The second wife of John Rogers, 2d, appears not to have been a Rogerene before marriage, and the same may be said of the second wife of John Bolles. If such facts are true of the chief leaders and their children, we may easily judge of the alliances of their followers with persons of other denominations, in this comparatively quiet interval.

The above particulars are important as showing the social status of the leading New London Rogerenes in the middle of the eighteenth century, and proving that, although holding strictly to their own opinions and customs, they are not only accounted honorable and esteemed members of the community, but are so liberally inclined as to be in a large degree connected with liberal members of other sects. John Rogers, 2d, has said: "I abhor the abusing of any sect."—*Answer to Peter Pratt.* It appears likely that he also abhors the isolation of any sect, believing men and women can differ on certain religious points, and yet be friends and even partners for life.

This ready association of the New London Rogerenes with friendly people of other denominations, is but one of many evidences that the chief contention of these people has not been regarding minor matters of church government and customs, nor even so much in regard to baptism and hireling ministers; but that the great struggle, from first to last, has been for religious liberty; in asserting which liberty they must oppose those who institute, enforce or uphold laws inimical to free expression of religious belief, or individual liberty in the form of worship. Having the high ground of apostolic doctrines and usages upon which to found a strong opposition to ecclesiastical tyranny, they have fought the good fight upon that sacred foundation.

The indications are strong that by the middle of the eighteenth century there is not so much friction between the Rogerenes and the authorities in regard to the gathering of rates for the Congregational ministry, but that the old, exorbitant methods of seizure have declined to less grievous proportions. Nor does there appear to be serious interference with Sunday labor or travelling, which argues that the Rogerenes are not driven, by close watch and frequent arrests, to any extraordinary demonstrations of their disapproval of governmental meddling in matters of conscience. It appears to be the policy at this period to let them alone on these sensitive points, in consequence of which toleration they do not consider it necessary to make their differences of belief so distinctly prominent. Evidently, a large measure of the freedom for which this sect has contended is already accorded; certain ecclesiastical laws, not yet erased from the statute book, are becoming, in the neighborhood of the Rogerenes at least, of the dead letter order, which is the case with many other laws still upon that book.

In June, 1753, occurs the death of John Rogers, 2d, in his eightieth year. He has made a long and heroic stand, since at the age of seventeen years he joined his father in this contest. To him is largely due the size and strength of a sect that has called for the bravest of the brave—and found them.

Fifteen children gather at Mamacock, to follow the remains of this honored and beloved father to the grave, eight sons and seven daughters, of the average age of thirty-four years, the eldest (son) being fifty-two and the youngest (son) fourteen years of age. Besides these, with their families, and the widow in her prime, is the large gathering of Bolleses and other friends and followers in the locality, also those of Groton and doubtless many from other places.

They lay the form of this patriarch beside his father, his wife Bathsheba and the children gone before, in the ground he has set apart, in the southeast corner of his farm, as a perpetual burial place for his descendants, close by the beautiful river that washes Mamacock. They mark his grave, like the others in this new ground, by two rough stones, from nature's wealth of granite in this locality, whose only tracery shall be the lichen's mossy green or tender mould.[155]

John Rogers, 2d, was a man of remarkable thrift and enterprise as well as of high moral and religious character.[156] His inventory is the largest of his time in New London and vicinity, and double that of many accounted rich, consisting mainly of a number of valuable farms on both sides of the Norwich road, including the enlarged Mamacock farm, the central part of which (Mamacock proper), his home farm, is shown by the inventory to be under a high state of cultivation and richly stocked with horses, cattle and sheep. His children had received liberal gifts from him in his lifetime.

Four of the eight sons of John Rogers, 2d, are now in the prime of life, and not only landed proprietors but men of excellent business ability. John, the youngest of the four, now in his thirtieth year, is appointed administrator of his father's estate and guardian of his two minor brothers. James, the eldest, is a very enterprising business man. That his coopering establishment is a large plant is shown by the fact that he is, immediately after the death of his father, the richest man in New London, his estate being nearly equal to that left by his father.[157] The preamble of his will proved in 1754, shows him to have been a Christian of no ordinary stamp. Thus soon, after the death of John Rogers, 2d, this worthy and capable son, who must have been a man of large influence in the Society, is removed. For some time previous to his death, he occupied, as a home farm, the southern third of the enlarged Mamacock[158]—which fell to him later by his father's will—upon which was a "mansion house" said to have been built of materials brought from Europe. His brother Samuel has inherited the northern third of the enlarged Mamacock, upon which he resided for some time previous to the death of his father. His brother John has inherited the central part, or Mamacock proper, which his father reserved for his own use.

All the sons of John Rogers have been well educated; John has marked literary talent; his brother Alexander appears to be a schoolmaster of uncommon ability, although farmer and shoemaker as well.[159]

The eight sons of John Bolles are among the wealthiest and most enterprising citizens of New London; several own valuable lands in the very heart of the town, as well as farms outside; they are business men as well as farmers. Ebenezer Bolles is one of the richest merchants in New London. The moral character of these sons of John Rogers and John Bolles is without reproach. They are professing Christians of the most evangelical stamp. Their sisters are wives of thrifty and upright men.

These people and their adherents are not only a strong business element in this community, but they are a strong moral and religious element. If the present policy of non-enforcement in regard to this sect of the ecclesiastical laws which they are bound to resist should be continued, there is every reason to expect that in another generation they will mingle with the rest of the community in so friendly a manner as to be willing to compromise regarding such minor differences as the observance or non-observance of days.

In 1754, John Bolles issued in pamphlet form "A Message to the General Court in Boston," in behalf of the principles of religious liberty. In a volume in which this pamphlet was republished are two other publications of this author, one of which (apparently written about this time) is the tract entitled "True Liberty of Conscience is in Bondage to no Flesh." In this tract, among accounts of persecution inflicted on the Rogerenes, is the following (also noted in Part I.):—

"To my knowledge was taken from a man, only for the cost of a justice's court and court charge for whipping him for breach of Sabbath (so called) a mare worth a hundred pounds, and nothing returned; and this is known by us yet living, to have been the general practice in Connecticut."

The "by us yet living" and "to have been" indicate that it was at a time considerably previous to this writing that such great cruelty and extortions were in vogue. Yet it also shows how easily, with no such publicity as would be incurred by presentation before the County Court, great persecutions could be carried on by town magistracy, a possibility always existing under the ecclesiastical laws relative to Sunday observances.

John Bolles took his "Message to the General Court" to Boston for presentation, in 1754, making the journey of two hundred miles on horseback, in his seventy-seventh year. (See Part I., Chap. VII.)

In the previous year—October, 1753—close following the death of John Rogers, 2d, had occurred the death of Rev. Eliphalet Adams, after a pastorate of over forty years in New London. It has been seen that since the death of Governor Saltonstall no virulent persecution of the Rogerenes has occurred, and that the character and policy of Mr. Adams have been favorable to compromise and conciliation. But very soon after the death of Mr. Adams there appear signs of a grievance on the part of the Rogerenes of a character to call forth one of their old-time warnings. Proof of this appears in the "Hempstead Diary":—

March 17, 1754. John Waterhouse of Groton and John Bolles and his sons and a company of Rogerenes came to meeting late in the forenoon service, and tarried and held their meeting after our meeting was over, and left off without any disorder before our afternoon meeting began.

It is thirty-three years since Mr. Hempstead has had occasion to note such a noon meeting on the part of the Rogerenes. By what official move this warning has been induced does not appear. Evidently no violence was offered the Rogerenes. This meeting will be a sufficient check for some time upon whatever attempts are on foot to disturb them.

Two years later, J. Hempstead writes in his Diary: "1756, May 30. John Waterhouse and a company came to our meeting."

There is evidently some call for another warning. The Congregational pulpit is, at this date, filled with temporary supply.

In this evident crisis, it is probable that none await the action of the Congregational church in their choice of a minister with more interest than do the Rogerenes. Upon the views and temper of Mr. Adam's successor will largely depend the continuance or discontinuance of the generally pacific attitude on both sides, which has continued for so many years. In the Congregational church membership are town officials as well as those in still more influential positions.

CHAPTER XII.
THE GRAND COUNTERMOVE (1764-1766).

It is not until 1757 that a new minister is installed over the Congregational church, in the person of Mr. Mather Byles, Jr., a talented and very resolute young man, twenty-three years of age.[160]

This youth is of such character and persuasion as to resemble, in this particular community, a firebrand in the neighborhood of a quantity of gunpowder. (After the gunpowder has exploded and Mr. Byles determines to remain no longer in this vicinity, in taking leave of the Congregational church he says: "If I have not the Sabbath, what have I? 'Tis the sweetest enjoyment of my whole life.")

This young man, whose "sweetest enjoyment" is the Puritan Sabbath so reprobated by the Rogerenes, naturally looks over the field to see how he can best distinguish himself as a zealous minister of the ruling order. He observes a large portion of this community taking sufficient pains to demonstrate to all beholders that they are pledged to follow no laws or customs, regarding religious affairs, other than those instituted by the Lord Jesus Christ and His inspired apostles, and that they are particularly called to bear witness against that so-called "holy day" first instituted by the emperor Constantine, which has, in an extreme form, been forced upon the people of New England as a necessary adjunct to the worship of God.

This zealous young minister appears to consider it his plain duty to stem this awful tide of anarchy as best he may, lest it become a torrent in New England that no man can stay. Thus he may distinguish himself in a pulpit once occupied by the famous Governor Saltonstall and succeed where even that dignitary failed. He will endeavor to bring such new odium and wrath upon this obstinate sect as shall effectually annihilate their Society.

Among the first efforts of Mr. Byles are sermons regarding the sanctity of the Sabbath, accompanied by other attempts to arouse his own people and the rest of the community (outside the Rogerene Society) to the duty and necessity of putting a stop to any desecration whatever of the "sacred" day.[161]

The Rogerenes soon find themselves not only preached to and against, but seriously meddled with by the town authorities in ways for a long time neglected. It is now again as in the days of John Rogers, when he stated that "the priests stirred up the people and the mob" against his Society.

The Rogerene countermove is almost unknown to this generation of rulers; as for traditions concerning it, or the mild warnings of 1745 and 1754, perchance certain officials would be nothing loath to see if they could not, by the trial of a more vigorous policy, succeed better than did their predecessors in such contests, nor would such officials be likely to anticipate lack of general public sympathy in such an effort. It is as important to the Baptist church as to the Congregational that Sunday should be accounted a sacred day, let it be accounted otherwise, where would be attendants on "divine worship"? Surely the young people would go to places of amusement or of mischief, rather than to meeting-houses. The object lesson presented by these upright and deeply religious Rogerenes, whose youth are among the most exemplary and godly in the land, is naturally lost upon a people who cannot trust the Lord himself to furnish sufficient guidance for His church.

Joseph Bolles (born 1701), eldest son of John Bolles, is a leader among the Rogerenes, standing shoulder to shoulder with his father and John Waterhouse. He is a talented man, holding, like his father, "the pen of a ready writer," and is clerk of the Rogerene Society. John Bolles being now over eighty years of age, this son largely takes his place in the active work of the Society, on the New London side. Yet the grand old patriarch, still vigorous in mind, sits prominent in the councils, giving these active men and youth the benefit of his experience, wisdom and piety, combined with an enthusiasm as ardent as that of the youngest of them all.

The more the magistrates, inspired by Mr. Byles, re-enforce his sermons by strict and unusual measures, the more do the Rogerenes, following their olden policy in such emergencies, add to their Sunday labors in the endeavor to fully convince their opponents that they are not to be coerced in this matter.

Ere long, the Rogerenes are severely fined, and in lieu of payment of such fines, which never have been voluntarily paid, are imprisoned, sometimes twenty at a time, many of them being kept in durance for a period of seven months. Their goods and the best of their cattle and horses are seized, to be sold at auction and nothing returned. Those having no such seizable property, are imprisoned for non-payment of minister's rates. In the midst of this strenuous attack, Mr. Byles preaches an elaborate sermon, to be published and circulated, in answer to what he calls the "Challenge" of the Rogerenes, viz., their reiterated requests that the besieging party will show them any Scriptural authority for the so-called religious observance of the first day of the week, or for any required "holy Sabbath" under the new dispensation. In this sermon he calls the Rogerenes "blind, deluded, obstinate," which terms are quite as applicable to the church party, from the Rogerene point of view. The onset continues, with added determination on the attacking side and no show of weakening on that of the defense.

Since the pen is mightier than the sword, it may do good service in such a time of peril as threatens the very existence of this devoted sect. Joseph

Bolles, sitting by his father's side, sharpens his quill to a fine point,[162] and the tremulous but earnest voice of the faithful patriarch not only aids the theme, but speaks words of comfort and of cheer; for is not this the cause of the Lord himself?

There is another, John Rogers (3d), who, like his father and grandfather before him, holds the pen of a ready writer. He was born in 1724, three years after the death of his illustrious grandfather. With the rapt attention, the retentive memory and the plastic mind of youth, he has received from his father's lips accounts of the thrilling experiences of the past; as a young man, he has followed the teachings and emulated the deeds of his people. He, too, will sharpen a quill ere long.

[Particular attention is here called to the following reference to Mr. Byles, in the "Reply of Joseph Bolles." See *Appendix* for full connection. "It is this sort of ministers that preach to the General Court to suppress or persecute them that walk by the apostle's doctrine, for not observing this Sabbath which he" (Byles) "says the apostles 'left to after discoveries.'" It is certain that the Rogerenes are under no difficulty in discerning from whence emanates the influence that has set this new persecution on foot and is continuing it to a crisis.]

The first efforts at repression proving ineffectual, severer measures are adopted by the attacking party. Yet there are several years more of patient endurance and forbearance on the part of the Rogerenes before they resolve to turn upon their foes the sole effectual means of defense at their command in times like these.

Among legal weapons available to the church party are four ecclesiastical laws, the strict application of which—as regards the Rogerenes, at least—have fallen into disuse, viz.: the law against Sunday labor, that against going from one's house on Sunday except to and from authorized meetings, the law against unauthorized meetings and those holding or attending such meetings, and the law by which any one not attending meetings of the ruling order or the services of some authorized Society of which he is a member, in a regular meeting-house on Sunday, can be fined for every such absence.[163] (Besides these are the large fines for baptizing and administering the Lord's Supper on the part of unauthorized persons.)

It is optional with the town magistrates to present persons guilty of breaking any of the above laws before the next County Court or to deal with such "at their own discretion," a discretion which in a number of instances has taken the form of lynch law, by giving the offenders over to a mischievous mob. It is not the policy at this time to present the Rogerenes before the County Court; not only would such publicity be liable to create outside sympathy with the Rogerenes, but the fines of this court for such offenses are limited to an inconsiderable amount, expressed in shillings, while the "discretion" of the town magistrates allows of serious fines, expressed in pounds, as well as imprisonment, stocks and stripes. The damaging effect of a friendly jury is also to be avoided. (But one reference to the Rogerenes is to be found on the records of the County Court during the more or less turbulent period between 1758 and 1766; this reference occurs in regard to the barring of the doors of the New London prison by the prisoners, for which the penalty is conspicuously slight.—See end of this Chapter.)

While this persecution, the most virulent that has ever been visited upon the Rogerenes as a Society, is nearing a crisis, occurs the death of Ebenezer Bolles, June 24, 1762, at the age of fifty-four, through contact with "poisonous wood."[164] An obituary notice, in the next issue of the *Connecticut Gazette*, attests to the wealth, integrity, hospitality and general worthiness of this New London merchant, and also states that no physician or medicines were allowed in his sickness,[165] he "belonging to the Society ofRogerenes."

The account of this death, as of that of John Rogers in 1721, is important; since it affords proof, more than forty years after the latter event, that this Society are as unswerving as ever in their adherence to Scriptural methods. How much reason has John Bolles, now in his 86th year, to discard this faith, even in the day of his great bereavement? He has still twelve children in health and vigor, between the ages of 60 and 20, eight of whom are destined to live to the following ages: 94, 91, 85, 84, 83, 82, 78, 75, and the other four beyond middle life. In the Rogers and other leading Rogerene families there appears a like flourishing condition.

After more than five year's continuance of aggravations instituted and continued under the leadership of Mr. Byles, which have finally reached a stage past endurance, the Rogerenes, on both sides of the river, are gathering in council about a common campfire, to consider the move that must be made, a countermove beside which the entrance of John Rogers and his wheelbarrow into the meeting-house in 1694 shall pale to insignificance.[166] The plan concluded upon bears the stamp of such veterans in the cause as John Bolles and John Waterhouse, as well as of keen young wits besides. They will give their enemies all the attendance upon meetings in "lawful assemblies" on their part, that these enemies will be likely to invite for some time to come; they will enter into those assemblies, and, if necessary, there will they testify against this "holy Sabbath," for the non-observance of which they are again so bitterly persecuted, and against such other features of the worship of their enemies as are opposed to the teachings of the New Testament. So long as the ecclesiastical laws which forced their sect into existence are executed against them, so long will they enter into those assemblies thus to testify. The unscriptural features against which they will testify are easily set forth, and to these the testimony shall be strictly confined, with no mention of themselves or their wrongs. For whatever comes of this testimony, made in the name of the Lord Jesus Christ in accordance with His teachings, and after the example of His apostles, they are prepared, even though it be martyrdom. The first attempt shall be of a tacit nature; if that avail as a warning, well and good; they will not disturb the meetings unless compelled to such extremity.

Mild indeed seems that first countermove (1685) when Capt. James Rogers, by the commotion which his "testimony" called forth in the meeting-house caused "some women to swound," in comparison with that of the Sunday, June 10, 1764, when a procession of Rogerenes from Quaker Hill, re-enforced by friends from Groton, and including men, women, and children, wends its solemn and portentous way into the town, to enter into the midst of their persecutors.

Upon reaching the meeting-house, a number quietly enter, others remain outside. The men who enter keep on their hats, in token of dissent to the doctrines of this church. If some of these hats chance to be broad-brimmed, so much the better. Wonderingly and fearfully must the larger part of the congregation behold this entrance and the quick-rising ire on the faces of such church members as are most responsible for its occurrence. As for Mr. Byles, his sensations may be imagined. He is in the midst of his usual long prayer[167] containing copious information to the Creator of the Universe, together with thanks and commendation to the same Almighty Power, for many circumstances which have been brought about by men in direct disobedience to His revealed Word; also petitions for the forgiveness of the sins of this congregation, some of the most serious of which—as persecution of their neighbors—they fully intend to commit over and over again. In all probability some portion of this prayer is aimed directly at the Rogerenes, in regard to keeping "holy" the Sabbath day.

Some commotion, caused by the entrance of the Rogerenes, compels Mr. Byles to open his eyes before this long prayer is at an end. When he does open them, he beholds these men with their hats on and these women engaged in knitting, or some small sewing, in token that they, too, areRogerenes.

How long certain officials, and other church members, restrain themselves is uncertain, even if they restrain themselves at all from vengeance dire; but before the prayer is regularly ended, the Rogerenes are fallen upon and driven out of the meeting-house with great violence and fury, while those in waiting outside are attacked with like rage, prominent church members and officials kicking and beating unresisting men, women and children and driving them to prison.

This treatment but deepens the determination of the Rogerenes. It is evident that merely keeping on their hats and doing a little knitting or sewing will not answer for an emergency like this. It must be no fault of theirs if this effort in the Master's cause shall fail. They now enter the assembly of their persecutors to declare, by word of mouth and with no lack of distinctness, against the false doctrines of this persecuting church. This testimony will they add to the silent mode of disapproval until these enemies desist from their unendurable attempts at coercion, and from these furious beatings, kickings, drivings, imprisonments, etc.

The party who renewed this almost forgotten contest, under the leadership of Mr. Byles and his friends, with the intention of making the position of the Rogerenes untenable, having brought affairs to this crisis, are resolved to conquer. They proceed in the line of violence which they have inaugurated, and in their rage even demand of these devoted people that—to escape torture—they recant their testimony against the doctrines and practices of this church. Their testimony being of a purely Scriptural character, how can they recant, even if they would, except by denying the truth of those declarations from the New Testament which they have proclaimed in the presence of their persecutors? The zeal of the Rogerenes is only redoubled. It is now a question whether they will obey men rather than God, for fear of what men may do to them. Yet, in their strict fidelity to the teachings of Christ, they make no resistance to the redoubled efforts of their enemies. Though their old men are scourged to the verge of death and their women insulted; though their brethren are suspended by the thumbs to be mercilessly whipped on the bare skin; though warm tar is poured on their heads; though men and women are driven through the streets more brutally than any cattle, to be thrown into the river; though they are given over to mobs of heartless children and youth to be whipped with thorny sticks and otherwise abused, not the smallest or weakest of their persecutors need fear the slightest violence in return.

With every attempt at a fresh testimony, the brutality of their enemies is increased and the terms of imprisonment doubled, until the prison is filled to suffocation and some of those within venture to bar the doors against the incarceration of fresh victims. It being impossible to further punish the offenders already in prison, other than through presentation to the County Court, those who have barred the door are presented at that court, probably on their own confession, by reason of which there is one court record, relating to this otherwise lawless contest of a year and a half in duration, which is to the following effect:—

"Samuel Rogers, John Rogers, Alexander Rogers, Nathaniel Rogers" (all sons of John Rogers, 2d) "and Joseph Bolles, of New London, Samuel Smith of Groton" (grandson of Bathsheba) "Timothy Waterhouse" (son of John of Groton) "bound over to the County Court to answer complaint of Christopher Christophers" (son of Chris. Chris.) "sheriff of New London, for that said persons, with sundry other persons, on Sunday, Aug. 12th, 1764, did, in a very high-handed, tumultuous manner, being in N. L. prison, bar up the doors of said prison on the justice, so that said sheriff and officers were denied and prevented admission into and possession of said prison, and made a most tumultuous noise and uproar &c. as pr. writ."

The sentence of the court is a fine of 40*s*. each and costs of prosecution, £2 each, which indicates more sympathy than severity on the part of this court.

[Since the early and the latter scenes of this long contest are shown to have been marked by unflinching endurance, unswerving courage and strategic measures on the part of the defence, it may be judged that during the entire period of unrelenting endeavors to continue to a successful issue the policy instigated by Mr. Byles, the assailants of the Rogerenes were encouraged by no signs of weakening on the part of the sufferers, while much discouraged by the disgrace attached to their church and the disapprobation of not a few of its own members, on account of the unprecedentedly severe policy that had brought on this countermove and the startlingly barbarous punishments for the same.]

After nearly two year's continuance of such heroic measures, under leadership of Mr. Byles and his friends, the Rogerenes, while many of their heads of families are in prison, institute a new kind of tactics, striking more directly at the very root of the matter, viz., at Mr. Byles. The plan is to have some of their people besiege Mr. Byles, at every conceivable opportunity, with attempts to converse with him in regard to the teachings of the New Testament, and to reason with him concerning the cruelties practised upon the Rogerenes. They are also to go to the meeting-house on Sunday and sit directly in his sight, and they are to linger in the neighborhood of his house or the meeting-house, where he may know of their vicinity and expect them to walk with him and talk to him "of the things of God," whenever he ventures outside.

Victory is now near at hand. Mr. Byles is driven nearly frantic. His tormentors are thrown into prison for declining to give bonds or to pay fines for attempts to approach this gentleman and converse with him. In this serio-comic crisis, parties of Rogerenes enter the meeting-house on Sunday and sit where Mr. Byles cannot fail to observe their grave, earnest and otherwise expressive faces, telling volumes at a glance, of inexpressible sufferings and losses, endured through tedious months and wasting years, of children left fatherless and motherless at home or wandering the streets tearful and hungry, and of many a bitter thing well known to Mr. Byles. But, most eloquent of all to him and most impressive, is the fixed determination in their faces to continue in his sight at every opportunity. Even a cat may look at a king without fear of consequences, and so do the Rogerenes look at Mr. Byles. Here is something that has been left out of the law books.

Ere long, the able-bodied men and women not in prison may attend to business and family duties, while a few old people, principally women, go on Sunday to sit in the meeting-house, or stand outside before and after meeting. Also on week days they sit or stand in the vicinity of Mr. Byle's house, until he will not venture out, if but one such person is near. Nor will he go to the church on Sunday, even if there are but two or three Rogerene women outside, until some official drives them away and escorts him to the meeting-house. The bell is sometimes kept tolling a full hour, until it is time the long service should be well under way, before the minister makes his appearance; he has been waiting for some one to drive these women away.

For the whole time—more than two months—that the men who have attempted to converse with Mr. Byles are kept in prison, these faithful women keep the watch on Mr. Byles. When the men are at length released, they renew their endeavors to talk with Mr. Byles. It is now not long before Mr. Byles has had more than enough opportunity to distinguish himself in an endeavor to extinguish the Rogerenes. He is determined not only to leave New London but to desert the Congregational ministry and denomination, and lays all the blame of his failure to conquer these people upon lack of execution of the ecclesiastical laws!!![168] His determination is sudden, so far as the knowledge of his parishioners is concerned, and his exit speedy in the extreme. (For particulars regarding his resignation, see extract from "Debate, etc.," in *Appendix*.)

The Rogerenes may now rest on their laurels. With Mr. Byles out of the way, we hear no more of harsh measures being employed against this sect. They may now attend their own meetings upon Sunday instead of those of their opponents, never neglecting, however, to give sufficient evidence that this is to them a holiday and not a "holy day."

John Bolles lived to praise God that He had granted His servants strength to continue faithful to the end and given them so signal a victory. This devout and heroic Christian was called to his reward in his ninetieth year, January 7, 1767.

In another decade, is heard the trumpet call of the Revolution. It is more than probable that a people of such courage and love of liberty have some difficulty at this time in keeping their sentiments within scriptural limits, and still more difficulty in holding back their youth from the fray. Not a few grandsons of John Rogers, 2d, and John Bolles, as well as other Rogerene youth, break away. One of them crosses the Delaware with Washington, and another is in the body-guard of the great general. The young volunteers of this blood and training fight bravely on land and sea. Some of them die on the field and some in loathsome prison ships.[169] Outside of the John Rogers descent, many are the descendants of James Rogers, 1st, that join the Continental army and navy. Yet, for the most part, the Rogerene youth hold firmly to the doctrine of non-resistance as set forth in the New Testament. Many of them are among the first to note the inconsistency between the sentence in the Declaration of Independence regarding the equal rights of all men and the clause in the Constitution countenancing slavery. As for the torch of religious liberty which this sect held aloft in the darkness, through many a weary contest,—a few years more, and the flame that it has helped to kindle leaps high, in the dim dawn of that day whose sun shall yet flood the heavens.

[For further elucidation of the events set forth in this chapter, there is presented in the *Appendix* an extract from the pamphlet published about 1759 by Joseph Bolles, describing some of the opening events of this persecution under the leadership of Mr. Byles, also several extracts from the pamphlet written by John Rogers, 3d, giving particulars of the merciless punishments inflicted upon those who took part in the countermove of 1764-66. This pamphlet is entitled "A Looking Glass for the Presbyterians of New London." The limits of this chapter have allowed of very brief presentation of those cruelties, expressed in general terms. Still other extracts from the pamphlet by John Rogers, 3d, may be found in the "History of New London"; but only a perusal of the whole work could give an adequate idea of the barbarous cruelties practised upon the Rogerenes in this contest, during the whole of which not one of the victims was charged with returning a single blow or making any resistance to the attacks of the lynching parties. There is also presented in the *Appendix*, in connection with this chapter, quotations from a pamphlet which appeared shortly after the resignation of Mr. Byles, under the auspices of the Congregational church, entitled *A Debate between Rev. Mr. Byles and the Brethren*, which portion relates to Mr. Byle's determination to leave that church and ministry, and shows his aversion to the Rogerenes who were his victors. It will be seen that from the three above-mentioned sources has been drawn the information contained in this chapter.]

CHAPTER XIII.
QUAKERTOWN.

In the new century, ecclesiastical persecutions are scarcely more than a tradition, save to the aged men and women still living who took part in their youth in the great countermove, the sufferings attendant upon which are now, even to them, as a nightmare dream. The laws that nerved to heroic protest a people resolved to obey no dictation of man in regard to the worship of God lie dead upon the statute book—although as yet not buried. The Rogerenes are taking all needful rest on Sunday, the day set apart for their meetings. Many of those on the New London side mingle as interested listeners in the various orthodox congregations. They walk where they please on Sunday, and are no longer molested. The merciless intolerance that brought this sect into existence being no longer itself tolerated, the chief mission of the Rogerenes is well nigh accomplished. The children may soon enter into that full Christian liberty, in the cause of which their fathers suffered and withstood, during the dark era of ecclesiastical despotism in New England.

After the last veterans in this cause have been gathered to their rest, the past is more and more crowded out by the busy present. Most of the male descendants of the New London Rogerenes remove to other parts. Many of them are among the hardiest and most enterprising of the western pioneers. From homes in New York and Pennsylvania they move farther and farther west, until no State but has a strain from Bolles and Quaker Hill. Descendants who remain in New London, lacking a leader of their own sect in this generation, join in a friendly manner with other denominations, affiliating most readily with the Baptists and being least associated with the still dominant church. In Groton, however, despite some emigration, is still to be found an unbroken band of Rogerenes, and a remnant upon Quaker Hill continues in fellowship with those of Groton.

As the region occupied by John Rogers, John Bolles and their neighborhood of followers received the name of Quaker Hill, so that district in Groton occupied chiefly by Rogerenes received the name of Quakertown.

We find no written account or authenticated tradition regarding the beginnings of Quakertown, save that here was the home of the Groton leader, John Waterhouse. Given a man of this stamp as resident for half a century, and we have abundant cause for the founding in this place of a community of Rogerenes as compact as that at Quaker Hill.

Quakertown occupies a district about two miles square in the southeastern part of the present town of Ledyard. It was formerly a part of Groton. Among the early Rogerenes of this vicinity was John Culver. Besides gifts of land from his father, John Culver had received a gift of land from Major John Pynchon of Springfield, Mass., in recognition of the "care, pains and service" of his father (John Culver, Sr.) in the division of Mr. Pynchon's lands (Groton Records) formerly owned in partnership with James Rogers. John Culver, Jr., did not, however, depend upon farming, being a "panel maker" by trade. As has been seen, John Culver and his family removed to New Jersey about 1735, there to found a Rogerene settlement. (See Chapter XII.) His daughter Esther, however, remained in Groton, as the wife of John Waterhouse.

Among other early Groton residents was Samuel Whipple from Providence, both of whose grandfathers were nonconformists who had removed to Rhode Island to escape persecution in Massachusetts. About 1712 this enterprising man purchased a large amount of land (said to be 1,000 acres) about eight miles from the present Quakertown locality, in or near the present village of Poquetannoc. Upon a stream belonging to this property, he built iron-works and a saw-mill. It is said that the product of the iron-works was of a superior quality, and that anchors and iron portions of some of the ships built in New London were made at these works.[170] Samuel Whipple's son Zacharia married a daughter (Elizabeth) of John Rogers, 2d; a grandson (Noah) of his son Samuel married a granddaughter (Hope Whipple) of the same leader, and a daughter (Anne) of his son Daniel married a grandson (William Rogers) of the same; while a daughter (Content) of his son Zachariah married Timothy Waterhouse, son of John Waterhouse. Yet it was not until early in the nineteenth century that descendants of Samuel Whipple in the male line became residents of Quakertown.[171] That the early affiliations of the Whipple family with the Rogerenes had fitted their descendants for close union with the native residents of the place is indicated by the prominent position accorded the Whipples in this community.

Other families of Groton and its neighborhood affiliated and intermarried with Rogerenes early in the nineteenth century. William Crouch of Groton married a daughter of John Bolles. This couple are ancestors of many of the later day Rogerenes of Quakertown. Two sons and two grandsons of Timothy Watrous married daughters of Alexander Rogers of Quaker Hill (one of the younger sons of John, 2d). Although there was a proportion of Rogers and Bolles lineage in this community at an early date, there was not one of the Rogers or Bolles name. Later, a son of Alexander Rogers, 2d, married in Quakertown and settled there; but this is not a representative name in that locality, while Watrous, Whipple and Crouch are to be distinctly classed as such.

As for other families who joined the founders of Quakertown or became associated with their descendants, it is safe to say that men and women who, on account of strict adherence to apostolic teachings, relinquished all hope of worldly pleasures and successes, to join the devoted people of this isolated district, were of a most religious and conscientious character.

Generally speaking, the New London descendants in the nineteenth century are a not uncompromising leaven, scattered far and wide among many people and congregations whose religious traditions and predilections are, unlike their own, of an ecclesiastical type. Every radical leaven of a truly Christian character is destined to have beneficial uses, for which reason it cannot so much be regretted that the fate of the New London community was to be broken up and widely disseminated.

While the New London Rogerenes were, through the mollifying influences of a liberal public opinion, as well as by a wide emigration and lack of a leader fitted to the emergency, slowly but surely blending with the world around them, quite a different policy was crystallizing upon the Groton side. That the Rogerene sect should continue and remain a separate people was undoubtedly the intention of John Rogers, John Rogers, 2d, John Bolles and their immediate followers; aye, a separate people until that day, should such day ever arrive, when there should be a general acceptance of the law of love instituted by Christ, in place of the old law of force and retaliation. Yet not only had these early leaders more than enough upon them in their desperate struggle for religious liberty, but they could not sufficiently foresee conditions ahead of their times, in order to establish their sect for a different era.

It was by the instinct of self-preservation combined with conscious inability to secure any adequate outside footing in the new state of affairs, that the small but compact band at Quakertown, beholding with dismay and disapproval the breaking up of the main body on the New London side, resolved to prevent such a disbanding of their own Society, by carefully bringing up their children in the faith and as carefully avoiding contact with other denominations. It was a heroic purpose, the more so because such a policy of isolation was so evidently perilous to the race. Not so evident was the fact that such exclusiveness must eventually destroy the sect which they so earnestly desired to preserve. Such, as has been seen, was not the policy of that founder whose flock were "scattered throughout New England," and some of the most efficient of whose co-workers were drawn from the midst of an antagonistic denomination; neither was it the policy of him who carried his Petition not only to the General Court of Connecticut, but to that of Massachusetts. Yet it was no ordinary man who carried out the policy above outlined, with a straightforward purpose and vigorous leadership, in the person of elder Zephania Watrous, a grandson of John Waterhouse.

John Waterhouse was living in 1773, at which date he was eighty-three years of age.[172] Considerably previous to that time he must have been succeeded by some younger man.

Elder Timothy Watrous, the Groton leader, who next appears to view, was a son of John Waterhouse, born in 1740. He is said to have been an able preacher and a man of the highest degree of probity.

Supposing John Waterhouse to have been in active service to his seventy-fifth year, Timothy could have succeeded him at the age of twenty-four, at which age the latter took part in the great countermove of 1764-66. His experience in this conflict is given in his own words:—

In the fore part of my life, the principal religion of the country was strongly defended by the civil power and many articles of the established worship were in opposition to the religion of Jesus Christ. Therefore I could not conform to them with a clear conscience. So I became a sufferer. I endured many sore imprisonments and cruel whippings. Once I received forty stripes save one with an instrument of prim, consisting of rods about three and a half feet long, with snags an inch long to tear the flesh. Once I was taken and my head and face covered with warm pitch, which filled my eyes and put me in great torment, and in that situation was turned out in the night and had two miles to go without the assistance of any person and but little help of my eyes. And many other things I have suffered, as spoiling of goods, mockings, etc. etc. But I do not pretend to relate particularly what I have suffered; for it would take a large book to contain it. But in these afflictions I have seen the hand of God in holding me up; and I have had a particular love to my persecutors at times, which so convicted them that they confessed that I was assisted with the spirit of Christ. But although I had so tender a feeling towards them that I could freely do them all the good in my power; yet the truth of my cause would not suffer me to conform to their worship, or flinch at their cruelty one jot, though my life was at stake; for many times they threatened to kill me. But, through the mercy of God, I have been kept alive to this day and am seventy years of age; and I am as strong in the defense of the truth as I was when I suffered. But my persecutors are all dead; there is not one of them left.

This extract is from a book entitled "The Battle Axe," written by the above Timothy, Sr., and his sons Timothy and Zacharia. Timothy, Jr., succeeded his father as leader and preacher in this Society. Zacharia was a schoolmaster of considerable note, and at one time taught school at "the head of the river." He invented the coffee mill so generally in use, which important invention, his widow, being ignorant of its worth, sold for forty dollars. Having discovered some copper ore in the vicinity of his house, he smelted it and made a kettle. After a vain search to find a printer willing to publish "The Battle Axe," he made a printing-press, by means of which, after his death, his brother Timothy published the book. Thus "The Battle Axe," even aside from its subject-matter, was a book of no ordinary description. At a later date it was reprinted by the ordinary means. Copies of the first edition are now exceedingly rare, and held at a high price. There is a copy of this edition in the Smithsonian Institute. We present an extract from the body of this work in the *Appendix*, but no adequate knowledge of the book can be obtained from so limited a space. Men who could venture to decry war in the very height of public exaltation over the success of the struggle for independence were too far ahead of their age, in this regard, to attract other than unfriendly attention. [173]

The first proof discovered, that the Rogerenes have conscientious scruples in regard to paying the military fine,[174] is a printed Petition issued by Alexander Rogers, one of the younger sons of John, 2d, of Quaker Hill, a thorough Rogerene, and, as has been seen, closely allied with those of Quakertown. This Petition is dated 1810, at which time Alexander Rogers was eighty-two years of age; his children, however, were comparatively young. The fine was for not allowing his son to enter the train-band. (This Petition will be found in *Appendix*.) It proves that, even at so late a date as this, the authorities were seizing Rogerene property in the same way as of old, taking in this instance for a fine of a few shillings the only cow in the possession of the family, and making no return. As of old, no attempt is made to sue for the amount taken over and above the legal fine, but this Petition is printed and probably well circulated in protest.[175]

Soon after the death of Timothy Watrous, Sr., and that of his son Zachariah, occurred the death of Timothy, Jr., in 1814. The latter was succeeded in leadership of the Society by his youngest brother, Zephania, then about thirty years of age.

By this time, the Quakertown Society had become so large that there was need of better accommodations for their meetings than could be afforded in an ordinary house. In 1815 the Quakertown meeting-house was built, that picturesque and not inartistic house of many gables, the first floor of which was for the occupation of the elder and his family, while the unpartitioned second story was for Rogerene meetings.

Materials and labor for the building of this meeting-house were furnished by members of the Society. The timber is said to have been supplied from a forest felled by the September gale of 1815, and sawed in a saw-mill owned by Rogerenes. The same gale had unroofed the old Watrous (John Waterhouse) dwelling which stood near the site of the meeting-house.[176]

The Quakertown people had a schoolhouse of their own as well as a meeting-house, and thus fully controlled the training of their youth and preserved them from outside influence. About the middle of the century, a regular meeting-house was built. The old meeting-house was turned entirely into a dwelling. The newer meeting-house resembles a schoolhouse.

Zephania Watrous was the last of the prominent leaders in this community. He was not only gifted as a religious teacher, but possessed much mechanical genius. By an ingenious device, water from a large spring was conducted into the cellar of the meeting-house and made to run the spinning-wheels in the living-room above, where were made linen thread and fine table linen, in handsome patterns. A daughter of this preacher (a sweet old lady, still living in this house in 1900) stated that she used often in her youth to spin sixty knots of thread a day.

It is alleged in Quakertown that Rogerenes were the first to decry slavery. This claim is not without foundation. Some of the Quakers censured this practice as early as 1750, although many of them held slaves for a considerable time after that date. Slavery was not publicly denounced in their Society until 1760. It was before 1730 that John Bolles came to the conclusion that slavery was not in accordance with the teachings of the New Testament. Copies of the papers by which he freed his slaves, bearing the above date, may be seen among the New London town records. His resolve to keep no more slaves and his reasons for it are among the traditions cherished by his descendants. Attention has previously been called to the evident aversion on the part of James Rogers and his son John to the practice of keeping slaves in life bondage. There is no indication that John Rogers, Sr., ever kept a slave, and many indications to the contrary. His son John, however, kept slaves to some extent, some of whom at least he freed for "faithful service" (New London Records). Two able-bodied "servants," are found in his inventory.[177] His son James mentions a servant, "Rose," in his will of 1754. His son John, however, never kept a slave, and his family were greatly opposed to that practice, by force of early teaching. With the exceptions here noted, no proof appears of the keeping of slaves among the early Rogerenes, although many of them were in circumstances to indulge in that practice, which was prevalent in their neighborhood. The date at which slavery was denounced by the Rogerene Society does not appear.

It is certain that the Rogerenes of Quakertown were not only among the first to declare against the brutality of war and the sanction it received from ministers and church members, but among the foremost in the denunciation of slavery. Nor were there those lacking on the New London side to join hands with their Groton friends on these grounds. The churches of New London, in common with others, would not listen to any meddling with slavery, partisanship on which question would surely have divided those churches. The Rogerenes saw no justifiable evasion, for Christians, of the rule to love God and your fellowmen, to serve God and not Mammon, and to leave the consequences with Him who gave the command.

At the period of the antislavery agitation, some of the descendants of John Rogers and John Bolles on the New London side (no longer called by the name of Rogerenes), and other sympathizers with those of Quakertown, attended meetings in the upper chamber of the house of many gables, and joined with them in antislavery and other Rogerene sentiments, declarations and endeavors. Among these visitors was William Bolles,[178] the enterprising book publisher of New London (Part I., Chapter VII.), who had become an attendant upon the services of the Baptist church of New London; but who withdrew from such attendance after discovery that the minister and leading members of that church expected those opposed to slavery to maintain silence upon that subject. He published a paper in this cause, in 1838, called *The Ultimatum*, with the following heading:—

ULTIMATUM.

THE PRESS MUZZLED: PULPIT GAGGED: LIBERTY OF SPEECH DESTROYED; THE CONSTITUTION TRAMPLED UNDER FOOT; MOBS TRIUMPHANT, AND CITIZENS BUTCHERED: OR, SLAVERY ABOLISHED—THE ONLY ALTERNATIVE.—FELLOW CITIZENS, MAKE YOUR ELECTION.

A few disconnected sentences (by way of brevity) selected from one of the editorial columns of this sheet, will give some idea of its style:—

It is with pleasure we make our second appearance before our fellow citizens, especially when we remember the avidity with which our first number was read, so that we were obliged to print a second edition. Our sheet is the organ of no association of men or body of men, but it is the friend of the oppressed and the uncompromising enemy of all abuses in Church and State. Our friends S. and J. must not be surprised that their communications are not admitted—the language is too harsh, and partakes a little too much of the denunciatory spirit for us. We care not how severely sin is rebuked, but we would remind them that a rebuke is severe in proportion as the spirit is kind and the language courteous—our object is to conciliate and reform, not to exasperate.

About the year 1850, several noted abolitionists came to New London to hold a meeting. Rogerenes from Quakertown gathered with others to hear the speeches. When the time for the meeting arrived, the use of the court-house, which had previously been promised them, was refused. In this dilemma, Mr. Bolles told the speakers they could go to the burying-ground and there speak, standing upon his mother's grave. The meeting took place, but during its continuance the speakers were pelted with rotten eggs.[179]

Mr. Bolles often entertained at his house speakers in the abolition cause. Such speakers were also entertained at Quakertown, where they frequently held meetings when not allowed to speak elsewhere in the region. The Rogerenes of this place also assisted in the escape of fugitive slaves, Quakertown being, between 1830 and 1850, one of the stations of the Underground Railroad. Fugitive slaves were brought here, under cover of darkness, concealed in the meeting-house and forwarded by night to the next station. For these daring deeds, the Quakertown people were repeatedly mobbed and suffered losses.

Rogerenes were also among the first in the cause of temperance, nor did they confine their temperance principles to the use of tobacco and intoxicating liquors, but advocated temperance in eating as well. Although never observing the fast days appointed by ecclesiastical law, they made use of fasting with prayer, and fasted for their physical as well as spiritual good, judging the highest degree of mental or spiritual power not to be obtained by persons who indulged in "fullness of bread." (See "Answer to Mr. Byles," by Joseph Bolles, in *Appendix.*) The Rogerenes of Quakertown have been and still are earnest advocates of temperance principles.

The isolation and exclusiveness of the Quakertown community in the nineteenth century has already been noted as a distinct departure from the liberal and outreaching policy of the early Rogerenes. There was yet another departure, in regard to freedom of speech, which culminated, about the middle of the nineteenth century, in a division of this community into two opposing parties. At this date, Elder Zephania Watrous was advanced in years; but he had been, and still was, a man of great force of character, and was accounted a rigid disciplinarian. Only a man of such type could have held this community to its strictly exclusive policy for so long a period.

Free inquiry, with expression of individual views, was favored by the Rogerenes from the first, and formed an important feature of their meetings for study and exposition of gospel truths. Largely by this very means were their youth trained to interest in, and knowledge of, the Scriptures. Such freedom had been instituted by the founder of the sect, with no restrictions save the boundary line between liberty and license.[180]

The elder did not favor free speech in the meetings of the Society; he undoubtedly judged that such freedom would tend to disorder and division. The sequel, however, proved that a Society which could be held firmly together, for more than a hundred years, under a remarkably liberal policy in this regard, could be seriously divided under the policy of repression.

The feeling upon this point became so intense that public meetings were held in Quakertown for full discussion of the subject pro and con. These meetings excited wide interest, and were attended by many persons from adjoining towns. The party for free speech won the victory; but the division tended to weaken the little church, the decline of which is said to date from that period.[181]

For nearly two hundred years, New Testament doctrines as expounded by John Rogers (in his writings) have been taught in Quakertown, and the Bible studied and restudied anew, with no evasion or explaining away of its apparent meanings. Morality has been taught not as a separate code, but as a principal part of the religion of Jesus Christ. Great prominence has been given to non-resistance and all forms of application of the law of love.

Women were from the first encouraged to speak in Rogerene meetings, the meetings referred to being those for exhortation, prayer and praise. It will be seen (*Appendix*) that John Bolles wrote a treatise in favor of allowing women to speak in such meetings. Mr. Bownas also quotes John Rogers as saying that women were admitted to speak in Rogerene meetings, "some of them being qualified by the gift of the Spirit."

Among the principles rigidly insisted upon in Quakertown are that persons shall not be esteemed on account of wealth, learning or position, but only for moral and religious characteristics; strict following of the Golden Rule by governments as well as by individuals, hence no going to war, or retaliatory punishments (correction should be kindly and beneficent); no profane language, or the taking of an oath under any circumstances; no voting for any man having principles contrary to the teachings of the New Testament; no set prayers in meetings, but dependence on the inspiration of the Holy Spirit; no divorce except for fornication; to suffer rather than to cause suffering. There has always been great disapprobation of "hireling ministers." None of the Rogerene elders ever received payment for preaching or for pastoral work.

A gentleman who has been prominent in the Quakertown Society being questioned, some years since, in regard to the lack of sympathy between the Rogerenes and other denominations, gave the following reasons for a state of feeling on both sides which is not wholly absent even at the present day.

"The other churches considered cessation of work on Sunday to be a part of the Christian religion, and to be forced upon all as such. Many of their preachers were led into the ministry as a learned and lucrative profession, with no spiritual call to preach, being educated by men for that purpose. In many instances these preachers were worldly-minded to a great extent. The churches believed in war and in training men to kill their fellowmen. Ministers and church members used liquor freely. Church members held slaves, and ministers upheld the practice. For a long time the Rogerenes were compelled to assist in the support of the Congregational church, to which of all churches they were most opposed, on account of its assumption of authority over others in the matter of religion. The Rogerenes were fined for not attending the regular meetings, and cruelly persecuted for not keeping sacred the 'idol Sabbath' so strictly observed by other denominations. Although persecution has ceased, prejudice still remains on both sides, partly inherited, as it were, and partly the result of continued differences of opinion."

At the present day, meetings in Quakertown are similar to Baptist or Methodist conference meetings. The Lord's Supper is observed once a quarter. In the old times the Rogerenes held a feast once a year, in imitation of the last passover with the disciples, at which time a lamb was killed and eaten with unleavened bread. The Sunday service consisted of preaching and exposition of Scripture, while prayers, singing of hymns, relation of experience, etc., were reserved for the evening meetings of the Society. The latter were meetings for the professing Christians, while the Sunday meetings were public meetings, where all were welcomed. It will be observed that this was according to the apostolic practice, and not materially different from the practice of other denominations at the present day.

If there was so decided an aversion to physicians on the part of the early Rogerenes as has been represented, it has not come down to the present time among the people of Quakertown, as have most of the oldtime sentiments and customs; yet evidence is not lacking to prove that their predecessors made use of faith and prayer in the healing of disease, and that there have been cases of such healing in this Society. One of the latter, within the memory of persons yet living, was recounted to us by the gentleman to whom we have referred, upon our inquiring of him if he had ever heard of any cures of this kind in Quakertown. Pointing to a portrait on the wall, he said, "That man was cured in a remarkable manner." He then stated the circumstances asfollows:—

"He had been sick with dysentery, and was so low that his death was momentarily expected; his wife had even taken out the clothes she wished placed upon him after death. While he lay in this seemingly last stage of the disease, he suddenly became able to speak, and said, in a natural tone, to his wife: 'Bring me my clothes.' She told him he was very ill and must not try to exert himself; but he continued so urgent that, to pacify him, she brought the clothes he usually wore. He at once arose, dressed himself and was apparently well, and so continued. He said that, while he lay there in that weak condition, he suddenly felt an invisible hand placed upon his head and heard a voice saying: 'Arise, my son, you are healed,' upon which he immediately felt a complete change, from extreme illness and weakness to health and strength; hence his request to his wife."

There are numerous traditions regarding the offering of prayers for recovery by the bedsides of the sick, on the part of the early elders of this community, who were sometimes desired to render this service outside of their own Society, and readily complied.

That the founders of this community, both men and women, were persons of no ordinary mental and physical vigor, is attested by the excellent mental and physical condition of their descendants, after generations of intermarriage within their own borders. At the present day, it would puzzle an expert to calculate their complicated relationships. In a visit to this locality, some years since, we met two of the handsomest, brightest and sweetest old ladies we ever beheld, each of whom had passed her eightieth year, and each of whom bore the name of Esther (as did the wife of John Waterhouse). Both were descendants of John Rogers, and of the first settlers of Quakertown, several times over.[182] One of them told us that her grandmother took a cap-border to meeting to hem in the time of the great countermove, at which time and for which cause she was whipped at the New London whipping-post; also that for chopping a few sticks of wood in his back yard, on Sunday, a Quakertown man was "dragged to New London prison." This is but a hint of the traditions that linger in this community regarding the days of persecution. The other lady, a daughter of Elder Zephania Watrous, lived in the old meeting-house, where she was born. In the room with this gentle and comely old lady were five generations of the Watrous family, herself the eldest, and a child of four or five years the youngest, all fair representatives of Quakertown people; healthy, intelligent and good-looking.

To a stranger in these parts, it is a wonder how the inhabitants have maintained themselves in such an apparently sterile and rocky region.[183] In fact, these people did not depend upon agriculture for a livelihood. Although thus isolated, they were from the first thrifty, ingenious and enterprising. The property of the first settlers having been divided and subdivided among large families, it was not long before their descendants must either desert their own community or invent methods of bringing into Quakertown adequate profits from without. Consequently, we find them, early in the nineteenth century, selling, in neighboring towns, cloths, threads, yarn and other commodities of their own manufacture. A large proportion of the men learned trades and worked away from home during the week. Many of them were stone-masons, a trade easily learned in this rocky region, and one in which they became experts. In later times, we find some of them extensively engaged in raising small fruits, especially strawberries.

Although, with the decline of persecution, no new leader arose to rank with those of the past, bright minds have not been lacking in later days in this fast thinning community, which, like other remote country places, has suffered by the emigration of its youth to more promising fields of action.

Timothy Watrous, 2d, invented the first machine for cutting cold iron into nails. He also made an entire dock himself.

Samuel Chapman, a descendant of John Rogers and John Waterhouse, is said to have made and sailed the first steamship on the Mississippi. He founded large iron-works in New Orleans. His son Nathan was one of the founders of the Standard Iron Works of Mystic.

Jonathan Whipple, a descendant of John Rogers, having a deaf and dumb son, conceived the idea of teaching him to speak and to understand by the motion of the lips, by which method he soon spoke sonorously and distinctly, and became a man of integrity and cultivation. Zerah C. Whipple, a grandson of Jonathan, becoming interested in this discovery, resolved to devote his life to its perfection. He invented the Whipple Natural Alphabet, and with the aid of his grandfather, Jonathan, founded The Home School for the deaf and dumb, at Mystic.

Julia Crouch, author of "Three Successful Girls" (a descendant of John Rogers and John Bolles), was a Rogerene of Quakertown.

Ida Whipple Benham, a well-known poet, and for many years an efficient member of the Peace Society, was of Quakertown origin.[184]

In recent years, the Rogerenes of Quakertown have given much attention to the cause of peace and arbitration. The Universal Peace Union having been established by the Quakers, soon after the rebellion, the people of Quakertown invited members of that Society to join them in holding a Peace Convention near Mystic, the most suitable available point in the vicinity of Quakertown. Accordingly, in August, 1868, the first of an unbroken series of yearly Peace Meetings was held in an attractive grove on a hill by the Mystic River. Including the invited guests, there were present forty-three persons. The second meeting, in September, 1869, showed such an increase of interest and attendance that the Connecticut Peace Society was organized, as a branch of The Universal Peace Union, and Jonathan Whipple of Quakertown was elected president. This venerable man (to whom we have before referred), besides publishing and circulating *The Bond of Peace* (a paper advocating peace principles), had long been active as a speaker and correspondent in the cause so dear to his heart.

In 1871, James E. Whipple, of Quakertown, a young man of high moral character, having refused from conscientious scruples to pay the military tax imposed upon him, was arrested by the town authorities of Ledyard and confined in the Norwich jail, where he remained several weeks.

About the same time, Zerah C. Whipple, being called upon to pay a military tax, refused to thus assist in upholding a system which he believed to be anti-Christian and a relic of barbarous ages. He was threatened with imprisonment; but some kindly disposed person, interfering without his knowledge, paid the tax.

In 1872 a petition, signed by members of the Peace Society, was presented to the legislature of Connecticut praying that body to make such changes in the laws of the State as should be necessary to secure the petitioners in the exercise of their conscientious convictions in this regard. The petition was not granted; but the subject excited no little interest and sympathy among some of the legislators.

In the summer of 1874, Zerah C. Whipple, still refusing to do what his conscience forbade, was taken from his home by the tax collector of Ledyard and placed in the New London jail. His arrest produced a profound impression, he being widely known as the principal of the school for teaching the dumb to speak, and also as a very honest, high-souled man.

During his six week's imprisonment, the young man appealed to the prisoners to reform their modes of life, reproved them for vulgarity and profanity, furnished them books to read, and began teaching English to a Portuguese confined there. The jailer himself said, to the commissioner, that although he regretted Mr. Whipple's confinement in jail on his own account, he should be sorry to have him leave, as the men had been more quiet and easy to manage since he had been with them. On the evening of the sixth day, an entire stranger called at the jail and desired to know the amount of the tax and costs, which he paid, saying he knew the worth of Mr. Whipple, that his family for generations back had never paid the military tax, and he wished to save the State the disgrace of imprisoning a person guilty of no crime. This man was not a member of the Peace Society. Mr. Whipple afterwards learned that his arrest was illegal, the laws of the State providing that where property is tendered, or can be found, the person shall be unmolested. The authorities of Groton did not compel the payment of this tax by persons conscientiously opposed to it.

In 1872, *The Bond of Peace* was removed to Quakertown and its name changed to *The Voice of Peace*. Zerah C. Whipple undertook its publication and continued it until 1874, when it was transferred to a committee of The Universal Peace Union. It is now published in Philadelphia as the official organ of that Society, under the title of *The Peacemaker*.

The call of Mrs. Julia Ward Howe for a woman's Peace Society was heartily responded to by the Connecticut Peace Society, and the 2d of June was for years celebrated, by appropriate exercises, as Mother's Day.

The annual grove meeting increased rapidly in attendance and interest. The number present at the tenth meeting was estimated at 2,500. In 1875, it was decided to prolong the time of the convention to a second day's session, and the two day's session was attended with unabated interest.

Jonathan Whipple, first president of the Connecticut Peace Society, died in March, 1875. Shortly before the end, he was heard to say: "Blessed are the peacemakers; but there has been no blessing promised to warriors."

The grove meeting is now held three days annually. It is the largest gathering of the kind in the world. The large tent used at first was replaced some years since by a commodious wooden structure, which is the property of the Universal Peace Union.

From the first, some of the most noted speakers on peace and kindred topics have occupied the platform, among them Belva Lockwood, Mary A. Livermore, Julia Ward Howe, Aaron M. Powell, Rowland B. Howard, Robert T. Paine, Delia S. Parnell, George T. Angell, H. L. Hastings, William Lloyd Garrison, etc. The Hutchinson family used frequently to sing at these meetings. The only one now remaining of that gifted choir, a gentleman as venerably beautiful as any bard of ancient times, has, in recent summers, favored the audience in the grove with several sweet songs appropriate to the occasion.

It is said that the winding road leading about Quakertown is in the shape of a horseshoe. May this be an omen of honors yet to come to this little battlefield, where an isolated, despised, yet all-devoted band have striven for nearly two centuries to be true to the pure and simple precepts of the New Testament as taught them by sufferers for obedience to those truths, beside many a fireside where tales of woes for past endeavors, mingled with prayers for future victories, have nerved young hearts to the old-time endurance, for His name's sake.

Many are the noble men and women who, from first to last, have been content to live and die in this obscure locality, unhonored by the world and sharing not its luxuries or pleasures, consoled by the promises of the New Testament: promises which are not to the rich and honored (as such), but chiefly to those who for obedience to the teachings of this Word are outcast and despised, poor and unlearned, and even, if need be, persecuted and slain.

Not because that good man, Jonathan Whipple, was more conscientious or talented than many another of the Rogerenes of this locality, but because he was a good specimen of the kind of men that have from time to time been reared in this Society, there is given in the following note[185] an abstract from a published account of his life, a copy of which was forwarded to us by his daughter, Mrs. Whaley, in 1893. In the letter containing this enclosure she said: "I hope that justice will at length be done our so long misunderstood and misrepresented people."

Presentation of facts belongs to the historian; but the effect and uses of the information thus afforded is for the reader. We have collected and set in order such attested facts as we have been able to discover relative to the history of the Rogerenes, of which sect the people of Quakertown are the only distinct representatives of the present day.

If at the end of this history it should be asked: "How can the Rogerene sect be described in briefest terms?" we reply:—

"The doctrines and customs of this sect were patterned as closely as possible after the early church of the Gentiles, instituted under apostolic effort and direction; hence it included the evangelical portions and excluded the unevangelical portions of the doctrines and customs of every sect known to Christendom. Should a new sect be brought into existence on strictly evangelical lines, it would, to all intents and purposes, be the same as the Rogerene Society." It is evident, however, that a marked feature of the Rogerene sect would be lacking to such a church in modern times, viz., the constant need of withstanding ecclesiastical laws whose unimpeded sway would have prevented the existence of any truly evangelical church. It is easy to perceive that the growth of such a spirit of close adherence to New Testament teachings as animated the Rogerenes would tend to the obliteration of sects.

Should the churches of Christendom ever awake to the fact that not one of them but has made and countenanced signal departures from the teachings of Christ and his apostles, both in principles and modes, and that their differences one from the other are founded upon variations from the first divinely instituted church, and should they, on thus awakening, join hands, in council assembled, with the purpose of uniting in one church of the apostolic model, fully devoted to the cause of peace on earth and good will to men, then would dawn the millennium.

It is plain that John Rogers had faith in the people at large for the realization of such a church universal, could adequate leadership be procured. He believed that of existing societies of the evangelical order having in his day a fair start, that of the Quakers (by its peace principles and dependence on the Holy Spirit) was best fitted to take the lead. For such an end he had urged upon that Society the instituting among them the ordinances of Baptism and the Lord's Supper, which they had rejected, and he expressed his opinion forcibly when he said to Mr. Bownas in 1703 that if the Quakers would take those two ordinances they could "carry all before them." (As quoted by Mr. Bownas.)

CHAPTER XIV.

DRAGON'S TEETH.

Mr. J. R. Bolles has aptly compared the falsehoods sown by the author of "The Prey Taken from the Strong," to dragon's teeth constantly springing up anew (Part I, Chapter I). When Peter Pratt wrote the book thus entitled, he was evidently stimulated and encouraged by the ecclesiastical demand for such a publication, and trusted that lack of correct information on the part of the general public would secure credence for it. The falsities evident in the work, through its contradictions in one part of statements made in another, must have been due either to lack of careful observation on the part of the writer or to his confidence of such lack on the part of the public to whom it was addressed.

There was an evident personal object in this deliberate attempt to malign the character of John Rogers three years after his death; by statements which Peter Pratt of all men knew to be false; he having himself been a Rogerene, closely allied and attached to one of the leaders of that Society. Having since become a prominent member of the ruling church, and intimate with leading ecclesiastics of that church, in what better way could he prove to his influential friends his regret at having been associated with the hated nonconformist than by lending himself to the ruling order in their endeavors to stamp out whatever respect for and interest in the Rogerenes and their cause had found lodgement in the minds of the public?

On the ecclesiastical side, who could address the public with better chance of being heard and credited than a popular lawyer, known to have had intimate acquaintance with the obnoxious sect? For despite the blunder in regard to computation of longitude (Part I, Chapter IV), Peter Pratt was a man of considerable note in Connecticut, both as a lawyer and speaker, at the time he wrote this singular book. Joshua Hempstead says in his Diary: "Nov. 25, 1730. Melancholy news of the death of Mr. Peter Pratt of ys Town,[186] Attorney at Law, is confirmed, who died at Hartford on Saturday last,—the finest Orator in the Colony of his Profession."

The literary ability of this man is shown to be far below that ascribed to his oratory, the style of this sole book of his authorship being very ordinary; while the reply of his half-brother John Rogers, 2d, as well as other works of that author, will bear comparison with some of the best works of his time, for clear, vigorous logic and expression, enlivened by sparkles of wit and acumen, which qualifies are not observable in the literary effort of this other son of his mother.

The principal point to be secured being an impeachment of the character of

John Rogers, free use is made by Peter Pratt of the accusation presented by the Griswolds in the petition for divorce, by way of declaring that the separation of John Rogers from his wife and children was on account of certain immoralities charged against him, which pretended immoralities Peter Pratt names, on no other authority than the entirely ambiguous statements of the records of the General Court regarding the Petition of Elizabeth in 1675, which Petition (according to said records) distinctly stated that the chief reason of her plea did not relate to breach of the marriage covenant, of which she admitted that she had small reason to complain.

The exact charges manufactured by the Griswolds under the head of "Breach of Covenant" may be found in the bill of damages still to be seen in the Connecticut State Library (see Chapter II), which bill was brought against John Rogers by Matthew Griswold during the trial for divorce, and in which is no imputation regarding the moral character of John Rogers. Peter Pratt, although avowing familiarity with these records, declares a serious breach of the marriage covenant to be one of the chief causes for this separation; while he does not in any sort intimate to the reader that the charge brought forward for the divorce related—as he well knew—to a period before marriage, and to some fault known only to John Rogers himself, until he divulged the same to his wife.

Peter Pratt also states that John Rogers owned out of court to the charge against him, and that the person intrusted with that confidence gave this evidence against him, for proof of which statement the reader is referred to files of the General Court. Evidently Peter Pratt did not expect any of his readers to consult said files; for although it is to this day on the files of that court that John Rogers was said to have owned out of court to the charge against him, it is stated in the same connection that the man who avowed this confidence on the part of John Rogers, upon being asked the time and place of the confession, gave such reply that John Rogers was able to prove an *alibi*.

The one other opportunity improved by Peter Pratt for an attack upon the moral character of John Rogers, is in regard to his marriage with Mary Ransford, twenty-five years after the charge made for the purpose of obtaining the divorce. In his account of this marriage, he not only falsifies and vulgarizes the circumstances in a very singular manner, but, while in one place he represents the marriage to Mary to have been less of choice than necessity, in another place he avers that he himself was, at the very time of this marriage, on friendly and intimate terms with John Rogers, and so continued, to the extreme of actual discipleship, for years after that marriage.

It would seem that any careful and intelligent reader of "The Prey Taken from the Strong," however prejudiced, could but note this singular inconsistency,—that Peter Pratt, while knowing to any such irregularity as he claims on the part of John Rogers, should, at that very time, have taken him as a spiritual guide, and continued, for years after, under his leadership. The readers of that day, in that locality, must have known that Peter Pratt's connection with the Rogerene Society was at a date following the marriage to Mary Ransford, which latter occurred in 1699, while his own declaration that when he was imprisoned with other Rogerenes in that cause he had a young wife at home, fixes the date of this imprisonment as late as 1709, which was the year of his marriage.

In order to appear to substantiate his calumnious intimations, Peter Pratt states that, to the best of his recollection, the first child of Mary Ransford was born "three or four months" after the ceremony before the County Court. He also states that she was complained of by the court on the birth of this child. As a lawyer in this town, he dwelt, so to speak, among the court records, and could easily have found the date of this child's birth, had he intended to make a truthful statement. The County Court record still remains distinct and easily to be found, which says that this child was born in January, 1700, exactly seven months after the marriage of John Rogers to Mary Ransford, and, as stated by John Rogers, 2d, "within the time allowed by law." It was born at the date at which John Rogers, 2d, brought his bride to Mamacock, to the great annoyance and irritation of Mary. It is well known that less disturbances than this have often hastened the birth of a child. Proof is evident that neither John Bolles, nor any other of the highly honorable friends and neighbors of John Rogers, who had the very best opportunity of knowing the facts of the case, showed the slightest diminution of allegiance to him at this date, and quite as evident that Peter Pratt himself continued right on to full discipleship.

The two chief calumnies in this work of Peter Pratt having been presented, attention is now called to two of a different character.

I saw him once brought into court,—he had contrived the matter so as tobe just without the door when he was called to answer. His features and gestures expressed more fury than I ever saw in a distracted person of any sort, and I soberly think that if a legion of devils had pushed him in headlong, his entrance had not been more horrid and ghastly, nor have seemed more preternatural.

John Roger's declaration that the indictment was a lie is brought out in similar style, also the exclamations of other Rogerenes present in the court-room.

This plainly refers to the trial before the County Court in November, 1719, when John Rogers is said (by court records) to have come into court "in a violent manner," etc., and, when the indictment was read, to have exclaimed that it was “a devilish ly” (see Chapter IX), for which contempt of court he was fined only twenty shillings, which nominal sum was never collected. Taking into consideration the evident sympathy of the jury on this occasion of “violent entrance,” etc., and the great ease with which Peter Pratt is proven capable of misstating and exaggerating facts, the reader will admit the probability that this entrance of John Rogers into the court-room, and his words there spoken, together with those of his followers, were neither more nor less than impassioned expressions of indignation and protest regarding the terrible cruelty to which the wife of John Bolles was then being subjected. She was, as will be remembered, at that moment lying in a critical condition in New London prison, where the death of her child had just occurred. Peter Pratt, then present in that court-room, by his own avowal, knew all of these facts, and knew also that the life of this woman was saved only by such determined efforts at full publicity on the part of the Rogerenes and their sympathizers. Yet he utterly conceals these circumstances from the reader, while he exaggerates the Rogerene protests, and represents them as being simply senseless and grotesque.

It is from this description by Peter Pratt that historians have borrowed their statements regarding the loud voice of John Rogers, and that Rogerenes were accustomed to charge dignitaries with lying, etc.[187]

The singularly false and indecent statements made by Peter Pratt—in regard to the divorce of John Rogers and the marriage to Mary Ransford—and his exaggerated description of the scene in the court-room, form almost the entire portion of the account of the Rogerenes contained in Trumbull's “History of Connecticut,” which is the standard history (first published, 1818) from which, as has been said, later historians have derived their ideas and representations in regard to this sect.

Of the many lesser aspersions cast by Peter Pratt upon the character and teachings of John Rogers, one of the most astonishing (seeing that Peter Pratt himself refutes it) is to the effect that John Rogers held that “a man dies even as a dog.” In another place he says John Rogers “held both to the resurrection and the day of judgment, although doubted whether the body to be raised would be the same that fell, yet owned it would have the same consciousness.”

The author guilty of the above (and many another) self-contradiction, says of the writings of John Rogers: “For that they are so perplexed and ambiguous, that he that will attend the rules of reason and speech can prove scarcely anything of the chief articles of his faith by his books.”

Careful perusal of the many extant writings of John Rogers will prove to any candid person that they are written in the clearest manner, having in them nothing which cannot be understood by the most ordinary reader. Peter Pratt, being unable to quote from these writings anything that could substantiate his statements concerning them, had need to manufacture some excuse for such omission of evidence.

It would be exceedingly difficult, if not wholly impossible, to find another book from which historians have condescended to quote which contains so many contradictions in itself, so many utterly and needlessly vulgar expressions, and so many easily proven falsehoods, as does this calumnious work of Peter Pratt. The favor it received in ecclesiastical quarters is proof that there was almost no device, however underhanded, of which the enemies of the Rogerenes would not stoop to avail themselves in branding this daring opponent of ecclesiastical rule.

Yet Peter Pratt's baldly dishonest account is not the only source of Rogerene calumny.

Backus, among others, in his "History of the Baptists," makes the statement that the Rogerenes were a sect whose practice it was to take work into meeting-houses. The Rogerenes were a sect nearly a century before 1764, when they first took work into a meeting-house, and have been a sect more than one hundred years since 1766, when they ceased to take work into a meeting-house, making in reality less than two years, of their more than two hundred years of existence, in which they (their women), in defence of their Society, took work into a meeting house.

The same historian asserts that it was their regular practice to enter the churches and interrupt the ministers, although it would have been evident, upon careful examination of the case, that they never entered any church in this manner except under stress of bitter persecution, and that, as a non-resistant people, they had in such emergencies no other efficient means of defence.

Historians have generally stated that the Rogerenes imitated the Quakers in dress and speech, apparently on no further evidence than that the name of Quakers had become attached to them.

That the Rogerenes did not imitate the Quakers in speech is shown by the testimony of those of their descendants most likely to be well informed in regard to the early customs of their people. That they did not imitate the Quakers in dress is proven by their inventories, which show the usual style of dress, wherever the wardrobe is itemized.

In the countermove of 1764-66, the men kept on their hats in the Congregational meeting-house. John Crandall and other early members of the First Baptist church in Newport had no affinity or sympathy with the

Quakers; yet, when attending service in a Congregational church, they kept on their hats, in token of dissent.

Historians inform us that the Rogerenes did not employ physicians, surgeons, or midwives, or make use of remedies in sickness, depending wholly upon the prayer of faith. As has been fully shown, the Rogerenes did not feel authorized to neglect any New Testament injunction; they undoubtedly believed in healing by the prayer of faith; yet, being a logical and discriminating people, they perceived that the prayer of faith is often a remedy most difficult to procure at a moment's notice, and that other modes of relief obtainable, in absence of this superior agency, are not to be despised. As opposed to statements that the Rogerenes had nothing to do with remedies, we have evidence that they were very attentive to the sick, which presumes aid of various kinds. They appear not to have disapproved of natural, ordinary means of restoration and alleviation. A striking proof is furnished in the description given by John Rogers of his illness, through cold and neglect, in the inner prison. On this occasion, we do not find his son standing by the prison window praying, though this son is a Rogerene of the Rogerenes; but we find him running out into the streets, crying loudly for help, and when help comes, in the form of hot stones, wine and cordial, as well as speedy removal to warm quarters, there is no indication of any lack of ready acceptance of these means of restoration. We find afterwards a grateful acknowledgment by John Rogers himself to Mr. Adams and wife for the wine and cordial.

Remarkable cases of divine healing appear to have occurred in this Society at an early date. The account given of the healing of a later day Rogerene in Quakertown (Chapter XIII) indicates that this was a result of faith, through teachings and experiences that had been in operation long before this man's day, descending from the first headers through intervening generations. The bringing of their sick, by the Rogerenes of New Jersey, to the "holy men" from Ephrata, to be healed, is also indicative of former experiences that had strengthened their faith even to a point like this.

As for surgery, there is no reason to suppose that the Rogerenes did not use the ordinary methods for a cut finger and for more serious wounds. These people must have had broken bones, yet we hear of none lame among them, except one who was "born lame." They had no New Testament directions regarding surgical cases. As for midwives, the size of their families of children by one mother prove that, whatever their mode, mothers and babes thrived to a very uncommon degree. We hear nothing of the prayer of faith in such cases, except in unauthenticated statements of "historians." There is abundance of traditional evidence that the Rogerenes were trained in the care of the sick, not only that they need not call for aid from without, but that they might assist in ministering to others.

The fact that it is appointed to all men once to die, of itself precludes the possibility of continual and invariable healing, even by the prayer of faith. But to suppose that such prayer is not as efficient as human remedies, is to declare incredible certain passages of Scripture which are as authentic as any other portion of the New Testament. Thus reasoned the Rogerenes.

While referring to Backus, we will note a statement made by him to the effect that some of the Rogerene youth having put an end to their own lives, this was a cause of the decline of their Society. Here is a curious dragon's tooth, and it is difficult to see how it was manufactured. Suffice it to say that, in extensive historical and genealogical researches for the purposes of this history (and in researches by the authors of the Rogers and the Bolles Genealogies, both of which works largely include allied families), there has been found but one instance of suicide among the Rogerenes, and this was that of a young man who took his own life while under the influence of melancholia which came upon him during a period of religious revival. This young man was not of Rogers descent. There was, however, in New London, at a somewhat later date, a young man of Rogers and Rogerene descent, who became hopelessly insane. Because of the devotion of his mother to a church in New London he was brought up in that church. It is said that he was a very bright and promising youth, and that no cause could be assigned to his derangement other than excitement induced by a revival in that church. This is mentioned to show that such instances are not confined to any denomination.

Backus also says that "as late as 1763" some Rogerenes "clapped shingles and pieces of wood together around the meeting-house" in Norwich. Since he gives no authority for this statement, it is likely to be one of the many fabrications imposed upon the public as "history." If any such thing occurred, it was doubtless a Rogerene warning to that church to desist certain meddling or persecutions. It will not only be remembered that the date given is during the height of the persecution that induced the great countermove, but that from the Norwich church had issued those who apprehended and scourged the party of Rogerenes on their way to Lebanon.[188] Mr. Backus, with the real or assumed lack of perception common to ecclesiastical historians when treating upon the Rogerenes, adds that "the rulers having learned so much wisdom as only to remove these people from disturbing others, without fines or corporeal punishment," they had ceased from such things in a great measure. It would have been contrary to the inclination of such writers to perceive that the Rogerenes disturbed no one but in defense of the truth for which they stood, and that when persecution on account of their own religion ceased, they had no further need to disturb the religious observances of others.

Barber, in his "Historical Collections of New Jersey," states that there is a tradition to the effect that, about eighty years before the date of the writing (which would give us the date of the great countermove at New London), some of the Rogerenes of Schooley's Mountain came into a neighboring meeting-house, bringing work and interrupting the minister. The latter statement is couched in the very words used by Miss Caulkins concerning the New London countermove of 1764-66, indicating the exact origin of this New Jersey "tradition," which is simply in line with the erroneous accounts of historians in general—derived from repetitions and alterations of statements concerning the New London movement—which represent the Rogerenes as always and everywhere taking work into meeting-houses and interrupting the ministers.

Could any such disturbance be proven in regard to the Rogerenes of New Jersey, it would show—as a known effect of a certain cause—that they had been subjected to unbearable annoyances from members of that church, on account of their own religious persuasion, and took that method to check their enemies. But no proof of any such New Jersey molestation or defense has been presented.

Rev. Mr. Field, in his "Bi-centennial Discourse," says the Rogerenes did not believe in the Sabbath "nor in public worship," whereas, from the first they held as regular public meetings as any of their neighbors. Their meetings were open to friends and enemies alike, even to Mr. Saltonstall and his fellow-conspirators. They had, moreover, a regular organization with record books and clerk, proof of which is still extant in Quakertown, by a book of records written by said clerk. This erroneous statement regarding public meetings is doubtless derived from the fact that the Rogerenes, in opposition to the ecclesiastical law against meetings in private houses, persisted in holding meetings in such houses, and also to the fact that the Rogerenes held evening meetings for prayer, praise, and testimony, which were particularly for believers.[189]

There remain but two more principal fangs to be dealt with. One of these is a fossil which was recently revived by Mr. Blake, minister of the "First Church of Christ, of New London;" while the other is quite a new production, which the same estimable gentleman himself manufactured and circulated, through a natural desire not to be behind other ministers and historians of that church, in endeavoring to perpetuate the odium cast upon those who are reputed to have suffered strange things from some of its members in times past.

The first of these statements is that it was the custom of the Rogerenes to marry without a lawful ceremony, upon which Mr. Blake undertakes to give a description of their manner of marrying, which description is modelled after a familiar anecdote,—combined with a current statement founded on the same anecdote, to the effect that the marriage of John Rogers to Mary Ransford was a ceremony invented for the Rogerene sect by its leader, regardless of the known fact ("History of New London") that upon his third marriage the intentions were regularly published in New London and the ceremony performed by a justice in Rhode Island. It may be seen by New London records that his son John, two years after the death of his father, was married by the Rev. Mr. Woodbridge, pastor of the Congregational church of Groton. Mr. John Bolles, the noted Rogerene leader, was married to his second wife, in 1736, by Mr. Joshua Hempstead, justice of the peace, John Rogers, 2d, taking Mr. Hempstead and Mr. Bolles over the river for that purpose. ("Hempstead Diary.")

The New London town and church records and the "Hempstead Diary" bear full evidence that the Rogerenes of New London were married by the regular ministers or by justices of the peace, after a regular publication.

At a comparatively late date it appears that some of the Rogerenes prefer to have their marriages solemnized in their own public religious meetings on Sunday, in Quaker fashion, a form allowable by law, under condition that the marriage intentions be regularly published. The first marriage of this kind which has been discovered was recorded in 1764, by Joseph Bolles, clerk of the Rogerene Society, in a church book.

By the will of Joseph Bolles (1785), it is shown that he left a chest of Rogerene books and papers to Timothy Waterhouse of Groton. The latter probably succeeded Joseph Bolles as clerk of the Society; hence a remnant of this church book is in the Watrous family, and from it was copied the following:—

At our public meeting in New London the 17th of the 6th month, 1764, Joseph Bolles was appointed clerk for our Society, to write, etc.

This may certify all persons whom it may concern, that I, Timothy Walterhouse[190], do take thee, Content Whipple, to be my lawful, wedded wife, for better or for worse, for richer or for poorer, in sickness and in health, and I promise to perform to thee all the duties of a husband according to the Scriptures, while death shall separate us.

And I, Content Whipple, do take thee, Timothy Walterhouse, to be my lawful, wedded husband, for better or for worse, for richer or for poorer, in sickness and in health, and I promise to perform to thee all the duties of a wife according to the Scriptures, while death shall separate us.

TIMOTHY WALTERHOUSE.

CONTENT WALTERHOUSE.

The above named couple have been lawfully published, and now at our public meeting in New London, the seventeenth day of the sixth month, 1764, they both acknowledged and signed this paper, after they heard it read. Thus they are man and wife, married, according to the laws of God, in our presence.

JOHN WALTERHOUSE.

JOSEPH BOLLES.

SAMUEL ROGERS.

JOHN ROGERS (3d).

Among the various marriages in this church book are two well-known New London Rogerenes,—Thomas Turner and Enoch Bolles (son of John). Both of these are second marriages and the brides of Quakertown affinity, one of them (bride of Thomas Turner) being widow of John Waterhouse, 2d. John Waterhouse, 2d, lived in New London at, or near, Quaker Hill.

By 1811, we find the paper to be signed reading as follows:—

GROTON, *August 4, 181* .

These lines certify all people whom they may concern that I, William Waterous, and I, Clarissa Cushman, both of said Groton, are joined together in a lawful covenant of marriage, not to be separated until God who hath joined us together shall separate us by death, and furthermore it is enjoined on us that we perform the duty due to each other as the Scripture doth teach.

WILLIAM WATROUS.

CLARISSA WATEROUS.

In presence of

AMOS WATERHOUSE.

SAMUEL CHAPMAN.

Copies of these and other records were furnished us by Mr. Jabez Watrous of Quakertown.

These marriages were, with the exceptions noted, of Rogerenes on the Groton side, although the public meetings in which the earlier ones were solemnized were held in New London, and most of the witnesses were of New London. The New London Rogerenes continued to be married by regular ministers or justices of the peace. Thus early, we find an exclusiveness on the part of the Groton Rogerenes not discoverable among those of New London. Yet all of the Rogerenes considered marriage a strictly religious ceremony, consisting of vows taken before God and not to be annulled save for the one cause stated in the New Testament, while all know for how comparatively slight causes marriages in other denominations have been set aside. By the Quakertown method, the parties took each other for husband and wife in the presence of their "elder" and the assembled congregation; the elder did not pronounce them man and wife, they having taken each other before God; but the marriage was recorded in the church book, with names of several witnesses attached. We find certificates of these marriages both on the New London and Groton town records, further showing their legal character. Among them the following:—

GROTON, *July 29, 1821.*

Personally appeared John Crouch and Rachel Watrous, both of Groton, and were married in presence of me

ZEPHANIA WATROUS.

Where the antique marriage anecdote to which reference has been made originated, or to what persons it was first applied, is a matter of uncertainty; but, as it has frequently been attached to others besides Rogerenes, it is likely to have originated in quite different quarters. It appears to have become attached to the Rogerenes through the fallacious notions previously mentioned. Even the talented and scholarly author of the Bolles Genealogy (Gen. J. A. Bolles) was misled by this anecdote, together with the current statement in regard to lack of marriage ceremony among the Rogerenes, and also by his failure to find a record of the marriage of Joseph Bolles.[191]

Marriage publications were not entered upon New London records; but the publication of Joseph Bolles and Martha Lewis, in the Congregational church, in 1731, is plainly recorded in the "Hempstead Diary." Mr. J. A. Bolles had no knowledge of the existence of this Diary.

The anecdote which Mr. J. A. Bolles judged too good to be spoiled for the sake of relationship, yet of which he said: "The story has been told of so many that I doubt its authenticity," has had so many versions, even as attached to the Rogerenes, that it cannot well be presented in this connection without laying before the reader several of the Rogerene versions that have become current. Space is given for these the more readily, because this is a good illustration of the scurrilous stories that have been told regarding this greatly abused sect.

ANECDOTE.

Version No. I. (From the Half-Century Sermon of Rev. Abel M. McEwen, 1857.)

Among the idols which it was the mission of these fanatics to demolish, was the Congregational ceremony of marriage. One of their sturdy zealots, a widower of middle age, announced his intention to take for his wife, without any formality of marriage, a widow in the neighborhood. Mr. Saltonstall remonstrated against the design of the man, but he stoutly maintained and declared his purpose. The clergyman, seeing him enter the house of his intended, also went in that he might see them together. "You, sir," said he to the man, "will not disgrace yourself and the neighborhood by taking this woman for your wife without marriage?" "Yes," he replied, "I will." "But you, madam," said the wily watchman, "will not consent to become his wife in this improper manner?" "Yes," said she, "I do." "Then," said he, "I pronounce you husband and wife; and I shall record your marriage in the records of the church."

The marriage records of the Congregational church, all of which are extant, give no record of any such Rogerene widower and widow. Any marriage of an irregular nature in those times, and to a much later date, would have been proven until this day by record of presentment at the County Court of the woman upon the birth of every child, with attendant fine or whipping. Since not a single such presentment in the case of a Rogerene (with the exception of Mary Ransford) is to be found on the court records, the opening statement of Mr. McEwen is even by that one evidence disproved.

Version No. II. (From Bi-Centennial Discourse (1870) by Rev. Mr. Field, successor to Mr. McEwen.)

Mr. Field tells above story in substantially the same manner, but causes the

Rogerene to say, at the close: "Ah, Gurdon, thou art a cunning creature!" Mr. Field adds, in a footnote to the printed Discourse, that "there can be no authority for the story except tradition," but that it bears "so many marks of probability that there can be no reason to doubt its correctness." Doubtless it was such "marks of probability" that induced Mr. Field to credit the story that the Rogerenes entered the churches unclothed, which he incorporated among the various erroneous statements relating to these people contained in this Discourse, although he had abundant means of knowing of its absence from all New London history or tradition.

Version No. III. (From Bolles Genealogy, 1865—concerning Joseph Bolles, son of John Bolles, proof of whose marriage has been given.)

There is a tradition in the family that Governor Saltonstall, who had a high regard for Mr. and Mrs. Bolles, contrived to marry them without their suspecting it. It is said that after Mr. and Mrs. Bolles had had one or two children, and been threatened by "some rude fellows of the baser sort" with prosecution, the Governor one day invited himself to dine with friends Joseph and Martha. As the dinner went on, friend Gurdon, in easy conversation, very adroitly led both Mr. and Mrs. Bolles severally to declare that they had taken each other as man and wife in a lifelong union, and regarded themselves bound by the marriage covenant before God and man. As Mrs. Bolles assented to her husband's declaration, with her smiling "Yea, yea," the Governor rose to his feet and spreading out his hands exclaimed: "By virtue of my office as civil magistrate, and as a minister of God, I declare you lawful husband and wife." "Ah, Gurdon," said Joseph, "thou art a cunning creature!"

It is strange that so intellectual and scholarly a man as Mr. John A. Bolles did not perceive that the best part of this joke was in the extreme friendship displayed between the ardent Rogerene leader, Joseph Bolles, and Governor Saltonstall, as well as in the fact that the governor must have risen from the dead to marry Joseph Bolles, the marriage of the latter having occurred seven years after the death of Governor Saltonstall; also that had there been a child born to such a couple in those days, no "fellows of the baser sort" of any less consequence than the regular town authorities would have needed to take them in hand.

Version No. IV. (From an article regarding the Rogerenes, by a talented historian of New London of the present date, which was published several years since in a New York paper.)

There was incessant war between John Rogers and the town because his wife had been divorced from him. Though she was twice married, he attempted to capture her by force, but finally married himself to his bond-servant Mary Ransford. This scandalized the community, and the pair were hauled before the several courts. No persuasion would induce them to be legally united, and almost in despair Gurdon Saltonstall, then minister, sent for the pair. "Do you really, John," said he, "take this woman, your bond-servant, bought with your money, for your wife?"

"Yes," said Rogers defiantly, "I do."

"Is it possible, Mary, that you take this man, so much older than yourself, for your husband?"

"Yes," said she doggedly, "I do."

"Then," said the minister solemnly, "I pronounce you, according to the law of this colony, man and wife."

"Ah, Gurdon," said Rogers, "thou art a cunning creature!"

Had this historian never read the famous history of the place in which she dwells, written by Miss Caulkins, wherein is proof absolute that John Rogers and Mary Ransford had not the honor of being married by Governor Saltonstall? Although Miss Caulkins herself gives a version of this story (History of New London), she calls attention to the fact that it could not be true, as proven by court records.

Version No. V. (In one of the editions of Barber's "Historical Collections of Connecticut.")

It is here stated that "one day as Gov. Saltonstall was sitting in his room, smoking his pipe," a man by the name of Gorton came in with a woman, and announced that he had taken her for his wife without any ceremony, upon which the governor, "taking his pipe from his mouth," went through the usual form in these anecdotes, whereupon Gorton exclaimed: "Thou art a cunning creature!" Barber gives this anecdote among his various false statements regarding the Rogerenes.

Version No. VI. (A solitary anecdote found in the Chicago Tribune of April, 1897, showing how dragon's teeth will spring up again and again, in one form or another.)

Alexander Bolles, one of the early itinerant preachers, who preached in three States among the Alleghany Mountains, says the *Argonaut,* was much tormented by the influence of one John Rogers, a Jerseyman, who openly taught atheism and the abolishment of marriage. On one occasion, while holding a meeting in the woods of Virginia, a young man and woman pushed their way up to the stump which served as a pulpit. The man, interrupting the sermon [of course], said defiantly:—

"I'd like you to know that we are Rogerenes." The old man looked at him over his spectacles and waited. "We don't believe in God, nor in marriage. This is my wife because I choose her to be; but I'll have no preacher nor squire meddling with us."

"Do you mean to tell me," thundered Father Bolles, "that you have taken this girl home as your wife?"

"Yes, I do," said the fellow doggedly.

"And have you gone willingly to live with him as your husband?"

"Yes," said the frightened girl.

"Then I pronounce you man and wife, and whom God hath joined together let no man put asunder. Be off with you. You are married now according to the law and the gospel."

This rehash of several aspersions, spiced by newspaper humor, has, as is perceived, for the best part of its joke (to those better informed than its writer) several amusing paradoxes; viz., that the opposing preacher should bear the name of *Bolles*; that John Rogers, instead of dying in New London a so-called religious fanatic, had a Rip Van Winkle sleep in New Jersey where he awoke an atheist and at the same time a Rogerene.

The dragon's tooth which Mr. Blake appears to have manufactured himself, with no assistance whatever, for his "History of the First Church of Christ, of New London," is of a more serious character than even such anecdotes as these. This new production is to the effect that the General Court (1684) granted Matthew Griswold and his daughter Elizabeth further guardianship of John Rogers, Jr., "on account Of the continuance of his father in *immoral practices*."

The manner in which Mr. Blake so easily manufactured a statement never before made by any historian in regard to John Rogers, is by having (doubtless inadvertently) placed together as contexts two court records which have no relation to each other. The continuance of John Rogers, Jr., in the custody of Matthew Griswold and Elizabeth, granted in 1784, because John Rogers was "continuing in his evil practices," etc., referred, as observed by previous historians, to the giving the two children into the mother's charge in 1677, on account (as distinctly stated in the records) of John Rogers "being so hettridox in his opinion and practice," even to breaking the holy Sabbath, etc. Mr. Blake went back of this the true context, to the alleged cause of the divorce suit in 1675, which cause was not so much as referred to by the court when the children were assigned to the care of the mother and grandfather, which assignment was wholly on the ground of the father's "hettridoxy." To have given the children to the care of the mother and grandfather on account of a charge against John Rogers of which he had been acquitted by the grand jury, would have been an impossible proceeding. His transgression of the ecclesiastical laws and usages were "evil practices" to the view of Matthew Griswold, Elizabeth, and the General Court.

There has now been demonstrated the unreliable character of the main charges that have been brought against John Rogers and the Rogerenes, to be repeated by succeeding "historians" and added to not infrequently, through prejudice, humor, or lack of examination into the facts. It is trusted that the evidence given in this present work will sufficiently prove it the result of painstaking research and studious investigation, with no worse bias than that in favor of the undoing of falsehood and misapprehension and the righting of grievous wrongs.

Is it too much to ask that every person who presents so-called history to the public shall be expected to present as clear evidence in support of his statements and assertions, as is demanded of a witness in a court-room, or forfeit the reputation of a reliable author? Only by such reasonable demand, on the part of readers, can past history be sifted of its chaff and future history deserve the name.

Times have changed since John Rogers, Jr., went "up and down the colony" selling his little book; but a public at large, to which this youth trusted for a fair hearing and for sympathy, still exists,—a public which, as a whole, is never deaf to a call for justice. In the hands of this court, of highest as of safest appeal, is left the "HISTORY OF THE ROGERENES."

APPENDIX.
EXTRACTS FROM "EPISTLES."

John Rogers, Sr.

Christian Reader:—

I direct this my book to thee, without any regard to one sect more than another, for the unity and fellowship of God's people is Love, and this Love is the bond of perfectness, and by this Love shall all men know that we are Christ's disciples; and if this Love be with us and dwell in us, by it we shall know that we are translated from death unto life; for that faith that purifies the soul works by this Love, and by this faith which works by Love we come to have the victory over the world.

Beloved brethren, Since that great apostacy hath been, which the holy apostles did in their day fore-tell of, which hath spread over nations and kingdoms, so that the very names of things in scripture hath been (and in many things yet are) wrongly applied and generally believed to be that which they are not; and those false customs which this great apostacy hath brought in hath been received (and yet are in many things) for truths; but God hath in these latter ages raised up such lights in the world at several times as hath discovered much of the great mystery of iniquity; but they have always been accounted (at their first appearing) as deceivers and seducers and the like, by the dark world in general, and met with great opposition from the powers of this world, even from the powers of darkness; but the God with whom all power is hath so borne them up, through their faith, that the gates of hell were not able to withstand them, nor all the powers of darkness able to gainsay them, so that Satan hath been forced to fit up a new form of pretended holiness to deceive the world with, at several times, yea, even at every such appearance of the light of the gospel; for so often as the Lord hath been pleased to reveal unto his Church the life and light of the gospel, by shining into the hearts of his children, so often hath there been a falling away, and that old serpent, called the Devil and Satan, which deceiveth the whole world, hath at such times endeavored to work in the hearts of governors and great men of the earth to set up that which they imagine to be the worship of God, and to maintain the same, and this hath ever been a snare and net whereby God's children have been ensnared and hypocrites set up; for the true worship of God is in righteousness and true holiness in the inner man, and none can thus worship God till he sets them free from the Egypt of sin, and works this righteousness in their own hearts by his own Spirit; and such as these cannot conform to any prescribed form set up by the powers of darkness of this world, without procuring the great displeasure of God; for they are to be God's witnesses of that worship which God hath set up in the hearts of his own children, who alone can worship God in spirit and in truth, and none else; and these are the light of the world, and yet are but strangers and pilgrims in the world; for their kingdom is not of this world. But those that fall away from the spirit of truth into the spirit of the world are the false prophets and antichrists, and these are they whom the world doth follow and close with, according to scripture testimony; for saith the scripture, They are of the world, and the world heareth them; he that is not of God heareth notus; by this we know, the spirit of truth and the spirit of error. Here is a plain description laid down for us to know the false prophets by, to wit, "for the world heareth them"; by this we know they are always the greatest number, because the body of the people will hear and speak well of them; but the world will not hear and speak well of the true, saith the scripture; and this is the description the scripture gives us to know them by. I John 4, 5, 6. Luke 6, 26. Mat. 5, 11, 12.

What I have written in this book to the churches of Christ called Quakers I did present to the ministry of the said people in the time of a general meeting at Rhode Island, desiring of them it might be read to the congregation at the said meeting, and so handed among them till it come to Wm. Penn and the rest of their ministry. But after the ministry had perused it, some of them told me that I knew they did look at water baptism useless after a person came to be baptised with the Spirit. To which I replied, Your argument is just contrary to the scripture; for said Peter, "Can any man forbid water, that these should not be baptised which have received the Holy Ghost as well as we? And he commanded them to be baptized in the name of the Lord." Acts 10, 47, 48. Another replied, saying, "Thou holds forth the light contrary to what we have done, both in our public testimonies and printed books." To which I answered, "If you can shew me wherein I have held it forth contrary to the holy Scriptures, it shall be rectified:" But I heard no further reply to that. I then told them that if they would be pleased to publish it among themselves, I should be satisfied, and proceed no further with it, otherwise my purpose was to print it. Whereupon, some of them asked me whether I would be satisfied if they read it in their private meeting. I told them Yes; for I directed it to them and not to the world. Upon which they appointed me to come to the same place the next morning at seven of the clock for an answer; accordingly I did, where my book was returned to me again, some saying "It holds forth things contrary to what we have done, both in our public testimonies and printed books, and may make a division among us." To which I answered, "If truth make a division among you, it is such a division as Christ came to make." But they thus refusing to publish it among themselves, I have thought it my duty to put it to public view, believing there is yet a remnant among them which have not defiled their garments.

I have also added something more at the end of that epistle which I presented to them, to show the difference between the ministration of the moral law (written in the hearts of all the children of Adam) and of the ministration of the gospel of Jesus Christ (written on the hearts of God's children by the spirit of the living God) the one being the light of condemnation, the other being the light of life, or the light of our justification, through faith in the blood of Jesus Christ, and both proceeding from the self-same God.

And as to what I have written to the observers of the Seventh Day Sabbath, these may certify thee that after it pleased God, through his rich grace in Christ Jesus, to take away the guilt of my sins from my conscience and to send the spirit of his Son into my heart, whereby he did reveal unto me his love and his acceptance of me in Jesus Christ, this unspeakable mercy did greatly engage my heart to love God and diligently to search the Scriptures, that thereby I might know how to serve God acceptably, for then I soon became a seeker how to worship God, though more zealous of the tradition of my fathers till I saw them to be traditions and no scripture precepts. I thus, upon diligent search of the Scriptures, found that the First-day Sabbath was nowhere commanded by any law of God, and the Scriptures telling me where no law is there can be no transgression, and that it is but vain to worship God by men's traditions, Mat. 15, 9, and also finding by Scripture that there was a commandment for the keeping of the seventh day, I then openly labored on the first day of the week, in faithfulness to God and my fellow creatures, and strictly kept the fourth commandment, which commanded labor on the first day of the week, and required rest on the seventh. But I continuing a diligent searcher of the holy Scriptures, and begging at the Throne of Grace for direction in the way of truth, it pleased God to open my understanding to understand the Scriptures and to see that the seventh day sabbath was but a sign (under the law) of a gospel rest that Christ gives the soul, and that the shadowing part of the law was nailed to the cross of Christ; I could then no longer observe the seventh day without defiling my conscience; for saith Christ, Mat. 10, 27: "What I tell you in darkness that speak ye in light; and what ye hear in the ear, that preach ye upon the housetops." I then wrote to those of my brethren that kept the seventh day sabbath, showing them how it was but a sign or shadow of a better thing that was to come by Jesus Christ, and since have writ this following Epistle to them, wherein is opened the covenant of the law and the covenant of grace, the first covenant being a figure of the second; which covenant, with all the rites and ceremonies of it, continued until the establishment of the new testament by the blood of Jesus

Christ; which testament contains the substance of those things shadowed out in the first covenant; and though the shadowing part of the law was nailed to the cross of Christ, and so ceased, as they were signs and shadows, yet it is as easy for heaven and earth to pass as it is for one tittle (of what was shadowed out by the law) to escape of being fulfilled by Christ in the substance of it; for what God had before determined should be fulfilled by Christ was prophesied of by the law, as well as by the prophets, as is to be seen, Mat. 2, 13. But John the Baptist came so near to him that he pointed at him saying, Behold the lamb of God that taketh away the sins of the world.

I have thought it my duty to put these things to public view, being sensible of the wiles of Satan, who is wont to work in the darkness of men, to mislead them to make idols of such things which God commanded to be observed as signs of instructions to his church as is to be seen, Numb. 21, 9, compared with II Kings 18, 4, and what it was a sign of is to be seen, John 3, 14, 15.

Then follows the Epistle to the Quakers and that to the Seventh Day Baptists.

EXTRACTS FROM "TWO MINISTRATIONS."

JOHN ROGERS, SR.

… But before he came into the world, those that were under the second ministration were led and taught by a shadowing law, and were under typical judges, kings and priests, who were types of Christ's kingly, prophetical and priestly offices; but since his coming in the flesh, they have ceased, and He himself is their alone King, Priest and Prophet, to rule and teach them, in a more evangelical or gospel way; and this was prophesied of before his coming into the world, Deut. 18, 15, Isa. 7, 6, Psal. 110, 4. Thus was He prophesied of before his coming in the flesh, to wit in his prophetical, kingly and priestly offices; but He being now already come, we are to hear Him in all things, and to follow Him in all exemplary things, and He alone is to rule in his church, being their King, Priest and Prophet.

… And although we are of another kingdom, and therefore are not to be concerned in the kingdom we do not belong to, either to sit in judgment with them, or to fight and kill under their kingdom, yet, as being in their country and limits, rather than to offend them we have liberty from our King to pay them tribute for the carrying on the affairs of their kingdom and government, both by his doctrine and example, Rom. 13, 6, 7 etc., Mat. 17, 24 etc.… But although the children of God are free, being of another kingdom, yet they are not to use their liberty for a cloak of maliciousness against them, but as they are the servants of God, and proper subjects of his kingdom, they are to honour all men, and to fear God and to honour the king, and to make conscience, as Christ did, not to offend them, but rather to give them their demand for carrying on their affairs in their own kingdom, …

Can it stand with Christianity, according to Christ's doctrine and example since He came into the world, for his church and people to join in with the powers of this world to resist evil, by judging and condemning sinners, and to destroy men's lives, by fighting against flesh and blood with carnal weapons; or to lord it over others by exercising authority over them, as the kings and judges of this world do?

No: for both his doctrine and example forbid his church all such things, as appeareth by these following Scriptures, … And thus are we to be followers of Him, and not to take the place of a judge upon us, from the hands of the children of this world, and to follow them in their kingdom, to sit with them in judgment, to judge and condemn sinners, whom Christ did not come to judge, or to condemn, but to save. And also seeing He who was without sin hath not executed justice upon us who were sinners, but hath extended his grace and mercy to us, in acquitting and forgiving us, so ought we to be followers of Him, and not now become judges and condemners of sinners, seeing he hath not judged nor condemned us for our sins. And seeing he who was without sin did not cast a stone at the woman taken in adultery, who was a sinner, so likewise let us, who were once sinners, learn of him to be merciful unto sinners, as he hath been merciful unto us, who came not to destroy men's lives but to save them....

... But Christ's doctrine doth not give his disciples so much liberty as to defend themselves by the law of justice from the hands of earthly judges, Mat. 5, 38 etc. "Ye have heard that it hath been said, 'An eye for an eye and a tooth for a tooth'; but I say unto you that ye resist not evil, etc," "And if any man will sue thee at the law, and take away thy coat, let him have thy cloak also, etc."... We are to love our enemies, and to bless them that curse us and to do good to them that hate us, and to pray for them that despitefully use us and persecute us, Mat. 5, 44, and to do violence to no man, and to live peaceably with all men, as much as in us lies, by suffering ourselves to be defrauded, Rom. 12, 18. I Cor. 6, 7.

Thus we may see, by the doctrine and example of Christ, that it cannot stand with perfect Christianity to be either governor, judge, executioner or jury man, or to be active in the making any laws which may be useful in the body of the kingdoms of this world, who are only under the ministration of the moral law, and their weapons are carnal, with which weapons they fight against flesh and blood only, punishing both the righteous and the wicked, according to what is written, "And he was numbered with the transgressors" (by the judges of this world) Mark 15, 28.

... And this His kingdom and peaceable government was before prophesied of, and how he should put an end to wars, and reconcile sinners to his church, ...

... Then said Jesus unto him, "Put up again thy sword into his place, for all they that take the sword shall perish with the sword." Matt. 26, 52. "He that leadeth into captivity shall go into captivity: he that killeth with the sword must be killed with the sword." Rev. 13, 10. Here He rebuketh the use of the sword, according to what was before prophesied of him, threatening them that use it to measure the same measure to them.... From hence it appears plainly that the very reason why Christ bid them provide swords was that He might fulfil those prophesies which prophesied of him beforehand; that He should rebuke the use of the sword when he should come, and cause them to beat their swords into plowshares and their spears into pruning hooks, and that they should learn war no more. For when they told Him there were two swords, He said, "It is enough;" but when they came to make use of them, he rebuked the use of them, saying, "Put up again thy sword into his place; for all they that take the sword shall perish with the sword." So that it appears he did not bid them provide swords to kill and slay with them, but put an end to the use of them in his church....

We thus seeing that Christ hath rebuked the use of the sword in his church, and that they are to learn war no more, but are to beat their swords into useful tools, for necessary uses, it is an evil thing for a Christian to practice any gesture that tendeth to war, as watching, warding or training, or exercising any posture leading to war; for it is some degree of contempt to the doctrine of Christ, who hath taught us to learn war no more, but to live the life of faith and love, who hath promised us his protection and preservation from famine, pestilence and sword, when we love him and keep his commandments, as throughout the 91st psalm, Job 5, 19, 20. Isa. 26, 1, 2, 3, 4. Rev. 3, 10.

... But forasmuch as we have obtained mercy and grace by Jesus Christ, and are thereby reconciled to God, and made heirs of a better kingdom, and are but strangers, pilgrims and sojourners here, we are not to mix ourselves with the children of this world, by joining with them in their kingdom, to judge, or condemn, or torture any man for his sin, seeing we are under another ministration, having not been condemned by Christ for our sins; neither are we to join with them to kill or slay our fellow creatures, seeing Christ hath rebuked the use of the sword in the hands of his followers; and except we deny ourselves in all these things, and take up our cross and follow him, we cannot be his disciples....

CONCERNING THE SABBATH.

Extracts from a Reply by John Rogers, Sr. (1721), to a Book by Benj. Wadsworth, entitled "The Lord's Day Proved to be the Christian Sabbath."

... When God's children were in a holy frame and agreed to fast and pray, they did it not with a mixt multitude in public assemblies, as hypocrites are wont to do; as appears Neh. 9, 1, 2. The children of Israel separated themselves from all strangers, in time of offering up their prayers unto God. Acts 1, 13, 14. And we nowhere read, throughout the whole Bible that God's children ever prayed in a public assembly, with a mixt multitude, and in a customary way, as hypocrites are wont to do, as throughout the whole scripture doth appear. Rom. 8, 26.

... This have I written that people may not be misled, by thinking they worship God in forms and set times of prayer, while they are in a state of sin; and that they may consider the publican, upon his first prayer, accompanied with true repentance, went away justified rather than the other that was zealous in his often fasting and prayers....

In page 5th sayth he: "The apostle doth not oppose the keeping one day in a week holy to God." To which I answer, It is not what the apostle doth not oppose, but what the apostle commands, I Pet. 1, 16, "Be ye holy for I am holy." An unholy man cannot do one holy act, no more than a corrupt tree can bring forth good fruit: but I have no where read in the books of the New Testament that we are commanded to keep one day more holy than another....

... And the next place, I shall shew that the first commandment that both the angel of God and Christ himself gave forth to his apostles was to make the first day of the week (the day of his resurrection) a day of labor by travelling out of one province into another.... Thus it appears that had they believed them that was sent by the angel of God and by Christ himself they should have set out on their journey early in the morning for Galilee, which was in another province, and by all probability more than one day's journey, as appears in the 2nd chapter of Luke, which shews that Christ's parents went a day's journey towards Galilee before they missed him.... So that it appears that Christ had no regard to the day, otherwise than to make it a day of labor ... through their unbelief they were disobedient to the message that Christ sent them and did not make it a day of labor by travelling, as they were required by the angel of God and by Christ himself; which journey according to history was above 40 miles and the message was sent them in haste, to set out upon this journey, upon the first day of the week, the day of Christ's resurrection.

In page 6th he quotes Gen. 2, 2, 3, which speaks only of God's resting from the works of creation, when all things were finished and "was very good" … and this God's Sabbath or rest from his works of creation had no evening or morning ascribed to it, because it was his eternal rest or Sabbath, all things being now finished. And it could be no Sabbath or rest to Adam, for he had done no work to rest from, for he was the finishing work, … So that Adam in his first creation entered into God's Sabbath and so continued, till he by sin brought labor upon himself … and we have no account in Scripture of any Sabbath commanded or kept from Adam till Mose's time, … For when God delivered the two tables of the ten commandments, he gave Moses a particular account about the seventh-day sabbath, how it was a sign, as is seen Exod. 31, 12 etc. compared with the last verse.… And a sign is not the thing signified by it, any more than a shadow of a thing is the substance.…

In page 19 he quotes … "I was in spirit on the Lord's day."… that is, I was spiritualized on the Lord's day of his revelation for that work he employed me in, but here is no account what day or days it was of the week or month, this God hath not revealed to us.… But for any to affect it to be on a first day of the week is presumption, seeing no such name in Scripture was imposed on the first day of the week in any other place of the Scripture.…

In page 27, he quotes Acts 20, 7, "And upon the first day of the week" … This text tells us the disciple's coming together was to break bread; it does not say to celebrate a Sabbath, or give the day any pre eminence above the five other working days … the word breaking of bread is used in common eating, Acts 2, 46.—"breaking bread from house to house,"—Christ brake bread to two of his disciples and also when Christ fed 5000.… And in this place it is said they came together to break bread, and Paul was at that time tending a ship, as appears.…

But as to the Lord's Supper, it was always attended at supper time, … It was first instituted by Christ at supper … And Paul, the Gentile apostle, hath left it on record that he did deliver it to the Gentiles to be attended in the night, as appears I Cor. 11, 23.… The Gentile churches attended the time and season, tho' they got into a disorderly way of partaking of it, yet they attended the season … "For in eating every one taketh before other his own supper."… So that we see this coming together to break bread, on the first day of the week, was not for preaching (but a feast of charity), for that was attended the night following (when the young man fell from the loft), nor for the Lord's supper.

The following is at the end of the book containing the answer to Benjamin Wadsworth. The "questions" were written in New London prison at the time John Rogers was confined there on account of troubles arising out of the arrest and imprisonment of Sarah Bolles for a "matter of conscience."

The following questions were presented as they are underwritten, but when I saw I could obtain no answer but persecution, I then presented them to a Superior Court in the colony New London, and from them to the next General Court in that Colony, and so to the Elders and Messengers of the churches of the Colony of Connecticut, requesting of them an answer, upon the consideration of the Confession of their own Faith and the good counsels there given, and printed in New London, in the year 1710. And here follows an account of some part of what I presented to them, taken out of the Confession of their own Faith.

In page 6. "First Counsel. That you be immovably and unchangeably agreed in the only sufficient and invariable rule of religion, which is the Holy Scriptures, the fixed canon, uncapable of addition and diminution. You ought to account nothing ancient that will not stand by this rule, nor anything new that will. Do not hold yourselves bound to unscriptural rites in religion, wherein custom itself doth many times misguide. Isai. 8, 20. To the law and to the testimony; if they speak not according to this word, it is because there is no light in them."

"Second Counsel. That you be determined by this rule in the whole of religion. That your faith be right and divine, that the Word of God must be the foundation of it and the authority of the Word the reason of it, etc. For an orthodox Christian to resolve his faith into education, instruction and the persuasion of others, is not an higher reason than a Papist, Mahometan or Pagan can produce for his religion."

Page 7. "Believe, in all divine worship, it is not enough that this or that act of worship is not forbidden in the word of God; if it be not commanded, and you perform it, you may fear you will be found guilty and be exposed to divine displeasure. Nadab and Abihu paid dear for offering in divine worship that which the Lord commanded them not. It is an honour done unto Christ, when you account that only decent, orderly and convenient in his house which depends upon the institution and appointment of Himself, who is the only head and lawgiver of his church."

Page 65. "God alone is Lord of the conscience, and hath left it free from the doctrines and commandments of men which are in anything contrary to his word, or not contained in it: so that to believe such doctrines, or to obey such commands out of conscience, is to betray true liberty of conscience; and the requiring an implicit faith and an absolute and blind obedience, is to destroy liberty of conscience and reason also. Acts 4, 19. Whether it be right in the sight of God to hearken unto you more than unto God, judge ye. Acts 5, 29. We ought to obey God rather than men. Jam. 4, 12. There is one Lawgiver, who is able to save and to destroy: Who art thou that judgeth another? Col. 2, 22. But in vain do they worship me, teaching for doctrines commandments of men? Mat. 15, 9. Which all are to perish with the using, after the commandments and doctrines of men. John 4, 22. Ye worship ye know not what. Hos. 5, 11. Ephraim is oppressed and broken in judgment because he willingly walked after the commandment."

These are the scriptures they quote for their proof, with many more. All these quotations, quoted out of the book of the Confession of their own Faith, with much more, was presented to the abovesaid Courts, Elders and Messengers of said churches, with the following questions, grounded upon the said Confession of their pretended Faith, but can obtain no answer but violence to compel us to rebel against it, as will appear by said questions as followeth.

To Richard Christophers Assistant, and from him to Gov. Saltonstall and Eliphalet Adams.

I request of you, as you profess yourselves to be Christians, and the Scripture to be your rule, to give me a direct answer to these scriptural questions, Rom. 4, 15. "For where no law is, there is no transgression."

My question is, Hath God any law to forbid labor on the first day of the week? If he hath, quote chapter and verse for it, to convict us of our error, or be convicted that you will be found fighters against God, in striving to compel us to worship the works of your own hands, which would be idolatry in us.

And consider the age and antiquity of an idol doth not make the sin one whit the less, but the greater; for God's patience and long suffering towards idolaters should lead them to repentance.

A second question I crave of you is, Whether the name "Sabbath" (which you impose upon the first day of the week in your law book) be a title that God by his word hath put upon it? If it be, pray quote the chapter and verse, where it is so named by God's word; if not, judge yourselves.

A third question I crave your answer to is, Whether the name Lord's Day (which you impose in your law book on the first day of the week) be a Scripture name peculiar to that day? And how you prove the revelations of Jesus Christ to John was upon the first day of the week?

And if you cannot answer the said questions by the holy Scriptures, then I request of you to read and to consider what is written, Psal. 94, 20, 21. "Shall the throne of iniquity have fellowship with thee, which frameth mischief by a law? They gather themselves together against the soul of the righteous, and condemn the innocent blood." From the New London Prison, the 17th of the

9th month, 1719.

And here follows a copy of my request to Court Elders and Messengers, wrote under the above questions as it is here.

My request to you is, That you will be pleased to see that an answer to my questions may be returned, by you or your elders, as you will answer it before God, the judge of Heaven and earth, and that we may not be compelled by the Authority to offer to God in divine worship that which he hath not commanded, against our consciences, and contrary to the Confession of your own Faith; and if God hath commanded the first day of the week to be kept for a Sabbath, to quote to us the place in Scripture where it is so commanded, and send it to us: And if there be no command of God for it in the Holy Scriptures, and only your own law in your Law Book, and your minister's doctrine for it, then I desire you to read and consider what is written, Mat. 15, 7th, 8th and 9th verses, "Ye hypocrites, well did Esaias prophesy of you, saying, This people draweth nigh unto me with their mouth, and honoureth me with their lips; but their heart is far from me. But in vain they do worship me, teaching for doctrines the commandments of men."

New London, the 7th of the third month, 1721. From him that wishes you well, and desires to see your salvation and not your destruction.

But I could obtain no answer from them; "For every one that doeth evil hateth the light, neither cometh to the light, lest his deeds should be reproved." John 3, 20.

And now my request to you, the said Courts, Elders and Messengers, is, in the presence and view of the world, to shew us chapter and verse, or verses, where God's command is which commands the keeping the first day of the week for a Sabbath, by which you are not in the same danger Nadab and Abihu was, that we may escape with you; for I can find no such commandment throughout the whole Bible: For you, in the Confession of your Faith, set before us the great danger we are in, if we offer to God that in divine worship which he hath not commanded; not only the loss of our lives, as Nadab and Abihu did theirs, but eternal damnation also; as appears in your "Confessions of Faith," Page 7, and in your second Counsel (before quoted).

Upon this consideration, I request this favor of you, so that we may venture in with you in keeping of it, by a commandment from God, if you know of any, for this will be more for your honour than to compel us against our own consciences (and your own counsels) by your own law, accompanied with your whips, stocks, fines and imprisonments; which hitherto you have been using to compel us to offer in divine worship that which God hath not commanded; and besides this, we are ashamed (I do not say you) to pretend to be "orthodox Christians" and "to resolve our faith into education, instruction, and the persuasion of others," seeing you say in your "Confession," page 6, that "this is no higher reason than a Papist, Mahometan or pagan can produce for his religion;" for we would not be like such spoken of in Zeph. 3, 5, "The unjust knoweth no shame."

Thus it appears nakedly before your eyes, and to your consciences, that either your Counsels, in the Confession of your Faith, is very erroneous, or else your first day Sabbath, if it have no command of God for it, which I can find nowhere throughout the whole Bible—and that which can be found nowhere may well be concluded not to be at all. And the said Counsels in the Confession of your Faith is so substantially grounded on the holy Scriptures that I think it most safe to conclude that it is your Sabbath that is erroneous and idolatry (except you have a commandment of God for it) by the Confession of your own Faith.

I having been treating upon your Sabbath, the foundation almost of all your worship, which is the works of your own hands, by your own Confession, except you can find a commandment of God for it....

The following from "A Midnight Cry," by John Rogers, Sr.

I desire that these following things may be well considered.

First, when God delivered the two tables of stone into the hands of Moses, he gave him a particular account about the Sabbath how it was a sign, as is to be seen Exod. 31, beginning at verse 12 to the end of the chapter, yea, it was a covenanted sign to that people, as is to be seen, verse 17. Ezek. 20, 12, 20.

Secondly, Moses testifieth to Israel that it was commanded to be kept upon the account of that deliverance out of Egypt, as is to be seen Deut. 5, comparing the 12, 13 and 14 verses with the 15th verse. So that as their deliverance was from a temporal bondage, so the sign of it was a temporal rest; and the sign was for a covenant between God and them, of his safe protecting them from the oppression of their enemies, in that inheritance which he gave them while they kept his laws.

Thirdly, Christ testifieth that the priests profaned the Sabbath in the temple and yet were blameless, Mat. 12, 5, compared with Numb. 28, 9, 10, so that we may well conclude those sacrifices by which they profaned the Sabbath, though they were but signs in themselves, yet the Sabbath which was of less value was to give place that the greater might not be omitted.

Fourthly; The man that bore a burden on the Sabbath day, to wit, his bed, John 5, 10, profaned it in so doing, and was as blameless as the priests; for that sign under the law was not the Sabbath, any more than that circumcision commanded to Abraham was the circumcision, and therefore, saith the apostle, That is not circumcision that is outward in the flesh, Rom. 4, 12. Thus we see he calls it the sign of circumcision, though the scriptures did no where call it a sign, but called it circumcision; but the 7th day Sabbath God declared to be a sign, yea, a covenanted sign with his people, as circumcision was, as is to be seen, by comparing these places of scripture together, Exod. 31, 13, 16, 17. Gen. 17, 10, 13 and 14.

Fifthly, Seeing that God testifieth that the weekly 7th day Sabbath is a sign, and gave no such plain demonstration of any other of the Sabbaths under the law, we have good and better reason to judge that Paul's words, Col. 2, 16, 17 (Let no man therefore judge you in meat or in drink, or in respect of a holy day, or of the new moon, or of the Sabbath days, which are a shadow of things to come, but the body is of Christ) comprehends the 7th day Sabbath in a special manner, seeing it agrees with God's testimony to Israel, that it was a sign to them, and a sign is not the substance; for a shadow is but the sign of the substance.

And lastly, Seeing that God testifieth to Israel that the 7th day Sabbath was a sign, so it was no more the Sabbath than the seven stars which John saw in the right hand of Christ were the angels of the seven churches, nor no more the Sabbath than the seven golden candlesticks were the seven churches, nor no more the Sabbath than those fat kine that Pharaoh saw were the seven plentiful years; which sort of creature (we afterwards read) they made an image of and worshipped; nor no more the Sabbath than the sign of circumcision was the circumcision; nor no more the Sabbath (under the first covenant) than the wine that Christ gave his disciples to drink was the blood of the New Testament or covenant; nor no more the Sabbath (under the first testament) than the bread that Christ gave to his disciples was his body under the second or new covenant.

Thus we see that signs (in the Scripture) bear the complete name of the substance or thing they signify; so the 7th day Sabbath was a sign under the first covenant, and so continued till the establishment of the second, and then both the covenant and signs under it ceased; for they were signs of instruction to the church, that they might impose their faith on the things they signified, which were to be fulfilled by Christ, who was the substance of them all; and so at his coming they were all nailed to his cross, and so ceased. Eph. 2, 15, 16. Col. 2, 14. And so likewise the signs that are now in being (under the new covenant) are to continue till Christ's coming in his manhood, I Cor. 11, 26, and then they will cease also.

"ADVERTISEMENT."

John Rogers, Sr.

Whereas there is a printed law in her Majesty's Colony of Connecticut, entitled only "Heriticks," in the preface to it they say "To prevent the danger persons are in of being poisoned in their judgments and principles by hereticks," etc.

Which said law the queen by advice of her council hath condemned, repealed and declared it void and of none effect, it being contrary to their charter. And indeed there is a good hand of God in the Queen's act, for I know of no sect worse poisoned in their judgments and principles by gross heresy than the Church of New England; and it is very evident that hereticks have ever persecuted the true church under abusive titles, as deceivers, hereticks, Quakers, and the like abusive titles, which they themselves are guilty of; for erroneous persons, principles and practices are condemned by the scriptures of truth; so that they have no other way to cloak themselves, under their delusion and heresy, but by casting such like odious titles on the children of God, and so persecute them and burn their books; for Satan's design in making use of these deluded persons, thus to act, is to suppress truth under pretense of heresy; as for instance I shall begin with the master of the house, whom they called Beelzebub, the prince of devils, Mat. 12, 24. He went by the name of "deceiver," Mat. 27, 63. Paul by the name of heretick, Acts 24, 14. Luther's books were burnt under pretense utterly to suppress heresy; the worthy martyrs in Queen Martyr Mary's time suffered death under the name of hereticks; and those worthy martyrs in Boston in New England under the name of Quakers and hereticks; and my books by this law now repealed have been condemned and burnt, under pretense of heresy, though I have made fair proffers at their General Court to reward any person well for their time and pains that would endeavor to show me any one error in them, but none have yet publickly appeared.

FOLLOWING FROM ACCOUNT OF SAMUEL BOWNAS OF HIS "CONVERSATION WITH JOHN ROGERS," 1703.

He (John Rogers) spoke very much of his satisfaction and unity with George Fox, John Stubbs, John Burnyeat and William Edmundson as the Lord's servants, with sundry others of the first visitors of that country, that he knew them to be sent of God, and that they had carried the reformation further than any of the Protestants ever did before them, since the general apostacy from the purity both of faith and doctrine; first the church of England they did nothing in the end but made an English translation of the Latin service used before, the Presbyterians they dissented and the Independants, but came not to the root of the matter; the Baptists dissented from the other three, but went not through. Upon which, though I could not wholly agree with him in his assertions, I queried if he thought that all these several steps of the English church from Popery, the Presbyterians and Independants from the English church, and the Baptists from all three of them, had not something of good in them, viz. I mean whether the first concerned in dissenting from Popery, though they afterwards rested too much in the form of worship in the Episcopal way, had not the aid of Christ's spirit to assist them in their dissent? And so for all the rest. This he did readily grant to be a great truth; and so allowing that the first reformers actuated by divine light, and being faithful to what was made known to them, had their reward; and their successors sat down in that form their predecessors had left them in, but did not regard that Power and Life by which they were actuated, and so became zealots for that form, but opposed the Power. "And this," said he, "is the true cause of the several steps of dissent one from another; and the reason why there is so little Christian love, and so much bitterness and envy one against another, is their sitting down contented, each in their own form without the Power, so that they are all in one and the same spirit, acting their part in the several forms of worship in their own wills and time, not only opposing the Spirit of Truth, but making it the object of their scorn and those who adhere to it the subject of their reproach, contempt and envy; and this is the foundation of persecution" said he....

FROM REPLY TO J. BACKUS.

JOHN ROGERS, 2D.

… Here I think he (Backus) does the government no honor by informing the world that they have made laws to debar such as differ from them in matters of religion the liberty of the king's highway to pass to their own meetings, since our lord the king hath granted equal liberty of conscience to all dissenters to hold their meetings and serve God according to their consciences….

In his 13th page he gives a record (of his own making) relating to John Bolles, which record declares that J. Bolles acknowledged that he came from New London, and was going to Lebanon, and that he knew it was contrary to our law, and that they did it in defiance of the law.

To which I answer, "That God's three children were cast into the fiery furnace for declaring their defiance to the king's law, which was made to force men's consciences in matters of religion; and all the prophets and apostles suffered for opposing those laws which were set up to force people's consciences in matters of worshipping God; And all the martyrs which have suffered the flames and other tortures ever since, it has been for manifesting their defiance to such laws as have been set up by the worldly government to uphold false worship, or to restrain them from worshipping God according to their consciences. Now for as much as God has justified all those sufferers above-mentioned, for their bold defiance of such laws as were set up by man to prevent people serving God according to their consciences, well may we have confidence that God will justify us for the same thing. We have also further to plead in our own justification in this matter than those sufferers above-mentioned had, inasmuch as our lord the king has granted us the same liberty to meet together and worship God according to our consciences as he has given to our persecutors: So that in the consideration of what is here expressed, I think J. Bolles and his brethren are highly commendable for their faithfulness to God, in manifesting their defiance against such laws as would restrain them from worshipping God according to their consciences.

… In his 14th chapter, he charges the sufferers to be most daring and malicious offenders, utterly disregarding those Scriptures, Rom. 13, Tit. 3, I Pet. 2, etc.

In the first place I shall fully grant from those Scriptures, and many more that might be mentioned, that the worldly government is set up of God, and are God's ministers to act in worldly matters between man and man, and that the law that God hath put into their hands is good, if they use it lawfully;…

according to what is written, I Tim. 1, 8, 9, 10. And while the worldly government act within their commission, God is with them and has put such carnal weapons in their hands as is sufficient to rule all carnal persons, which are stocks, fines, prisons, whip and gallows, which above-named weapons are sufficient to conquer and subdue all carnal and guilty persons, so that rulers are a terror to evil-doers.

And forasmuch as we acknowledge the worldly government to be set up by God, we have always paid all public demands for upholding the same; as town rates, county-rates and all other demands, excepting such as are for the upholding hireling ministers and false teachers which God has called us to testify against. Now when the worldly rulers take upon themselves to make laws relating to God's worship, and thereby force men's consciences, and so turn their sword against God's children, they then act beyond their commission and out of their jurisdiction; and are so far from being God's ministers that they are fighters against God and his church; and God is so far from making them a terror to his church that he gives his church and people faith and boldness to withstand them to their faces....

... Here I think he (Backus) does the government no honor by informing the world that they have made laws to debar such as differ from them in matters of religion the liberty of the king's highway to pass to their own meetings, since our lord the king hath granted equal liberty of conscience to all dissenters to hold their meetings and serve God according to their consciences.

FROM ANSWER TO A PAMPHLET BY COTTON MATHER.

BY JOHN ROGERS, 2D.

… A travelling ministry are sent from town to town and from city to city, and from country to country, and over sea, so that they are not only taken from their own employment, but are also sent upon charges; their state and condition is like a man that is prest a soldier and sent away from his own living on charges and therefore maintained at the king's charge. And hath not this man power to forbear work? though he tarry some days at a place, must he therefore maintain himself by his own labor? is not this the very state of a travelling ministry of the gospel?…

… I have thus proved by Scripture that a traveling ministry of the Gospel hath power to forbear work. And secondly that the churches ought to relieve them: And thirdly have shewed their differing state from settled elders.

… In the second place, I shall now prove by Scripture that settled elders are commanded to work with their hands and thereby to support the weak; by being givers rather than receivers.—We find that the apostle sends for the elders of the church.—He saith to them, I have coveted no man's silver or gold, or apparel; ye yourselves know that these hands of mine have ministered unto my necessities and to them that were with me; I have showed you all things, how that so laboring, ye ought to support the weak, and to remember the words of the Lord Jesus, how he said, it is more blessed to give than to receive….

… And 3rdly Whereas Christ, upon sending them forth to preach the gospel, forbids them making any provision for their journey, requiring them to expect their meat and reward from his hands….

… From hence we may see by Scripture that Christ's ministers, whom he calls and sends to preach the Gospel, are so well provided for by Him that they have no need to be hired by the children of the world; for in so doing they would reproach their Lord and Master and shew themselves not only faithless, but wickedly covetous, in practising contrary to this doctrine of Christ, and to come under the condemnation of this great sin so much condemned in Scripture, "The priests whereof teach for hire, and the prophets whereof divine for money, yet they will lean upon the Lord, and say, is not the Lord among us; none evil can come upon us. Therefore shall Zion for your sakes be plowed as a field, and Jerusalem shall become heaps, and the mountains of the house as the high places of the forest … yea they are greedy dogs, which can never have enough, they are shepherds that cannot understand; they all look to their own way, every one for his gain from his quarter."… Christ calls them hirelings and ravening wolves.

And though the nameless authors of the said Pamphlet are pleased to call such (as join with Christ and his shepherds, to testify against these hirelings) by the name of wolves, yet these hirelings, or at least their shearers, the collectors, have always taken them for sheep, especially about shearing time.... Now we that join with Christ and the true shepherds to testify against these hirelings, we come under the blessing of Christ ... Blessed are ye when men shall revile you and persecute you, for so persecuted they the prophets which were before you; yea this must we suffer all the time that these hireling prophets are under this curse of Christ. Wo unto you when all men shall speak well of you, for so did their fathers to the false prophets.

... In page 8, they assert ... "That he be given to hospitality" and say they, "how is it possible for him to be so, if you be given to covetousness, and given to dishonesty and cheat him of his maintainance?"

To which I answer If it be the people's gift, its their hospitality and not the ministers: the churl may be liberal, if other men's purses make him so. But the ministers of the Gospel are given to hospitality of that which their own hands have ministered to them, and are obedient to their Master's words, who hath said unto them, "It is more blessed to give than to receive."

... And it is a shame for you to tell of the galling of your hands with inferior labor for the getting of bread; it is your duty to do so, and if the people be the cause, as you say, of your laboring with your hands, they are worthy of praise in causing you to do your duty, and you ought to have done it without their causing you to do it, and therefore you proclaim your shame. For you ought to have taken the holy prophets, and Christ and his apostles for your example, to have labored with your hands, and not the false prophets and false teachers, who sought to live upon the people,... Christ shews that such stewards as those could not dig for their living, and to beg they were ashamed....

And the true prophets, and Christ with his apostles have set us better example.... Here you may see that Elijah was plowing ... here Elisha went to Jordan with the sons of the prophets and cut down wood.... Amos was a husbandman and a gatherer of wild figs.... Christ was a carpenter.... Paul was a tayler or tent-maker and worked at it tho' he were a travelling minister of the gospel,—and so did the rest of the apostles, as is to be seen.... These examples, with that apostolical command (to the elders of the church) Acts 20, 34, 35, ought to be attended by Christ's ministers....

FROM REPLY TO PETER PRATT.

JOHN ROGERS, 2D.

As it has ever been allowed that the defaming of the dead is a mark of the most unmanly and base spirit of a coward and ought to be abhorred by all persons who bear the image of man; then how much more abominable is it of P. P. to sport himself with his own lies over a man in his grave? And I think no person of common reason will expect any apology of me on account of this my undertaking, since my silence in this matter would have rendered me very unmanly....

... If John Roger's books contain "but few of his principles" then how comes P. P. to know what his principles are, several years after his death? except the same spirit which once deceived him in the matter of longitude has again deceived him concerning J. R.'s principles; and we have as much reason to question the truth of what he tells us of J. R.'s principles (since he has no better proof than his own bare word) as the General Assembly had to question the truth of longitude, which soon after proved a delusion of Satan....

Now by these foolish and vain pretended reasons, the reader may plainly see that he only wanted an excuse to evade J. R.'s books, that he might take his full swing to bely and abuse him at his pleasure; because he well knew that if he had quoted his books, they would have discovered his falsehoods....

But I should not have enlarged so much upon this head, were it not that I am sensible that there are many thousands of grown persons in this Colony that for want of opportunity to be informed in the principles of other sects remain so ignorant that they know no difference between the Church of England and the Papists, nor between the Quakers and the Baptists, but esteem each couple to be alike. And now is it possible that such persons should be able to discern the ignorance of P. P.?...

... Now how marvellous is it that P. P., who knew himself to be a man so inconstant and changeable, not only in his worldly concerns from his very childhood, but also in matters of religion since he has arrived to riper years, should presume to put out a book only on his bare word, without any proof at all. Surely he might reasonably have thought that all who knew him would expect better proof from such an inconstant person than from any other man....

FROM ANSWER TO MR. BYLES, BY JOHN AND JOSEPH BOLLES.

Considerable light is thrown upon the "Outbreak" of 1764-66 by a Rogerene pamphlet (of about 1759), which appeared in several editions, sometimes ascribed on the title-page to John Bolles, sometimes to his son Joseph, and probably the joint work of father and son, written out by the latter; thus having a style noticeably different from that of John Bolles, although equally clear-cut and forcible. John Bolles, being at the date of this work eighty-two years of age, may be supposed to have welcomed the aid of his son Joseph, both as collaborator and amanuensis. The following is from a copy of this work to be found in the New London Public Library:—

An Answer to A Book entitled The Christian Sabbath, explained and vindicated in a discourse on Exodus XX. 8.[192] Jan. 14, 1759, upon a particular occasion, by Mather Byles, pastor of "The First Church of Christ" (as he saith) in New London, written by Joseph Bolles, in behalf of the rest which suffer persecution for breaking said pretended sabbath.

In page 5 of Mather Byles sermon, he says: The Christian Sabbath has of late been publickly attacked; and those who observe it have been challenged to show any scripture warrant for the practice.

Ans.

We have been imprisoned 23 at a time, 8 of us about 7 months, and some of the best of our cattle and horses and other goods taken away, and 3 of us cruelly whipped, near 20 stripes apiece, for doing the business of our ordinary calling on the 1st day of the week, which he calls the Sabbath, all within 9 months. And in these persecutions we have continually desired our persecutors to show any Scripture warrant for their practice; we have also sent forth advertisements promising ten pounds reward to any person that could show us one word in the Bible that forbids labor on this pretended Sabbath; which we suppose he calls "a challenge;" and because he cannot find a word in the Bible that forbids labor on his pretended Sabbath he has preached a sermon instead thereof, and though he calls it the Christian Sabbath, it is not called so in Scripture; by which it is evident it was not the Christian Sabbath in the apostles time; for if it had been they would have called it so. Also his text is part of the commandment to labor six days and rest the seventh; so that his own text that he builds his Sabbath upon requires labor on his pretended Sabbath. For it says six days shalt thou labor; and we know that this pretended Sabbath is the first of the six days….

… In page 18 he says, "And lastly to assign a reason why there is no command for this Sabbath in the New Test.;" and in his next page he says, "The apostles left it to after discoveries," which will be answered in its place. But neither God nor man require us to keep a Sabbath without a law, "For where no law is, there is no transgression." Rom. IV. 15. And sin is not imputed when there is no law: And the "Confession of Faith" of this Colony requires a command for all the worship we perform to God, in page 7, and there is no discovery of this pretended Sabbath in the Bible; for he says, "the apostles left it to after discoveries," and the first command that we have discovered for this pretended Sabbath was more than 300 years after Christ by Constantine the emperor, recorded in "Fox's Acts and Monuments," Vol. I. p. 134, in these words: "The Sunday he commanded to be kept holy by all men and free from all judiciary causes, from markets, marts, fairs and other manual labors, only husbandry excepted." Here we may observe no husbandry labor is forbidden, in this "after discovery."

Also king Inas, who reigned in England, in the year of our Lord 712, commanded that infants should be baptised within 30 days, and that no man should labor on Sunday. "Fox's Acts etc." Vol. I, P. 1016. Observe in this after discovery all labour is forbidden; as popish darkness increased, this Sabbath strengthened and infant baptism was also "discovered."

Also king Edgar, who began his reign in England in the year of our Lord 959, he ordained that Sunday should be kept holy from Saturday noon till Monday morning, and he ordained and decreed for holy days and fasting days. "Fox's Acts," Vol. I. P. 1017. Observe this "after discovery" being in midnight popish darkness, this Sabbath was kept more strict and they also discovered half a day more, and holy days and fasting days to be observed. Also king Canutus, who began to reign in England in the year 1016, he commanded celebration of the Sabbath from Saturday noon till Monday morning. This king "discovered" it by the name of "Sabbath"; but the other three "discovered" it by the name of "Sunday."

Also in our Colony there is an ample "after discovery" of it by the name of Sabbath or Lord's day, which exceeds the four other "after discoveries;" with a famous law to torture the bodies of them that break this pretended Sabbath, by whipping, not exceeding 20 stripes if they refuse to pay a fine; and doubtless there has been more "after discoveries" by express commands, for this pretended Sabbath, in Rome, France and Spain. Therefore if M. B. will preach up this pretended Sabbath, which he says the apostles left to "after discoveries," he ought to have taken his text out of the forementioned "after discoveries," where there are express commands to build their Sabbath upon; but, as he builds it on God's commandment, which commands labor on his pretended Sabbath, it has no foundation to stand upon, and therefore stands upon nothing. No "after discovery," neither this pretended Sabbath, infant baptism, nor the mass nor purgatory, ought to be built on any text in the Bible. But whoever preaches up any of these "after discoveries" they ought to take a text out of the law book, where they are instituted and commanded, and not out of the Bible where they are not "discovered."

How fully Mr. Byles had endeavored to stir up the authorities to take the offenders strenuously in hand will be inferred from the following, from the same pamphlet.

... He calls us deluded, blind, obstinate, because we suffer persecution for breaking a Sabbath which he says the apostles left to "after discoveries." But it is this sort of ministers that preach to our General Court to suppress or persecute them that walk by the apostle's doctrine, for not observing this Sabbath which he says the apostles left to "after discoveries."

He further says:

"Take away the Sabbath and what will be the consequence?"

Ans. He speaks like the idolaters of old. Judges XVIII. 24. "Ye have taken away my gods which I made, and the priests,—and what have I more?" Here we may see the idolaters speak all with one voice; their heart is after their idols and their priests more than after God.

Next he says: "Errors in doctrine and corruption in practice would break in upon us like a flood, immorality would triumph without control."

Ans.

It is such a time now, for there are errors in doctrine, manifest errors indeed, in this and other sermons; and corruption in practice is already broken in upon us like a flood, and immorality triumphs almost without control among the people, who are encouraged to it by the example of their priests, which live immoral lives in covetousness, pride, fulness of bread and abundance of idleness.... Also the observers of this pretended Sabbath do allow that there is more immorality amongst themselves than there is among us who do not observe it. Immorality triumphs in a high degree, even in gathering money for the priests of many poor people to whom there is more need to give, and casting some into prison to force them against their conscience to pay money to maintain such priests in idleness,[193] which they know God hath not sent to teach them.

EXTRACTS FROM "LOOKING GLASS FOR THE PRESBYTERIANS OF NEW LONDON."

JOHN ROGERS, 3D.

To see their Worship and worshippers Weighed in the balance and Found Wanting.—With a true account of what the people called Rogerenes have suffered in that town, from the 10th of June 1764 to the 13th of December 1766. Who suffered for testifying, That it was contrary to Scripture for ministers of the gospel to teach for hire. That the first day of the week was no Sabbath by God's appointment. That sprinkling infants is no baptism and nothing short of blasphemy, being contrary to the example set us by Christ and his holy apostles. That long public prayers in synagogues is forbidden by Christ. Also for reproving their church and minister for their great pride, vain-glory and friendship of the world they lived in.—With a brief discourse in favour of women's prophesying or teaching in the church.—Written by John Rogers, New London. Providence N.E. Printed by the author 1767.

June 10, 1764. We went to the meeting house at New London, and some of our people went into the house and sat down, others tarried without and sat upon the ground some distance from the house. And when Mather Byles their priest began to say over his formal, synagogue prayer, forbidden by Christ, Mat. VI. 5 etc., some of our women began to knit, others to sew, that it might be made manifest they had no fellowship with such unfruitful works of darkness. But justice Coit and the congregation were much offended by this testimony, and fell upon them in the very time of prayer and pretended divine worship; also they fell upon all the rest of our people that were sitting quietly in the house, making no difference between them that transgressed the law and them that transgressed not; for they drove us all out of the house in a most furious manner; pushing, kicking, striking etc., so that the meeting was broken up for some considerable time and the house in great confusion: Moreover, they fell upon our friends that were sitting abroad, striking and kicking both men and women, old and young, driving all of us to prison in a furious and tumultuous manner.

... The authority and minister and some of the people were greatly offended at our opposing their false worship; for they carried on their worship in such pride, and so contrary to the Holy Scriptures that they could no ways defend it by the Scriptures and therefore took another way to defend it never practised by Christ or any of his followers. For justice Coit did continually fall upon us when we came among them and drive us to prison, in an angry and furious manner; sometimes twenty sometimes thirty in a day, striking and kicking both men and women, pulling off women's caps and bonnets and tearing them to pieces with their hands, setting an example to the rest of the people; also he made no difference between them that spoke at the meeting house against their worship and those that did not speak; for his constant practice was to fall upon all our friends that came to the meeting house and all that he could see in sight of the house and drive them to prison, he and his company, in a most furious and tumultuous manner, stopping their mouths when they went to speak, choking them etc. Also he doubled our imprisonments every time we came among them; but this method he took added no peace to them, for some of our friends were always coming out of prison, as well as going in, … However, this was the method they took, and after this manner they celebrated their Sabbaths from the 10th of June to the 12th of August.

… February 16. Some of our friends were sitting quietly in the meeting house, between meetings, and Col. Saltonstall[194] came in and laid hold of an old man that had the numb palsy, aged 73 years, and with great violence hauled him out of the seat, setting an example to others, who fell upon them and drove them out of the house and to the court house, in a furious manner, and carried them up through a trap door into a dark garret and locked them in, and at night a company of their base men got together, among which were … This base company went into the court house and shut themselves in and took our friends out of the attic and offered shameful abuse to our women in the dark…. Now after this shameful abuse to the women, they took two men and stripped off their clothes and tied them to a post in the court house and whipped them in a most unmerciful manner, especially one of them, which they struck unmerciful blows with a staff and with bunches of rods on his back, till it was like a jelly, also they rubbed tar into their wounds and whipped upon the tar, forcing it into their flesh, also they rubbed tar in the mouths of the men and women when they went to speak. When these two men were first tied to the post they sang praises to God, and in the time of their torment they called upon God to strengthen them. After this, they laid hold on these two men and forced them to run down near to the town wharf and threw them into the water several times; also they took their hats and threw water on them for some considerable time. Moreover, they threw the women into the water. And after this the sheriff's eldest son and another man with him took a poor weakly woman, forty odd years of age, and forced her to run through the streets till she dropped down, and then they left her….

Now the next first day of the week, after Col. Saltonstall shut our friends up in the court house and set his son Dudley and others to abuse us, it being the 23d of February, we were coming to the meeting house again, but as soon as we appeared in sight, Col. Saltonstall run out and met us, and a great company with him, and fell upon us in a very angry manner, before we had spoke one word, to drive us to the court house, as he did the week before, when our friends were sitting quietly in the house between meetings. But as soon as they fell on us, we spoke and made a great noise, and refused to go with them, telling them we chose to be killed publickly before the people, rather than to be murdered privately in the court house.

Now the tumult grew very great, so that the meeting was broken up for some considerable time, and they dragged both men and women on the ground to the court house;[195] some by their hands, some by their legs, and some by the hair of their heads, striking them with their fists, kicking them, striking and punching them with staffs and tearing the clothes from their backs, and they dragged them into the court house and hauled both men and women up two pair of stairs, and hauled them up through a trap door into that dark loft that they had shut our friends up in the week before, and they locked them in. In this tumult an aged woman was so overcome that she fainted away and they left her lying on the ground. Now there were present in this riot justice ——, justice ——, justice ——, the high-sheriff and Col. ——, besides constables and grandjurymen: There was also a deacon among them, which makes us write as follows.

The deacon and the justices
Were busy in this fray,
Church members and grandjurymen
Forgot their Sabbath day.

After the tumult was over, these church members remembered their Sabbath, and returned to their pretended worship again: But as soon as that was over, the authority consulted together at the meeting house, and sent the high-sheriff, who came with a company of men and took down ten women out of that dark loft that the authority had shut them up in (two of these women had young children with them and another was big with child)[196] and committed them to prison, leaving near twenty small children motherless at their homes. Now as the high-sheriff was going from the meeting house, to commit these women to prison, some of the people of the town asked him what they were going to do with our friends; the sheriff answered that the women were to be committed to prison, but he said the men were to be delivered up to Satan to be buffetted. So the authority kept the men locked up in that dark garret till night, and then they were delivered up to the authority's children and a rude company of young men, who came and unlocked the trap door and abused our friends in the manner following: They took down one man first out of this dark loft and brought him down into the lower room of the court-house, and tied his hands round a post, also they tied another line to his hands and hoisted him up by a tackle, then they brought his knees round the post and tied them with a line, and stripped his clothes up over his head and tied them also; then they whipped him in a very barbarous manner by the light of a candle. And when they had done torturing him, they let him down and shut him up in one of the court house chambers. They then brought down another out of the garret, and tortured him after the same manner as they did the first, and then shut him up also, pretending they would whip them all over again, except they would recant and promise not to come among them any more. There were twelve whippers that took turns at the whip, and commonly three or four to whip one man, one after another. They pretended to give those men thirty nine stripes each, but they used several sorts of whips, especially one unmerciful instrument made of cow-hide, also they whipped them with large rods tied together, some of which had ten in a bunch, so that they far exceeded thirty nine stripes, for they struck each person thirty nine times with that cruel instrument, except one man, which after they had struck him thirty unmerciful blows, one of the spectators ran and untied him, telling the whippers he was an old man and they ought to use some discretion towards him. Nine men were thus used this night, all heads of families, some of which were elderly men that had great families of children.

This whipping was executed in a very barbarous manner, for the rods were trimmed, and long sharp fangs left on them, to tear the flesh of the sufferers, also these men that whipped our friends struck them in such a violent manner with these heavy bunches of rods that they beat and bruised their flesh till it was like jelly. Moreover some of their wrists were so cut and their sinews so much hurt with the line they hung by, that several of their hands were numb for more than two months after. Also the two men that had been so unmercifully whipped by this company in the court house the week before, and otherwise abused, were of these men that suffered that night: And they struck one of these men, he that had been the most abused the week before, forty three cruel blows on his old sores, and ten or twelve of these blows were after he had swooned away. Our persecutors cut these rods upon their Sabbath, and fitted them at the court house, and Colonel Saltonstall was at the court house among them when they were preparing the rods.... When their persecutors heard them praying and calling on Christ for strength, they would threaten them, and whip them with all their might, endeavoring to make them promise to renounce their testimony against their worship, but were not able to make one of them renounce their testimony, or make any promise at all. But the sufferers told them to this effect, that what they did against their worship was for no other end but to please God and keep a good conscience, and that if they should promise to renounce their testimony God would renounce their souls forever. Also when some of the men that had suffered this cruel whipping were shut up in the court house chamber, they prayed earnestly to God to strengthen their brethren that were to suffer, also they prayed for their persecutors, for God gave them more than a common love to those that were tormenting them.

So after these nine men had suffered, they were set at liberty. Their persecutors threatened them to double their whipping every time they came to the meeting house among them. And no doubt they would have gone further, had not God prevented them by making a division among the people; the neighboring towns crying out against such barbarous and unlawful behavior; also it was a common saying among the people that they were sorry their rulers had resigned up their authority to a company of boys and set them to defend their worship....

The above is but a small part of such blood-curdling accounts, filling a good-sized pamphlet. Portions will be found in the "History of New London," not quoted here. Near the end is something less thrilling.

Sept. 14, 1766. Some of our people went and sat down some distance from the priest's house, and when he came out to go to meeting, they walked with him and endeavored to have some friendly discourse with him concerning the things of God; But the priest would not talk with them about the things of God. However, they walked with him and talked to him, but before they came to the meeting house, justice Coit began to kick them in a furious manner, especially the women. Also one of the townsmen fell upon them, punching both men and women with a staff in a cruel manner, so they were driven by some of the people to the upper end of the town.

The next first day of the week, being the 21st of Sept., as some of us were setting by the side of a house, between meetings, about four or five rods from the priest's house, saying nothing to any person, the high-sheriff came, with some assistants and took us and sent for justice Coit, who came and committed eight men of us to prison. And on the 26th day of the same month, justice Coit came to the prison, and we were taken out and brought before him, and he charged us with disturbing the minister's peace. We told him we had no thought of doing the minister any hurt. Justice Coit answered, that he did not suppose that we intended to strike him or wrestle with him, nor did he suppose we intended to hurt a hair of his head, but he supposed that we intended, when the minister came out, to go along by his side and talk with him. So when justice Coit had confessed that he did not suppose we intended to hurt a hair of the priest's head, he fined us five shillings each, and required bonds of good behavior towards all his majesty's subjects; but especially towards the priest. But we refused to give such bonds, looking upon the judgment to be very absurd, and that justice Coit's supposing that we intended to talk with the priest was not breach of the peace in us, so he committed seven of us to prison again, all heads of families, one of which men was in his 75th year. Four of these men were kept in prison till the 13th of December following, and two were set at liberty about the 28th of November, and one within a few days after we were committed to prison.

Now after these men were committed to prison, our friends that were at liberty thought it necessary that some of our people should go on the first days of the week and set in the priest's sight and not fear them that persecute the body. But when the priest saw them sitting in sight, if it were but a few women, he would not come out of his house to go to meeting.... Also this behavior of the priest occasioned much trouble to his poor flock, for sometimes the bell would ring and the people sit waiting for their priest till it was time for meeting to be half done: And then justice Coit, or some of the rest of his sheep, were obliged to come and move the women out of the priest's sight, and guard their shepherd to the meeting house, lest these women should speak to him of the things of God.

It was almost every day of the first days of the week for the whole time of this imprisonment, which was near three months, that this shepherd was kept in his house by the sight of our friends, and sometimes only at the sight of a few women, and he never ventured to come out till some of his sheep came and drove the women away. But justice Coit committed no more of our friends to prison under bonds of good behavior because he supposed they intended to talk with the priest, after these men above mentioned. But the 23rd of November, one of our men told the priest, after he was come out of the meeting house, that he came to put him in mind how they kept God's children in prison, and that their worship was upheld by cruelty. The priest answered to this effect, that they could uphold it in no other way. Then the man replied it must certainly be of the devil, if there was no other way to uphold it but by cruelty. But the sheriff struck him twice on the head, and punched him with his staff to prevent his speaking with the priest. And he and three women were committed to prison, but at night they were set at liberty.... God said, Jer. 1, 7,—"Thou shalt go to all that I shall send thee, and whatsoever I command thee thou shalt speak." Also the apostle Paul exhorteth us to be followers of him as he was of Christ, I Cor. XI. 1. And Paul spent much time in going from place to place, disputing in the synagogues on the Sabbath days, as appears in the Acts of the Apostles. And no doubt they built their synagogues, and thought, as our neighbors do, that they had a natural right to worship in them and that the apostle had no right to oppose them in their worship, for they were as much offended at the apostle as our neighbors are at us, for they called him a pestilent fellow, and said he was a mover of sedition throughout the world, Acts XXIV. 5. Also speaking of Paul and Silas they said, Acts XVII, "These that have turned the world upside down, are come hither also."

EXTRACTS FROM "A DEBATE BETWEEN REV. MR. BYLES AND THE CHURCH."

Minister.

I have no particular objection to this church; but believe it to be a true church of our Lord etc.—but it is this mysterious call of Providence etc.—the churches of this and old England are equal to me. I am called from one to another where I can be of more usefulness, which is my duty.... And I believe you had better dismiss me, as you may get one that will do much better. You want one that will visit his parishioners—preach a lecture once in a while.... I was not made for a country minister.... I am weak and infirm[197] ... to come up this tedious hill all weathers—come in all out of breath ... obliged to preach till all in a sweat ... then go out in the cold, on this bleak place ... run the risk of my health etc.... And then to be treated as I have been by the Quakers ... disturbed upon the holy Sabbath. If I have not the Sabbath, what have I? tis the sweetest enjoyment of my whole life!—Insulted by them almost continually, surrounding my house. Many a time has the bell tolled for hours together, and at last one single man condescends to come down and drive them off. I would not live such a life over again for no consideration.... I see no prospect of amendment ... our laws are not put in full execution. (And then he went on to show wherein the civil authority, in his opinion, were deficient in duty with regard to the Quakers etc.[198])—My salary is not sufficient[199] etc.... My friends are in Boston. Etc.

People. These objections are nothing to the purpose, and what you say about the Quakers is a mere cobweb. As to the call of Providence, it plainly appears to be money.... Conscience! with what conscience can you leave this church of Christ? (They then set forth the obligations he was under to walk with this church; the connection between them was of a sacred nature etc.)

Minister. There are ministers enough to be had.

People. Yes, such as you are—We never could conceive nor imagine how you could spend your time before now, for you never visited any of your parishioners, but very seldom—seldom preached a new sermon; but old sermons over and over, again and again; and behold all this time you have been studying controversies, about modes and forms, rites and ceremonies! Is it for this we have been paying you this three years past, when you should have been about your ministry?... In regard to the Quakers insulting you etc. Is any man wholly free from persecution? If that is all you have, you ought to be very thankful that you have no more than a few poor old women sitting round your gate.

EXTRACTS FROM "THE BATTLE AXE,"

By Timothy Watrous, Sr., and Timothy, Jr.

Satan, to all classes of the Ecclesiastical system that profess Christ's name and prove traitors to his service.

I now address you as my sworn subjects, under full power of my authority; feeling much gratified to see my kingdom established on the ruins of God's creation. Though I have been wounded by Christ, the invader of my possessions, yet I hold before you the greatness of my power and the glory of my kingdom. I am the great and high prince and god of this world.... I am your god, and I warn you of my great enemy Christ; that you be not found obedient to any of the requirements of his contracted plan. My ways are broad and easy. I am high in heart and teach the same to you. That in all nations you may set my worship in high places, that it may be adorned with all the splendid glory which belongs to the prince that offered Christ all the glory of this world. That your places of worship may appear beautiful to men. And let my servants, your ministers, be men of the best gifts and talents; for so were your fathers the false prophets. And be not like Christ's apostles, who were ignorant, unlearned men. Even his great apostle, Paul, (they said) in bodily presence was weak and his speech contemptible. But let it not be so with you.... For it is my will that you should have the praise of men; and receive from them titles of honor. For the ways of Christ, our great enemy, are contrary to all men, and even to nature itself, as you may see throughout all his precepts; for example I Cor. I, 26, 27, 28. "For ye see your calling, brethren, how that not many wise men after the flesh, not many mighty, not many noble are called; but God hath chosen the foolish things of the world to confound the wise; and God hath chosen the weak things of the world to confound the things that are mighty; and base things of the world and things which are despised hath God chosen."

This is no description of an accomplished member of society. Faithful subjects, when you execute the priest's office in my service, put on a dress suitable to your ministration; and let your bodily presence be amiable and your speech affable, and your countenance grave and solemn. Salute the people with a comely behavior, that you may glory in your own presence. For verily I say unto you, except your outward appearance of righteousness shall exceed that of Christ's ministers, you shall in no case deserve the world....

Agreeably to my counsel, in all cases resent an insult from your fellows and go forth to war with them; embody yourselves and march to the field of battle, with religion at your right; and appoint one of my servants, your ministers, a chaplain to pray for your success. And there encamp, one against the other; and let my servants, your priests, on both sides, put up a prayer to the God of heaven that you may gain the victory over each other; cherishing the belief that all that die gloriously in battle go immediately to heaven. And when you are coming together to do the work of human butchery, if a sense of the horrid piece of work which you are about to perform shall fill your soldiery with terror, benumb their senses with intoxicating liquor; and put on confusion and distraction, under the name of courage and valor; and fear not, for I will be with you and fill your hearts with such vengeance, through the immediate influence of my spirit, that you shall be able to perform all my will and pleasure. And, when you have sufficiently soaked the ground with the blood of your fellow men, and humbled their hearts and have gotten your wills upon them; then return and let my servant, your minister, lift up his voice before you, unto the God of heaven, with praise and thanks for the victory; that you have been able to do such deeds as to bereave parents of their sons, wives of their husbands and children of their fathers…. And then return home full of the glory of your own shame, and tell your rulers you have saved their pride, gratified their ambition and saved a little of the trash of this world; for which you have taken the lives of your fellow creatures, each one of whom is worth more than all the treasures of India. For all such things belong to the religion that I delight in.

Ye fathers, I exhort that you exercise yourselves in laying up treasure on earth. And ye, young men, that you likewise embrace every opportunity to get riches, which are an honor to youth; that in the performance thereof your hearts may be raised higher in pride.

And ye, ministers of the civil law, I counsel that you swerve not from mutual confederacy with the ecclesiastical system. That, for the sake of your honor, you strictly attend to your oaths; and put in motion all laws and modes of punishments which may tend to compel all kinds of people to submit to our precepts, which are in opposition to the rules of Christ.

A SERMON TO THE PRIESTS.

It is well known that the Christian religion has been in the world 18 centuries, since she first visited the earth, and also that 300 yrs. of the first part of the time, altho' she stood in opposition to the powers of this world, and under cruel persecutions, yet she mightily grew and flourished until about the 4th century, at which time, a general revolution took place through the governing parts of the earth and she was delivered from her persecution, being a great church and standing on her own foundation. And from that day down to this the priesthood of this religion (falsely so called) has been preaching to us a sinful world, though broken in sect, but under one lineage of ordination. Yet they have not brought the world, nor the church to a state of perfection; but much to the contrary. For when they first took the Christian church by the hand to lead her through the ensuing ages of the world, she then stood on her own feet, enjoying a well-united system of her own. And what is she now?… she is now broken all to pieces and become a house divided against herself. And this unparalleled circumstance has rendered it necessary that the sinful world unto whom you, the said priests, have been preaching, should have somewhat to preach unto you….

THE SUBSCRIBERS PETITION TO HIS COUNTRYMEN FOR HIS RIGHTS AND PRIVILEGES.

Whereas I am once more called to suffer for conscience's sake, in defense of the gospel of Christ; on the account of my son, who is under age, in that it is against my conscience to send him into the train-band. For which cause, I have sustained the loss of my only cow that gave milk for my family; through the hands of William Stewart, who came and took her from me and the same day sold her at the post. Which circumstance, together with the infirmity of old age, has prevented my making my usual defence at such occasion. I have therefore thought proper and now do (for myself and in behalf of all my brethren that shall stand manfully with me in defense of the gospel of Christ) publish the following as a petition to my countrymen for my rights and privileges; and especially to those that have or shall have any hand in causing me to suffer.

Fellow Countrymen:

You esteem it a great blessing of heaven that you live in a country of light, where your rights and privileges are not invaded by a tyrannical Government. And for this great blessing of heaven do you not feel yourselves under obligation of obedience to heaven's laws; to do unto all men as you would that men should do unto you? Or which of you on whom our Lord hath bestowed ten thousand talents should find his fellow servant that owed him fifty pence and take him by the throat, saying, "Pay that thou owest me," and, on refusal, command his wife and children to be sold and payment to be made?

Fellow Countrymen, this case between you and me I shall now lay open before your eyes, seeing it is pending before the judgment seat of the same Lord. Our Lord and Master hath commanded us not to hate our enemies, like them of old times under the law of Moses. But hath, under the dear gospel dispensation, commanded us, saying: "I say unto you love your enemies, do good to them that hate you and pray for them that despitefully use you and persecute you, and if any man shall sue you at the law and take away your coat, forbid him not to take your cloak also." "If thine enemy hunger, feed him, if he thirst, give him drink." And again: "I say unto you that ye resist not evil."

For these, and many other like commands of our Saviour, Christ, I have refused to bear arms against any man in defense of my rights and privileges of this world. For which cause, you have now taken me by the throat, saying:

"Go break the laws of your Lord and Master." And because I have refused to obey man rather than God, you have taken away the principal part of the support of my family and commanded it to be sold at the post.

And thus you, my fellow-servants (under equal obligation of obedience to the same laws of our Master) have invaded my rights and privileges and robbed me of my living, for no other reason but because I will not bear the sword to defend it. And if a servant shall be thought worthy of punishment for transgressing his master's laws, of how much punishment shall he be thought worthy that shall smite his fellow servant, because he will not partake with him in his transgression? But I wist that through ignorance you have done it, as have also your rulers; and for this cause do I hold the case before you, that you may not stand in your own light, to stretch out against me the sword of persecution; but agree with your adversary whilst you are in the way with him. But if you shall refuse to hear this my righteous cause and shall pursue your fellow servant that owes you nothing, and who wishes you no evil, neither would hurt one hair of your head, and although you take away his goods, yet he asks them not again; but commits his cause to Him that shall judge righteously; I say if you shall follow hard after him, as the Egyptians did after Israel, God shall trouble your host and take off your chariot wheels, so that you shall drive them heavily. For I know, by experience, that no device shall stand against the counsel of God; for I am not a stranger in this warfare, neither is it only the loss of goods that I have suffered heretofore; but extreme torments of body, while my life lay at stake under the threat of my persecutors, and yet God, through his mighty power, has never suffered me to flee before my enemies, but has brought me to the 83d year of my age, though all my persecutors have been dead these many years.

ALEXANDER ROGERS.

January 7th, 1810. Waterford, New London County.

Lightning Source UK Ltd.
Milton Keynes UK
UKHW042316030123
414627UK00018B/378